Blue Ruin

BLUE RUIN

*A Novel of the 1919
World Series*

Brendan Boyd

W. W. Norton & Company
New York · London

Copyright © 1991 by Brendan Boyd
All rights reserved.

Printed in the United States of America.
The text of this book is composed in Bodoni Book, with the
display set in Bodoni Open. Composition and manufacturing
by the Haddon Craftsmen, Inc.
Book design by Charlotte Staub
First Edition.

Library of Congress Cataloging-in-Publication Data
Boyd, Brendan C.
  Blue ruin: a novel of the 1919 World Series / Brendan
Boyd.
    p.   cm.
  1. Chicago White Sox (Baseball team)—History—Fiction.
2. Cincinnati Reds (Baseball team)—History—Fiction.
3. World series (Baseball)—History—Fiction. I. Title.
  PS3552.087755B5 1991
  813'.54—dc20   91–2487

ISBN 0-393-03020-2
W.W. Norton & Company, Inc.
500 Fifth Avenue, New York, N.Y. 10110
W.W. Norton & Company, Ltd.
10 Coptic Street, London WC1A 1PU
1 2 3 4 5 6 7 8 9 0

For Elaine

From the first day I looked upon her face
in this life, to this present sight of her,
my song has followed her to sing her praise.

—Dante, "Paradiso"

Blue ruin 1. Inferior liquor, esp. gin. *Archaic and dial. since c1920.* 2. A catastrophe; complete ruin, failure, or disgrace.

—*The Pocket Dictionary of American Slang,* compiled by Harold Wentworth and Stuart Berg Flexner

FIXERS

Joseph "Sport" Sullivan *Boston gambler*
Arnold Rothstein *New York gambler*
Nat Evans *Assistant to Rothstein*
Abe Attell *Former lightweight champion*
Sleepy Bill Burns *Former major league pitcher*

WHITE SOX PLAYERS

Chick Gandil *First baseman*
Swede Riisberg *Shortstop*
Shoeless Joe Jackson *Left fielder*
Happy Felsch *Center fielder*
Eddie Cicotte *Pitcher*
Lefty Williams *Pitcher*
Buck Weaver *Third baseman*
Fred McMullin *Utility infielder*

WHITE SOX MANAGEMENT

Charles Comiskey *Owner*
Kid Gleason *Manager*
Alfred Austrian *Counsel*

August
1919

1

In the summer of my thirty-seventh year, when the air began leaking so conspicuously from my life that remaining oblivious to it soon required my full attention, my father fell into a pig-rendering fire and, of his unspeakable injuries, perished.

It is difficult to say how long my father had been dead before he actually died.

Perhaps he died when I was born; I wouldn't know. Perhaps he didn't die until my mother died; I have no memory of this. Perhaps, as seems more likely, he was simply born dead, or rather, having begun life as a mere suggestion of himself, a suggestion he neither wished, nor felt compelled, to expand upon, he simply faded beneath life's predictable disappointments until only his resentments, and his resignation to them, remained.

It's all a mystery to me, Christ knows.

As is the matter of how, and for how long, I'd been retracing his footsteps in the guise of obliterating them, like an anarchist circling the block to flee a time bomb.

The sole witness to my father's flaming exit, a coworker named McGafferty, told me this of the rescue efforts:

"By the time we'd cooled his bacon, Sport, Jerusalem Slim himself couldn't have said which was your old man and which was the pig."

1

It is a measure of my detachment from this episode that I didn't kill McGafferty on the spot.

They put what was left of my father into a far corner of St. Chrysostom's, where his screams wouldn't disturb the convalescent. There he lay, in a seaman's hammock, secreting strange liquids and strong smells, attended to by a Cistercian nun who bore a disquieting resemblance to Battling Siki, the light heavyweight. Several of the Great War's more imaginatively maimed veterans surrounded him, expiring under morphine.

Occasional visitors brought flowers; one, a crib of blood oranges.

I visited him every day at first, compelled by some residue of filial responsibility. Distant relatives sometimes accompanied me, small old people with vaguely familiar faces who insisted on engaging me in encouraging conversation. Soon I'd abandoned regular visiting hours entirely.

But I couldn't abandon my father.

Not yet at least.

The night nurse was married to one of my slower payers. In exchange for shrinking his tab, she let me sneak onto the ward every third night. There, in the consoling darkness, I would stand at the foot of his bed, watching his remnants stir in their shell.

The night before he died he spoke my name.

"Jo-seph."

His voice was so distorted I might have mistaken it for another's had anyone else been present. I moved closer, bending to the carnage, shunning the fumes. He said one more word.

It could have been "see," or perhaps "be," or maybe even "flee." If I'd thought it mattered, I'd have given it more thought. But it was definitely a warning. My father only

2

communicated by warnings, and recriminations. And this one was a warning.

I think he wanted very much for me to understand him then. I didn't care whether I did or not. It wasn't warnings I needed anymore, but signs. And he was more beyond signs than he'd ever been. I looked deep into the one eye he had left. I surveyed the skin on my palms, which was mottled, but firm. I turned and walked off the ward, intending never to return.

A doctor called the next morning and said, "He's gone."

"Gone?" I asked. "Gone where?"

"Your father has passed away, Mr. Sullivan. I'm sorry."

"That's all right," I said. "Feel free to say he's dead."

Then I hung up.

So I didn't even get a chance not to go back.

Occasionally, after his funeral, I'd catch myself wondering what he'd tried to tell me that night, though my greater curiosity was why I didn't wonder more. Shortly I stopped wondering entirely. It didn't seem that important.

Only three times before had my father spoken to me from what might loosely be called the heart. Each of these conversations occurred before I stopped believing anything he told me was true, or even important.

Once he cautioned me never to dream, because if my dreams didn't come true, I'd be disappointed, and if they did, I'd be even more disappointed.

Another time he told me not to get used to happiness. I forget what his rationale for this was. I credited it to the solace he'd always drawn from failure.

The last time he gave me advice was the only time I ever sought it.

I'd gone to him to ask whether I should marry a girl I later married and who subsequently abandoned me when she discovered how little there was to me beyond the animosity I bore him. I thought I was seeking his approval for this union; I was really seeking his disapproval so I could defy it.

I got neither.

I received instead the cryptic admonition that "every man's story has three beginnings: when he's born, when he leaves home, when he discovers what he really wants. Marrying has nothing to do with it. But if you must marry, take the bitch on your wedding night, tie her to the bedpost, pry her flanks apart as you would a mare in heat, and take your pleasure in those quarters. After that she'll do anything you want her to."

My brother, Eugene, never visited my father's deathbed. He didn't attend the funeral either. He did send an enormous box of chocolates to the wake, however, which the undertaker, after animated consultation with his assistants, placed unopened at the foot of the bier. Everybody thought Eugene intended this as an insult. I knew he just meant it as a joke.

Eugene is two years my junior. He spent his entire childhood trying to steal my father's affections. When he finally realized there were no affections to steal he turned mordant. It was during this period that he made the remark which severed me forever from the lingering delusions of my youth.

"Your father," Eugene said, picking his toenails with a paring knife, "is the kind of guy who writes things down on little scraps of paper."

It was a hyperbolically dismissive summary—the sort only a boy about to bury his life in carelessness makes about a man who's already buried his in caution.

And it *was* caution my father died of, make no mistake on that, the reckless sort of caution that confuses opportunity with danger. When they plucked him from his pyre he was wearing an extra safety harness. It had become entangled in the tackle, dragging him into the flames.

I knew what Eugene said about the scraps of paper was true, of course, before he'd even said it. I'd always known. I'd just been waiting to hear someone say it out loud.

The day after Eugene did, the day before my fifteenth birthday, I activated my deepest occupational fantasy and took a job running numbers for Jocko Kielty. It was a position far riskier than any my father ever warned me against. It had other attractions as well: solitude, furtiveness, an unlimited potential for manipulation and gain. It seemed like something I might eventually be good at.

Eugene's remark, then, marked one beginning to this story; the second, actually.

The first was my birth, on April 26, 1883.

The third was the day Chick Gandil, the White Sox first baseman, sauntered up to me in the bar of the Buckminster Hotel in Boston and said, "Let's jive up the Series with a little Jewish lightning, Sport."

That was July 1, 1919, two weeks before my father's incineration. I'd been pretending to weigh Gandil's proposition in the meantime, while actually allowing it to atrophy beyond all likelihood.

Until the day this story had its fourth beginning.

For there was, indeed, a fourth beginning.

My father was wrong about that too.

The fourth beginning, the true beginning, occurred the day after my father's funeral. I was working my way through his effects—cheap furniture, frayed suits, the sort of pitifully inconsequential paperwork the timid always hoard

5

against oblivion. I was half hoping to find something valuable, half fearing to find something poignant. I discovered instead a small Chinese lacquered chest, a three-drawered affair of uncharacteristic daintiness. I assumed it had belonged to my mother, and so opened it with lascivious foreboding.

The first drawer held a small nest of my father's notes to himself, the "scraps of paper" that had elicited Eugene's scorn.

The second held a like number of my own betting slips, all of recent vintage. How, or why, my father had acquired them I can't imagine.

The third drawer held a tiny unchained cameo which, when opened, revealed a yellowing daguerreotype of my mother and father together.

They were almost young in this picture. They were at the seaside, dressed in white. The sky was cloudless. There were balloons, a rickshaw, sprigs of sea moss. My mother gazed at my father as if inventing him. My father seemed lost in concurrent ardor. He looked more alive than I ever remember seeing him, not at all like the man who had raised me, not like someone who'd tie anyone to a bedpost.

I held the cameo to the late-afternoon light. Then I picked up one of my father's notes to himself, and one of my own betting slips. I placed them side by side, like lantern slides. They were the same size, the same shape, contained nearly the same number of words. The handwriting on them was undeniably similar.

I went downstairs and called Chick Gandil in Chicago, told him I was ready to do that business he'd suggested, ready to take on a project with scope. He asked what had taken me so long to get back to him. I told him I'd had a death in the family.

6

2

So much is lost in shadow now, though parts remain resolutely visible. In those days every detail seemed so plain to me that I never dreamed any would require illumination. Volumes have been written about the fix. Those who didn't squeal confided in those who did. I've read it all—the memoirs, the depositions, the speculations—hoping to learn what occurred beyond my sight. It's amazing what people will admit to, in what detail, to justify themselves. No one will ever know the whole story, I suppose. There will always be gaps, to be filled in, as I have tried to, over the years. There is no truth, only versions. This is mine.

The day after I called Gandil I visited my father's cupola. It was the first time I'd been alone in his house, though I often might as well have been.

The cupola was full of objects awaiting repair, obsolete items anticipating unlikely needs. I'd hidden there often as a child. From its window I'd imagined the edge of the universe.

My future lay straight before me now. I'd run out of reasons for avoiding it, for probing its boundaries only in my dreams. I wouldn't let its inevitability paralyze me, though. Anticipation eventually turns into nothing too, or less than nothing.

I'd been dreaming of it forever, it seemed, or some equivalent of it, something transcendent, imperishable. I'd only been waiting for some signal of my readiness. But while I'd

7

waited I'd grown steadily less ready. Now I had my sign. To ignore it would be to call my life a dream.

I'd come to the cupola to discard my baseball pictures, florid portraits cut from the backs of Red Man chaws. As a boy I'd invented games for them, slid them around countless invisible diamonds, in patterns existing solely in my eye. I'd long needed to junk them; now seemed the time.

When I removed them from their box, however, I found I couldn't part with them. Time had fused them to me, as second skin. They'd been immortalized by gray layers of attic silt, made indispensable by the pungent aroma of domestic mildew. I discarded the duplicates, neatened the stacks, transferred the entire collection to a smaller carton. Then I threw out several objects I didn't recognize and sat down for a long stare out the double glaze.

It was the thick middle of a listless afternoon. The neighborhood was its invariable self. Gray sheets stiffened on slack lines. Sunlight bounced off half-shaded windows. A single cloud raced to the horizon. Beneath me the house creaked, then grew silent. I listened, listened hard. My heart filled with the power of my plans. Beyond that, I neither felt nor heard a thing.

You can tell a lot about any man, I've always felt, by the way he lolls around a hotel lobby.

Some spread themselves across divans, as though contemplating bids on the place. Others sit bolt upright in wing chairs, as if anticipating the house detective's summons. Chick Gandil assumed the basic ballplayer's lobby-sitting posture that airless Monday morning. Knees splayed, shoulders hunched, he looked like Elmo Lincoln's understudy awaiting the proctologist's finger.

8

Gandil had suggested meeting at the Buckminster. The White Sox were in Boston for three games. They were six and a half in front, and coasting. It seemed a perfect chance to open discussions. I, of course, would have preferred a more discreet rendezvous, but Chick liked his conniving on the high side. He didn't rise to greet me.

"Sport."

"Chick."

Our exchange required a courteous touch it would never receive. Chick's posture radiated tension, all the more menacing for lacking specificity. Gamblers sense such things. Emotion is bad for our business.

Several other White Sox players lined the walls, eyeing the molls, hoping to be eyed. They looked quite unlikely in their street clothes, looked too big, in fact, for their own bodies.

Gandil motioned me theatrically toward the stairwell. I had the feeling I was being paraded for someone's benefit. Kid Gleason, the manager, was standing beside the checkout desk, excavating his fingernails with an incisor.

"Bump up to my den for a moment, Sport," Gandil bellowed. "I got something there could make Woodrow Wilson's dick hard."

What is it about cheap hotels, I've often wondered, that makes the shabbiest tenement seem palatial by comparison? Does catering to transients accent their squalor? Is institutional inadequacy more threatening than our own? Not that the Buckminster was Boston's shoddiest scratch house. It was just ragged enough to make its customers feel they belonged there. The dump didn't even have an elevator. I trailed Gandil's rump up five flights to his room. Since I find it difficult to address even the comeliest backside, our ascent was made in absolute silence.

9

Chick's room fulfilled the lobby's seedy promise, its shortcomings limited solely by its size. Two steel cots slouched in opposite corners, exuding rust. One held a battered cardboard binder. There were no chairs.

"We could've done this downstairs, Sport. They all know. They don't know what, they just know something."

We sat down on one of the cots. He placed the binder squarely on my lap.

I don't keep a scrapbook myself. In my line it would hardly be advisable. And though I'm unjustifiably attached to my history, I've never required relics to evoke it. Gandil struck me as similarly uncommemorative. I couldn't imagine him preserving anything more touching than a grudge.

There it all was, though—a horsehider's life in effigy, perpetuated in sepia prints and rabbit-skin glue.

Chick at seventeen, with his St. Paul high school team, looking like an angry child impersonating a hangman. At eighteen, tending first base in Amarillo, the year he hopped a freight to seek perpetuity. Toiling for a Mexican outlaw team in 1906, and as a boxer during spare moments of this period.

Only in his first major league portrait, with the 1910 White Sox, does his face suggest its later liverish adamancy—the flintiness about the eyes, the skin pulled back to amplify the skull. With the Senators, after his trade, the effect is even more disquieting. (This was around the time I first encountered him, in a pool hall two blocks from the Gaiety, and began coaxing injury tips from him for $10 apiece.)

The most striking tintype, however, dates from his return to Chicago, in 1917. It suggests an elemental sourness ripening slowly into malice. In it he is seen sliding into second base, spikes up, teeth bared. No ball appears in the frame.

The portfolio revealed one further chilling idiosyncrasy. It contained no family pictures, no likenesses of teammates. In all cases where other people had been portrayed, their presence had been neatly cropped from existence.

"That's my life, Sport, in that book, and in this room. I wanted you to see it. I'll be thirty-two tomorrow."

This wasn't quite true, but I understood his need to exaggerate. He was building himself a case.

"Comiskey says this shitbin is 'convenient.' He don't mention it costs ninety cents a night. They change the sheets every fucking Groundhog Day. See that No Smoking sign? In a real hotel it would say 'No Smoking, Please.' I made four thousand dollars this year. That ass-boil Chase made six thousand finessing half the Giants' schedule. I worked fourteen years for that book, Sport. I'm going to hock it now to get out of this coop. After October, every fucking sign I read is going to say 'please.' "

It was more lip than he'd served me in any ten previous meetings. He was working himself into a high latitude.

"I want a hundred thousand, Sport. Fifty for palm oil, fifty for myself. You'll bet the second fifty for me, twenty-five on the Series, five on separate games. I don't care what else you do, just don't bruise my odds. We've always been finger-and-thumb, Sport. That's why you're getting first call on this deal."

He paused briefly. I nursed my silence.

This apparently was it, then, in outline, and particular, what all my dreams would come to. It was transcendent enough, I suppose, unless you figured in my waiting.

"We're having a team meeting next week. Comiskey owes us bonus money. We should strike for it, but we won't. These buttercups are afraid to even wish for things. I'll line my guys up after that. You talk to your guys. I know you

11

don't keep that kind of dough in your pocket."

He gave no signal that our meeting was over, but it was. I had nothing I wanted to ask him, and less to tell. We would be partners, not friends. I left him sitting on the bed, balancing his memories on his knee bones.

The players' eyes tracked my retreat through the lobby. They would be there until noon, when a bus would carry them six blocks to the park.

Out on the sidewalk a rush of late-morning heat engulfed me. It was like emerging from a tomb into daylight. My steps had a springiness I couldn't credit. I was having trouble focusing my thoughts. It had started, after all this time, and already it was moving beyond my grasp, like a moth released from darkness into daylight.

A trolley rumbled by. A squirrel lunched in the gutter. Church chimes marked the odd hour.

I paused to observe things I rarely took note of. Beyond their novelty they held little significance. Still I wanted to acknowledge them, to remember everything that happened that day.

I wondered, briefly, if I should have bargained with Gandil. But why? He'd already offered me more than I'd have thought to ask for.

For several minutes I wandered in a daze of my own devising, lost in good fortune and the fix's lack of limit. I had little idea where I was going, and less desire to learn. I knew I was making progress, trusted my instincts to extend it.

Suddenly the former world intruded, as a rag of flame flashed quietly past my ear. It hit the sidewalk, flipped over, smoldering.

It was Gandil's scrapbook.

I turned a page with my toe. The photographs had turned to ash. Only the binding remained to identify it. I looked up to see where it had come from. And there, to my horror, stood the Buckminster. I'd been wandering in circles for twenty minutes beneath it.

Only then did I realize the first complication had presented itself. I'd agreed to get back to my guys. But, in truth, I had no guys to get back to.

3

But of course everybody has at least one guy to get back to. So the next morning I took the trolley to South Boston to get the inside bang from Sleepy Bill Burns.

I had no way of communicating with Bill. Nobody did. He had no fixed address, no telephone. Most mornings, during the baseball season at least, he made an appearance in the Cathedral of Sighs, to take in the eight-o'clock Mass. Bill was an incorrigible daily communicant.

After the service he d often remain alone in the sacristy, fussing with votive candles, receiving financial supplicants. He had a lot of money out on the street. I have no idea what his understanding with the cathedral was on this, or if the irony of the situation occurred to him. Bill was a very literal man.

That morning I had him all to myself. He was sprinkling some religious-looking powder on several chasubles, folding them into an Italianate armoire. I experienced a slight pang on approaching him, but attributed it to indigestion, and proceeded. Bill didn't look up. As always, he addressed me as if we'd last conversed fifteen minutes earlier.

"Yes, well, there's the gambler's life for you, Sport, Shinola one minute, shit the next. And yourself? Up to something with scale, I see. I can tell by the enthusiasm with which you consumed the wafer."

Bill had pitched five years in the big leagues, for five different teams, without once achieving a winning season. His 30–52 lifetime record included a 7–13 stint with the 1909 White Sox. When he retired, in 1912, he went straight to Texas and, improbably, struck oil. It wasn't a big hit, just substantial enough to ensure his perpetual ease, and fund his passion for low-level conspiracies.

Bill was a tall, deceptively lethargic-looking man with a wren's nest of prematurely white hair. He spoke habitually from the side of his mouth, as if hinting at secrets too delicate for broadcast. If you asked him what time it was, he'd glance around the room, lean to within inches of your ear, and whisper: "Eight forty-seven." Everything he said thus had an air of shared intimacy. He never *really* shared anything, of course, but only told you what everybody knew, hoping to learn something he didn't. He was, in short, a cozy Irishman. I should know.

I outlined the parameters of my opportunity to him as he continued his folding. When I finished he looked directly at me with a wry smile, which I could have interpreted as either conspiratorial or condescending had I chosen to make a distinction.

"You don't need many players, Sport. Three's plenty. Gandil. Cicotte. Jackson. More players, more complications. Gandil's a hard guy—he'll keep the others straight. I don't know if he's up to the complexities, though. Cicotte can be trusted. If he says he'll dump, he'll dump. And he could start three games. Jackson's so stupid he's almost legally dead. But he's half the team. The others would be more

trouble than they're worth. Riisberg's a mean little cunt—
he'll throw it just to spite Comiskey, then double-cross you
for the buzz of it. Williams talks too much, Felsch is an idiot,
Weaver I have no sense of."

It was a typical Burnsian synopsis, reams of common
knowledge wrapped in layers of conventional wisdom. The
clipped delivery was meant to mask its banality. Bill would
have made a good Pope.

"You've got three problems as I see it, Sport. Raising the
money, controlling the players, keeping it quiet. Then
there's Comiskey's long nose, and the papers, and the odds.
They'll drop like the Kaiser's arches when tall jack moves
against Chicago. I don't know, Sport. The Series. A lot of
people could get annoyed at you for this."

I was tempted to stop him then, but didn't. I needed any
counsel too much to reject the gloomiest.

"If you want my hit on it, though, here it is. Cut it to
Gandil, Cicotte, and Jackson. Keep Gandil between you and
the others. Stay away from Riisberg. Bet early, on the Series, not on individual games. Anything can happen in one
game. Spread it around. And don't go to Rothstein for the
cash. He'll dry-shave you before your piggies hit the pavement."

He paused then, as if conjuring up a memory.

"And if you want somebody to set it up for you, Sport, I
might be able to spare you the odd moment."

He looked me almost straight in the eye then, as if to
soften his offer. It was the one contingency I hadn't bargained on—a request for inclusion. I'd thought just seeking
his advice would be compensation enough.

"Good luck no matter what you decide, though, Sport. It's
a pretty big order. You could have a mile of fun with it, or
you could get your pud fed to the fishes."

15

I knew then that he realized he was out. My silence had said what my tongue hadn't dared to.

I couldn't help being struck by his assessment, though, and by how profoundly it differed from Gandil's. It always astounds me when similar men disagree completely, especially when I agree with both. I think it has something to do with diction.

On the trolley going home I sensed I'd made my first mistake. I had no idea how damaging it was, so I wasn't too worried. It just bothered me that it had come so soon.

Every mistake seems predictable once you've made it. Maybe I should have kept my own counsel in this matter. But I thought expansion required guidance. I was a victim of my isolation, my lack of contacts. I wanted to change, but could only change what I had.

I suppose I chose Burns because he was available. He'd never helped me much before. But neither had my father. What I probably really wanted from him was reassurance, the sort of reassurance you only get by sharing a dangerous secret with somebody exactly like yourself. I suppose I thought that's what "getting back to your guys" meant.

Still, I had learned a few useful things during our talk.

I'd learned how big this deal could be, by how much Burns wanted in on it.

I'd learned how deeply I was committed to it, by how much I wanted to exclude him.

And I'd learned that I should head straight to Arnold Rothstein for my capital, by how violently Burns's jaw had bobbed when he'd warned me not to.

4

For a week after that I slept in my father's house. I'd be leaving it soon and not returning. I wanted to get as much benefit from my remaining time as possible.

I talked to no one during this period, saw no one.

I rose every morning before dawn. In the early light I wandered his house, room to room, window to window. After lunch I strolled around his garden. On the second day I cut five red peonies low on the stem and placed them in a glass of water on the kitchen table. The next day I came down to find them open. Each day after that they opened in the morning, closed in the late afternoon. In the evenings I put on my Argentine tango records and danced by myself around the parlor. Late at night I bicycled out to the countryside and walked unfamiliar back roads in the moonlight.

Gradually this routine crushed my apprehension. Like a frazzled pitcher whose inshoot begins sinking, my mind gained clarity as my nervous energy dissipated. I began noticing how I made time disappear, keeping life always safely out in front of me, endlessly preparing for what I feared had to fail. Or succeed.

On the fifth night I dreamed an evil dream. A pockmarked stranger who claimed to be Sergeant York stuck a silver bayonet into my esophagus. He cut out the back of my pharynx and I died, drowning in my blood. I awoke at the peak of my terror and went downstairs and prepared a large meal.

I don't know how to cook, and have little desire to learn. I simply collected all the food in the house and launched into it with insolent abandon.

I stuffed an avocado with cheese and random herbs. I cooked a small fowl in a great pot—either basting or braising it (whichever is which) in sloe gin and *crème de marron.* I constructed a substantial ratatouille from all sorts of indistinguishable vegetables. Then, inspired by the power of my ignorance, and cheered by my total indifference to it, I attempted an angel food cake which didn't rise because I forgot to put something important in it. I washed this all down with three bottles of Hale's lager. By the time I finished it was six A.M. The sun was creeping in beneath the shades. Birds were singing on their wires. It was time to go upstairs and pack. I would be taking the B train to Saratoga, to where Arnold Rothstein was summering, as always, living the expansive life I'd long coveted at a distance.

I left the uneaten food scattered about the kitchen, where it would rot and settle in interesting patterns. Or vandals would compromise the basement and smear it on the walls. Or the agent I'd engaged to sell the house would clean it up to charm a prospect.

Whichever, it was no longer my concern.

I walked the half mile to the station, carrying the possessions that still interested me in two valises. Principal among these were a copy of *Spalding's Baseball Register,* a pair of black patent-leather dancing pumps, and my Smith & Wesson .38 barking iron. The sky was pure azure, the breezes past perfection. Saratoga's four-week race meet would begin tomorrow. Rothstein would surely be there.

Midway through my walk a small brown mongrel joined me, sniffing my bags dismissively, racing ahead to explore alternative diversions, then reclaiming me at every corner.

Ordinarily I try to discourage such society, but he was a pleasant enough companion, and we weren't going that far.

When we reached the station he spotted a pigeon loitering on the tarmac. He barked once; the bird took flight. The dog pursued it to the edge of the retaining wall, leaped at its beating wings, then disappeared over the side without a sound. He had no way of knowing the drop was fifty feet; I had no way of knowing he would risk it. My heart and voice froze simultaneously. I walked slowly to the wall and peered over. No body was visible below, no blood, no trace. In the distance the Lake Shore Limited curled slowly past the roundhouse.

I sat in the parlor car and read the New York papers. The White Sox had swept the A's the day before. They were pictured celebrating in the clubhouse. Only Kid Gleason seemed unreservedly pleased.

The man in the seat next to me, who looked like a recent retiree from a particularly debilitating profession, stuck his stubby finger into the headline. He informed me that an inside guy had told him all ballgames were fixed. I said, "Don't defame our national pastime, Jasper, or I'll piss on your wing tips." Then I walked out to the rear platform to insulate myself from fatuous society.

The Berkshire hills rolled by as in a moonscape. Farmhands trudged aimlessly across ledge-filled meadows. Sunlight caressed my face.

When we entered a tunnel just before the Hudson, I went to the club car and ordered a drink. I'd heard it was the longest railroad tunnel in the world. But the man who'd told me this was addicted to paregoric and thus given to superlatives.

The darkie who served my scotch was from Key Largo.

We had a brief conversation about conches and trade winds. His distracted manner quickly loosened my tongue.

"I'm about to change my life, Roland," I told him, before he could ask.

"Is that right, sir. Well isn't that just palatable."

"Actually I'm about to *begin* my life, as it happens. What I've been doing so far has been mainly preparation."

"Preparation is important, sir. It's the mother of invention, like they say."

"Exactly, Roland. It's just that now I'm panting to get on with it, to swap anticipation for action. I walked to South Station today, Roland. And as I did I thought: 'If I pass this sad way just one more time I will sink to the ground sobbing, possibly never to rise.' I'm still doing what I've always done, Roland. Nothing changes, except the dates. But now I'm well on my way to revising that condition."

"Lovely. Lovely."

"It will be lovely, Roland, and exciting too. I feel this talk we're having is just its preamble, the calm before the uproar, as it were."

"I'm glad you feel that way, sir. I'm always happy to be of service if I can help it."

He was drying glasses as we talked. Every third one gave that little squeal. A tiny piece of roughage marred his smile. I tried to guess which tooth it would land on next.

"Have you ever noticed, Roland, that when you start doing something you've put off for a long time, you can't imagine how to proceed? It seems such an impossible undertaking, you can't even think of how to begin."

"Yes, sir, I've noticed that. It's like tying a four-in-hand."

"So naturally the question becomes—now what?"

"Exactly. That's the question Roland asks the face in the mirror every single morning."

"Still, I do imagine, Roland, if I place one foot in front of the other, eventually it will all put itself straight. Then I'll wonder what I was waiting for. I'll ask myself: 'What could you possibly have been doing before you did this?'"

"Like tying a four-in-hand."

"I've got the general idea all worked out, Roland, plus some big shots to help me with the particulars. Have you heard of Jocko Kielty, Roland?"

"Jocko Kelly, sir? Is that the gent that plants his keister up on flagpoles?"

"Kielty, Roland, *Kielty*. He just happens to be the top numbers man in Boston, the nonpareil. I was his right-hand man, more or less, for fifteen years. I outgrew him, though, quite a while back actually."

"Did you, sir?"

"Yes. I did. But I stayed with him. Don't know why exactly. Loyalty, I expect. Loyalty is very important to me, Roland."

"Loyalty's important to everybody, sir."

"Ever heard of Arnold Rothstein, Roland?"

But of course he hadn't. Roland hadn't heard of much of anybody. That was his principal charm. Talking to him was like talking to an obtuse version of myself. He kept on polishing his stemware, smiling, nodding, hearing me, but not actually listening, just part of his job. It wasn't really a conversation, it was more like a précis for a conversation. He was a blackbird, we were traveling. It could easily not have been happening.

I stopped talking when I heard myself mention Rothstein, though. This was ground too dangerous to tread on even in jest.

I left Roland an oversized tip then and headed back to the parlor car. He grinned as if he knew how much he'd helped.

And he had helped, too, allowing me to amuse myself, which I need to do, and permitting me to taste my excitement, by acting as if he shared it. Somebody would have to be excited, after all, if I was to get myself profitably through these next few weeks.

I took a cab from the Saratoga station to my rooming house. All the better hotels had been booked to the gills. I wasn't particularly anxious to be seen in one anyway, happy to cede the spotlight to those who required it.

My driver was lathered with opening-week lowdown. Lillian Russell was ensconced at the Grand Union. Sam Rosoff had downed an entire steer at Canfield's. Three new whorehouses were soliciting Elmers on lower Broadway.

"The mummers will parade at dawn tomorrow, bub. They're the ones that grease their kissers up like spearchuckers."

Our swing through town confirmed his vulgar summary. The streets roiled with romantics and advantage-seekers. Two lines wound around the Adelphi, one hoping to see Theda Bara in *Camille,* the other awaiting the arrival of the racing form. My heart was with the latter, though I denied it my body. There would be ample time for handicapping tomorrow. I had a sudden urge for a vanilla phosphate, but let it pass.

We swung out past the racetrack and into silence. The elms on Union Avenue refracted the late-afternoon sun. Twenty-five thousand souls would fill the old course tomorrow. Now it was resolutely serene. Two workmen sewed wind socks, four planted calla lilies. The infield lake teemed with *trompe l'oeil* swans.

High overhead a lone falcon circled, then paused before

22

heading into its dive. It hit the water at a ninety-degree angle, its entire body vanishing beneath the surface. The swans rocked in inanimate contentment, insulated by their woodenness. I waited breathlessly for the falcon to re-emerge, but it didn't. I kept staring at the lake, but it didn't help. It was simply gone.

The driver pointed to a tiny figure running beside the road. "That's Earl Sande, the greatest living jockey in America. He don't eat nothing but spinach and skim milk, then he drinks Worcestershire to make himself puke."

I knew this was untrue. I'd once stood Sande a major meal at Lindy's. Two eye ribs, three baked murphies, half a keg of porter, and a quart of ginger sherbet to seal the bribe.

It was worth it, though. The horse paid $26.80.

I slept well that evening. The crickets sang in their slings outside my window. For the first time in a long while I didn't French-rub the fix while drifting off.

The last thing I did consider was something Bill Burns had said before I'd left him.

He'd escorted me up the cathedral's middle aisle, slipping a folded bill into the mission box on passing. I think it was a single.

"For the starving pygmies in Boboland, Sport. I don't want you to think my heart is on permanent vacation."

He didn't smile as he said this. He might have been serious.

"I think God looks a bit like me, don't you, Sport? Tall, herring-gutted individual with a slightly distracted air, hangs around the backs of basilicas, doesn't seem to have much else to do."

I'd had no answer for him then. But now, lying there in

the cool Saratoga twilight, with sleep approaching like a reward for all my dreams, I suddenly thought of one. I didn't intend to waste it.

"How could God look anything like you, Bill," I growled at the frayed outline of his memory, "when everybody knows he's the spitting image of Arnold Rothstein?"

5

Ten A.M. Bright. Calm.

A large Jew, a small Jew, and a medium-sized Irishman sit in the garden of the Saratoga Reading Room. The large Jew, Arnold Rothstein, drinks bourbon from a tumbler. The small Jew, Abe Attell, drinks rye from a shot glass. The Irishman, myself, does not imbibe.

Around us the rich lounge with characteristic insouciance. Half look like men who owe me money, the other half look like they've never owed anybody anything.

"Capital at play," Rothstein whispers. "When thieves develop affectations they're ripe for picking, Sport. And these are thieves. Never mistake understatement for quality. They just got here two hundred years before us ethnics."

Rothstein liked addressing his inferiors donnishly, suggesting camaraderie while maintaining distance. Since he considered nearly everybody his inferior, it was a style he was much given to.

I'd been assured I'd find him in this nook, his morning headquarters in Saratoga. The Reading Room wasn't really for reading. It wasn't even a room. It was, rather, a rambling frame cottage next to the main entrance to the track. In

1875 it had been converted by its owner, an aging dandy of indeterminate gender, into a hot spot for the amusement of his drinking companions. Attell and I weren't well-bred. Rothstein had few friends. But he *was* rich enough to compensate for all our shortcomings.

We sat on white wicker furniture with our racing forms spread out before us. We wore identical cream-colored straddlers and straw boaters with black satin bows. It was the accepted affectation of the moment. Rothstein had placed us in the southernmost corner of the garden, as far from the other guests as seemed possible. The wind blew through his wayward forelock, then up through the clematis. Or perhaps I've reversed the sequence. The sun made evocative patterns on his forehead.

I'd often passed this club while approaching the track, and always coveted admission. Now that I had it, it seemed a particularly insipid ambition.

I'd risen at dawn that morning, taken my breakfast on the Gideon Putnam veranda. Afterward I'd walked the gravel paths of its grounds, preparing myself for the forenoon's confrontation. I wanted the specifics of my desire to be lucid, as well as what I'd be willing to settle for. I didn't want to know exactly what to say, though. Spontaneity has always fueled my ardor, or such ardor as I've ever been able to summon. I did want to know what *not* to say, though, to make my omissions a major feature of my argument. I had command of a significant opportunity. Its gravity could support the deepest silence. I didn't want my natural anxiety at any chance subverted by Rothstein's native power over every chance. He assumed rights I had to talk myself into.

After an hour of reflection I felt ready. I lay down under an oak and took a nap. Its dander soon covered my body.

When I awoke I took a cab straight to the Reading Room. Rothstein was always there the first day of every meeting. He thought it helped people forget he was a Jew.

"Did you come up from New York on the Special, Sport?" he asked me now, laying aside his racing form.

"No, I came straight from Boston, Mr. Rothstein."

"Ah yes, Boston. You missed a grand trip then, Sport. Six specially fitted coaches. Three sleeping cars without uppers. One hundred sportsmen. Two hundred bottles of Lafite-Rothschild. Three hundred Antiguan lobsters. Eight hundred Havana panatelas. Fifteen of Flo Ziegfeld's finest. And enough domestic help to staff the mating shed at Versailles. Harry Sinclair, the oil wallet, sponsored it. None of the boys reached the old Spa intact, am I right, Abe?"

Attell nodded, but didn't speak.

This was vintage Rothstein, a brilliant slice of his social attack in miniature. He'd inquired of my trip to warm me, detailed his own to impress me, explained who Harry Sinclair was to show how little I knew, forgotten I came from Boston to show how little I mattered. It was a burlesque calculated to charm and demean simultaneously, to leave me feeling I was enjoying company I didn't deserve to be in. I sat back and waited for the question he *really* wanted to ask.

"What brings you bouncing our way today, then, Sport?"

"I'm going to fix the World Series, Mr. Rothstein."

"Yes, I suppose you are. How much do you need?"

"One hundred thousand."

He'd pounced. I'd parried. He'd remained unruffled. I'd ignored his calm. It was an exchange I could never have anticipated, which is precisely why I felt so ready for it. George M. Cohan taught me to bandy budgets with the prosperous: "Guess their limit, then double it, and add ten percent. You'll be shy at first, but don't flinch, or explain. When you see how cheap they still think they're getting you, you'll know exactly how long you've been playing in the bush leagues."

"Who's your contact?" Rothstein asked now, looking off into the distance.

"Gandil," I replied. "The first baseman."

"It would be."

I gave no answer.

"How many players do you need?"

"Five, maybe six."

"How many pitchers?"

"Two."

"Why would they do such a thing?"

"For the money."

This seemed to surprise him, though profit was the self-evident motive. Yet it did sound somehow inadequate to the circumstances.

"A hundred thousand isn't much."

"Enough."

"Can Gandil get the others?"

"Yes."

"Can he be trusted?"

"No."

This seemed to please him. If Gandil could be trusted, after all, he'd be no use to either of us.

I was growing gradually more comfortable. Yet every exchange made me feel less in charge. Rothstein had a genius for the enslaving calmative.

"Who are the other players?"

"I'd rather not say."

"Of course."

"I hope you don't mind."

I *was* losing control. Rothstein looked directly at me, and smiled.

We all gazed away then, across the broad expanse of lawn. Beside the goldfish pool various trust fund managers exchanged pleasantries with assorted beneficiaries. Miscellaneous wives tossed slivers of croissant to the frogs. Colored waiters in white jackets moved languidly along the hedgerows.

This, then, was what I'd always coveted in this place, the air of easeful timelessness, parasoled tables widely spaced in random patterns, frosted drinks, fresh strawberries, soft breezes, amiable conversations discreetly muffled. It was the perfect spot for mounting genteel intrigues, especially on the first morning of the racing season.

"I don't think it can be done," he said finally, as if to himself.

Attell traced his lower lip with a thumbnail.

"Something about it isn't quite right."

He took out his pocket watch.

"It throws everything off."

He stared at the watch for a moment, then returned it to his vest.

"No more talk of it now."

He'd clearly not wanted me there in the first place. I intruded on his notion of the ideal. He'd only indulged me out of the mock courtesy common interests dictate, and because he knew of me, knew that timid tinkerers like me only approach expansive operators like him with projects worthy of their time. Now he'd heard my case, and dismissed it. Not that I considered his rejection permanent. I knew his disdain would eventually yield to his greed. He might have begun to imitate old money, but he still knew what he was.

We passed the next two hours handicapping the horses,

our silence broken only by the soft laughter of rich women and the reassuring rustle of seersucker against stone. Between calculations I gazed up at the swaying trees, keeping track of the shadows as they slid across the garden.

I was surprised at how familiar I was with Rothstein. I shouldn't have been. I'd been following his career clandestinely for years. He was what I would have been, if I could have been anything.

Once he looked up from his figuring, and, apropos of nothing, said: "It's a big risk."

I smiled, but held my tongue. It was seeping in.

At twelve-thirty he stood abruptly and folded his racing form, tucking it like a riding crop beneath his arm.

"Gentlemen, we'll want to be there when the first horse reaches the paddock."

He didn't wait for a response, but strode purposefully across the garden, through the rose trellis at its entrance. A shower of petals fell in his wake. After a moment's hesitation, Attell and I followed, one at each elbow, in provisional symmetry. Nobody in the garden looked up to watch us go.

"Riisberg and Williams I can imagine, but Cicotte and Jackson are a puzzlement. I suppose Felsch is going along for the ride. The sixth, if there is one, eludes me."

No response was required. We made the rest of our way in silence. I knew I'd made a good start then, done the first of the many things I would need to do, made some small part of him, at long last, my own.

6

I have a dream of the perfect scam.

I've had it for as long as I can remember. It involves small-town banks and kited checks and a horse race won by a ringer and several dozen square-toes fleeced within inches of their lives, yet incapable of revenge because I've evaporated. I'll speak no more of it now. I may still attempt it.

Its key elements are solitude, escape, and perfection. The solitude and escape are mine. The perfection lies in its intricacies.

For years I've entertained this fantasy, savoring its basics, revising its details. In tight quarters and lone moments, in men's-room stalls and flappers' arms, I've savored its geometric simplicity.

I plan for months, then act sequentially, fleeing with unheard-of sums into remote areas, losing myself in the isolation of the solvent, undertaking a life of restrained and reflective elegance.

I garden, sketch, read voraciously, travel sporadically, take long lunches and regular naps, living off my interest, which is considerable.

I'd been dreaming this dream so long it no longer felt like a dream to me, but like some part of my life I'd decided not to live. When I finally had to live it, it came out crooked. There were no small-town banks, no kited checks, no horse races, just a kraut first baseman with his own larcenous agenda, and two Hebrew slug-duckers with self-aggrandizements to be cannibalized.

30

Is it only by accident that anybody ever accomplishes anything?

That week in Saratoga was the closest I've ever come to really living. Even the unlikeliest goals seemed temporarily attainable.

The tone was set the day after I met with Rothstein.

I rose at six and breakfasted again on the Putnam terrace. John D. Rockefeller, Jr., loitered opposite me, tonguing his concubine. At seven Jimmy Walker whirled puckishly through the lobby, as if in flight from his own enthusiasms. I made prune juice and one-way eggs my meal.

At nine I strolled to the track to watch the workouts. The clubhouse was already frantic with luminaries; I felt like one just being there. Several ingenues played kiss-the-king in the loges. I couldn't tell if they were beautiful, or just young.

At Art du Temps an exhibit of marine oils was in progress. Will Rogers perused it, looking neither amusing nor amused. Several lesser Vanderbilts had cornered the *artiste*, who resembled a miniature rodent specifically bred for the occasion.

A cup of slumgullion in the track kitchen reoriented me. The word was out that speed was holding up. After the Camembert I strolled to the lake for a quick bummy dunk, dog-paddling in a deserted corner in my underwear. Then I dressed and strode back through the darkening maples to the track. The sky was cloudless, as it would be all week. Quick breezes made fugitive furrows in the Bermuda. I took several flutters, losing each.

In the sixth, the Sanford, I backed a two-year-old named Upset. He beat Man o' War by a fast-diminishing neck. Man o' War paused at the start, surrendered fifteen pounds, yet still almost got up to get the job done. He'd won all six races previously, would win all fourteen after.

I don't ordinarily defy perfection. Faultlessness deserves to run its particular course. But Upset's name intrigued me, and his odds (19–1) were irresistible. I doubled up on a steeplechaser in the next race, for the kick of it. He led over every fence, at 7–2. I fled the track feeling cheeky and indomitable, as impervious to defeat as only heedless plungers deserve to feel.

After a gin fizz at the Grand Union I walked to Niggertown for Veal Oscar beneath the grape vines. The evening light was fading into the courtyards, the streets slowly filling with Hasidim. Sunny Jim Fitzsimmons dined beside me, extolling his two-year-olds. I didn't listen. Trainers always overestimate their young.

Down at Fasig-Tipton, lines of limousines ringed the auction barns, their headlights piercing the swaying arborvitae. White-jacketed grooms paraded yearlings outside their stalls. The auctioneer's voice drifted tonelessly from the pavilion. Buddy Ensor arrived with his entourage, looking tastelessly natty in an ill-advised suit. Damon Runyon surveyed the action, chatting up the hot walkers, larding on the charm, collecting color no doubt.

My last stop was at Rothstein's casino, the Brook.

It filled a four-story Norman cottage on the town's northern edge. Rothstein had refurbished it with his usual restrained expansiveness, filling the common rooms with unexpected artifacts, painting the woodwork in somber, neutral colors. Its sole banal touch was an overly evocative oil of Mrs. Rothstein, the slim and untalented actress Carolyn Green. In it she looked like an Episcopal nun impersonating Salome.

Rothstein wasn't due until midnight. I decided to wait. I made a tentative pass at chemin de fer, risking only coins. A gaunt, brassy woman whom everybody called the Countess was running amok at dice. I bought my day's final drink and hit the south lawn with a vengeance. Viola notes drifted up from the orangerie. The klieg lights lit the milling chauffeurs' faces.

I need to say something more of Rothstein now, if only for my own sake.

He and I were the same age, the same height, the same temperament. We shared several interests, a background, a profession. Yet I had remained adamantly the fantasist, while he'd stepped out steadily deeper into his longings.

How was this? By chance? By predestination? By force of circumstance?

I'd met him only once before, in 1911, at a muffin worry for Jaunty Callahan. I was in the midst of concocting myself then, desperate for clues. Rothstein looked like the man who'd invented money. We brushed over the boiled ham. It did the trick. The next day I began my file on him.

These are excerpts, but give the flavor.

8/27/11.   His father, "Rothstein the Just," cuts pants, cultivates piety. No wonder the kid craves the rackets. After Ellis Island they head straight to Delancey Street. A.R. quits school at fourteen, like myself.

A street-corner ascetic in his apprenticeship, hoarding capital, and favors, shylocking at 25 percent, fencing for yeggs. He doesn't just consider action, he takes it. In 1902 he opens a casino with Augie Doran, in Murray Hill no less. Ten-thou-

sand-dollar handles nightly. It's not enough though. Nothing is. He starts skimming. Doran demurs. A.R. opens his own joint the next night.

9/23/11.   Running the whole East Side by 1906, girls, numbers, you name it. Meanwhile I'm cadging dime raises from Jocko. He insulates himself with subordinates, mythologizes himself through banty nicknames: Mr. Big, The Brain, The Bankroll, The Man Uptown, The Man To See (this last my favorite).

1/3/14.   At last a photo of him, clipped from the Traveler, in profile, unfocused, a lower brow than remembered, thicker nostrils; unsettling, actually—refuting any fable. Though I'm sure my mind will quickly rearrange it. The suit, at least, is as imagined: pearl-gray, tailored by God; the hair cut hourly; both arms crooked permanently, prepared for any blonde. The soul, in short, of streetwise swank.

3/8/17.   Thirty-five today, twenty years a gambler, seven a millionaire, the east's largest racing stable, extensive real estate holdings (Florida, California), knows everybody, man of will, and substance, can fix anything. Does he appreciate what he has, or even know it? Perhaps he takes fruition for granted. That would be unbearable, that he has everything without desiring it. Does he dream of things, of me perhaps, of what I might be doing at any particular moment?

Read again, years later, my reports betray a certain lack of rigor. I'd omitted so many things. For example; nothing about others interested him, unless he could profit by it. Naturally I resented this, naturally I wished to emulate it.

I'd kept similar files before, I blush to admit, on women I'd desired, on eras I'd missed, once on a former schoolmate shredded at Château-Thierry. I kept no file on myself, though. What would it say?

34

Six years with the nuns, two at Latin School; a voracious reader, to distance himself from his world. A numbers runner for six years, a bag man for two, touting since 1912, thin, reclusive, a careful dresser, his father's son, nobody's best friend.

The last entry I made in any file was this one made in Rothstein's, one month, short a day, before our rendezvous.

7/1/19. Quiet lately, sponsoring no mayhem, opening no fronts. Is ambivalence contagious? I imagine him sitting in his penthouse, above the Hudson, staring out at the pigeons. Last night I called. He answered. I held the line, without speaking, for thirty seconds, like a pervert. Did I imagine he said: "I know you're out there, Sport"? Whose desire was that I felt pulsing along the wire?

Finally my curiosity had justified itself, in the uncertainty I'd sensed in his response. I now knew something about Rothstein nobody else knew. I knew he doubted.

At midnight his cinnamon Stutz rolled imperiously through the portico, disgorging him, then Attell. They bounded up the marble staircase in fluid unison, disappearing quickly into the casino. It was what I'd come for, to see him again, to be sure.

I left immediately, walked downtown to the telegraph office, sent a wire to Gandil in Chicago.

FUNDS SECURED, COMMENCE ARRANGEMENTS. FONDLY, SPORT.

It wasn't exactly true, but soon it could be.

I bought the vanilla phosphate I'd been denying myself then, and a copy of the next day's racing form. I'd study it briefly before I slept. It had been a satisfying day, full of the airy gratifications self-contained atmospheres generate. I'd mingled with, but not pandered to, stimulating society. I stood poised on the brink of a grand adventure, calm in the knowledge I could still elude it, yet aware that to do so now would cost me everything.

I drifted back to my room through the empty, quiet streets. The air was thick with the scent of unknown flowers. An owl called. The gas lamps dimmed. In Chicago, events I only learned of years later prepared to unfold in concert with my dreams. I wouldn't have deferred to them even if I'd known of them, though. This interval of lush anticipation deserved its precedence.

7

If the White Sox ever held a victory banquet," Ring Lardner once told Heywood Broun, "they'd ask the caterer for twenty separate checks."

It was true. The Sox rarely did anything together, except win.

That morning, as I mooned voluptuously around Saratoga, the fixers drifted glumly toward their park, their conveyances as diverse as their routes.

Gandil took a cab, Riisberg was driven by his wife (a neat, dyspeptic woman who habitually confused Swede's desires with her own), Cicotte came by trolley (the conductor often let him ride for free), Lefty Williams hitched, Happy Felsch bicycled, Joe Jackson and Buck Weaver walked, though not together.

When they arrived they went straight to the clubhouse, where Kid Gleason was waiting for them in the can, his chin cupped like a boiled egg in his palm. This was an authentic reflection of the Kid's present predicament, if slightly bar-numized.

Gleason had reached the park at nine-thirty, via Comiskey's Packard. Comiskey had ridden up front, skimming the stock pages. He'd already talked to the Kid more than he cared to at breakfast, though he assumed he owed him the ride.

The players gathered around Gleason now, loyalists to the right, dissidents to the left. Those who didn't know, or care, how they felt, mingled.

"He wouldn't talk about it," Gleason mumbled, barely audible.

It was the specific lie he and Comiskey had settled on, though it had sounded a lot less bald at 6:00 A.M.

"You mean he said no?" asked Riisberg, almost glee-fully.

"He said you boys signed contracts, you should honor them. He said he'll cash in all your chips when the time comes."

The players wanted to laugh at this, but lacked the strength. They were about to win another pennant. Two of them would enter the Hall of Fame. Two others would be diverted by circumstance. Yet they had an almost irrelevant payroll. Now they also had an answer to their bluffs, an answer whose bluntness was draining their tongues of moisture. They weren't even worth *real* deception anymore.

"We'll go out, Kid," Riisberg said.

"No you won't, Swede. You'll never play again if you do."

Gleason's tone was more wistful than dismissive. He hadn't imagined their faces when he'd rehearsed this.

"Mr. Comiskey says he'll give you all bonuses after the Series. He says all things comes to every guy that waits."

The *Mr.* was all the players heard of this. Gleason bent quickly to retie his shoelaces.

"I'm still waiting for my 1917 bonus," Cicotte said.

The Kid coughed quietly into his palm. He'd done what they'd asked him to, and what Comiskey had *told* him to. What else did they want from him?

He wished he could say something encouraging to the boys, though, something peppy, even fatherly, some phrase with the words "overcome" and "ultimately" in it, some chin-off-the-floor that might possibly begin: "When I was a fledgling second sacker in Sheboygan . . ."

But no jaunty homily occurred to him just then, and he feared bending his heart in the pursuit of one. He didn't want to sound even sadder than he already had, like an old man foisting his compromises on the feckless.

When he finally did say something it was almost luxuriantly beside the point.

"If any of you want a good deal on a lawn mower," he whispered hoarsely, "my cousin August recently married into the business."

Gandil stood impassively by his locker, unwilling to grasp his perfect moment openly. He knew the players wouldn't strike unless he told them to; he wouldn't tell them to. Cashless vengeance no longer held much appeal for Chick.

The crowd around Gleason slowly dispersed, clearly shocked at the depths of their submissiveness. They would play today, as they always played, and they would win too, as they always seemed to win. Later they would deal with Comiskey's cramp-handedness, as Chick determined.

In the corner Gandil stood catching up on his reading. Inside his locker, behind the Absorbo Miracle Liniment, someone had taped a 1917 Series box score. All the White

Sox statistics had been inked over with zeros.

Gandil looked over at Riisberg. Riisberg winked, then flicked his flaccid genitals. Gandil permitted himself a quick grin, before a chilling hint of what he could become expunged it. Eddie Cicotte sat crouching in the corner, his forehead resting against his locker, one oyster eye turned magically to the room, fixing Chick with the deadest deadman stare imaginable.

8

They won, of course. Over Cleveland, or Detroit, or some such. Cicotte didn't pitch. When Gleason saw him warming up he thought better of it. Eddie's action seemed a trifle abstract, as if he'd recently been in a minor accident, or witnessed a major one.

Lefty Williams took his place, allowing just three hits. Joe Jackson and Happy Felsch hit home runs, Chick Gandil went three for four.

Sixteen thousand four hundred and twenty-three fans watched the game. Six hundred thousand would fill Comiskey's park that season. He'd make more money than several major railroads.

In the clubhouse, after the final out, the players dressed somberly, then left. They would be setting out on the season's last road trip that evening.

When the last player had fled, Kid Gleason donned his humblest homburg and his sincerest cardigan and disciplined his fugitive locks with dabs of Viso-cream. He had another appointment with Comiskey to endure.

He walked down the tunnel, out across the infield. The

late-summer sun was halfway behind the scoreboard. A lone attendant was redefining the third base line with crushed limestone.

Gleason walked the length of the yard, climbed the right field barrier, then trudged up the stone rows to the top. Comiskey liked sitting there alone after winning games, watching his park evacuating its innards.

"There's nothing better than seeing your park filling up," he liked to say. "Except maybe watching it emptying out afterward. It's like some gorgeous doll unaware she's being cased."

From his seat in the last row, Comiskey could scan Chicago's expanding skyline, whose scale his holdings now did so much to define. He was eating a veal chop grilled by his secretary, Nadine. Gleason lowered himself to the wooden slat beside him.

"They won't strike."

"Of course not. Why did you start Williams?"

"Cicotte seemed upset."

"Upset?"

"Distracted."

"It was his turn."

"Yes."

"Then?"

There were many answers Gleason could have made to this. He made none. He talked instead about his plans for the road trip, his pitching rotation, Weaver's batting slump. These were artificial problems his real problems could hide in. Later he told his wife he actually had said many of the things he'd merely wanted to say. Only his insistence on the point proved to her he hadn't.

Comiskey let him prattle on. The strike threat was all he'd really cared about. Now it had passed. He didn't actually yawn, though his jaw assumed a presomnolent set. When his shoulders began tilting toward his breastbone, Gleason took it as a signal of dismissal. He headed back the same way he'd come, through the long shadows that had begun blackening the diamond.

Comiskey watched the Kid walk away, a small, fidgety figure making his overly cautious way across the outfield. He was the only other person left in the stadium, unless you counted (and Comiskey certainly didn't) an elderly usher sweeping beneath the first base boxes.

Comiskey knew he could rely on the Kid. He was the ideal intermediary.

"He craves affection enough to befriend subordinates," Lardner once told me, "but covets approval too much not to betray them. It's what allowed him to rise through the ranks without leaving them. Plus he's cheap."

Comiskey burrowed deeper into his detachment then, digesting his veal, watching the sudden twilight subjugating his park. He took out his notebook and made three additions to his lists. This notebook, bound in opossum skin, had been a Christmas present from Marshall Field, Jr.

Under *Management, Immediate,* he wrote: "Gleason, haircut." He'd noticed the Kid's fringe needed cropping. He'd have an office boy lay down the law.

Under *Players, Long-Term,* he wrote: "Praise Cicotte, watch Gandil." Shameless flattery neutralized any resentment, Comiskey felt, while the silent foe always holds the steepest peril. Riisberg had been making all kinds of noise lately, it was true, but noise was all that little pissant could make. Comiskey underlined Gandil's name before returning the notebook to his pocket.

Full darkness now stole over the field. The linden trees had lost much of their definition. For not the first time

Comiskey noted how uncannily they resembled the groves on his uncle's ranch in Wyoming, trees that lined the creek where he'd speared walleyes as a boy, and whose branches filled with the drowned bodies of mouflon sheep every year after the spring floods subsided.

9

I received Gandil's return telegram that evening. It was the essence of economy.

THIS END SET. CHICK G.

So we both lied right from the get-go, claiming cooperation we could only have been hoping for. Such lies are inevitable, I suppose, as is believing them. We would both exaggerate increasingly throughout the Series, until even we came to believe our own distortions. That's the only way anything gets done, I'm afraid. Doubt must be dispelled, like any disease.

I was sitting on the back porch of my Saratoga boardinghouse when the wire arrived, gazing up at the stars, wondering if anything they said about them was true. Cicadas were chanting; honeysuckle breath hung seductively in the air. If I had any doubts about Gandil's message, I kept them from myself. At the very least my dream required that *I* believe in it. So for the moment, and with all my might, I did.

10

How many Chicago fans, asked how their star pitcher, Eddie Cicotte, spent the final hour of August 2, 1919, would have guessed: "Examining his laugh lines in a pocket mirror while passing through the Poconos in an upper"?

Yet he did.

Cicotte had sensed his skin shriveling for months, though he hadn't admitted it to himself until recently. It was an intriguing development, he had to admit, like discovering yourself rusting out from the inside.

How could there be so many of them? he wondered, staring at the lines. Had they just appeared overnight? Or had he been too distracted to notice them until now? Maybe he'd thought they were something else, shadows perhaps, or windburns. They meant his skin was losing something, he knew. *But what?*

When he caught himself reexamining them a fourth time he replaced the mirror and killed the light. He was worrying the same ground obsessively, he knew, applying futile attentions to irreversible trends. That was something he'd been doing too often lately, postponing sleep with pointless ritual. He seemed increasingly reluctant to end old days, or face new ones.

He lay now with his sheet beneath his chin, trying to conjure up some pleasantly neutral prospect. But there didn't seem to be any. Thus the clawing sound, when it came, was less unwelcome than it might have been, suggesting a small domestic animal seeking asylum in his berth.

43

Swede Riisberg's head popped abruptly through the curtains.

"What the fuck are you doing here, Swede?"

"Come to kiss you good night, Eddie. Comiskey sends his love. It don't cost nothing after all. How'd you like that dinner tonight, kiddo? Ain't often you see meat with that degree of mystery."

Riisberg sniggered softly at his jest, blinking in rhythm to the ticking of the road ties.

"I'd like to get some sleep if you don't mind, Swede."

"So would we all, Eddie, so would we all. Which is exactly why we should get down to business here. How's five thousand sound?"

"Five thousand what?"

"Dollars, Eddie. Christ on a crutch, are you Polish?"

"What are you talking about?"

"Ramming a garden hose three miles up Charley Comiskey's poop chute, that's what I'm talking about, and you pitching the Series just good enough to lose it."

"You're drunk."

"On the contrary, I intend never to be quite this sober again."

It seemed to Cicotte that he'd heard this song before. It had the familiar lilt of long-suppressed desire. Outside the black hills rolled steadily by in the moonlight.

"Six thousand's about what you make for the whole year, ain't it, Eddie? Correct me if I'm damp on that. I get twenty-seven hundred myself. But I'm just a kid. When I'm thirty-five I'll probably be making six thousand too. Then I can buy two packs of gum every week instead of one."

"Gandil's behind this, isn't he?"

An almost imperceptible ripple of annoyance passed over Riisberg's features then, without in any way compromising

44

his composure. It was like a chill wind skimming a late-August lawn party, disappearing before the guests have even noticed.

"I'd like to make an observation or two here, Eddie, if you'd permit me the indulgence. Okay?"

"No."

"Good. Here goes. I have this peculiar habit of dividing the world into two types of individual. Probably you didn't know that about me. Very few people do. For example, some guys' belly buttons stick out, others don't. The same with broads. Personally, mine does. I noticed yours does too. I hope you don't mind my mentioning this situation. There's twenty-five guys on this team. Thirteen have belly buttons that stick out, twelve have the other kind. I draw no conclusions from this, it's just a fact."

He paused briefly, rubbing his abdomen for emphasis.

"I've also noticed two sorts of guys when it comes to listening to safety lectures, like the one we got on the train tonight. Some guys listen the first time, other guys listen every time. I listened the first time, you listen every time. That's good. When you die in a wreck you'll go knowing exactly what you should have done if you'd only had time to do anything."

"What's your point, Swede?"

"My point? Well, my point is another difference I've noticed lately, Eddie. It concerns pissing. Some guys look down when they piss, like they've never seen the thing. Other guys just stare straight ahead, like they don't even have one. I haven't checked on you in this regard, Eddie, but I'll lay a month in the country to a dose of cupid's itch you never sneak a peek. Cincinnati's going to win the Series, Eddie. It's been arranged. Get on and get rich, stay off and get left. It's going to happen regardless."

45

Here, then, was the cool core of Gandil's logic, Cicotte realized. Resentment. Greed. Collusion. Exclusion. Riisberg's delivery was cruder than necessary, but undeniably effective. He was like a child molester stalking an orphanage.

"Let me paint you a quick picture of your predicament here, Eddie, if I might. You're going to make less dough this year winning thirty games than Bernie Boland made winning thirteen games for Detroit last year. That's *last* year, Eddie. For *thirteen* games. I happen to know because Bernie himself told me. And the minute you start losing two-to-one instead of winning one-to-nothing, which shouldn't be too long now by my watch and chain, Charlie Comiskey will drop you straight through the shithouse floor, as if God himself had eaten away the timbers. You'll be lucky to get one-fifty a month coaching yannigans in Toledo. You can make five thousand here for three days' work, Eddie, then buy that fucking farm you're always boring everybody's ass off about, and tell Comiskey to kiss the wrong end of your business. Get smart, Eddie."

Cicotte didn't answer. He couldn't. Riisberg's argument precluded speech. If he said no, he was a chump. If he said yes, he was a thief. It was like everything connected with money, he thought resentfully, both adding to, and subtracting from, simultaneously.

He suddenly wished it wasn't so late, or so hot, and that Riisberg hadn't caught him in the cradle. He also wished he wasn't so frazzled by old problems that new opportunities only promised fresh peril. But most of all he wished Riisberg would leave him alone for a while, but only for a while.

"You don't have to be obvious about it either, Eddie, just some little slips. You'll get plenty of help, and a thousand dollars after every game. Nobody will ever know. There'll be other Series, Eddie, even for you."

Cicotte heard none of this. He was too busy watching Riisberg's lips move, and noting the insolent way his rear end was saluting the ceiling. He'd have given any passerby a rich horse's laugh, Eddie thought, with his imitation of the most hot-pants lover imaginable.

"How about the fans?"

"They forget everything in fifteen minutes. Grow up."

"I don't think so, Swede. This just doesn't seem right to me. I've always played it straight."

"I know."

Riisberg reached over and plucked Cicotte's boater from its hook then, fingering the frayed brim, disdaining subtlety.

"I know you don't study yourself when you pee, Eddie, but you must've seen those little disks they put in pissers, the ones made from the same stuff as mothballs. Those things get whizzed on all day, Eddie. Eventually you don't see them anymore. Think about it."

He was revving up for a big finish, Cicotte sensed, baiting the hook no mortal man spurns lightly.

"Do it for your family, Eddie, if you won't do it for yourself."

And there it was, Cicotte noted bitterly, the one care any carelessness can hide behind.

Riisberg's skull pulled back through the curtain then, and was gone.

Cicotte turned to stare out at the moonlight. The pale orange globe seemed to be following him around. He took out his mirror again, held it up in front of him. The lines were still there, but the expression framing them had darkened considerably, underlining rather than softening, his decay. What previously had seemed the glare of the insurgent now looked like the smirk of the adherent, a man who'd never have anything he wanted unless he did everything someone he hated ordered him to do.

Eddie knew that he wouldn't sleep until dawn then. So in patient resignation to the fate he'd made his habit he settled back in his pillows to await it.

11

The next morning, at nine sharp by the porter's gong, Cicotte blew into the dining car, high on the muscle. Without hesitating he marched straight to Gandil's table and sat down next to Riisberg.

"Ten thousand, cash, before the Series."

Again he didn't pause, but rose and retraced his footsteps daintily.

"Pretty quick," Riisberg said.

"As I expected," Gandil answered.

Chick had expected no such thing, Riisberg knew. He hadn't even set a time limit. Still it was a minor vanity, thus easily accommodated.

"He'll flop for eight grand easy," Riisberg said. "I can smell it. He's beyond eagerness. He'll drop his drawers for us and call it haberdashery."

"Maybe, maybe not. We'll pay the ten grand anyway. The road to Nowheresville is paved with five-and-diming."

Riisberg doubted there was a road to Nowheresville, but he knew Gandil hated economizing. He'd dodged poverty too long to act like he still had to.

Riisberg had only a partial picture of Chick's finances, as

it happened. He knew about the first $50,000 ($12,500 for each of them, $5,000 apiece for Cicotte and the boys). The second $50,000 remained Chick's little mystery.

Swede was recalibrating the numbers when Fred McMullin stole up behind him. The brackish gray outline of Manhattan was just rising across the pale Jersey meadows.

"Swede. Chick."

Neither looked up. McMullin was a utility infielder.

"I'll get right to the point, boys," Fred said briskly. "I'd like to share in this little promenade you've got percolating. It strikes me as an excellent opportunity for advancement."

Fred's eyes were bulging beyond their lids, Riisberg noted, his voice wavering like a schoolboy's. He sounded like a mental defective peddling suppositories to a bank president.

"What the fuck are you talking about, Fred?"

"Don't take that tone with me, Swede. You're not half the big bag of brains you seem to think you are. You don't even know somebody sleeps in the bottom half of every upper."

Gandil glanced over at Riisberg.

Riisberg peered down at his fingertips.

McMullin folded his arms and stared straight ahead, smiling. For the first time in as long as he could remember, he didn't have to say another thing.

12

My Saratoga days passed blissfully. I wasn't aware of the conflict in Chicago. When I became aware of it I still couldn't credit it. It sounded like part of another scam, some other's dream.

49

Whenever I conjure up the past only pleasant images present themselves. The rest bear too much weight. What I recall of that week are the singular moments: a thunderstorm, early on, pouring unannounced from a brilliant afternoon sky, a marble doorway providing me shelter, a bank perhaps, the streets emptying in seconds, leaving me alone in a sudden wind.

Or the racetrack, the next afternoon, the limp sunlight hanging on the eighth pole, the crowd growing progressively quieter, watching time folding into itself.

Or the Brook, aglow, the following evening, Scriabin drifting faintly across its herb gardens, an unknown boy, his life still awaiting him, leaning against a fence post, unaware that disappointment is possible, at least for him.

Occasionally now, sensations accompany these images, a twinge of desire, a hint of joy; memories of possibility pierce my torpor. But only briefly. They are unsustainable, like the week itself, like all those years preceding it, that other life, that rehearsal.

There were several compulsions, besides lasciviousness and parsimony, which drew Lefty Williams to the corner of 79th and Broadway the following morning. Chief among them was surely force of habit.

Williams was both a lecher and a miser. He valued the economies of quiff shooting as much as its thrills. So each morning when the White Sox were in New York, Lefty parked himself outside Handleman's Quality Lingerie to verbally molest the female servant class. The girls weren't likely to report him, given their stations, and even less likely to take him up on it. It was a free ride.

The day's first prospect did nothing for Williams's glands. The second did, but seemed menacing. The third girl wasn't a girl at all, but Chick Gandil, out scouting up confederates.

"How's it hanging, Lefty, you cozy cut-and-dry you? Having any luck scaring up a sheetmate?"

Williams was embarrassed to be caught billy-goating in public, though the excuse he offered turned quickly into a confession.

"That's not it, Chick, that's not it at all. They never come, or they have a story, or a disease, or they want money. They always need more than they have, Chick. You know that."

Gandil was shocked by Lefty's vehemence, but, smelling profit in it, let him ramble.

"Nothing's ever good enough, is it, Chick? I don't have to tell *you* that. I wanted to play ball. I figured I wasn't good enough, but it's *it* that isn't good enough. What a joke."

Gandil nodded sympathetically. Soul-baring was clearly in the air. It took him exactly ninety seconds to turn Lefty's doubts his way. He began by mentioning Comiskey's millions, followed with hints of Cicotte's willingness, then closed with a brief judicial opinion.

"There's no law against not trying, Lefty. Look it up."

Williams took very little convincing. Cicotte's participation piqued his interest; the idea of shafting Comiskey fanned the flame. When he heard $5,000 mentioned in this connection he almost bent double to caress Gandil's Florsheims.

Instead he invited Chick into the Hibernian for a near beer. And there, over pickled eggs and wisecracks, they formalized their mutual resentments. By the time the last governess had paraded unmolested past Handleman's, Gandil had both his pitchers' peckers in his poke.

13

The next morning I took the waters at Ballston. A titanic attendant twiddled me with palm fronds. It was a circumstance that fairly cried out for rumination.

It astounds me now how confident I was of Rothstein's help. It felt like a woman I could desire into possessing. Might I actually have believed in myself then? Or merely known how few plots ever get beyond the plotting stage?

"Losers think everything is fixed," Jocko once told me. "Cheap cynicism is every failure's armor."

He was right. Only fixers know how random fixes are, how resistant even the simplest events are to rigging.

I had no illusions about Gandil's efficiency, either. I knew he'd make five mistakes for everything he did half right. Still I trusted. Who'd believe it possible soon enough to put a stop to it?

So.

On the evening of August 6, 1919, eight ballplayers with everything to lose met to begin losing it.

The White Sox beat the Yankees 8–5 that afternoon. Cicotte started, but didn't last. He seemed alienated from his rhythms, as if playing some other game. Gandil began wondering if he'd even have to be bribed.

Gandil and Riisberg went straight from the field to an Alsatian restaurant on West 82nd Street. It was a watercress-and-finger-bowl sort of endeavor named, impudently enough, Fleur de Lys. Gandil had stumbled on it while pricing marital aids. He'd instinctively pegged it an unlikely spot for ballplayers (though he had scant idea *how* unlikely) and thus the ideal spot for finalizing up their plans.

In the dining room they were seated with four other couples, all male. Eight sets of eyes rose to appraise them as they ordered.

For the next two hours they ventilated their con. Even casual observers, had there been casual observers in attendance, could have distinguished between their styles.

Gandil spoke seldom, and slowly, his dour thoroughness emphasizing each detail. Riisberg spoke often, and aggressively, belaboring even the broadest nuance ruthlessly. Gandil's concerns were secrecy and timing; Riisberg's concern was the money. Gandil was clearly in charge, the patient tutor curbing the avid pupil. Riisberg was pressing his position, the weekend guest who's begun rearranging the lawn furniture.

Gandil never had any doubts about recruiting Riisberg. It was the first thing he'd done after contacting me. Swede was the ideal second-in-command, Chick believed: mean, efficient, unimaginative.

They both had steak *au poivre* with rösti potatoes and leeks. Chick longed to order peach cobbler, but thought better of it.

When the waiter observed, with a coquettish toss of a forelock, how "endearing" he found their identical tastes, they suddenly had a name for his unlikeliness.

They paid the check and scrammed.

Back in Chick's room they sat quietly, in opposite corners, awaiting their company.

Cicotte arrived first, walking like a man (and indeed he

was that man) who'd had indigestion for months. McMullin followed, looking even less confident than usual. He'd been rehearsing his pitch for a full cut since noon. Williams came next, reciting a joke about three Negroes and a porcupine. Buck Weaver arrived at eight, Jackson and Felsch fifteen minutes later.

"Each of you will get five thousand before the Series," Gandil began crisply, "except Eddie, who'll get ten thousand, and Fred, who'll get four thousand. Eddie because he'll pitch more, Fred because he's Fred. Any questions?"

There apparently were none. Nobody seemed to begrudge Cicotte his extra; all clearly begrudged McMullin anything. Fred didn't press for a full share either. He could smell dog-eye building in the room.

"Don't discuss this with anyone, even with each other. We'll decide which games to tilt, and how, later."

Jackson and Felsch glanced instinctively at Cicotte. Everybody else just studied the carpet. They seemed chastened, either by the plan, or by what had driven them to it.

"It's all set then. We tried to reason with him, but . . ."

This was a mistake, Gandil realized instantly—rationalizing it. It sent the players scuttling headlong toward the door. Only Jackson and Felsch paused for clarification.

"Chick," Jackson began, wetting his lower lip, "there is one question I would like to bring up here."

"What's that, Joe?"

"Kid Gleason—how does he feel about this particular deal?"

Stupidity is its own rationale, Gandil knew, makes its own relentless way through the universe. No amount of reflection could have anticipated this question. It was just Jackson.

"What do you mean, Joe?"

"Well, I always felt partial to the Kid, you know, Chick. He reads me the Sunday snickers, buys me college ices, don't yell at me every time I miss a sign. I wouldn't want to do anything to upset him."

"I understand, Joe. Of course not. The Kid thinks this is a top-notch idea, in fact. He can't get involved with it himself, of course, for obvious reasons, but he would if he could. And he does want all you boys to take advantage of it, as long as you never discuss it with him, in any way, never, ever, not even once. He made that as plain as death when I talked to him about it. Because then he *would* be mad, mad as anything. Because of Comiskey and all that sort of thing. You understand?"

"Sure, Chick. I understand."

He didn't, of course. But he knew he should. It was a lie he often told. He tried to adopt a knowing stride as he shuffled off down the corridor.

Gandil stood watching him disappear, before wheeling to face Felsch's vacant grin.

"I got a question too, Chick."

"I bet you do, Hap."

"I was just wondering, could I maybe get my personal cut in thousand-dollar bills? I never seen a grand note before. I think it would be interesting."

"Sure, Hap. I'll write that down right now. 'Grand notes for Hap.' There it is."

"Thanks, Chick, I appreciate it. Good night."

"Good night, Hap."

Gandil closed the door again, and turned to speak to Riisberg. He assumed they were alone. But they weren't. Weaver was standing insolently between them, smiling his high-horse smile. It was a grin that said, I know your little

55

secret, Chick, and you'll never get away with it.

"I know your little secret, Chick," Buck whispered, "and you'll never get away with it."

Then he too vanished out the door, as cockily, and inscrutably, as he'd entered.

14

I watch.

It's my business to watch. That's part of it. But I'd watch anyway. It's my nature.

Some people watch to excite themselves, others out of fear. I watch because it interests me, noting the distinctions.

While Gandil was spinning his webs in Chicago, I was busy watching in Saratoga, observing how powerful men exert subtle influences. I caught on quickly. It seemed like something I might eventually be good at.

There was a reason why everything worked for them, I could see, or rather several reasons stitched into a seamless plait of circumstance. It was better to be born knowing, I knew, but I hadn't been. Watching would have to do for me.

Mostly I watched Rothstein; only later did I come to watch Attell.

I watched them every day at the races, where they had a private box, and I didn't. I observed them varnishing the Brook's clientele, romancing the amateurs, reining in the pros. I remained inconspicuous. That's the key to watching, I believe, maintaining presence and distance simultaneously. Saratoga fosters such equilibrium, providing both worldly diversions and the room to reflect on them.

Rothstein was the master of this milieu. He approached

every room as if he'd designed it, treating hosts like guests at their own parties. Few resented this. Weren't they fortunate just to be in his presence?

In his velveteen jerkin and calfskin toe mittens he oozed authenticity. He'd give any clod ninety seconds of counterfeit charm, leaving even skeptics panting for an encore. He never peered over anyone's shoulder, either, but got you to look over *your* shoulder for him, seeking someone almost as fascinating as you to introduce him to.

"He'd make an immortal producer," Cohan often said, "if he could bring himself to stroke the other yids, or *anyone* with under ten million for that matter. You'd think he was born in Windsor Castle, for Judas' sake, instead of over some moyl's den on Mott Street. But the fucking guy can sell hemorrhoids to the assless."

His élan was almost calculatedly facile, his perpetual motion like constant repose. He peddled oil leases over breakfast on his veranda, fenced counterfeit bonds at the track in the afternoon, hosed chorus girls between gin hands at the Brook. All without straining. He made every gesture seem like a small kindness he'd do anyone because they'd eventually do something even more beguiling for him.

Attell was a different trick entirely. It took me three days to figure out their link.

Attell's real name was Albert Knoehr. For twelve years he'd been the featherweight champion of the world. He won his first fight at sixteen, took the title from Harry Forbes at seventeen, stood five feet four, 116 pounds, coat and shoeless. The world called him "the Little Hebrew"; Rothstein addressed him as "Little Champ."

Abe was a sagacious boxer who could punish with either hand. When he retired, at twenty-nine, after 365 bouts, he retained few souvenirs of his career—two ropes of scar tis-

sue under each eye, two ears soldered to his skull, a taste for
high living on the cuff, and so little cash as to make no
particular difference.

He'd gotten $15,000 for some fights, but the money never
stayed his for long. Abe considered his championship a public trust to be funded. He never thought it would end.

He'd met Rothstein in New York in 1905, at the very
peak of his aplomb. Rothstein was only getting started then,
but Attell sensed his gravity instantly. It was like a specter
standing beside him in the room. The two shared many attributes; each knew the other could do him justice. When
Attell's skill deserted him he quickly sought Rothstein's
counsel. Rothstein granted it. It was that natural.

They made a curious match, those disparate Israelites—
the somberly elegant Rothstein with his predator's distant
manner, the flashy bantam Attell with his plug-ugly pa-
nache. Attell's body had betrayed him, so he revered Rothstein's stamina. Rothstein lacked physical courage, so he
basked in Attell's menace. They traveled in tandem.

Gradually, of course, their emphasis shifted. As Rothstein's world expanded, Attell's shrank in sympathy. Rothstein began asking favors of Attell, making demands on him,
sending him on errands. Shortly Abe had become something
of a mascot.

Abe had his reasons for acquiescing, of course. He was
making contacts, learning the ropes. When he was ready he
would move out on his own. In a word, a word he might even
have used himself, he was *watching*.

That's how they struck me that brilliant August morning
in Saratoga, the day I realized how far beyond respect Abe's
emulation of the Bankroll had grown.

They were coming out of Shuster's Gym on Caroline

Street, having endured an intimate rendezvous with the weights. Rothstein was vain about his physique; Attell always stayed in fighting trim. I hadn't been following them, had no idea they even frequented the joint. I was seated on a bench across from the Adelphi, reading the second volume of Melbourne's interminable memoirs. I'd borrowed it on the sly from the Brook's library.

It was one of the loveliest mornings of my stay. The sky was sheer blue. A slight breeze ruffled every visible awning. Junior celebrities and veteran poseurs patrolled lower Broadway. I had a pleasant morning's reading behind me, a serene afternoon's racing yet to go. I wouldn't have noticed either hoodlum if their chauffeur hadn't honked them his welcome.

They came strolling from the gym, fastening collar stays, massaging deltoids. Rothstein led, as always. When they reached the car the driver jerked the door open for them. Rothstein leaned forward, rolling his shoulders flamboyantly, simultaneously cocking his off foot for leverage. It was such an eccentrically baroque gesture, so needlessly complex, that I'd have had to search my memory for a precedent, had one not leaped so readily to mind.

It was the way Attell always entered the ring.

Attell followed, mimicking Rothstein perfectly. Only a few details differed, differed from Rothstein's style and from Abe's own historic one. It was a moment before I realized what I'd seen. Attell was imitating Rothstein's imitation of him. From that instant I grasped their kinship perfectly.

That Rothstein was a watcher I had known. He could hardly have been otherwise. That Attell was a watcher surprised me. But he was, and a ruthless one at that, the sort who'd bare any subject's bones with scrutiny, crush any rival's longings with his own.

That evening Gandil phoned me in my digs, collect, to tell me that all the players were in line. He'd told me this before, of course, but now it was true.

He suggested we get together again before the Series, to settle on procedures. He asked if I had the money yet. I said I'd have it by the end of the week. I, too, had begun to call my wishes facts.

He said he was a little surprised how well things were going.

I said I had to admit I was a bit surprised myself.

After I hung up I had my first attack of ambivalence. I was ready to proceed, but wished I wasn't. I've always wished I wasn't.

But being *almost* ready no longer seemed advisable. I had to be *completely* ready now. I'd stepped off the ledge, exhausted my remaining reasons to procrastinate. If I hadn't I'd probably still be sitting in that alcove, beneath those creaky rooming-house stairs, twirling that phone cord endlessly around my ring finger, waiting for yet another impediment to deliver me.

Recollections, from those days, of differences detected, between those born to money, and those not, written, I fear, on tiny scraps of paper:

"They speak deliberately, drawling, seeking the ideal phrase, stuttering slightly, affecting a defect, making us wait."

"They dress plainly, yet substantially, seemingly without care, in clothes chosen to last, disdaining fashion, suggesting shabbiness without quite achieving it. But no dirt, except after gardening, and certainly no sweat. Aging, they come to resemble their help."

"They speak first, loudly, though not boisterously, talk to

us of our concerns, compliment us mildly, refer to their friends by given name, as if we should know them."

"They display no great interest, except in the interests of others. They're always smiling, nodding, appearing on occasion to actually recognize us."

Rothstein had many of these attributes.

I had none.

15

If I really *was* surprised at how well things were going, it was only because I didn't know they weren't. I didn't even know Bill Burns was now among us.

I only learned of Bill's treachery much later. My picture of it is hardly complete, just complete enough to sponsor one conclusion: that I was a fucking fool for ever talking to him in the first place.

Apparently Bill had drawn few deep breaths since we'd parted. The day I left Boston he called Eddie Cicotte in Chicago, to ask him how my pipe was being laid.

"Search me, Bill. I don't even know the guy."

"Do you think . . .?"

"Thinking's not my line, Bill. Call Gandil."

So Burns did.

"I can raise whatever's necessary by next Thursday, Chick. Give it some thought."

"I will, Bill. I will indeed."

"Do you have Jackson?"

"On my hip."

When I first learned of Burns's betrayal, I assumed Gandil, too, had gone south on me. Only later did I realize he was just doubling up, billing Burns for what he'd already sold to me. He'd begun thinking of the fix as a franchise.

Burns spent that evening phoning his stand-behinds. Many expressed interest, all wanted control. Bill spurned them.

At midnight he rang up B. G. Maharg in Philadelphia. Maharg was a retired club fighter with a sideline in gorilla-ing. His real name was Graham, but he'd reversed the spelling on turning professional. ("What a peachy tip-off on his career," Jocko once remarked, "and what an A-one example of how his noodle works.") Maharg's face was so ravaged by the ring that it frightened people who'd only heard about it. This made him an ideal accomplice, and Burns needed accomplices as much as I needed mentors.

"Meet me in Saratoga next Thursday, B.G.. We'll head straight to Rothstein for the dough. He's a smart Jew—he won't double-cross us right off, but try to lose us gradual. Our challenge will be to seem luxuries worth paying for."

So Burns came to the Spa with his musket cocked, having taken one week to accomplish what had taken me fifteen years.

"I should have known" is the world's least useful epitaph. We should all know just about everything; that we don't is nobody in particular's fault. Yet in this case I really should have known. The secret was unkeepable, the payoff idyllic. It bothers me that I didn't anticipate Burns's back-handling, though not nearly as much as the possibility that I did.

The confrontation between Burns and Rothstein was a classic of discrepancy. One might have expected Bill to be lavishly serpentine. In fact, he was repulsively candid. Rothstein was his usual courtly self. He even offered Sleepy Bill a licorice whip. That's why the sharpies revered the Bankroll so. They knew what his courtesy hid, but appreciated his discretion in hiding it.

Bill waylaid Rothstein in his loge. Attell was there, as was Mrs. Rothstein, and two Queens ward heelers peddling more influence than they had. Burns's presence was affront enough; he quickly compounded it with the cheekiest gaff imaginable, addressing Rothstein by his given name.

"Arnold, how's tricks? Bill Burns here. Perhaps you've heard of me. We're more or less in the same line of endeavor, you and me. This here's my associate, Mr. Maharg. We're here to discuss an important matter of enterprise, Arnold. We think you'll be magnetized by the details."

The first "Arnold" froze Rothstein's jaw mid-smile. The second set it twitching like a rabbit's.

"Mr. Burns, I'm sure your reputation precedes you in most quarters, but I'm afraid it hasn't yet fought its way over the Berkshires."

Rothstein knew exactly who Burns was, and what he wanted.

"Arnold, how amazed I am to hear that. I assumed a man of your prosperity would be familiar with everyone in his line."

Burns was busy making a bad situation irredeemable, rebuking Rothstein for not recognizing their parity. He seemed immune to all self-consciousness about it, too, prattling on as though his pitch was taking wings.

"Arnold, I'm a former big league ballplayer, a pitcher in particular. I was with the Senators, the Reds, the Phillies, the Tigers, and the White Sox."

His voice rose in singsong emphasis here. Could he be about to address Rothstein as "Arnie"?

"My career was a little short on the distinction angle, it's true, due to circumstances. But since I retired I've had a lion's share of success. I've made a shitload, Arnold. I have extensive oil interests in Texas. Harry Sinclair's a partner in several. You've heard of him, I'd imagine?"

He paused, inviting affirmation. Mrs. Rothstein tinkled the ice in her glass. Attell tapped a molar with his thumbnail.

"I also have extensive real estate holdings up and down the Eastern Seaboard." (He owned a three-decker in South Boston.) "Yet I still keep up my interest in the pastime, strictly from a business point of view. That's what I'm here to talk to you about, Arnold. Unless your enthusiasm for the bats and balls has dwindled."

His voice was wavering now. Explaining himself was growing a trifle wearing. For who, when all was said and done, was he? A sudden gust blew his Windsor over his shoulder. Mrs. Rothstein's fragrance became a stronger presence in the box.

"As you no doubt know, our mutual acquaintance Sport Sullivan—"

But this was as far as Bill's pitch ever got him. Rothstein cut it off with a snort.

"Mr. Burns, I've heard of Mr. Sullivan's plan, though not from him. I've determined it is in nobody's best interest, least of all mine. My guests and I would like to return to our handicapping now. Thank you so much for stopping by. Mr. Attell, please show Mr. Burns and . . . this other gentleman . . . to the clubhouse bar. Fidel can introduce them to the limitless possibilities of lemon squash."

By all accounts the ensuing silence was brutally absolute. Even the Queens ward heelers had to glance away in sympathy. I blush just thinking about it. Burns would have gasped if he'd had breath. He looked like a vicar who'd caught his wife blowing the paperboy.

In the bar the Little Hebrew ordered three scotches "neat." He was no lemon squash man himself; he doubted Burns and Maharg were either. He'd copped the anglicized phrasing from Rothstein.

Maharg quaffed his shot in one gulp. He was ignorant of the controversy's origins, but sensed it meant the free hootch was limited.

Burns stared at his glass. He shouldn't have approached Rothstein cold, he now realized. Men like Rothstein don't indulge others' whims. He shouldn't have made his pitch at the track either. That was where the Bankroll did his dallying. But his biggest miscalculation lay in the slope of his ambition. He was pursuing a goal he no longer wanted, as if achieving it might make him want it again.

He sat there now, hefting his uncertainty, as Attell leaned forward with a reprieve.

"Slip me a number where I can catch you tonight, Sleepy Billy. That pasting you just took was strictly for the dime seats."

16

If the confrontation between Burns and Rothstein suggested the miles between the Back Bay and Manhattan, the diddling of Burns by Attell confirmed the light-years between South Boston and the Bronx.

Abe called Bill at seven-thirty.

"I'll be up in two shakes, Sleepy Billy. Be lonesome."

Attell's attitude again echoed Rothstein's, though his tone betrayed his own pie-eyed raffishness. He sounded like a dock walloper crooning Shelley to the gulls.

Abe arrived on the hour, bearing Chivas.

"Always grease seductions with gratuities," Rothstein once counseled him. "Inappropriate generosity undermines any victim's will."

Attell seemed alert to this effect. It was the cause he was having trouble grasping. He betrayed his confusion now by pouring a stiff drink for *himself.*

"Mr. Rothstein sends his apologies, Billy. He regrets having to lean on you this afternoon, but the conditions dictated it. People are going to connect him up with this deal no matter what he does. So he needs to put a few miles between himself and the truth. Believe me, though, he's definitely nuts for your dodge."

Burns's brain bought this alibi, but his gut sounded a four-bell alarm. It was too pat. The sweat on Attell's upper lip confirmed this.

"How much would you need to pull it off, Billy?"

"A hundred thousand."

Attell nodded, as at a customary sum.

The heavy money isn't always that smart, Abe knew. Slick, mulish, but no savvier than the average. This gink sure wasn't. Even Rothstein wasn't all the time. People just liked to think he was, so they could yearn.

Burns didn't elaborate on his needs. He was too busy enjoying Attell's discomfort, dunning him for the shame his boss had caused him.

"Have you got enough players?"

"Of course."

"Then Mr. Rothstein will stake you to your ramble, Billy. He don't want his name too pertinent, though. You'll do all your dealing through me. I'll meet you later to cook up the details. You'll get your dough then."

For thirty-seven years I'd roamed life's lower corridors, assuming I'd never reach its upper tiers. Men like Rothstein seemed to have been born there, men like Burns to have scrambled up on brass, while men like me just watched and waited, straining to perfect the imperfectible in our dreams.

What happened that week suggested I'd been shortchanging myself.

I'd never have called Rothstein "Arnold," for example, or taken anything Attell said on faith. Attell must have sensed my latent shrewdness. Why else would he have passed me by for Burns?

When Attell quit Burns's room shortly after nine, his skivvies soaked through with discomfort, his anxieties cradled in an alcoholic brume, he felt sure he had Burns in his side vent. Burns assumed the reverse. He was so elated by his success, in fact, that he decided to send Gandil a night letter, the exuberance of its text betraying the depths of his misjudgment:

MONEY ADVANCED, AWAIT INSTRUCTIONS. BURNS.

It was the third such wire to cross Lake Erie that weekend. It brought no one closer to the truth than either of its predecessors.

17

When I awoke the next morning, my confidence ripening, Gandil's assurances lying on my nightstand, the well-known emptiness was upon me. I wasn't aware of Attell's deception. There was no connection.

I've come to expect the emptiness, without learning to anticipate it. It's as likely to follow good days as bad, is irregular, and thus indeterminate.

I call it emptiness because no other name suggests itself. It's not exactly sadness, but more an absence of happiness, a complete absence. When evolved from my dreams, as on that morning, it evokes an almost thrilling sense of hopelessness.

I used to try to repel it, but that only seemed to encourage it. Now I just wait until it subsides. It always has.

The best way to dilute it, I've found, is to flee to the racetrack. There simulated problems replace real problems. Anonymous crowds distract by their rapacity.

I enjoy going to the track under most circumstances, actually. It's how I got started in the life. I only converted to baseball when the war closed the tracks. I'd been thinking of switching back recently, having grown weary of sucking up to ball hawks, of varnishing men I could hardly bear to meet.

"Never bet on anything that talks," Jocko once advised me. "Stick to the ponies. They're as close to a cure for futility as you'll find."

So when I awoke that luminous morning, I pointed myself straight at the course. I was a bit surprised at feeling that vacant. Everything had been going so well.

I could have danced on the head of that particular pin for hours, I knew. In the past I would have. But if I did I knew I'd begin feeling blank again. And that was the last thing I needed at that point.

The day was a perfect example of its type—bone-dry air, an east wind signaling the remote possibility of autumn. I chanced the first five races, without success.

I didn't bet heavily, though. I never try to overwhelm the emptiness. Even winning can't displace it. Nothing can, except time. Upping the ante only amplifies the tension.

Between bets I wandered aimlessly about the track, chewing on a chicken wing, dropping dimes into a blind beggar's cup, for luck. I meandered out back, beneath the elms, to watch the trainers saddle their charges. That's where I discovered what was missing. It was solitude. I needed it, feared losing it. Meeting with Rothstein hadn't doubled my expectations, it had diluted them, by introducing another presence into the scam.

As soon as I realized this the emptiness passed from me. I looked up from my figures to face the sun. Rothstein's profile blocked me from its warmth.

"Good afternoon, Mr. Sullivan. Cultivating your formidable lack of gregariousness, I see."

"Yes, Mr. Rothstein. I find avoiding the crowd helps keep my greed in check."

"I agree. And how is your judgment treating you this ideal afternoon?"

"I'm losing, but not much. And you?"

"I'm winning, but even less. I'll spare you the details. Nothing is as tedious as a gambler's near misses, except a golfer talking about anything."

"I don't play golf."

"How wonderful. Nor bridge either, I'd imagine?"

"No, no bridge."

"Too clubbable, no doubt. That's something I detected in you instantly, Sullivan, your abhorrence of conviviality. I share the strain, though I mask it for business purposes. I appreciate the purity of your particular aloofness. It tells me a lot about how your cap is set."

69

His presumption was quickly restoring my balance. I knew the moment I'd long anticipated was at hand.

"What was the largest amount you ever won, Sullivan?"

"Twenty-five hundred."

"When?"

"May 8, 1916, the Cardinals over the Giants."

"What was your line on Dempsey–Willard?"

"Six to five, Dempsey."

"Where do you store your cash when you travel?"

"I don't."

He smiled. He'd known each answer, yet he'd asked. I'd responded as if I recognized my worth. He'd approached me, after all, and alone.

"How would you divide the money between them?"

"That's Gandil's problem, though it should be fair. Ten for Cicotte maybe, five for the rest. Gandil expects fifty, but will take fifteen. Jackson's hunky enough to do it for beers. That wouldn't do though. We'd demean the enterprise by economizing."

I'd said "we" deliberately, just as I'd assumed his "them" referred to the players. Men like Rothstein are sticklers for the subtleties. I stood there waiting for my nickel to hit its slot. It never did, though. Instead he said something no amount of research could have prepared me for.

"Isn't it a queer piece of business, Mr. Sullivan, how one can stop doing something one loves without noticing it? I now do something from habit which I once did strictly from ardor, as if affection was still its primary impetus. You know how that feels, I'm sure, Mr. Sullivan. That's why I'm discussing it with you now. That's why I'll be funding your little project, start to finish."

Of course, I knew what he meant. I too had turned my

70

passion into my livelihood, and seen the need drain all the pigment from its flesh. But I hadn't just stopped doing what I enjoyed without knowing it, I'd stopped doing everything without knowing it. Almost.

I wanted to tell him this now, to assure him that I knew what his standards were costing him. But I couldn't. His confession held too many perils. I hadn't come here seeking an equal, after all, but a man to make myself equal to.

Then, as abruptly as he'd ceded it, he retook control.

"So, you'll have your little score, Mr. Sullivan, and all the gelt to fund it with. Meet me tomorrow morning at the Brook, ten o'clock, and do be prompt."

He stopped just short of saying "like a good boy."

"I'm hardly surprised Sleepy Bill Burns fears you so profoundly, Sport. Your capacity for reticence is positively heroic. You and I are going to have an awful lot not to talk about."

That was my first indication that Sleepy Bill was afoot. It gave me something else to fret about, as I'm sure it was meant to. Otherwise Rothstein's remarks were pure air.

He started to leave then, but apparently thought better of it.

"Did you play the game as a boy, Mr. Sullivan?"

"What game?"

"*The* game."

"A bit."

"And did it sow visions of immortality in your dreams?"

"I suppose so."

"And do you remember the exact moment those longings turned to dust?"

"Well . . ."

"So do we all, Mr. Sullivan, so do we all. Every wine would be champagne if it could, Mr. Sullivan, and every boy would be a center fielder if allowed to. Some deny it, but they lie. The droll thing is that the ballplayers seem to envy us. Can you believe it?"

"I don't . . ."

"Never mind, it's not important. Ten o'clock then."

He turned again and walked away. The sun flashed several messages off his cufflinks. A blue jay jumped the flagstones in his path. He still had time to bet the sixth race.

It was only then that I thought to wonder how he'd found me, to suspect I was being watched as much as I'd been watching. I didn't have long to ponder this suspicion, though, for a more disquieting concern replaced it almost instantly.

Rothstein's assent ended my Saratoga idyll. Tomorrow I'd begin pursuing the fix in earnest, taking steps, launching measures. I'd be putting my beloved longings into practice, as if passion had never been their ruling force.

18

I arrived at the Brook promptly at ten. A one-armed doorman anticipated my knock.

The Brook didn't play well to the morning, like so many nocturnal fantasies exposed to daylight. Its rooms seemed smaller, its appointments shabbier. Stripped of its context, it was imposing, yet prosaic. Back-lot Negroes stacked crockery in its hallways, their chatter suggestive of auction blocks and leg irons.

I was led through a foyer to the library, where Rothstein stood posed in left profile. His lieutenant, Nat Evans, occupied a banquette in the corner.

"Mr. Sullivan, I was just telling my associate, Mr. Evans here, how seldom I conduct business at the Brook. It's my home in Saratoga, as you know, and I loathe blurring such distinctions. It cheapens both milieus, I feel, erases the boundaries. So every morning, whether I feel like it or not, I play the split-tailed devil on myself, walking out the front door as if forever, then returning almost immediately through the back. It creates the illusion of a cross-county commute for me, converting my brain into a Dobbs Ferry wage slave's."

Self-mockery was a notorious Rothstein ruse. Funning himself prevented others from trying to. Evans quickly picked up the thread.

"I know exactly what you mean, A.R. I felt the same way running rye in Honduras. You oughta build yourself one of those little cabanas down by the stables there—that way you wouldn't have to shit where you eat."

Evans's demeanor was deceptively cultivated. Only his words betrayed his basic savagery. I should have dwelled on this contrast, but couldn't. I was too busy trying to think of something to say.

"It's a nice day," was what I finally came up with.

"Yes," Rothstein agreed. "Yes, it is."

There seemed nowhere to take this bland assessment. Evans jiggled his testicles. Rothstein surveyed his lawn.

"The track seems to be favoring the inside," I finally said.

"It does indeed," Rothstein replied. "Very much so."

I was quickly running out of regional banalities. My brain felt like speech hadn't been invented.

"That's a handsome tree," Rothstein offered, pointing yardward.

I strained to see it, but couldn't quite.

"Yes," I replied. "It's a honey. What's it called?"

"They live about two hundred years."

"Do they really?"

"On average."

"Imagine that."

"That one's about seventy-five."

"How can you tell?"

He glanced down at the floor, smiled, drummed his temple.

"You just can."

This was my introduction to verbal retention as a strategy, to the clever use cagey tongues can make of silence. At first it unsettled me, then it calmed me, absolving me of any responsibility to speak.

We kept at it for almost twenty minutes, staring out the window, counting the gardeners. Occasionally Rothstein commented on the shrubbery. Twice I complimented him on his furnishings. Evans didn't say another word.

Just as I'd relaxed almost to the point of semiconsciousness, Rothstein rose and walked dramatically to the door, opening it violently enough to split both hinges.

"You don't happen to believe in happiness, do you, Sullivan? Please tell me you're not one of those. You might as well put a spike in your aorta. I never let satisfaction grab me personally, or sorrow either, but toss both out the window with the birdseed. Still, you'd better get one thing straight before you leave here today. If you pull this off your life will be over. You'll have gotten exactly what you wanted."

He paused, to let his little homily sink in. I didn't blink.

"Gamblers aren't supposed to *do* things, Sport. They're supposed to *bet on* things. I thought you knew that. But I suppose your tiny heart is set on immortality."

I said nothing, learning fast.

74

"All right, then, Mr. Evans, if you and Mr. Sullivan intend to catch the midnight speedball to Chicago, you'd better run home and do a little packing. The money will be waiting for you on Division Street."

There was no anger in his mandate, no tone of any sort. Nothing gave Rothstein more pleasure than puncturing underlings, except finding one who might efficiently do his bidding.

I *was* displeased, though, clear up to my eyeballs—miffed to be going straight to Chicago, distraught at going anywhere with Evans, and furious at having my assent taken for granted. But what griped my liver more than bile itself was to learn *I* wouldn't be dispensing Rothstein's money, Rothstein would.

If I was a different sort of man I might have bucked his impudence, clamped it before it made my dream his own. But I am not a different sort of man. And so I didn't.

19

How awful a man was Nat Evans?

Reader, he was awful beyond any epithet to encapsulate.

He referred to Rothstein as "the kike."

He wore matching spats and hankies.

He whistled.

He sweated.

He said everything loudly, and twice.

"Sully, the kike has got your number, Sully. He's got your fucking number, all right."

He called me Sully. Nobody ever called me Sully. He touched me when he talked, showering me with warm drops of spittle. Half his conversation consisted of unsolicited advice—by turns obvious, inapplicable, and wrong. The other half consisted of dirty jokes, all told as if they'd actually happened to him. He looked, in fact, like one of his own most scurrilous punch lines.

From the moment we left Saratoga he held me helpless, like a large dog with a small bone. Rothstein must have told him to gumshoe me, but his vigilance exceeded all reason. He seemed intoxicated by his responsibility. I don't ordinarily suffer fools gladly, but I did that week. I thought Rothstein might be testing me, weighing my mettle. Was this cowardice on my part, or cunning? And where, if anywhere, lay the difference?

"This can't go on," I kept assuring myself. "Nobody can be this bad." But he was. And it did.

"Sully, you look like a pretty smart cookie to me, Sully. But you lack ginger. There's no difference between cutting small deals and cutting big deals, Sully, just arithmetic, and balls. You could handle this whole deal yourself, Sully. Instead you run it bashfully by the kike. You need to think big, Sully, think big. You're going to be dead an awfully long fucking time, you know."

"Sure, Nat."

He'd brush my wrist for emphasis as he counseled me, his moist fingers amplifying my revulsion.

I knew everything couldn't happen as I'd imagined. I was prepared for some deviation, within reason. But this wasn't reasonable. And I couldn't do anything about it. If I objected, my dream might die. If I didn't it might flourish without me. I suddenly wished I'd had more experience with partners.

"Did you notice that dolly in the dining car, Sully, the one with the big headlights? Sure you did, you slit-licking devil.

76

Imagine what a mouthful like that could do for you, especially if she knew we had a hundred thousand dollars waiting for us on Division Street. She'd drench her bloomers, Sully, that's what she'd do. You know how to make time with a cooz like that, don't you, Sully? I'll tell you." (Answering his own repellent questions was another of Evans's charms.) "You put it right to her, Sully. You walk right up to her and say: Hey, honey, let's fuck. That's right. You walk right up to her and say: Hey, honey, let's fuck. More often than not, they will."

"Sure, Nat."

As the train crawled dispiritedly into Cleveland, I made another stab at numbing my misgivings. But it was hopeless. The lake might have diverted me on a more agreeable occasion, but it couldn't help me that day. I was too disgusted by my inertia to fight it. I kept thinking about how much more devoted I was to dreaming my dreams than to fulfilling them. I feared this attitude doomed me, but there you are.

Trains usually take twenty-six hours to reach Chicago.

This one seemed to take half my life.

We booked two rooms at the Warner, back to back. Evans wanted to share; I wouldn't hear of it. I called Gandil as soon as we checked in. His wife said he was out digging night crawlers.

"It usually takes him about three hours to fill his bucket, bub, unless he starts right in on the gargle. Then it could take half the night. I'll have him call you as soon as he falls in."

We walked to the telegraph office on Division Street. But the money hadn't come.

"This is typical of the kike," Evans said. "He'd mark the prayer cards at his own mother's funeral."

"I don't believe Mrs. Rothstein would have prayer cards at her funeral, Nat. That's a Christian custom."

"Oh."

We returned to the hotel and ordered lamb chops from room service. For dessert Evans went out to get drunk. He couldn't even manage that properly, though, and returned within the hour, minus a shoe. His breath, heretofore merely fetid, had by now achieved a full and grand putrescence. I remained in my room, reading Chesterton, waiting for Gandil to call, which he didn't.

We duplicated this burlesque each of the next three days, sleeping until noon, tramping to Western Union, finding the money hadn't arrived, returning to the hotel, calling Gandil, speaking to his wife, waiting for his call, playing gin, reading the papers.

It had a certain ritualistic appeal to it, I had to admit. If Evans hadn't been there I'd have enjoyed it, even clung to it.

Then on the fourth day, the money arrived. An hour later Gandil called my room.

"Got the cash, Sport?"

"Yes."

"All of it?"

"Every cent."

"Good. We'll be up in fifteen minutes."

I should have told him about Evans right there and then. But shame at my subservience made me hesitate. Before I could shake it he'd broken the connection.

I lay back on my bed to read the sporting pages. Long shots were hitting the board at Saratoga. I'd have given almost anything to be back there.

They arrived twenty minutes later—Gandil, Riisberg, Cicotte, Williams. Jackson and Felsch had gone bowling. Nobody had been able to reach Weaver. McMullin hadn't been invited.

I'd asked Evans not to mention the money, for discretion's sake. Before the players could ask who he was I told them.

"Gentlemen, this is Nat Evans, the man with the cash, not its source, actually, but its conduit. For practical purposes, though, these definitions are synonymous. Mr. Evans, this is Chick Gandil, Swede Riisberg, Eddie Cicotte, Lefty Williams."

"Where's the dough?" Riisberg asked, glowering.

"It's right here, Mr. Riisberg," Evans told him. "Not in this room, but nearby. Before I fill your pockets, though, I'd like to ask a few questions."

"Go ahead," said Gandil, "but make it peppy."

Evans flashed him an assistant headmaster's smile.

"How much will each of you be making from this project?"

"That's our fucking business," Gandil snapped. "It's got nothing to do with what you're anteing up for."

I ventured a little cough. Evans had apparently forgotten my request for discretion. Or had he?

"How many of you are involved?"

"Eight."

"Including Jackson?"

"Including Jackson."

"Where are the others?"

"Getting laid."

"Why are they doing it?"

"For the money. And you?"

"I'm here because I have to be, Mr. Gandil. Believe me, there are many other places I'd much rather be."

"Who the fuck *are* you, anyway?"

79

At this point some intervention seemed advisable. My subtly orchestrated intrigue was edging dangerously toward a punch-up.

"Chick, Mr. Evans is here to see we get what's coming to us. A little cooperation might speed things along nicely."

"Where's the money?" This again, and much louder, from Riisberg.

And that exact moment marked the end of Evans's patience with my charges.

"The money is here, gentlemen, waiting. But I won't be dispensing it this afternoon. I've been instructed to await further developments. You'll be hearing from Mr. Sullivan on this shortly. From now on all our contacts will be through him. Thank you so much for your patience. I think we've made substantial progress toward our common goals this afternoon."

Today I know it's so difficult to anticipate anything that you might as well stop trying to foresee everything. But in those days I still nursed an innocent's faith in prescience. That trust received a swift kick in the nuts just then as I realized Evans was coming up with the empties. And who was this revised version of Nat the Vile I saw before me now, this oily tactician growing more ministerial by the minute? He bore less resemblance to his boorish predecessor than Attell did on his jakest day to Rothstein. If he resembled anyone, actually, it was Rothstein himself. Everybody seemed to lately.

I didn't have to worry about a beak bust breaking out just then, though. All four players, led by Riisberg, were hitting the bricks. For a moment I considered yelling something reassuring at their backsides. But I feared my inflection would only betray my gloom. Evans wasn't much help. He just stood there, smiling, imperious, unflappable.

80

"That's exactly how the kike would have handled it, Sully," he said dryly. "Now your playmates know who's throwing this particular stick, and now we all know who's supposed to be fetching it."

20

Had I thought of any conciliatory messages, I could have flashed them straight to the lobby bar. The players headed right for it, too full of anger not to vent some on each other.

Gandil was ready to kill, but remained calm. He was the leader. Riisberg was ready to kill, period. Williams was too surprised to speak. He kept rubbing his keys against the rosewood bar, tracing teethmarks the size of his disgruntlement in its polish. Only Cicotte seemed resigned. It was about what he'd expected.

No one said a word until the drinks came, hoping some contradictory rationale would float forth unbidden. When none did, Riisberg made the suggestion he always felt most comfortable with.

"Let's go back up there and break their fucking backs."

Violence was Swede's favorite antidote to intransigence. Only larceny gave him more satisfaction than mayhem.

"We can do that anytime," Gandil said. "We can't make an easy five grand anytime."

"Including now," Riisberg said.

"We can make them give us the money," Williams said. "We'll hire a lawyer."

Nobody contradicted this suggestion. It contained too little logic to refute.

"I never had any trouble with Sullivan before," Gandil whispered, almost to himself. "I figured he could raise the money easy. I don't know who this fucking guy Evans is supposed to be."

"Nobody's blaming you, Chick," Williams said.

"Nobody's blaming you at all, Chick," Riisberg agreed.

Their resolve was fading fast into the night, Gandil sensed, their disappointment turning dangerously inward. Soon they'd be assuring each other they didn't need the fix, that it was "too much trouble."

"I know what they're trying to pull," Gandil blurted suddenly. He didn't, but surely needed to. Any solution now seemed the correct one.

"They think we can get the money someplace else. They're looking for a free ride."

Gandil felt momentarily exhilarated. His lie made the truth seem almost extraneous.

"That's right," Riisberg said. "They're trying to get a fucking free ride."

"We'll just get the money someplace else then," Gandil continued. "We won't say a goddam word to anybody."

"Not one goddam word," Williams said.

"Not a single goddam fucking word," Riisberg agreed.

Cicotte kept his mouth shut. He believed in Chick's revision even less than in the original. He shifted his seat a few stools toward the door, turning his full and unqualified attention to his drinking.

They stayed in the bar for forty-five more minutes, rationalizing every chink in Gandil's fable. Riisberg and Williams got drunker and louder. Cicotte got drunker and quieter. Gandil kept his hard eye on the door, hoping Evans would stroll by and see them plotting. He wanted Nat to know that they, too, had alternatives.

At ten sharp, Chick walked purposefully to the bar phone, to dial a number Sleepy Bill Burns had given him. He may not have intended to take Bill's offer until then. Nobody ever knew, least of all Chick.

There's one thing I do know as sure as gun is iron, though. Gandil took more of a chance on that vague possibility just then than I could have on any number of certainties.

I was sitting alone in my cootie cage, paralyzed, perspiring. Evans had left all my hopes dangling, my mind as white as my belly with the shock.

This is the real difference between Rothstein and me, I was thinking: He adds to things, I subtract.

Everything had been racing along so smoothly, as though A.R. himself were pulling the strings. Now this. I wish I could say I felt only disappointment. But I didn't. My losses never come unattended by relief.

I didn't consider my original dream rebutted, however, or even modified. What *was* threatened was Rothstein's version of it. I still saw the basic plan succeeding. Nothing could deter it, not even refutation.

The fading light slipped slowly past my shade. Hesitant footsteps made little mysteries on my ceiling. My lids grew heavy, my mind foggy. I rolled over and tucked my legs beneath my chin. I could reconsider it all tomorrow, the causes, the cures. What I needed now was to pass the night successfully. Salvation lay on the far side of its borders, I felt. For now sleep seemed the most ambitious goal imaginable.

21

Everybody knew.

But nobody *really* knew.

I certainly didn't, and I'd put the whole gag in gear.

I didn't know, for example, that Evans was calling Rothstein that very moment. How could I? Nat phoned from his closet, after stuffing the transom with wads of cotton sheets.

"Hello, Mr. Rothstein. It's me, Nat Evans, out here in Chicago."

"Nat. How are you? How's everything going out there in Hogopolis?"

"Swell, Mr. Rothstein, very swell indeed. We had a pleasant trip west on the Limited. The weather was tiptop, the meals a bit less so. A man with tattoos covering his schnoz—"

"That's splendid, Nat. Now let's get to the point, shall we?"

"You bet, Mr. Rothstein. Well, Sullivan's convinced I've got rats in my attic. He can't decide whether he's more disgusted or terrified."

"Good, Nat. Did the funds arrive promptly?"

"Four days after we got here, Mr. Rothstein, as promised."

"Have you met with the players?"

"Just a few minutes ago, Mr. Rothstein. They're serious about it. Whether they're up to it is another matter."

"And Sullivan?"

"As expected. He's the sort who prefers plotting things to

doing them. It'll take him two days to demand the money. Even then he'll be showing more gumption than he feels."

"Give him the dough tonight, Nat."

"If you say so, Mr. Rothstein."

"I say so, Nat. Give him the first fifty thousand. Leave the other fifty thousand in the hotel safe. We'll use it to pay the players after the Series. If I know Gandil, he's haunting the wires this very moment, auditioning alternatives. I wouldn't mind sharing expenses, Nat, as long as we get down first on the books."

"Okay, Mr. Rothstein. I'll take care of it right away."

"Good. And incidentally, Nat, there's one other thing you should be aware of."

"What's that, Mr. Rothstein?"

"Abe Attell has strayed off the path a bit on this one. I'd seen it coming. Abe's cock is much bigger than his brain. I like him, though. One can't help liking the Little Champ. And he still has his uses. So I'm not as peeved as I might be. I just don't want him pissing in our punch bowl, as it were. Abe treats the daintiest opportunity like a thirty-round knuckle mill with Gaspipe Gannigan. He can't raise enough cash to do anything really serious, of course. And I've instructed anyone who could give him credit not to. Still, he bears watching."

"Has he started betting yet, Mr. Rothstein?"

"No, he has no idea I'm on to him yet. So he hasn't felt the coercive press of time. But he'll be coming out to Chicago later this week. Keep an eye on him, like a good fellow. He shouldn't be too difficult to spot."

"He never is, Mr. Rothstein."

"I know, Nat. That's one of the Little Champ's most endearing attributes."

"Very good, Mr. Rothstein. Will there be anything else?"

"I don't believe so, Nat. Just get Sullivan that cash right away."

"I will, Mr. Rothstein, and I'll call you as soon as he's distributed it."

"That won't be necessary, Nat. I'll call you at the end of the week."

"Okay."

"Okay, what?"

"Okay, Mr. Rothstein."

"Goodbye, Nat."

"Goodbye, Mr. Rothstein."

Evans never met Burns.

Rothstein never met Gandil.

I never met Kid Gleason.

None of us ever met Comiskey.

Everyone was making his own plans, none knew where they all intersected.

After he hung up, Evans poured himself a stiff drink. He'd just gotten two very vivid messages in one laconic call. Individually they radiated potential, together they constituted the good thing of a lifetime.

Chicago really was going to lose the Series. And Abe Attell was being pardoned a betrayal.

Nat downed his shot to animate his courage, and to muffle his mounting qualms at Rothstein's motives.

It took him exactly two hours to get his own bets down, at odds ranging from 3–1 to 7–2. The line in New York was 13–5, but the White Sox were all the rage in Chicago.

Nat spread the cash around judiciously, no wager exceeding $2,000. He guessed it was the first money bet on the

Series with inside wire. He had every reason to believe this was true. It just wasn't.

When Rothstein finished massaging Evans's greed he got right back on the horn to his price-makers. The receiver never cooled in his palm. Within seconds he was moving somber amounts behind Cincinnati. He found the odds a steady 13–5. Evans would do better, but Rothstein was betting harder, and stood a much better chance of collecting. In fact, he stood a 100 percent chance of collecting.

He bet $100,000 in New York, $50,000 each in St. Louis, Los Angeles, and Havana, and more modest sums in several smaller wire centers. He found everyone eager for his action, though puzzled at his enthusiasm for the Reds. They considered both him and the White Sox invincible.

He waited three hours before calling Chicago again, assuming it had taken Evans an hour to get the point, then two more to talk himself into pressing it.

The first man he called hadn't seen Nat in three years.

"He's the one without the chin, ain't he, Mr. Rothstein?"

"That's right, Emilio."

"No, I ain't seen him since . . ."

"Thanks so much, Emilio."

"Mr. R.?"

"Yes, Emilio."

"Is there any truth to this breeze we've all been hearin' . . ."

"Not an ounce, Emilio. Those are just the indiscriminate warblings of the novices, men who believe everything is crooked just because they're not in on it. You know the type, Emilio, guys who hang around the buffet table slandering celebrities, applying devious logic to inappropriate topics."

"Sure, Mr. Rothstein."

"But we know everything isn't fixed, don't we Emilio?"

"Well . . ."

"Indeed we do. And that taking the dough is often the naivest option. Have I satisfied your curiosity, Emilio?"

"Well . . ."

"Very fine indeed, and *gut Shabbes* to you, Emilio."

The second man he called had taken $1,500 from Evans not twenty minutes earlier.

"I sure hope he's good for it, Mr. Rothstein. I got a wife out here who needs her pipes rerouted."

Rothstein assured him Evans had the cash, then rang off with several breezy aphorisms.

He was pleased. Having Evans bet was easier than cutting him in on it, and twice the fun. Straight cons had begun to bore the Bankroll. Watching small-timers imitate big-timers always amused him. It was like watching children dressing themselves up in evening clothes.

Evans would proceed more cautiously than Attell, Rothstein knew, his meticulousness providing a diverting counterpoint. He'd never had two candle-holders sell him out simultaneously. It gave him more control over them in a curious sort of way. He found it easier to trust men he *knew* were betraying him.

Rothstein made all his calls from the Brook's library. From its window he could see small knots of workmen constructing a temporary trellis. He was giving a reception tonight for some dago duke.

He settled back in his new morocco davenport, crossed his legs, massaged an ankle. He always enjoyed watching other men work, especially if their labors benefited him, and if a sheet of glass insulated him from their yammering.

He also enjoyed dealing on the phone, conning a mark he couldn't even see.

"With one black telephone, and a pot of heavy java," he'd tell dinner guests, "I could make a running start at taking over the universe."

He strutted to his sideboard then and lit himself a stogie. It felt stimulating to be trying something new again, something cheekier, in a sense, than anything he'd ever tried before. He was manipulating an event the whole country cared about, queering it without precedent or sponsorship, from one tiny room in a tiny town in the Adirondacks.

And nobody knew.

Five minutes into his second cigar a valet arrived from the west wing with a pneumatic:

"Mr. Daldonis awaits you in the refectory."

Daldonis was Nick the Greek's tag before sundown. He'd come seeking some of that easy Cincy money.

The word was out.

That evening was the high point of the Saratoga social season. Two hundred top people filled the Brook. One filled Rothstein's dream sack.

Flo Delvaney (Delvancey, actually; Rothstein hadn't caught the elided consonant) was a bottle blonde with a legendary pudendum. She'd hooked the Bankroll's arm as he'd skimmed the receiving line, pronouncing herself eager to break into "the arts."

"Any of the seven lively ones, Mr. Rothstein, though naturally I'd prefer the very liveliest."

Rothstein assumed she itched to be a Folly Dolly.

Mrs. Rothstein was in New York pricing pearls. Rothstein evoked her memory in his traditional fashion, keeping Flo's heels saluting the ceiling until daybreak.

Fifteen violinists strolled languidly about the lawn. A pair of desperately unattractive debutantes frolicked naked in the frog pond. Three proposals were accepted, two engagements were broken. A crippled racehorse was sold to an oleomargarine heir who was a bit too drunk, and much too rich, to care. The war was over. The new decade was four months from its inception.

Every third banty who approached Rothstein departed fiscally committed to Chicago. They all knew something was up, but none believed the Series could be contaminated.

By the time the darkies had swept up the last shattered jeroboam, Rothstein had sold the Sox short to the hilt.

Everybody knew.

But nobody really knew.

22

All right then, baseball.

It seems the simplest prospect to the shorthorn. But human frailty makes it a labyrinth for the bettor. One pitcher may reach the park hungover, another may be fresh from divorce court. Such contingencies rarely influence the odds, though. The bleakest prospect seldom fetches 3–1.

That's one reason I prefer betting horses. Each race has several potential winners; every long shot generates delusory odds. It's a simple game that merely appears complex, whereas baseball's plainness veils a swamp of intricacy.

Still, baseball was the people's choice just then. So it had to be mine. I employed men like Gandil to keep me informed. Soon they were cooking more facts than they were reporting. I didn't mind. Their manipulations often proved more profitable than their tips.

Our collaboration was simplicity itself. They iced the games, I bet them. They took reasonable cuts, I an irrational one. My clients were the cream of the era's bowwows (George M. Cohan, two U.S. senators, and several industrial hooligans among them).

But then greed, as it will, intruded. The more the players made, the more they needed. Their shadiness soon became part of the hazard. They always charged, but delivered sporadically. That's another reason I prefer backing the ponies. When you buy a racetracker, he stays good and bought.

I've a further complication with baseball, of course. I love the game, played it endlessly as a child, would be playing it still if allowed to. That's the regret Rothstein sensed in me right off.

The next morning found me again fully conscious, yet still detached. Sleep hadn't softened Evans's double cross. Waking up just made it seem fresh news.

I've always handled loss better than danger. Reversals I've dreaded for years arrive benignly. Still, this one would require heroic rationalization, I knew. Giving up didn't seem to hold as much appeal as usual.

When Evans burst through my door at nine-thirty, then, his intrusion didn't seem all that intrusive. The room was as black as my mood, its walls sweating, its fan creaking. I lay in my shorts, beneath my sheets, the hall light draping Nat's outline in its aura. He tossed an oblong package blithely my way, without moving more than a foot inside the door.

"Compliments of the kike," he drawled unctuously. "Spend it like you earned it."

Then, like the soft-heeled root-sucker he was, he was gone.

Is it not the eighth and ninth wonders of the world combined, reader, how money converts despair into rapture? There I lay, the same man, in the same shorts, beneath the same sheets, contemplating the same dispiriting circumstances. But where the absence of $50,000 had legitimized my gloom, its presence rendered it instantly superfluous.

I'd been raised from the depths to the heights by a salami-sized package of green parchment decorated with pictures of dead politicians.

Money has very little smell, it's often said. Yet its appeal to me is oddly olfactory. I catch its scent on the men, and in the places, it calls home. It colors my perceptions, creating unsustainable images: of fair women with dark, throaty laughs; of bright secrets no mortal can live up to. It lends a sunny cast to even the darkest moods, making deep differences in even the shabbiest existences.

I'd like to be above such banal reactions, but can't seem to be. How cheaply even the hardest heart may be bought. A smile, a kind word, a slip of paper.

I'd never had any serious money before, just gambled and won, gambled and lost, seemingly content just to stay enough ahead. But now I wanted more. Rothstein's $50,000 could buy me back my dreams, I felt. If that bound me to cash, so be it. I'd rather be obligated to its presence than its lack.

I wrapped my arms around it then, savoring its warmth, ran my thumb along the seam between the packets, hefted its weight, rifled its edges, stopped just short of plunging my tongue between its folds. It did have a smell, faint, but lush with promise, a musky odor, like damp leaves in an abandoned convent. I fell right back asleep clutching it to my chest, dreaming light-colored dreams of unlikely transformations.

When I awoke again, at noon, I felt in need of fresh odds. So I called three of the eagerest slip-snatchers on the South Side. Local enthusiasm for the White Sox was peaking. It should have brought 7–2, but fell far short; 9–5 was the best the boys could manage.

I was tempted to blame Evans for this, but didn't. It was simply the culmination of my cumulative indiscretions. I'd been sharing the buzz to spread the burden. Now collusion was stripping the profit from my bones.

To my credit I didn't sit down and sulk about this, though, rehashing alternatives, or even worse, adding to them. To lose momentum now, I knew, would be to forfeit it forever. Instead I plunged straight to the heart of my ambivalence, to the action I habitually sacrifice to it. I called a cab to take me to the Chicago Board of Trade. And when it came, by God and glory, I *took* the frigging thing.

Just as my heart leads me where money is romanced, my head takes me where it is accumulated. The stock exchange was enjoying a flush period then, its operatives behaving less discreetly than they should have. Little distinguished them from common turf accountants, actually, except their striped ties and gin-with-a-twist demeanors.

I trailed my $50,000 behind me in a Warner's pillowcase. It's the small chances I can't seem to take.

I went straight to the most imaginatively named firm, and asked to see the least imaginatively named broker.

The most imaginatively named firm was R. Ugguz; its least imaginatively named broker was Robert Jones. (R.

93

Ugguz sounded like a Russian wrestling bear to me, Robert Jones like the man who cleaned its cage.) I was clearly seeking an ironist, not a sharpie, a man who could wink at the world, but rarely had to. I'd planned to seek the dullest-looking individual at R. Ugguz, but in the lobby every man looked the dullest.

The Robert Jones who greeted me was even drearier than his handle, his hair restrained by lavish sheets of brilliantine, his expression fixed in a tradesman's steely grimace. When I asked him for a price on Cincinnati, though, he responded as to the query of the moment.

"How much action can you stand up to, Clem?"

"Thirty-five thousand."

I'd almost gone the whole fifty grand, before remembering I'd need a little bit for Chick.

R. Jones disappeared importantly into his office. When he returned he looked, if possible, even less animated.

"Eight-to-five Chicago," he said, not moving his lips, his tone suggesting a lot less taking than leaving, "plus a six percent commission for my runner, and five hundred off the top for this and that. I had to call twenty-five sheet writers to scare this up."

This was the standard closer's line, I knew. Still, time *was* racing on. The price had tumbled 15 percent in one hour. I'd have to get down pretty quick, I sensed, or not at all. I didn't want to give this creep my business, though. His manner seemed a snare for the unwary, his price a sop contemptuously thrown a chump. So I excused myself to check on my alternatives, crossing the street to (God help me) the Blarney Pub.

In that dive I asked the bartender for a boilermaker, and enough change for an afternoon on the phone.

"You're a White Sox backer, aren't you?" he asked, not looking up.

"How'd you know?" I wondered, hoping not to learn.

"Because only gamblers dress that half-cocked on purpose, and because a shot and a beer this early any day is pretty disgruntled drinking."

"What happened to the odds?"

"It's in the bag," he said, as if he himself had arranged it. "Everybody knows. I got two-to-one on the Reds yesterday afternoon."

I thanked him, retrieved my change, then bolted out the door, abandoning my drink. The news elsewhere would surely be even harsher.

I stumbled back to R. Ugguz, bereft of options. I'd swallow my pride, grant bargain-hunting a holiday, take 8–5 on the Reds and be glad as glad could be of it. By that time, of course, the odds had fallen to 7–5. I drew $40,000 from my pillowcase before they could fall even further.

"Stick every penny of that straight behind Cincinnati," I instructed Jones. "And be quick about it too, my worthy fellow. I have important people to see on the trading floor."

I bet the extra $5,000 to make up for the odds, added the pathetic little fib to salve my dignity.

It was too late for either, of course. The day's delay had halved my potential profit, depleting my remaining capital almost to the level of irrelevance. My trek back to the hotel was a despondent one. Every nobody I encountered looked like somebody else who knew.

23

Rarely, if ever, have I seen a city so divided by success. Self-congratulatory cant filled the papers. Foreboding bubbled from beneath every headline. My room-service waiter spoke of no one but Jackson. The maître d' averted his eyes at the name.

My ambivalence mirrored the city's. I was contemplating my coming triumph funereally, having taken a short price on an underdog I'd levitated.

The final insult was Jones's commission. He'd extracted it up front, like a pawnbroker. No bookie would have done such a thing. Or if he had he'd have done it with a smile. Stock butchers take their shakedowns much too seriously.

I called Gandil when I got back to the hotel.

"Waltz up to my room for a moment, Chick. There've been developments."

I didn't outline the specifics, although he came dangerously close to asking.

I passed the moments before his arrival woolgathering, watching two sparrows contesting a pebble on my windowsill.

How consoling it must be, I thought languorously, to have a brain so small such controversies can engross it.

Chick arrived wearing an impertinent gray Stetson, and an expression of equally contrived umbrage. Burns's promises had reinflated his airs.

"If I don't get all the juice by tomorrow," he announced, "you can kiss this whole fucking deal goodbye."

He tossed the Stetson on my bed by way of emphasis. It was a predictable gesture, yet oddly compelling, drawing its persuasive power, in fact, from its very triteness.

"I think you'll find something appealing on that bureau over there, Chick. Something heartening."

He stared at the package, then back at me, seeming uncertain whether to ignore it or embrace it. Lifting it was the compromise he finally settled on. Only a slight twitch in his jaw betrayed his ardor.

"Where's the rest of it?" he asked, halfway through his count. "There's only ten thousand fucking dollars here."

His words were harsh, his tone conciliatory. I knew from the first syllable he was mine.

"You'll get it after every game you throw, Chick. Ten thousand per, fifty at the end."

"Throw" was a word I'd chosen carefully. I wanted him to know exactly what I was paying him for.

"This isn't how we talked about it, Sport."

"This isn't how I'd planned it either, Chick. But a hundred thousand dollars makes for an awful lot of amendment. The people spending it have a right to their misgivings. I trust you, Chick, but they don't even *know* you."

I could almost feel him wilting beneath my will. His history made him a natural for concession.

"I don't know, Sport. I promised the guys their payday up front."

"Jesus C. on a pogo stick, Chick. I had to cornhole myself to get you a dime from these pricks. You're pretty brassy for a light-purse."

This was my favorite closing ploy, attacking the man who already considers himself the victim. It's always worked on me.

"I'm not squeezing you, Sport. I just promised the guys."

"Okay, Chick, okay, listen, let's have dinner at the Century Club after the first game. I'll give you the second ten grand then, and introduce you to J. P. Morgan in the bargain. How does that sound?"

I was sure it sounded peachy. Chick's contempt for the prosperous masked a parallel reverence. That's something you can always count on from working stiffs.

"I don't know, Sport. I suppose the boys could wait a little longer. But tell that doofus Evans I want a full ten grand after every game."

"I'll tell him, Chick, and see he keeps to it, too. I want to get something out of all of this myself, you know, besides a back-ass view of half the world's foul temper."

I'd achieved more compromise here than seemed possible, and in less time than I usually took to *fail.* I unveiled a bottle of Haig & Haig to seal our bargain. I didn't know if I could deliver the money. I knew I couldn't deliver J. P. Morgan. Just reaching that point seemed challenge enough for now.

I have scant memory of the balance of that evening, beyond several blurred images of random violence:

Gandil, penitent in his cups over a woodchuck flayed alive in his childhood; the horrified expression of the room-service waiter when he saw what we'd done to his station; drained bourbon bottles flying from our twelfth-story window, exploding below like glass flares dropped in glycerine.

Gandil proved an even less desirable companion drunk than sober. The crassness of his cheer made me nostalgic for his rancor.

When I awoke beneath the bed the next afternoon he was gone, as was the cash.

I made myself as presentable as possible before shuffling off to hunt for Evans. But he'd also disappeared, ceding his room to a party-favors salesman with the least efficiently repaired harelip in my experience.

The desk clerk told me Evans had checked out, leaving no messages, except a terse one suggesting I'd be tickled to pay his bill.

I have a tendency, dangerous in any entrepreneur, lethal in one of visionary temperament, to abandon realities that fall short of my wishes for them. This rigidity has cost me many chances, as I'm sure it was meant to.

But when Evans flew our coop, then salted the wound by sticking me with the tab, I knew I'd had it with my unwillingness to improvise.

I spent the rest of the day revising my strategy. If they could waffle, I could waffle too. If they could stiff me, I'd stiff them at a quick step.

I outlined my new plan on a piece of hotel stationery, in violet ink, using talcum as a blotter. It varied little from its predecessor. Only my desire that it be different made it seem so.

When I finished I folded it in neat quarters, put it in the pocket of my pajamas, crawled into bed, squeezed my pillow between my knees. The talcum scent filled the room up to the ceiling, almost compensating me for this latest setback's cost.

24

That evening, as I scribbled away obliviously in my digs, Gandil combed the South Side's seedier precincts, searching for Eddie Cicotte's rooming house. Eddie always lived alone during the season, while his family stayed on thriftily in Michigan.

Chick had decided to give Eddie the whole $10,000, hoping his contentment would seep down through the ranks.

Cicotte wasn't in, but his landlady admitted Gandil anyway. She recognized him from his mug shots in the tabloids. Gandil tiptoed up to Cicotte's room, like a hysteric approaching a crypt. The bed was just inside the door, as in any ascetic's cell.

Gandil slipped the $10,000 beneath Cicotte's pillow, still wrapped in Sunday's rotogravure. He left a note with it:

Here's yours, awaiting ours. Regards—Chick.

No other explanation seemed necessary; Chick didn't force one. He couldn't help noticing the absence of sporting mementos, though, and that the linoleum had long since surrendered its pattern. He killed the light before he could notice more, then stole back downstairs to face the landlady's enthusiasm.

"You're so much handsomer than your pictures make you out as, Mr. Gandil. That one in yesterday's *Tribune* made you look like a chink."

Gandil thanked her, opened the door, and skipped out

onto the sidewalk. Ten minutes later he was safe inside Venachio's, flushing Eddie's coop from his memory with liquid amnesia.

Cicotte returned from his own soak-up at midnight. He wasn't drunk, just muddled enough to feel cozily indifferent. He threw himself down, fully clothed, on his bed, his head striking the sharp edge of Gandil's gift.

I wish I had a quarter for every quack question I've answered about that summer, since its events went so spectacularly awry. Had I even a dime for every chump who's asked me "Why'd they do it, Sport?" I'd be a very, very wealthy man indeed.

"Why'd they do it, Sport?"

As if anybody ever does anything for one reason.

Nobody ever asks me why I did it. They assume they know. I did it for the money. Why else do gamblers do anything?

But the players? They were assumed to make millions already. I knew different. I knew exactly what they did make. And that the discrepancy was beginning to drive them around the bend.

That was part of it. But only part. Another part was that they thought they cóuld get away with it. And that nothing is ever *really* quite enough.

Eddie Cicotte, then, nuzzling his rasping box spring in a thick haze of craw rot and night thoughts, fingered the bills while calculating their cost. His heart was tempering his lust with liquorish logic. He realized he could get something new, but that he'd have to surrender something old to keep it. Propriety held momentary sway, before an ancient memory won the day for desire.

It was of the most graphic image of his youth, his Aunt Lurie, groaning, beneath him.

She was a slate-haired spinster about his mother's house, a fading beauty, a straightener of hems. On her fortieth birthday, two weeks past his fourteenth, she invited him through her door, and onto her mattress.

She stood breathlessly, two feet opposite, slowly removing her crinoline. At first he was puzzled, then alarmed. He kept hoping it was a game, or even a joke. By the time he realized it wasn't, he no longer wanted her to stop. He'd never dreamed such possibilities existed, certainly not in this most familiar of guises. She turned and stretched athletically for his inspection, then beckoned him forward.

He hesitated, then went. Soon he was lost in a world beyond imagining. It seemed to take a month; it took a minute. He never told anyone. Two weeks later she moved to Canada.

Even now certain pressures evoked her image, the struggle for breath, the longing for oblivion.

He gathered the money now and stuffed it beneath his mattress. Some things, he recalled, were worth throwing everything away for.

25

Every style awaits the age that fits it.

I'm convinced of that now. I just don't *need* to believe it anymore.

I could have undertaken a major project long ago. But I wasn't ready. My father's death didn't allow me to do it, it forced me to do it. There's the difference.

You don't change until you have to, I believe. I'd never imagined there were other ways of doing things, of revising. If I'd known Evans's intentions I'd have changed even more. But I didn't. One can't know everything.

I passed the next two days locked in my room, reworking my strategy. I wanted it to be a model of concision, a conspiratorial clockwork.

Here's what I came up with:

1. *Stop mooning about the Jones bet.*
2. *Raise more dough, in small pieces, from old contacts.*
3. *Fix each game separately, pyramiding the profits.*
4. *Keep your trap shut.*

It amazes me now that I ever thought of this as a new plan, failed to recognize it as just my old plan in effigy. So smitten was I by my alleged transformation, in fact, that when Burns and Attell blew into the Warner dining room the next afternoon, I assumed they'd come in response to my metamorphosis.

All *is* vanity.

I'd descended to the salon to air my reflexes, and to treat myself to a celebrational feed. I already sensed my new approach succeeding, though it scarcely existed beyond my optimism for it.

I should have been shocked to see Bill and Abe together. I hadn't introduced them, after all. Yet somehow their collusion seemed inevitable.

They sat huddled in the corner, inhaling vichyssoise. Burns had been very busy since we'd parted, trying to shake his stake from Attell. Attell had been even busier, trying to raise it. All of Rothstein's contacts had dried up on him. He'd reached Chicago with neither his bets made nor his bribes raised.

The last thing any gambler wants to hear is that a man who's promised him money doesn't have it. That's almost what Burns was hearing just then. Attell wasn't exactly saying he didn't have the money though; he was just saying he didn't have it *now*.

"Mr. Rothstein wants to test your good faith on this, Billy. He'll chalk the lamppost with twenty thousand dollars after every game. You know he's good for it. His credit's as solid as Johnny Torrio's."

"Sure, but . . ."

"I'll talk to Gandil myself, square it personally. A Jew and an Irishman can talk a heinie into anything."

We all made mistakes that summer.

Gandil shouldn't have approached me.

I shouldn't have told Burns.

Burns shouldn't have believed Attell.

Attell shouldn't have crossed Rothstein.

Only Rothstein made no mistakes. He didn't believe in them.

Two of the biggest errors were being made right there in front of me. Attell was trying to con a con man, and Burns was going along with the gag.

And then suddenly, in that feverishly ornate dining room, among the potted palms and the cheroot smoke and the bric-a-brac, I had an irresistible desire to be away. It felt much like the impulse that had drawn me to Chicago in the first place, except it clearly sprang from a much deeper source. What it resembled most was the escape part of my dream, freeing itself since I obviously wouldn't let it.

I simply couldn't watch these two mugs scheme any longer, oblivious to even the possibility of my presence. It made me fear there were too many things that *I* didn't know.

I went upstairs to pack.

Two hours later I was skimming the rails back to Saratoga.

Attell had no such option, of course. He had to reassure the players, since he couldn't trust Burns to. After lunch he and Bill went up to Gandil's room to try.

"Is a fix this size a delicate operation?" Abe asked Chick right off. "You bet it is," he answered himself without hesitating. "Could anybody finance it better than Arnold Rothstein? Not another man in this country, or Canada. Would a man even close to his right mind—"

"It's getting late, short rocks," Gandil interjected. "I got palms to grease."

"What's that, Chick? I'm afraid I didn't quite hear you."

The entire confrontation went along like that, Attell interviewing himself, Gandil interrupting, Attell feigning deafness.

Abe never said "I *can't* hear you," either, but always "I *don't* hear you," as if his abstraction was strictly a matter of choice. This was another Rothstein stratagem.

Through this swamp of cross-purposes and veiled threats Abe and Chick stalked their avaricious compromise. It took them forty-five minutes to reach it.

Burns wisely kept his oar out.

In the end Attell made the same deal with Gandil that I had, at double the cost. I had that much on the Little Champ, at least. He had to promise twice what neither of us could deliver.

Gandil left the room irrationally satisfied. He'd be getting $10,000 from me after every game, then another $20,000

105

from Attell. If any of it had been true he'd have been over the hump going sixty.

Attell departed feeling decidedly less elated, yet encouraged. He still had no idea where his stake was coming from, but at least he had Gandil's commitment. That had to be worth something.

Burns exited feeling thoroughly confused. He didn't have any money, Attell didn't have any money, Gandil didn't have any money. Yet the odds on Cincy were falling through the floor.

26

On my train a man was selling small cats for a quarter. He carried them in a Lourie's gelatin box. When he reached my seat only one remained. I declined it and returned to my paper. The conductor asked for his ticket. As he reached for it, the cat made its move. The man grabbed it by its throat and held it, squirming, as the conductor punched his stub.

That cat's convulsions remain with me to this hour, struggling for freedom, yet powerless in its circumstance. Its captor was equally memorable, a dirt farmer diluted by mortgages, reduced to begging and calling it commerce.

My mind reverts easily to past indignities. Sharp sensations evoke them. The scent of spearmint recalls my school days, the fear of death my father's face. Some associations are obvious, others less so. I cannot escape them; they are my history.

Whenever I see a small cat now, it is *that* cat, its keeper baring his incisors for my benefit, the sun falling in weak streams across the forest, the scent the lavender of my seat-mate.

Whenever I think of the fix I think of Saratoga, of the boundless promise of my first visit. Contemplating the money only evokes my sad return, reminding me never to return to anyplace where I've been happy.

The train pulled in at 8:30 P.M. I hoped to reencounter some expectancy, but didn't expect to.

I sensed its absence instantly. The porters didn't squabble over my bags. My cabbie never spoke. The streets were as still as death, even around the grand hotels. We took the short route, didn't pass the track. I slept lightly, despite my weariness. The thick heat hung like a warning over my mattress.

In the morning all my worst fears were exceeded. I toured the hotel lobbies, foraging for capital. There was none. The big-timers had loaded up on the Series, the lesser lights had tapped out at the track. The odds had settled at 9–10. I lacked the courage to ask who was favored.

Everybody knew.

By eight I'd discarded what remained of my dignity. I began approaching old Boston contacts. Everywhere the answer was the same. The cash was out, the odds were down; everyone would make more from my scam than I would.

I took tea on the Gideon Putnam veranda. My scone arrived cold; it grew cloudy. I saw no one more famous than I.

At nine I rushed to the Brook to see Rothstein. His doorman said he was gone.

"Mr. Rothstein never stays in Saratoga for the last week, sir. He feels all the important people have already left."

That's how I learned of my mistake. The last week was for those who stay everywhere too long.

I thanked him, then fled. I was tempted to peek in through the curtains, to see if Evans and I were still loitering about. But I didn't. All looked as it had on my previous visits, except the south lawn seemed in need of a trimming.

I wasn't quite sure where to go then. So I headed back to town. I knew I'd eventually punish myself for my obliviousness, though not directly. I took it out, instead, on my prior visits' memory, savaging it through remorseless reenactment. The result was almost thrillingly pathetic, like a great beauty's face reconstructed after a fire.

I went first to watch the workouts on the track. A few inferior runners loafed through their breezes. Waiters banged crockery to ward off customers. Hand melon was declared prematurely out of season.

No tennis babies decorated the Skidmore courts. Art du Temps was shuttered. The lake teemed with paupers, discouraging bathing. What rich remained had sought refuge at the track. Even these were the wrong sort of rich, though— new rich unused to their money, old rich unused to anything else.

I lost $150 before leaving after five races. None of my runners got a call. At the Bijou I endured twenty minutes of *Shoulder Arms,* then hit the streets. The sun was sinking, the sidewalks filling—with locals, with tourists, with every imaginable inappropriate type.

I knew it was too early to revisit the Brook. I went anyway.

I had a few snorts among the troubadors and the freeloaders. Everyone seemed to be playing out the string. By ten the evening's end was blessedly in sight. The people who only come after nine hadn't come at all. A handful of regulars milled listlessly around the baccarat tables. I made a cursory pass at dice, without any luck.

At eleven I finally admitted I was bored and walked home through the damp, fetid streets. I was resigned to being in bed by midnight, to making yet another fresh start in the morning. I didn't glance back at the Brook as I left, reluctant to surrender that particular image to revision.

The next day was getaway day, the last day of the racing season, the traditional day for the least likely of long shots.

I awoke newly determined to face reality, to fling myself into the flow of new circumstances, even if there were no new circumstances to fling myself into. My determination lasted halfway through my bran.

The morning light had that dead sheen about it, that flatness that defines the back of August. It was the first sign that summer was really ending. The breezes were cooler, more vigorous, bearing hints of fall from the graves of prior years. I took my coffee at a small grease trap opposite the track, then tramped the woods behind the society stables. I wanted to fix the sun's declining angle. My new plans seemed to be vanishing in its haze.

I know I sometimes feel nostalgic without reason, tend to think of even the brightest prospects as memories. But this time I knew the loss was real. I had only to glance around me to confirm it.

When I reached the track it was ringed by livery wagons. They were clearing out before the day even began. The whole place seemed headed for cold storage.

I lost the first four races, but took it calmly. I'd decided to stop pretending there was anything to be cheerful about, to seek satisfaction in seeing the world as it was.

My horse in the fifth race broke his leg. He was only fifty yards from the finish, two lengths to the good. The leg snapped with a finality audible in the clubhouse. He went quickly to his knees, struggling to finish, not done racing.

He lunged to his feet, but the leg wouldn't hold. He started to stagger. The splintered bones stuck crazily through the skin. The crowd gasped. The jockey dismounted, reining in the panic. The great eyes rolled wildly. The bloody leg dangled foolishly. The jockey gentled him, though the horse seemed to know.

Grooms ran onto the track from every angle. The horse van arrived, but wasn't needed. They threw a screen around him and shot him on the track. The report was muffled, but unmistakable. The crowd hushed. Only the livery vans out back disrupted the silence.

He was the jumper who'd won for me the first week. He'd switched to the flat track today, gone off at 9–1. He was very fast, but unused to sprinting. He'd jumped a shadow inside the sixteenth pole. It cost me $200. It would have been a little extra to bet against the Sox.

I didn't watch them shoot him; I'm not that type. When they put up the screen I headed out back immediately. I'd make my pick for the next race under the saddling trees.

And then, as often happens when I'm ducking reality, and even more often when I need a reason to, a woman passed into my life.

Two women, actually, though only one was to matter for long.

They were standing near each other, though not together, theirs the lone figures in the rear landscape besides my own. They, too, had fled the execution of the steeplechaser. Neither flaunted her discretion.

One was tall, disorientingly beautiful, carrying a fawn parasol to shield her from the sun. Her features were delicate and sensual, her form so flawless it could have been cast. She took my breath and tossed it off somewhere behind me.

The other was slimmer, more serious, less studied, her hair a bit disheveled, her complexion a trifle wan. Her appeal was less immediate, less accessible. She was as pretty now, I could see, as she would ever be.

Something in her stance suggested danger, though, hinted at a passion well beyond regulating. I wouldn't reach it, I knew, probably wouldn't even try to. But you don't need to reach passion to use it. I learned that long ago.

Both of these women would surprise me. Most of their surprises would be unpleasant. But I sensed the slim girl's surprises wouldn't be calculated. So I didn't hesitate. That is, I didn't hesitate in my choice. I did hesitate in making *any* choice. I knew it wouldn't work; it never does. There would be endless complications, countless disappointments, ultimately great sorrow. I paused to weigh the benefit against the cost. I guessed the cost would be greater, but I knew the benefit would be now.

I walked slowly toward the girl with the parasol. Her perfume roused me, but only briefly. It was already just a memory as I passed her, fixing my course resolutely on the slim girl, comforting words concerning dead horses and barbarous crowds already fully formed on my lips.

We spent September in Saratoga together, in her rented room, behind a farrier's. She taught me to saddle a horse; I taught her to read the box scores. Her room wasn't big enough for two. Often we slept in the forest, beside the lake, beneath the box poplars.

By the time the sun set on getaway day all the August people had fled farther south. The streets reverted to the hillbillies and the jigaboos. We bicycled into town every morning and ate breakfast at a crumb castle opposite the backstretch. We went to the track itself many afternoons, indulging ourselves in wordless audits of its emptiness. She was something of a gambler herself. Once we even snuck inside and made love in Harry Payne Whitney's private box. I got splinters in my backside; she got a side stitch from laughing. I never asked her her age. It didn't seem to matter.

She was as full of surprises as I'd imagined. None were surprises I'd ever had before. She yodeled. She could speak French. She was willfully naive, yet her guilelessness seemed irrefutably logical. I came to depend on her, as I will. Her name was Rose.

At night we lay on the Brook's empty lawns, gazing up at the deep, shimmering star fields. There was frequently a low lamp in one of the casino windows. The watchman's shadow played periodically over her limbs. We could easily have been lovers.

We lived on my last few dollars, and on my unspoken hopes that the fix would soon multiply them. I know now that I was just tricking myself into contentment, diverting attention from the disillusionment I feared must follow. I'd spent my entire life preparing to do something memorable, ignoring the suspicion that I really didn't want to. I'd extracted woe from elation, then burrowed deeper and deeper into it. I was anxious to try something different. I think she was too. It's an easy ambition in any out-of-season town.

The month passed quickly. I seemed happy. Before I knew it it was time to go.

The night before I left I told her about the fix. Or at least everything I knew about it then, which seems pitifully little now.

She nurtured some surprisingly conventional instincts beneath her surface bonhomie. Her initial response was guardedly disapproving. But soon her audacity made all the right adjustments. She grew less timid with each inflaming detail. Danger does that to women. Money helps.

For an hour she quizzed me breathlessly on my plan. I made it sound more promising than I now considered it. Or perhaps she'd already revived my flagging hopes. I just knew I wanted to see it through. I owed it that much.

I told her I was leaving for Chicago the next day. I said she should lie low, not try to contact me. I said the Series could take two to three weeks, collecting the money another couple of days. I said we'd go off someplace nice when it was over, someplace hot and foreign, someplace neither of us had ever been before, where we could spend our money without thinking much about it, on red wine, and vast hotel suites and all manner of foolish and transitory pleasures. I seemed to have forgotten the modest rewards of my perfect scam. Or perhaps I only omitted them for her benefit. I told her I would wire her when it was time, with instructions on where to meet me.

She stared at me with a willfully tranquil expression, then nodded. A thin membrane of emotion passed quickly over her eyes. It might have been the grief even the briefest passion prefigures; or maybe it was just the light. I touched her lips with a fingertip to dispel it. As I did, I felt it pass from her to me. She pressed her tongue to my flesh then, and licked it softly.

It was at that moment that the two questions I'd avoided all month finally caught up to me:

When did you stop feeling this way without realizing it, Sport?

and

Could the illusion that you might wish to feel this way again possibly propel you through the next three weeks?

October
1919

1

I may have reached that point in my narrative, reader, where the facts begin playing havoc with the truth.

The next three weeks were quite eventful. Remembering them is difficult, explaining them out of the question. Yet I'm tempted to try. They were so ripe with contrary significance that I might easily allegorize them out of existence.

I left Saratoga at eight the next evening, a gold moon sheathing my silver Pullman. The White Sox would be leaving Chicago in thirty-six hours. I would accompany them.

My trip west was instructive in several respects.

In Schenectady a legless veteran requested an aisle seat for his prosthesis. He was refused. The conductor denied responsibility for phantom pains.

Outside Sandusky a young nigger with an apprentice pimp's bravura assured me it was the *Reds* who were about to take the gas.

"This is the gilt-edge buy on it, my man. I got it straight from a guy who's pokin' Edd Roush's missus."

He could have told me Carry Nation was a rumdum and been believed, so skeptical of all my old assumptions had I become. I checked the sweatband of my boater for reassurance. My new plans were stenciled boldly in its felt:

I'd take even money to extricate my stake, then bet the remaining games individually.

I also intended to be more spontaneous in my new guise. Planning seemed to distract me from my plans. I made a list of impetuous things to do, seeing no irony in this.

The coach emptied as we pushed farther west. Straw hats replaced fedoras. The fall landscape drifted by benignly: amber fields, azure hills, copper timberlands. Calm horses raised their heads from shallow streams, surveying our progress with pitiless detachment.

In Chicago I went straight to the Sherman Hotel, booking a small room under an assumed name. The Sherman was just central enough to catch the current drift, yet not so downtown as to get itself caught up in it.

One turn of the lobby confirmed my suspicions. The odds had settled at pick 'em. So much cash was flowing toward the Reds that skepticism now gripped the deeper thinkers. Reason said Chicago, the juice said Cincinnati. Nobody knew which fact to fight. It was a muddle Rothstein would have made a pile in.

I downed a glass of buttermilk and retired early.

The next morning hell in a handbag broke out across the Midway.

Model T caravans formed spontaneously in the streets, White Sox backers massed raucously in my hallway. Chants were chanted, banners unfurled. From nowhere zeal for the Series had spiked a fever.

I liked the idea of this, and some of the reality. It was animal happiness, pure and simple. To savor its specifics I

118

sought shelter in the breakfast room, where I struck up a conversation with my waitress, Marge from Cicero.

"Griddle cakes for the special today, hon, and Wheatena cooked just the way boys like it. With shirred eggs you get repeats on the java."

"Sounds ideal, Marge, but I think I'll stick to raisin toast this morning, and tomato juice to put some acid in my outlook. Does it always sound like recess at the geek farm around here?"

"That's just the local boys getting ready for the Series, hon. Those Redlegs are about to take a licking."

"Not if I have anything to do with it, Marge, and by the way, I do. I've put all my influence behind the Reds, as it happens."

"Why would you do something like that, hon?"

"To be different."

"There's modern life in a nutshell for you. Everybody wants to be different. It's the latest thing that makes everybody the same."

She had me there, so she left me, deflated, and with my coffee black and icy. I downed it, and my toast, then hailed a hansom to the terminal and my train.

Half of Chicago filled Union Station that morning, and hardly the sedate half. Three bands—two brass, one philharmonic—bounced modish anthems off the dank retaining walls. Masked jugglers kept hundreds of baseballs improbably airborne. Troops of Ukrainian Boy Scouts marched gravely around the news kiosks. The atmosphere suggested fifty thousand truants excused permanently from shop class. The sun shone benevolently on the city and its fans. It was a day on which no misgiving stood a chance.

I arrived at eleven and watched bemusedly from the loge.

119

I'd felt no guilt at past manipulations, but this one made me queasy. Here were thousands of innocents nursing one common delusion. I alone knew how delusory, for I alone had ordained it. It was a brief twinge, but a genuine one. I'm nothing if not human.

It was clear from the chaos that we wouldn't be leaving soon. So I bought a lime cooler and settled in for the spectacle. Pickpockets dipped three-piece-suiters on the fringes; rival aldermen elbowed each other out of camera range. Long lines formed spontaneously at the ticket windows. Hundreds of Chicagoans would awake sober, and broke, in Cincinnati tomorrow.

Once I peered down into the multitude and thought I saw Rose. But it wasn't her. On closer inspection, it didn't even look like her.

It was a time . . .

But of course, I'm not sure just what kind of time it was. Subsequent events have colored my perceptions. And I'm reluctant to introduce a laundry list of happenstance just to fix the period's character in my memory. But it was a genuine time, that much is clear.

Fourteen million corpses were oxidizing in Europe. Valentino was mouthing sweet nothings from the screen. Girls bared ivory limbs on public strandways. The whole world was busy reinventing itself. In the transition my Series scam nestled, both postscript and prelude simultaneously.

They called us aboard at one-fifteen. The players made their feisty way forward. My eight lacked the decency to even *feign* modesty. I liked that.

Comiskey and his retainers followed quickly, looking like

close relatives of a recently elevated commoner. Next came the press, accompanied by a smattering of celebrities: John Barrymore (looking as beautiful as his wishes); Frank Lloyd Wright (*sans* his traditional hauteur); John Dewey (seemingly invigorated by reality, a state he usually preferred examining to experiencing). All were just fans for the occasion.

It was a time . . .

Well, it was a time when the mighty mingled for recreation.

The train finally pulled away at three. I took an aisle seat next to Aimee Semple McPherson's cousin. He tried to sell me opium. We ignored the fanatics clinging to the car; their pounding only reinforced our serenity.

A few passengers decanted their hootch straightaway, others set about playing backgammon. I drew a berth over William Z. Foster in the sleeping car. Dorothy Speare sat opposite me in the diner.

He snored.

She didn't.

2

We sped out across the flat, featureless countryside, an island of light in an ambiguous landscape.

It was a familiar trip for the Chicagoans, an unprecedented one for us easterners. We'd anticipated a short jog across the wheat fields, assuming Cincinnati was just Chicago's southernmost suburb. Once faced with reality, however, we settled in to bear it. Clouds broke out playfully across the horizon. Porters circulated complicated canapés. Christy Mathewson wandered over from his pinochle game.

Mathewson had been a great pitcher for the Giants, an indifferent manager of the Reds, a drinking companion to stateside enthusiasts of the Big War. Now he was composing loutishly vivid Series reportage for the *New York World.*

"Up to something your mother wouldn't approve of, Sport?"

It wasn't a venomous question, just a rib, a needle I was supposed to prick my composure on.

"Just along for the ride, Matty. And yourself?"

"That's what you said when I caught Hal Chase's thumb up my heinie in '17, Sport."

"Hal Chase is nothing to me, Matt. I never managed the guy. He never fixed any games on me."

"He's even less to me these days, Sport, although I still find myself fascinated by his schedule, and that of his bunkies, an uncommon number of whom I see lounging along these aisles. Don't dick around with me, Sport. Everybody knows there's toe jam in the mulligan."

"Everybody but me, Matt. I only know what I read in the *World.* They say the White Sox could win it in their sleep."

"They could, too, Sport. But unfortunately they're going to be awake."

"It's beyond unlikely, Matt. How could anybody fix the Series?"

"With money, Sport. And precious little if Chick Gandil is tending the register."

"But everybody would know."

"Everybody *does* know, Sport. I played this game, remember? It's duck soup to pull a fast one. Hang an inshoot, drop a can of corn, before you can say Arnold Rothstein you're knee deep in the short weight."

He smirked when he mentioned Rothstein's name. I didn't flinch.

"It's out of the question, Matt. I'd have heard, and I haven't. Now please excuse me. I have to see a man about fixing the Ice Frolics."

His inquiries had grown jarringly insistent. I had nothing to gain from parrying them, except further innuendo. So I withdrew. I'd wanted to survey my fellow passengers anyway. There suddenly seemed no time like the present.

I didn't have far to go to find someone relevant. Monte Tennes was sitting just four seats forward.

Tennes was Chicago's definitive yentzer, a corpulent sharpie given to oracular misstatements. He'd gathered the usual felons around him, their cuticles glowing, their aftershave humming.

"What's the good word on the Series, *mon frère?*"

Tennes called everybody *mon frère.* He thought it made him sound continental. It might have, if he hadn't pronounced the *e.*

"There's no good word, Monte. Cincinnati can't win, Chicago mightn't, though a few perilous rumors are afloat."

"Rumors?"

"Rumors. Nothing definitive. I'm standing clear until crisper patterns emerge."

I'd been feeding wire to Tennes for years. I didn't want to pollute this arrangement with fibs, or cut the odds even further with the truth. Straddling such fences is how we sharpies last.

"Sport, this," he said, pointing window-ward without turning, "is Nicky Arnstein. Nicky, stick a mitt to Sport O'Sullivan. Sport operates strictly out of Boston. He knows more about baseball than Arnold Doubleday."

Tennes's flattery was typically hyperbolic, and even more

123

predictably inaccurate. Could there be any doubt which "Arnold" he had in mind? Arnstein gave my paw a quick undertaker's pass.

I'd heard of him, of course, the dapper Semite who'd done time with Fanny Brice. He'd long been associated with Rothstein, especially in people's minds. What he did for a living wasn't clear. He didn't look like a man who had to do anything for a living.

We exchanged bogus pleasantries before I fled, offering my weak bladder as an excuse. I think Arnstein understood. I was reluctant to talk to any pal of Rothstein's, to risk making myself feel more the pump than its primer.

It seems so unlikely now, looking back on it from this great distance, that so many celebrities could have shared such close proximity, and for so frivolous a purpose.

But they did.

Our train was a veritable riot of democracy. Film impresarios mingled with Harvard deans, oil barons with third base coaches. Everybody seemed to be somebody, if only fleetingly.

The most conspicuous presence was that of the gamblers, at least a dozen of whom I spotted gossiping in my coach. Afterward everyone claimed amnesia of them, but that day they were the toast of the Soo Line. That's how it worked back then. Baseball and gambling mixed seamlessly. We were good company, and good copy; we brought thousands of otherwise reluctant spectators through the turnstiles.

I combed the rear compartments for another hour or so, seeking more pertinent figures. I found a few. Evans, Attell, and Burns weren't among them. I thought this relieved me a bit, though my comfort felt curiously like alarm.

I did spot Gandil in the bar car, alone, aping Iscariot. I

slid down beside him and ordered a round. It was a gesture based on our now discredited comradeship. I knew it was a mistake even as I made it.

"How's tricks, Chick?"

"What tricks?"

"It's just an expression, Chick."

"Like 'The check is in the mail,' Sport?"

"Don't worry, Chick. You'll get all your dough Thursday."

In fact I'd taken no further fiscal action. Could my lie's specificity possibly mask its scope?

"I had to give Cicotte the whole ten grand, Sport. The other boys weren't too wild for the arithmetic."

Our repartee was rapidly exhausting its potential. Gandil was nursing a palliative rancor. The boilermakers weren't helping. I didn't wait for an exit line to flee on, but patted him on the shoulder and slid from sight.

As I hit the door I saw Kid Gleason in the corner, watching me, as he'd watched me that morning in Boston. His expression was blank, yet oddly penetrating. My fingernails suddenly seemed in need of close inspection.

In the parlor car a much less awkward confrontation was brewing. Comiskey was holding court for his admirers— reporters, owners, flunkies. The reporters and owners didn't interest me; I didn't recognize the flunkies. I only knew they were flunkies from their hats, which were expensive and worn ostentatiously low.

A few players milled uncomfortably about—Eddie Collins, Dickie Kerr, Ray Schalk. I sensed instantly that they knew nothing of the fix. They had the moony obliviousness of calves headed bladeward. I resented their detachment. Who were they to be so impervious to their doom?

125

Between the dining car and the smoker a bumptious stranger accosted me, a large, formless man with a round, featureless face. He wore a clerical collar and pronounced all his *r*'s as *w*'s.

"Excuse me, young fellow, would you, by any chance, by any stwetch of the imagination, you wouldn't be, you couldn't be . . ."

"Sport Sullivan, Father, none other, and glad of it. How may I be of service to Holy Mother the Church this peerless afternoon?"

"Well, yes, thank you, Mr. Sullivan. Thank you so much. Although it's not pwecisely an ecclesiastical mission I've undertaken today. But I certainly appweciate your courtesy in asking. I hate to bother you. I know you must be vewy busy. Especially now, today that is, considewing the cwowds, and the noise, and the heat. Well, Mr. Sullivan, it's this, I was just wondewing if, well, if it wouldn't be asking too much, could you, by any chance, indicate, and of course, bear in mind . . ."

"The Reds, Father, on a velvet swing, bet the rectory, at any price. Now, do excuse me. I think I hear the rosary beginning in the baggage car."

I glanced down at his hands as we parted. Several crumpled bills dangled from each. I recognized them instantly as hundreds. It was dark, but that's something I can always tell. Visions of pilfered collection plates and rigged bingo nights eased my bumpy jaunt back to my coach.

Ring Lardner was sitting in my seat when I returned, as if he'd paid hard cash for the privilege. I didn't mind. Lardner's was one curiosity I could usually profit from. His questions often told me more than others' answers. He didn't

126

interrogate me this time, though, but reached over and dropped a telegram in my lap.

ADVISE ALL NOT TO BET ON SERIES. UGLY RUMORS AFLOAT. HUGH FULLERTON, HERALD AND EXAMINER SYNDICATE.

"That came over the wire just before we left, Sport."

I didn't deny him a response; I just didn't have one.

"I only know two things that float like ugly rumors, Sport. Shit. And corpses."

Today hard guys talk nailish almost instinctively. It's in the air. But in those days boiled language took some effort. Lardner's had its desired effect on me. He didn't risk it by waiting for a response, but rose and sauntered haughtily toward the honey house.

I sought no other company that evening, and no one else sought mine. I pretended to doze, while all around me conviviality ran rampant.

Six Michigan Avenue cloak-and-suiters staged a mock infield drill in the dining car. Soup tureens and salt cellars served as bases. Two masseuses did piggy things to three probate judges in the sleeper. A group of sportswriters started a $2 pool on how high Joe Jackson could count. The consensus was he wouldn't know where to start.

I paid no attention to any of this, hoping some illuminating intelligence would drift forth spontaneously. When none did, my doubts grew proportionately more pressing.

How long would it be, I wondered, before everyone knew what *almost* everyone seemed to know already?

And what would happen if Robert Jones wouldn't pay me off early?

I made a mental note to ponder these riddles later. For

127

now they seemed much too much to grapple with. So I let my thoughts drift back to Saratoga, to before I knew, or even dreamed, of such complexities.

I realized I hadn't been truly happy then; but it was enough to imagine that I could have been. I leaned back in my seat and closed my eyes. The couplings clicked consolingly beneath me. My body grew lighter, my eyelids heavier. Before long my feigned sleep had turned authentic. I was back to where all illusions pass for genuine.

3

You never saw Hal Chase unless he wanted something. So it was with unalloyed foreboding that I watched Hal pick his tricky way across the Sinton lobby the next afternoon, his greedy gaze undeniably on me, his rapaciousness untempered by discretion.

Hal always wanted what you were least likely to give him.

We'd reached Cincinnati at eight that morning. I'd slept six fitful hours in a room the size of a Jacob's biscuit tin. Now I was eager for fresh information, though probably not rested enough to grasp it. I certainly wasn't eager for Chase's company. His insatiable cravings could only mock my own.

"Hi there, Sport. Nice weather we're having. My mother just had her gallbladder out. Seen the new Tom Mix? I got five hundred down on the Reds at even money. Look at those tits. What do you hear from Rothstein? They never have enough spittoons in these dumps. Where'd you get those pants? Gabardine, ain't they? I know a guy wants to bet five thousand on Al Smith. Haven't seen this many gamblers in one place since T.R. was in jodhpurs."

This was Prince Hal at his crudest. Battery by babble, Cohan called it. Rothstein's whereabouts were his true concern. The rest was just camouflage.

"There certainly are a lot of sharpies about, Hal. There's no denying that."

As indeed there were. Of the two hundred bodies in the lobby, easily a quarter belonged to angle-shooters.

"But I haven't seen Rothstein yet, Sport. I wonder where he could be. Hmmm . . ."

Hal was no paragon of subtlety. I flashed him a pout to signal my indifference.

"Rumors are swirling, Sport. What's to believe? That's a nice boutonnière, very jaunty. A guy from New Jersey told me Cicotte's got a spongy wing. Have a pink gin on me, Sport. He said his wife's cousin is Cicotte's doctor's brother. Eels don't have peckers, did you know that, Sport? They just rub up against the broad. Who do you favor in the Series, Sport? Christ, everybody's got an inside on this one. It reminds me of the 1910 Highlanders."

Chase came by his cynicism honestly. He'd done fifteen hard years in the majors, dealing from the start. I'd been involved in a few of his rigs myself. I'd never warmed to Hal personally, though. He seemed more interested in vengeance than in profit.

"Rumblings have even reached Comiskey, Sport. His secretary tipped me. Do you think Charlie Chaplin's a fag? Comiskey told Lardner the stories are just greeneye. Still, he's worried. Have you eaten in that new wop joint around the corner? I heard he is. Chaplin, I mean. Who'd imagine the Series could be buggered, Sport? I spilled cranberry juice on my tie last night. Rube Benton told me piss would take it out. Here comes Harry Zork. That guy can hear toenails grow."

I let him ramble on, hoping he'd eventually exhaust himself. But my inattentiveness only seemed to encourage him. His patter didn't annoy me as much as it usually did, though. Its screwy animation was distracting me from my woes.

Just then an even greater diversion presented itself. Weaver and Williams came bouncing from the elevator, surrounded by the traditional swarm of press hounds. All eyes tracked their progress toward the sidewalk.

"That's how it was with New York in '06, Sport. They can't get enough of you when you're hot. Do you think niggers get poison ivy?"

I felt a touch of sympathy for Chase just then. Such starblowing would never pass his way again. His scheming seemed scant compensation.

"Abe Attell's been here for a week, Sport. Bill Burns is with him. When hummingbirds fly they . . ."

But I never did find out what hummingbirds do when they fly. The news of Attell's and Burns's presence had jarred me, sending a spasm of anxiety sweeping through my limbs. Its effect registered instantly in Chase's smile. He'd hit home. From now on his questions would be much blunter. None would concern the mating habits of film stars.

"I hear Abe's been all over the East Coast, Sport, trying to raise boodle to back the Reds. He hasn't come up with much, though. Wouldn't you think Rothstein would help his little pal? Wouldn'tcha, wouldn'tcha, wouldn'tcha? Unless Abe is pulling this particular stunt solo. What's your hunch, Sport?"

"I don't have one, Hal."

"That's not what I heard, Sport. I heard you're right up to your cute little chin dimple in this one."

"You heard wrong, Hal."

"Burns is an old playmate of yours, ain't he, Sport? I heard they bet fifty thousand on the Reds. They'll parlay another fifty thousand on each game. I was talking to Nat Evans about it in the bar just this morning."

The shocks were coming in waves now. Chase loved seeing them hit. It made him feel foxy.

"You know, Sport, if I was just a little bit clearer on this deal, I could help a guy. I can tug a lot of ropes nobody else can."

"I'm sure you can, Hal. That's why you should stop pestering me on this. I'm just an innocent bystander, clean and sober. Although if you want my hit on it—bet Chicago. Attell's advertising Cincinnati too publicly to be credited."

Chase's grin shut down at this remark. He'd obviously never considered the possibility. It was a fitting note to end our little chat on. But I had a parting shot I'd been hoarding for such an occasion. So I fired it.

"You know, Hal, I had an interesting dream the other night. In it you had an original idea. That's how I knew it was a dream."

I rose to leave, but hesitated slightly. A revisionist thought had just occurred to me. What if Attell really was backing Chicago?

I was at sea for an answer, or even a clue. I was already three shocks behind, and fading. The door that spun me wordlessly from the lobby placed me smack outside in the steamy border air, with no hint to my imagined destination.

"There's that faggot Chaplin now," I thought I heard Chase whisper behind me. But it could just as easily have been the breeze.

I didn't expect to sleep much that night. Humidity filled my suite like an emetic. I passed the early evening walking the strange city, hoping to put Chase's remarks in some perspective. But I lacked any precedent to measure them against.

I returned to the lobby at eight and lolled for a while among the layabouts, trying to detect any shift in public sentiment. Chicago remained a 6–5 favorite. Everybody agreed they were a great bet, but nobody wanted to back them. No explanation of this paradox was forthcoming.

In my bed, after midnight, I lay calm and resigned. The hotel hummed with self-contained intensity, the streets echoing with the shrieks of the believers. There was a muffled tension in the air, as in the interval before a howitzer meets its target. What I'd waited for so long was about to happen. I could scarcely believe it, that this quiet night, in this quiet room, in this quiet town, could precede any heart's ultimate desire.

This, then, was what my life would be, I now realized, the event which would define it. Whether it succeeded or failed, it would bear me along with it. I feared that, thrilled at it, surrendered to it.

Did Rothstein ever feel quite this uncertain? I wondered. Were his dreams ever crushed by their fulfillment?

At three I ordered a dozen oysters from room service, downing them greedily, propped up in bed, with half a bottle of Moët as encouragement. I was congratulating myself for having propelled my scheme this far, consoling myself for having done it so imperfectly.

When the food was gone I turned on the reading light and wrote a note to Rose. It was our first communication since we'd parted.

132

Dear Rose,

I am here now, as is everyone else it seems. The air is thick enough to grow potatoes in. My room is high. I can see the river from it.

This is what I've waited all my life for, this chance, and, of course, you.

Everything is happening much too fast though. Sometimes it seems too confusing to enjoy. I suppose that's its attraction for some fellows, but not me. There's the difference between dreaming and doing, I suppose. You do something, it passes, you can't hold it, revise it, perfect it. It's just gone.

The food is good here, as is the weather.

Well, I suppose I'd better close now. I miss you, and love you . . . well, as much as anything, really. I am thinking now of the whiteness of your thighs, etc., etc. I may not enjoy doing things as much as some, but I enjoy thinking about things as much as any.

Your

Sport

When I finished this note I ripped it into hundreds of pieces and drifted off to sleep, dreaming vividly of the latter years of my childhood. The river barges blew their warnings through the dark, accentuating, rather than piercing, my serenity.

4

Game One

T he next morning the Series exploded all around me. Braying bullhorns shook me from my flop. Unfamiliar figures on important-looking missions flew up and down my corridor. Dozens of all-night newsboys screamed headlines beneath my window.

"Redlegs Open Quest."

"Reuther Duels Cicotte in Opener."

"Sox Favored in Best-of-Nine Matchup."

There are no headier hours than those preceding a World Series. Cincinnati was suddenly the center of the universe, its citizens propelled, unwittingly, from their torpor.

I passed the morning in the lobby, reading Tarkington. I had nothing else to do, no place else to go. I'd made my bribes, placed my bets. Whatever happened now would have happened anyway.

In the Crystal Salon, journalists tapped out last-minute dispatches. Gamblers waved wads of surplus currency, enticing waverers. This was the action I lived for, the artificial pulse that gives the real pulse its meaning.

The day was here.

At noon I surrendered to the inevitable and strolled out into the high, welcoming sun. Liverymen solicited me from every angle. I resisted their appeals to walk the full mile to the park.

The action in the streets was unprecedented.

Thousands of partisans flowed up Race Avenue, screaming and chanting, pounding backs, tossing flares, rolling like nature itself toward the outline of the park. Outside the stadium hundreds of urchins hung from parapets. Scalpers circled beneath them, soliciting tickets. The sidewalk filled with peddlers, the air with powder blossoms. The sun hung at its apex, like a warning.

I longed to buy myself into this conviviality, but didn't know how to. I thought for a moment of making a side bet. But with whom, and on what? To salve my confusion I took it briskly through the turnstiles. There the mood was equally intense, but not as frenzied. Every seat seemed to hold two fans; each fan seemed gripped by three emotions. Proletarians jammed the galleries, dignitaries clogged the boxes. Incomprehensible cheers broke out at unlikely intervals. The crowd seemed to be celebrating its own expectancy.

And then, inexplicably, my thoughts returned to Rose. I'd passed an eye-catcher in an arch, a honey blonde looking confused, and also alone. I didn't equivocate, but broached her desirability point-blank.

"Excuse me, Miss, may I be of some assistance? You look like you just swallowed a shoe."

"Thanks no, mister, I'm just commencing my menses. That always gets me flummoxed. I had a vinegar gargle this morning to push it along. Now a boil the size of Delaware is chafing my thigh. I also suspect I'm coming down with gingivitis. Some giant pustules have commandeered my gum line. Care for a peek?"

She rolled down her bottom lip like a horse tattooer. I declined her offer and scurried up the ramp. She was either mad, or a medical anomaly, or the most ingenious deflector of mashers in my experience.

I took a seat behind Comiskey in Section A. If he was anticipating any irregularities, he didn't show it. Attell, improbably, sat in front of him, with Sleepy Bill Burns and Maharg at either side. Attell appeared agitated, Burns restrained; Maharg just looked pleased to be there. Maharg always looked pleased to be anywhere.

Only Evans, among the finaglers, was invisible. Then I spotted him, in an obscure seat, up the line. He'd chosen a perfect spot for seeing without being seen. Chase sat two sections over, picking his teeth.

I had to hand it to Hal. Every hint he'd dropped had

proved out so far. If many more of his speculations turned true my bark was cooked.

On the field the players were concluding their preliminaries. My eyes fell instinctively on the fixers. Gandil's presence particularly affected me. I'd forgotten he actually *played* the game.

Riisberg stretched his biceps, Jackson his vocal cords. In front of the dugout Cicotte rehearsed his delivery, his attention never wavering from his task. Each pitch struck Ray Schalk's mitt with unwavering accuracy.

It was the most evocative of tableaux—the players, the fans, the park, the soft afternoon on the forward edge of autumn. I tried to fix it precisely in my heart's cold eye, for later, when its effects would blur its memory.

And then suddenly, almost inappropriately, it was time.

I'd been counting the minutes apprehensively, knowing it would begin too soon, which it did, by thirty minutes. I'd assumed two was the starting hour, not one-thirty. Foreboding gripped my intestines. One miscalculation made me fear I'd made a thousand.

The umpires took the field, the players yielded it. The crowd hushed. The army band sounded its As.

How tragic, I thought, buying my first hot dog. It will happen, like anything else.

The last box holders settled into their seats. The Cincinnati fielders burst from their dugout. A single white cloud floated past the sun.

5

In New York City, at exactly that moment, Arnold Rothstein ambled into the Ansonia. He'd just come from a schmooze with Louis Lepke. They'd agreed to stop killing each other's help.

Rothstein had a four-o'clock appointment with his tailor, second fittings on four Fair Isle suits.

The Bankroll enjoyed roaming the city during working hours, tweaking drudges, mimicking truancy. Hands thrust invasively into his chesterfield, panama hat curled raffishly over one eyelid, he now defined the enigmaticism he'd once merely cultivated. Men approached him warily, women's nipples stiffened at his gaze. He'd become the elusive specter all wished to embody.

In the Ansonia ballroom the Series awaited simulation. A bank of teletypes lined one wall, a green felt baseball diamond another. Four bellboys in full mail stood chewing their tongues. They'd be moving magnets around the felt momentarily, mimicking the evolving action in Cincinnati.

The room was packed with sporting types, cigar smoke and speculative chatter predominating. Rothstein took up a spot inside the door, tipping a Bushmills to give his hands employment.

From across the room a tall man with no eyebrows coughed a warning. He'd risked three steps toward Rothstein before the Bankroll's stare deterred him. The slug's smile and wave froze simultaneously, as he reoriented his swaggering stride toward the can.

Rothstein checked his watch. Twelve twenty-eight. He'd

timed his arrival perfectly. He didn't intend to be there very long, just half an inning and one batter, if God was good. His eyes passed nonchalantly over the crowd. He knew instantly there was no one there worth noticing.

At one-thirty a small bellboy with intricately pitted teeth wrote "Our National Anthem" on the blackboard beside the diamond. The crowd hushed. Those not standing, stood. Rothstein smirked. Patriotism! A pisher's solace.

Another bellboy put Shano Collins's number at home plate. The crowd cheered. Rothstein smiled again. They were such sheep. They never did anything they hadn't done before.

The bellboy wiped the blackboard with a napkin, then wrote "ball one" on it.

The game was on.

The first half-inning took three minutes. Chicago didn't score. Rothstein took no notice. Cicotte's intentions were his sole concern.

In the bottom half, Morrie Rath led off for Cincinnati. Rath was a tiny second baseman, ineffectual with the bat. Cicotte's first pitch was a strike. Rothstein squeezed his glass. He wasn't nervous, just impatient. He'd come to learn one thing; he wanted to learn it quickly. With the next pitch he did.

Cicotte threw a roundhouse that never broke, hitting Rath in the middle of the back. Rothstein put his glass down, shoved his hands into his pockets, and walked out of the ballroom, through the lobby, and into the street. It was raining. The sidewalk smelled like lemon peel and naphtha. A troop of trained marsupials was entertaining the gadabouts behind the Dorilton.

Rothstein hailed a cab and headed uptown. He would bet

another $100,000 that night. His tailor wouldn't have to be kept waiting.

In Cincinnati, deep down the third base line, Nat Evans allowed his spine to touch his seat. He knew something Rothstein didn't know: Cicotte was supposed to hit Rath with his *first* pitch. He hoped this improvisation didn't mean what he feared it might.

In their box Attell and Burns exchanged shrugs. They weren't sure what Cicotte's blunder meant either; they just knew it meant something. Eddie never hit leadoff men. He had *control*.

Comiskey, too, felt suddenly frazzled. A small knot of apprehension was winding around his colon. He began trying to dissolve it without actually acknowledging it.

In the press box Ring Lardner leaned coquettishly toward Mathewson.

"You could have won five hundred games with an aim like that, Matty. How many pitchers can plunk a .250 lead-off man when they have to?"

My own reaction was a bit more proprietary. As Rath trotted daintily toward first, I felt a brief twinge of pride at having put him there.

The final score was 9–1. Cicotte didn't last the fourth inning.

I left after the seventh, fleeing the indelicacies vicious beatings often generate. The crowd's delight was rapidly turning swinish. I don't share success well under the best of circumstances; rejoicing with troglodytes always makes me dyspeptic. Besides, I prefer leaving emotional scenes unconsummated, stunting my sentiment before it's had a chance to stunt itself.

139

I took the same route back to the Sinton as I'd come by. Knots of celebrants ringed the park, like genial lynch mobs. A few blocks west, though, the streets were strangely empty. It seemed a different world there. A gypsy woman napped on her quilts, feral dogs shredded bags of bovine entrails. It was a day like any other.

I had the first one in hand, I could admit. And high hopes for the second. I'd call Jones now and make my buyout pitch. If he bit I'd begin betting the individual games tomorrow. I felt optimistic. Yes, I suppose I felt very optimistic indeed.

6

I've spoken little of the loyalists until now.

Fans forget their disappointments, owners deserve theirs. But players neither weather nor merit betrayal. Only the defense of my dream justified savaging theirs.

It's not the particular players I ache for, of course, but the idea of them. The actual loyalists inspired scant compassion.

Only three, as Rothstein would have said, mattered: Eddie Collins, the second baseman; Ray Schalk, the catcher; Dickie Kerr, the kid pitcher.

All three sat staring into their lockers after the game, their silence the loudest indictment imaginable. When the tension became unbearable, Collins strode over to where Gandil was standing and tapped him on the shoulder. Chick turned. Collins deepened his glower. A faint smirk broke out on Gandil's lips then, a retributional tic. Collins didn't react to it, but just kept staring at Gandil's hairline, as if remorse might somehow break out there involuntarily.

When it didn't, Collins turned and walked away. The other players resumed dressing. Ten minutes later, the room looked as if no one had ever been in it.

Kid Gleason strolled into the Sinton bar at six-thirty, trailed by the immutable band of scribblers. The Kid was trying to put a poised face on his panic.

"This will get my boys' attention, gents, snap their gaffs, make them surly. Now we know Cincy won't just roll over and die for us."

"Somebody's beating them to it, Kid."

Gleason ignored this razz. He already had more doubts than he felt up to.

"What are you planning to do in here, anyway, Kid?" the *Trib* cub asked. "You don't drink."

Gleason looked befuddled. It was true, he hated hootch. So why, indeed, had he wandered into this bottleshop?

He began scanning its clientele for an answer. Riisberg was most conspicuous among them, bellying up to the bar, chortling as if he had some reason to. Gleason strode over to him on a trot.

"How's the old potato, Swede?"

Riisberg's smile evaporated.

"That was a tough one to take out there today, wasn't it, Swede?"

"It surely was, Kid."

"We'll stick it to them tomorrow, though, boyo, don't you worry. We're twice their hat size. Just bum luck today is all it amounts to."

"You bet, Kid, we'll stick them good tomorrow."

"Don't blame yourself for your part in it either, Swede, for that error in the second, or that bad throw in the fourth, or for taking the collar against a short-armer like Reuther.

Nothing you did out there today should mortify a spastic."

As Gleason filled the room with false condolence his hands began moving Riisberg's way. Riisberg seemed hypnotized by their progress, so orderly, so controlled, so unlike the blunt intentions pushing them forward.

It took three writers to pry the Kid from Riisberg's windpipe. Gleason wanted to kill, not to fight. Riisberg was too shocked to resist. No one could think of anything to say, not even the *Times* man. They all just stood there, mimicking detachment.

Gleason suddenly felt in need of a nap. He excused himself and headed up to his room.

Comiskey phoned John Heydler from his penthouse after the game. He knew what was happening, but craved corroboration. He hoped the National League president might have some for him.

"That wasn't my ball club out there today, John. Some chiseler's pounding icicles up my ass."

"Get hold of yourself, Charlie. It's only one game."

Heydler, too, had heard the rumors, though he'd shrunk from believing them. It could only make him trouble.

"A ten-strike tomorrow will make today a memory, Charlie. Have a chocolate malt and point yourself straight at blanket class."

"All right, John. I just wanted you to know. It might matter later."

As soon as Heydler hung up he dialed the Commission office. Something gruesome was in the works. He couldn't dodge responsibility for it fast enough.

Comiskey sat with the phone in his lap, counting to fifty. Then he dialed room service and ordered a piece of calf's liver. Yelling at somebody had settled his nerves, but he still didn't feel up to visiting the dining room.

In Alfredo's, three blocks north, Nat Evans was eating a steak the size of his head. At precisely eight he told his waiter to fetch him a telephone.

"Rothstein residence."

"This is Nat Evans calling from Cincinnati for Mr. Rothstein."

"Mr. Rothstein ain't here just now, Mr. Evans. This is Tilly, Mr. Rothstein's personal stenographer. Is there any message you'd care to leave for Mr. R.?"

"No, I guess not, Tilly. I was just wondering if Mr. Rothstein had any more instructions for me."

"Not that I've heard of, Mr. Evans. I'll be sure to ask him when he comes in."

Evans thought he detected ambiguity trailing saucily behind this final preposition. He thanked Tilly and hung up. As he did Rothstein moved his tongue even deeper into heaven.

Evans was glad there were no further instructions. Not that he'd expected any. Rothstein never called when things were humming.

Tilly, he thought disapprovingly. What a bimbo name for a high-hat like the Bankroll.

In my room, at precisely that hour, the twenty-third Robert Jones in the Chicago phone book finally proved the correct one. He didn't seem too pleased to be reached at home. He seemed, in fact, to have momentarily misplaced my identity.

"Sullivan. S-U-L-L . . ."

143

"I can spell, Mr. Sullivan."

"The man who bet forty thousand dollars on the Reds."

"I handle many wagers, Mr. Sullivan."

"Yes, I imagine you do. I was just wondering, considering today's outcome, if you might be interested in settling our transaction at a reduced rate of—"

"No."

"—of say fifty percent."

"No."

"Or perhaps forty percent."

"No thank you, Mr. Sullivan, nor ten percent either. It takes five victories to settle this particular question, I believe."

"But surely, given the way Chicago played today, it all seems so . . . well . . . did you happen to see the game?"

"No, I'm afraid I didn't, Mr. Sullivan. I never attend baseball matches. I detest sports."

Then he hung up.

7

And that exact moment, that exquisitely demeaning instant when my rival refused me his neck, marked the end to my pretensions of ascendancy. At least in that matter.

My body sank like a cobblestone into the bed. Tensions seeped from major and minor muscles. I experienced that great peace which must greet drowning men when they finally stop fighting the sea to join it.

From here on in, I told myself, I'd impose no order on the fix. I'd allow circumstance to bear it along on its impulse.

I didn't move from that position all night long, but slept atop the covers, wheezing, gyrating. I'd need a full night of bye-bye at the very least, I knew from experience, if my passivity was to extract its usual tariff.

It could easily have been the violent pounding of my heart that awakened me the next morning. It wasn't. It was Gandil's insistent fist on my doorframe.

Six-fifteen! An unprecedented hour for a first baseman. I was shocked to find myself where I'd left me, outside the blankets, fully clothed, palm on pecker. Gelid sweat coated my underthings; the rank taste of an unanticipated dawn lined my tongue.

I leaped up, eager to be awake, or at least to seem so. I straightened the bedspread, parted my hair, smoothed my flannels. In one minute I felt as ready for the world as I usually do in thirty. Yet I still couldn't feign composure. A fresh threat had clearly caught me napping. By rising in yesterday's garments I'd labeled my will regressive. I was sure Gandil would notice, though I grinned ferociously to distract him.

I needn't have; his sole concern was the money. I might as well have been standing there with Rothstein's dick in my ear.

"Where's the ten thousand, Sport?"

"Why Chick, hello, how nice to see you. Won't you come in? You and I must be the only souls up and about this—"

"The money, Sport. I don't have time to pick daisies from your bull's-eye."

"Yes, well, aren't you the charming fellow to put it just that way. You know, I was telling George M. Cohan only the other evening—"

145

"The money, Sport."

"I don't have it, Chick. There's the horrid truth, not a cent, not just yet, not now."

His insistence was wilting my equanimity. I began circling the room like a cabin steward, straightening things that required no alignment.

"What do you mean, you don't have it?"

There are men who explain self-explanatory remarks convincingly. I'm not one of them. I picked up the pace of my tidying.

"I just don't have it, Chick. That's the size of it. I'm terribly sorry. I thought I'd have it, I certainly meant to have it, but I don't. May I offer you a saltine?"

I thought I might cry then, but men don't cry, so I sighed instead, just forcefully enough to evacuate one adenoid.

Why hadn't I prepared some plausible excuse? Or better yet, several dazzlingly implausible ones? Instead I just stood there, exuding inertia, making admissions more alienating than any lie.

I must have looked as pathetic as I felt, too. For Gandil pressed me no further. He just gave a small shrug, and his own sigh, then spun on his heel to leave. I was just about to place my water pitcher in my bureau drawer.

"No, Chick, wait. I'll have it for you tomorrow, all of it. There's been a small misunderstanding, that's all."

"I don't believe so, Sport. I just made a mistake about you is all it amounts to."

Then he was gone.

I might have borne his fury, or even his contempt, but his regret was too appropriate to tolerate. It pronounced me a small-timer in hopelessly over my head.

"Please stay a minute, Chick," I almost shrieked in desperation. "Please give me one more chance."

But his patience with me had clearly run its course. The click of my latch was morbid with finality.

I sat back on the bed to inventory my losses, which were considerable. I'd forfeited my remaining self-respect, for openers, and set a world's record for crumbling resolve in the process. I'd also alienated my sole ally, my in with the players. I could feel the old desire to fold my tent blowing seductively in my ear.

If Chicago won today I'd lose my leverage with Jones. If they kept winning I'd lose everything. No matter what, though, I'd have to call Rothstein. He was my sole remaining source of capital.

Six-thirty seemed an inappropriate hour to disturb him, though. So I stretched out on my mattress, still in my weeds, and with a speed almost obscene in its impertinence, regained the sleep I'd surrendered just moments earlier.

Gandil raced from my suite to Attell's. But Abe wasn't in. Not for the Little Hebrew to laze about in his worsteds, with opportunities for tainted profits in the breeze.

Chick eventually tracked him to the lobby, to the shoe-shine stand, to Burns's side.

"Where's my twenty thousand?"

"Why Chick, hello, how nice to see you. I was just telling Bill here how suave it is to be back among the sporting class. It reminds me of the time I whacked out Jailbait Minahan in Salinas."

"Where's the money, Abe? I got to be at the park in twenty minutes."

"Indeed you do. Well, I don't have it, Chick, not right now, not with me, not here. It's still out on bets. I got nifty odds by letting the whole roll ride. Double or nothing, don't you know. That'll mean a hatful for you tonight, Chick. Forty grand instead of twenty."

Gandil looked more startled than angered. One double cross per morning was his limit.

"I can't run this scam on promises, Abe. I need some ready for the guys."

Attell pulled a telegram from his pocket then, and handed it without explanation to Gandil. He, unlike me, had prepared.

$40K ARRIVING THIS A.M. FOR C.G. ET AL. CHEERS. A.R.

Within the context of Gandil's needs, this made no sense whatsoever. That's why it convinced Chick so easily. Outlandish lies beat shy ones six ways from Sunday, Attell knew. He knew this because Rothstein had told him. Abe's fame helped. Gandil couldn't imagine a former world champion of anything turning on his word.

Burns dipped into *his* pocket for the clincher, handing it to Gandil with a flourish.

"That's an oil lease, Chick, one hundred thousand dollars' worth. Tape it to your rear end for collateral."

"I guess I just won't, Bill. I don't know nothing about oil. But I can spot a fish story from either end of the line. Get up the whole forty tomorrow, Billy, or this deal is dead."

With that he left the lobby on a trot, to hunt for a cab to take him to the ballyard. He had fifteen minutes to think up a good alibi, to make his timidity sound like cunning to the boys.

Burns went straight from the lobby to Western Union, hoping to authenticate Rothstein's wire. It held as much promise for him as for Gandil. There was no record of it, of course. It was as fraudulent as the oil deed he'd fabricated.

148

Rothstein's "personal stenographer" Tilly answered all my calls that morning. She said Mr. Rothstein would ring me when he could.

He did not.

To keep from calling back every forty-five seconds or so, I began counting the water veins on my ceiling. The shades were drawn, the curtains joined, the morning's first light filtering bravely through them. The room was ripe with the scents of former occupants: the despair of shoe salesmen, the rut of newlyweds, the blood of suicides.

I tried to distract myself by imagining what Rothstein might be doing then. Riding down Broadway in an open Dusenberg perhaps, or plodding the brown boards of the Brooklyn Bridge, staring down at the city he'd now subjugated.

I liked that one, so I froze it, transferring my bland features to his face. Soon his failure to call seemed entirely understandable, though I jumped like a gaffed trout when he did.

"Mr. Rothstein. I—"

"This is the house operator, Mr. Sullivan. You said you wanted to leave for the ballpark at ten-thirty."

8

Game Two

The second game was yielded more discreetly.

Williams allowed only four hits, but walked six. His teammates always seemed about to score, they just never did.

Comiskey sprawled in front of me again, grimly auditing the innings. He looked like a man watching lantern slides of his own funeral. When McMullin's pop fly ended the ninth, he rose and walked silently to his limousine. They were taking it away from him, and he couldn't stop them.

John Heydler left after the seventh, convinced now that there really *were* dinges in Comiskey's woodpile. He wouldn't do anything about it, though. He was by nature a factotum, an administrator of things requiring no administration. A scandal like this could only bring him woe.

"Everybody wants baseball to be kosher," he told his wife that evening over dinner. "They'll skin the sap who proves to them it ain't."

In their bunker the Cincinnati players strained to celebrate. They'd been assured Chicago was unbeatable. Beating them seemed just a shade unnatural.

Ivy Wingo, alone, recognized this emotion. He'd once stopped his father from molesting his sister. The ease with which he'd knocked the old man senseless had felt like more power than he'd really wanted to have.

In Chicago's clubhouse no celebration ever again seemed possible.

Kid Gleason locked himself in his office, humming "Nola." He had the kind of headache he associated with an argument he wanted to have, but couldn't. He decided not to open his door again until his noodle felt more rational.

When he finally did emerge he spotted Chick Gandil sitting in the corner, simulating grief. A stranger's tongue leaped from the Kid's throat straight at him.

"You, you, you, you, you . . ."

Gleason regained his office in two little hops, resigned to remaining there until the snow flew. He wanted a cigarette, but couldn't find one. He tried to visualize his mother's face, but couldn't remember her. Was she a small woman with a large, pockmarked nose, or a gangly individual who braided her hair like Olive Newsome?

The one mug he *could* recall clearly was Comiskey's, gloating at the gulling of his players. Gleason put a finger to his own lips then, to make sure Comiskey's malice hadn't spread.

The last player to leave the locker room was Lefty Williams. When he reached the end of the tunnel he found his catcher, Ray Schalk, waiting for him in the darkness. Schalk didn't breathe a word, but stepped forward as if to relieve Williams of a package. But Lefty wasn't carrying anything. Schalk's fist found the dead center of Williams's abdomen, collapsing it like a dime-store concertina.

As Lefty bent, gasping, to his knees, Schalk aimed more punches thoughtfully his way. They bounced nonchalantly off Williams's cranium, like hailstones off a chicken coop. Williams gained the relative safety of the floor, squirming, drooling like a haddock.

Schalk was unsure of his next move. Pummeling Lefty seemed undignified, kicking him was out of the question (though, in truth, a tempting option). If he intended to await Williams's revival, he knew, he should be prepared to wait at least until dawn.

So he just stood there, breathing heavily, twitching his shoulders. Finally he bent down and pried Williams's lips open and placed a buffalo-head nickel squarely between them, as coroners separate the molars of stiffening corpses.

151

Then he spit once on Lefty's left breast, and skipped down the tunnel toward the daylight. He had no idea what any of this meant. But it felt good.

I myself floated from the stadium on a cloud of fresh optimism, like John Q. Public about to bed a film queen. All my encumbrances suddenly felt like advantages. I would at least make *something* for all my trouble.

There were no messages for me at the front desk. I checked twice. I would have traded two years from the far side of my salad days for a positive word from Rothstein. But even this didn't seem as important as it once had.

In the function room they were holding an exhibition of salt cellars. I passed an hour there, finding it all quite interesting.

9

It would be futile to speculate on which of his elaborately inappropriate impulses Bill Burns drew when he dragged B. G. Maharg to Attell's suite that evening.

It certainly wasn't menace.

On his lamest day the Little Champ could have cold-cocked Maharg with one mitt.

Bill had anticipated some double-shuffling from Abe. His worst suspicions quickly proved underestimates. Attell's room was swarming with break-a-leg men, of a ferocity Bill didn't even permit in his fears.

They sat on cane chairs, in tight semicircles, counting and recounting piles of moolah. Abe had finally found a sucker to take his bets on credit. Cash, in almost farcical amounts, had become the room's motif. It wasn't more money than Burns had ever seen before, just more than he thought it wise to see. Attell didn't acknowledge his arrival.

"I'll take forty thousand of that for Chick and his boys, Abe."

"The fuck you will, my shoneen friend. This jack is already out working on the third game."

Maharg stood uselessly in the doorway, immobilized by fear. Each of Attell's apes was larger around than anyone who'd ever pulverized him in the ring.

"What should I tell Gandil then, Abe? He'll be spitting ink."

"Tell him all first basemen are dickheads, Bill. He'll believe that."

The counters guffawed at this. Apparently they'd never heard such a droll rejoinder.

"Where's my cut, Abe? Where's the slice of the motive I got coming?"

Attell tossed a packet Burns's way, over his shoulder, like a tip.

"This isn't enough, Abe. This isn't halfway to the answer."

"It's all I can manage just now, Bill. Times are tough."

The heavies sniggered again, but kept on counting.

"How about the rest of the Series, Abe? How will we keep them dixieing on the cuff?"

"They'll play along, Bill. They're in too deep to queer things on us now."

"Is this how the great Arnold Rothstein conducts his business, Abe? Is this all that courtly shit I've heard so much about?"

Burns knew he'd hit home with this slur. Hired smiles snapped off all over the room.

"I think it's time for you to run along now, Sleepy Billy. You must have tons of regrets to pass along to Chick."

Burns did indeed wish to commiserate with Gandil, though his message had just turned itself inside out.

On his way to Chick's room, Burns's imagination ran riot. He hadn't taken Attell's words literally. The real lesson lay in what Abe *wanted* him to think. The recoiling at Rothstein's name was the key.

Burns assumed he had twenty-four hours to devise a new plan. He had forty-five seconds. And he didn't make it.

In room 802, Gandil lay stretched out on his dream sack, nibbling pistachios, letting farts, miming the reform-school scholar contemplating elopement. His bags, neatly packed, flanked the dresser. Burns launched into his spiel without preamble.

"I don't have the dough, Chick. There was some trouble with the wire. It got sent to Chicago. I haven't even got mine yet. We'll both get paid tomorrow. I just checked. Hope you understand."

It was a pure piece of extemporized flapdoodle, part truth, part misemphasis, part cavalier embellishment dependent on Gandil's ignorance. Burns was no longer lying straightforwardly, he was tap-dancing, hoping to buy some time.

Gandil's expression remained eerily tranquil. He lay on his back, cracking nuts, flexing his anal sphincter.

"That's okay, Bill. These things happen. Don't worry. Meet me at the Warner day after tomorrow. Have a pistachio."

Burns couldn't believe his ears. He'd sold it, and without having to beg. He was tempted to seal the deal with more excuses, to obliterate objections Gandil hadn't even raised.

154

"Great, Chick, just great. I'll have it all for you then, five sharp, with bells and balls on."

Bill backed out the door on this promise, leaving no room for either reply or reversal. Gandil said nothing. He seemed almost, in fact, not to be listening.

As the reality of Gandil's assent fled Burns's brain, a parallel thought sped forward to replace it: This *has* to work.

Bill now believed he could talk anybody into anything. And that was fatal.

In my own room there were no more mysteries to solve, except the location of the most elusive mosquito that side of the Mississippi. Each click of the current made it one with my wallpaper.

Rothstein continued not returning my calls. I packed early and sat in the dark, next to the telephone, imagining how I'd spend whatever I *would* make from the fix.

Fifty grand is a shitload, I kept telling myself, even for someone who's imagined making millions. Maybe the only way to make as much as Rothstein would make from my scam, I rationalized, was to begin with as much as Rothstein had begun with.

The phone never rang, though I gave it every chance to. It just sat there, like a sullen child, defying me.

At ten sharp I left the hotel for my train.

No bands played the White Sox off that evening. All their celebrity fans had abandoned them. Ditching failures is a given with the smart set.

The players were sequestered from the public. Though I did spot Happy Felsch in the bar car, alone, his expression belying his nickname. I took the hint and gave his stool a major miss.

155

The night passed without incident or color. A cool drizzle marked our reunion with Chicago. None of the previous week's well-wishers greeted us. It felt like a two-car funeral absent the lead vehicle.

Isn't it a kick in the pants (and a threat to the presumptions) how empty previously filled train stations can seem, in the morning, in the rain, when the home team has dropped two straight to a pushover?

The players got off last, an unnecessary precaution. The few souls haunting the platform dodged them studiously. Two youths icing carp cut them deader than last week's catch.

The last thing I saw as my cab headed down Division Street was Eddie Cicotte standing at a bus stop outside the terminal. He was pressing his chin to his chest to thwart detection while converting a copy of that morning's *Tribune* into a rain hat.

Attell took the red-eye back to Chicago. Before he left he phoned in his bets: $50,000 on the Reds to win the Series, five games to three, at 4–1; and $100,000 on Chicago, straight up, to take the third game. He got just 6–5 for that one but didn't argue. Any price on a lock seemed the right price.

Before he bet he dismissed his "enforcers," returning them to the docks where he'd found them, twenty bucks and a bankable tip the better.

Burns killed his ride north trying to deduce Attell's motives. He longed to make Abe's desires match his own. Twenty minutes outside Oaklawn he finally did.

"The little kike is dealing behind my backside," he told

156

himself. "He and Rothstein want *all* the goyim off their lawn."

It was a shimmering revelation, a pure equation of punk attitude. It even made a kind of sense.

Burns phoned his deductions back east from the terminal, betting $5,000 on Cincinnati to win again.

10

Alfred Austrian based his law practice on two principles: That no point is too minor to be litigated, and that the real dough is made keeping plunderers out of court.

It was in the service of this second precept that Austrian visited Comiskey's house that evening, hoping to set the old man straight by midnight. The whining of the prosperous always made his piles throb.

Austrian had grown up in Chicago, then returned to it after finishing Harvard Law School. At forty-seven he was already a top corporate lip. Comiskey had hired him after meeting him on the golf course. He'd been impressed by Austrian's diverse accomplishments—his art collection, his stock portfolio, his five handicap. Austrian hadn't been impressed by Comiskey of course, just aroused. A.A. wasn't even a baseball fan. To him it was just a business, like everything else.

"You have three options, Charles," he began now soothingly. "Accuse them publicly, dissuade them privately, or sit on your hands."

"I won't—"

"Going public will destroy your team, negotiating will

157

destroy your power. I suggest inaction."

Austrian put a finger to his pulse then, to time his pause. He always dreaded telling sharks to run. Their bloodlust could so easily turn on him.

Austrian knew very well where the Series was headed; he'd seen what Comiskey had seen; he knew what Gandil was. He was Charles Comiskey without benefit of counsel.

"But I can't just sit here and let them eat my liver, Al," Comiskey told him. "In two weeks they'll have me waxing their Maxwells."

Austrian nodded sympathetically. He knew Comiskey's arguments were pure reflex, the complaint of the thief discovering himself burglarized. Still he listened. It was his job.

Within an hour, Comiskey's bluster had turned philosophical. When Austrian left at half-past nine, he knew the old man had resigned himself to inaction. Gandil and company would get their way for now. After the Series, he and Comiskey would destroy them.

Comiskey poked at his fire for several minutes after Austrian left, watching its embers die their little deaths. Then he walked into his trophy room and removed all his team pictures from their frames. With rusted pinking shears he cut Gandil's and Riisberg's faces from each.

He wanted to throw each little head into the fire, but feared the smell. He couldn't toss them into his wastebasket either; his housekeeper might find them. But mostly he couldn't just stand there holding them. Metaphorically it felt like much too much to bear. Finally he stuffed them into an unused bureau drawer, intending to chuck them out in the morning. But he forgot, and they probably remain there to this day.

The fixers met at the Full Moon bar that evening, agreeing, though hardly unanimously, to win the third game. They weren't abandoning the fix, just limiting its credit, drawing the line.

Their double cross had three immediate aims: to ruin Attell, to scare me, and to bring Rothstein running with his checkbook. Instead it finished Burns, made Attell rich, and hardly affected Rothstein or me one iota.

The next morning, at nine sharp, a messenger appeared at my door, bearing a cashier's check for $60,776. A handwritten note from Robert Jones accompanied it.

Enclosed find full payment as per our discussion of August 6, 1919, amended October 3, 1919. If this is satisfactory, sign this waiver and return it via my man. If not, return the check and we will proceed as previously outlined. Hoping all is well with you.

R. Jones

It was too late to bet on the third game with these profits, but at least they gave me a strong rooting interest. A Chicago win today would leave me three more games to influence.

I was suddenly $20,000 ahead, without a hitch. I'd pulled it off, put myself back in the catbird seat. I felt a full minute's joy at this accomplishment, before the usual afterthoughts began sawing on the limb.

11

Game Three

The third game took just eighty-seven minutes.

Chicago won 3–0. Riisberg, Jackson, and Felsch scored the runs.

By the second inning, Chicago's superiority seemed irrefutable. When I sensed this, my imagination boiled over. There seemed no limit to how much I might now make, just as hours earlier no profit of any sort had seemed possible.

Up the line Nat Evans picked at his shingles. He knew Chicago should win a game or two, but not this convincingly.

The innings melted softly into the autumn afternoon. The smell of slaughter drifted up from the stockyards. The air grew heavier, the sun murkier. In the eighth inning someone whispered Rose's name. Not my Rose, just some Rose. My groin stiffened appreciably at the sound, as it hadn't at any previous memory of her.

In their locker room, the White Sox hailed their comeback. Kid Gleason smoked an extravagant cigar, congratulating himself for his nonexistent patience. The press floated flattering questions forward. Prodigal fans lined the hallways, demanding bows. Squaring the Series seemed a foregone conclusion.

The fixers didn't linger, but dressed hurriedly and left the stadium. One victory hadn't changed their plans; they hoped to find it had altered a few others.

160

12

Sleepy Bill Burns didn't hunt up Attell that evening. What would he have said to him? "Point to you, you little doofus, see you in shul."

He'd figured wrong, that's all. Attell hadn't been greasing the boys. Nobody had. Their compliance had been assumed.

Bill knew exactly where he'd gone wrong, too. He hadn't needed the money. His misjudgments were the blunders of a dilettante.

At six he crossed the hall to Maharg's room. B.G. was sprawled coquettishly across a throw pillow, exaggerating his fistic career to a bellhop.

"We'll be going back east tomorrow, B.G.," Burns began, in a tone he used to coax stray cats from trees. "We won't be making that big score, I'm afraid. It just wasn't in the cards. Maybe next year. Let's stroll down to Michigan Avenue for a beer or two. I'll rent you a molly there who can lick postage stamps through keyholes."

Maharg looked distraught at this news, until the prospect of free gash reached his privates. Then he jumped to his feet, as at the bell.

As they descended to the lobby, Burns grew momentarily contemplative. Two misgivings were queering his complacency.

Would he risk a million by welching on twenty thousand? And if he wouldn't, why would a wisenheimer like Rothstein?

161

When Attell didn't hear from Burns by eight he assumed he never would again. He called the front desk to confirm this suspicion. The night clerk said Burns had checked out at seven. Abe clicked his tiny heels. He felt like a rum sponge who'd reinvented bicarbonate.

He quickly requested an outside line. Within minutes he'd bet $100,000 on the fourth game, on Chicago, on the nose.

Before the sun set tomorrow he'd be $400,000 up, he figured. This was proving even easier than Rothstein's version of it. He didn't know apprentice gamblers always feel this cocky, just before the floorboards disappear beneath their feet.

13

There was only one lie I could have told Gandil that evening that might have kept him from hanging up on me. I was lucky enough, or cagey enough, to tell it.

"Come and get it, Chick. It's here burning a serious hole in my rompers."

I'd been dialing his number for hours, with receding expectations. When he finally answered I blurted out the news, no hello, how's the family, guess who this is, just "Come and get it," as if he'd been hanging on my call.

"Do you now, Sport, right there, right this minute?"

"Every cent, Chick, awaiting you and your little wheelbarrow."

"And is it green, Sport, with tiny gray lines in its margins, and does it fold like Valentino's britches when you bend it?"

"As green as last month's veal, Chick, and it will fold any way you have in mind."

"In the amount agreed on, Sport?"

"That exact sum, Chick, down to the final penny."

"And will it have skipped off on some mysterious errand by the time I get there?"

"Not at all, Chick. It's not going anyplace without you. It and I await your presence with bated breath."

I'd prepared no alibi for my delay. I was thinking of giving the truth a brief audition, or at least as much of the truth as I felt Chick might reasonably profit by. This was another Rothstein tactic: resorting to veracity when his antagonist least expected it.

When Chick appeared, what seemed like moments later, I treated him, and his greed, to some outsized hospitality. I'd ordered coffee and Napoleons from room service and placed the $10,000 on a trivet, like the Baptist's head. I took Chick's coat and offered him a pastry, then launched into my gloss without delay.

Midway through, an urge to confide in him swept over me, the well-known itch to seek sympathy where none exists. I banished it though, as Rothstein surely would have.

Gandil let me ramble on unedited. Only after he'd done a count did his doubts begin to perk.

"This is nice enough, Sport, but where's the rest of it?"

It was the line I would have written for him if I could have.

"Not fifteen minutes ago, Chick, the biggest book in Cook County filled that very seat, quoting me two to one on Cincinnati tomorrow, put his tuchis on the table, as it were. I'm just waiting for the okay from you, Chick. Meet me in Delano's tomorrow at seven. I'll have it then. This is my big

163

chance, Chick. I'd be putting the lights out on my own party by stiffing you."

He seemed stunned by my frankness. I wasn't courting his approval any longer, but demanding it, with the confidence cash on the barrel always brings. I felt as in control of the situation as I'd always pretended to be.

"All right, Sport, but that's seven o'clock tomorrow, *central* time."

His compliance didn't surprise me, even after all my evasions. He knew it would be pointless to argue, and what other choice did he have? That's one thing years of gambling had taught me: You can postpone a payoff almost indefinitely, if the amount you've promised in the first place is considerable enough.

And so it happened that at the precise moment that Bill Burns quit Chicago (and vacated my scam), and ten minutes before Attell finished speculating (on an outcome I was now paying to refute), Chick Gandil and I reforged our misalliance. He promised me Chicago would lose tomorrow. I promised him another $10,000 if they did. We even shook on it.

I, for one, meant every word I said. But just as the first time you leave a woman is the real time, the first knife you plunge into a co-conspirator's back is the thrust no subsequent gesture ever reconciles.

The night was unseasonably cool. The spiders in my closet quit spinning early. I put on a cardigan and went downstairs to celebrate.

I was stunned by the shifts my scam was experiencing, day to day, hour to hour. One moment triumph seemed assured, the next instant ruin appeared inevitable. It was disorienting, yet stimulating. It felt like life.

As I bounced along Division Street, toward God knows what gratuitous destination, a tall blonde in a lustrous chemise stepped fetchingly from a doorway. She was flaunting an umbrella, and a knee-weakening smile.

I smiled back; she flaunted harder. It made perfect sense. It was my day.

Just as I'd halved the distance between us, a blurred figure overtook me from the rear, threw his arms around her, violently, possessively, his ardor forcing an even broader smile to my lips.

I didn't begrudge them each other, not that night at least. For that night I already had as much company as I cared for.

Steam hissed reassuringly from beneath buildings. Packard tires skimmed the moisture from the asphalt. My face met the wind. My heart bore me forward. In the plush night my ancient dreams of ascendancy lived on.

14

Game Four

Each Chicago book I called the next morning seemed ravenous for my business. It took just ten minutes to wheel $40,000 on the Reds for that afternoon's game. At 3–2 yet. One small-timer said Chicago scratch was everywhere. He said the word was out that whatever was on was off.

I greeted this confluence of prepositions with a noncommittal snort. He'd held his tongue, after all, until I'd bet. I took his affront in stride, though. I'd soon be rich enough to disdain all such trap-handedness. Besides, I knew something he and his kind couldn't possibly have known. I knew that whatever had been off was now very, very much back on.

I left for the park a bit earlier than usual, eager to savor the bumptiousness in the stands. It seemed much more picturesque now that I had complete control of it. The Chicago crowd was much like Cincinnati's, only harsher. Their cynicism couldn't mask their renewed enthusiasm, though. Even Comiskey appeared encouraged by yesterday's score.

The game itself was baldly anticlimactic. Cicotte pitched well, but made two fielding errors. Cincinnati scored on each, and won 2–0.

The silence that greeted the final out resembled the hush following a distant relative's death rattle. I'd never heard such quiet. The departing fans tiptoed weightlessly up the aisles, looking drained of blood. Comiskey appeared jubilant by comparison. He hadn't been fooled by yesterday's win after all. He seemed as pleased as my father always did whenever I disappointed him.

Still, the day's operative image was of Attell, straddling his pew, arms akimbo, contemplating his toe tops.

The seats around him had emptied quickly. An elderly usher approached him from the rear, whether commiseratively or expulsively seemed uncertain. The old man bent slowly to Abe's ear. Attell whirled, sprung to a crouch, then brought his fist quickly to the pink cheek. The geezer dropped into a clatter of cane chairs.

I scurried down the tunnel, feigning myopia.

Cincinnati was ahead now, three games to one.

Burns was gone, Attell going. Rothstein ahead, I gaining. It was just the two of us now.

There would be at least two more games, probably three, maybe even five. I couldn't imagine losing any. It was all there for my asking, and my desiring.

15

In Delano's, on Division Street, third booth from the rear, half past six, I sat, as advertised.

Gandil rolled in twenty minutes later, trailing his Airedales. They looked less like victims than victimizers. Forty fingers were instantly in my salad.

"How's it going, Sport?"

"What's the good word, Sport?"

"Long time no see, Sport."

Seven of us filled a booth meant for four. Our neighbors shot us the usual killing glances.

"Kiss my ass, Sport, let's get drunk."

This was Williams, flaunting his buckupishness. Felsch and Jackson nodded. McMullin just stared at me, smirking.

I asked Gandil to accompany me to the men's room, feeling in no mood to make it any easier for him.

"What the fuck is this, the chiseler's novena?"

"They wanted to come, Sport. It don't hurt nothing."

"It don't help nothing either. In six minutes every blossom-nose in Chicago will know you've been in here hailing Columbia, and with a well-known professional gambler yet."

"Well-known, Sport? By who?"

He had me there, but only temporarily. I was resolved to keep his fat ass in the dock.

"Where are Weaver and Cicotte, Chick? Out parading around the *Tribune* with sandwich boards?"

"Weaver assed out, Sport. I thought I told you that. Cicotte has a migraine. Stop screaming, will you, for the love of Christ? The bartender already thinks you're lighter than air."

It hadn't sounded like screaming to me; still I hushed. One can have too much the upper hand as well.

"And don't call my associates chiselers, either, Sport. It has a peculiar ring sliding out your particular pipe."

I drew $20,000 from my jacket then to muffle him. It seemed an uncedable sum, but had to go. I'd be collecting $109,000 in an hour to make amends.

Gandil took it, riffled it, tallied it, before slapping half of it back in my palm without a word. We were no longer even feigning trust.

"Drop this back on Cincinnati tomorrow, Sport, and don't try anything amusing with the odds."

"And your associates?"

"I'll worry about them, you worry about this."

I left him then, in the shortest shrift imaginable. Nothing seemed the best thing I could say.

As I pushed through the swinging doors the fixers peered up at me, as they had that legendary forenoon in Boston. Again I snubbed them, as they deserved. Sharing success with such louts felt almost like failure to me. They were too brash, too common. Everything made them happier than anything seemed to make me.

Abe Attell wasn't hobbled by such qualms, of course. He'd have traded his mood just then for any other. He'd just lost a fast hundred grand, plus his recently refurbished sense of inevitability. Now he had the trots.

When he reached his hotel he went straight to the crapper, to calm his colon and examine his options. Unfortunately he could think of few options. He kept turning his attention to alternate corners of the head, scrutinizing the antique rosettes on the wallpaper.

He was furious, but at whom? He felt lost, but here he was.

The one man who could soothe his throbbing gut was the one man he could least afford to talk to. So in panicked submission to the futility of his circumstances he dialed that individual's number. Instantly his bowels stabilized beneath him.

"Rothstein here."

"Mr. Rothstein, Abe Attell."

"Yes, Abe. How are you?"

The tone was calm, almost dispassionate. It was as if Attell had recently stepped out for cigarettes, and was now calling back to verify Rothstein's brand.

"I'm in Chicago, Mr. Rothstein."

"You certainly are, Abe."

"I just thought I'd come out here to take in some of the Series. I never had time to before, always in training, in bed with the birdies, this thing and that. You know the story, Mr. Rothstein. The games have been pretty good so far. I'm enjoying them quite a bit. Cincinnati's ahead three games to one. They won again today. I suppose you know that already. I've seen a lot of our mutual friends out here, Mr. Rothstein. Carl Zork was just—"

"Say what you have to say, Abe."

The voice was fiercely indifferent, as if recorded.

"What?"

"You called to ask for something, Abe. Ask for it."

There seemed nowhere for Attell to forge but forward, as

in the ring. To seek cover now was to solicit devastation.

"Well, you see, Mr. Rothstein, I've been speculating on some of these Series games, you see. Not a lot, you understand, but maybe a bit more than I should have. And I seem to have gotten in a little deep here. Nothing I can't maneuver out of, naturally, as long as Chicago doesn't win the Series. Chicago isn't going to win the Series, are they, Mr. Rothstein?"

He'd been struggling to sound casual, or at least composed. But there it was, pure panic, flapping like a severed head in the breeze. He might as well have tacked a red flag to his butt end.

"Are they, Mr. Rothstein?"

A profound silence settled over the wires then. Abe feared Rothstein had hung up. But then he heard him breathing, a measured, rhythmic sound as calculated as a dying mother's sighs.

Attell wanted to start speaking again, to fill the void. But he lacked a theme. Perhaps, he thought, he might sing.

"Mr. Rothstein?"

"Yes, Abe?"

"Am I going to lose everything, Mr. Rothstein?"

"No, you're not going to lose everything, Abe. And do you know *why* you're not going to lose everything, Abe? Because it wouldn't suit me to have you lose everything, Abe, not just now, that is. Do you understand what I'm saying, Abe?"

"Yes, Mr. Rothstein. I understand."

And he did, not in the precise way Rothstein intended, perhaps, but close enough. He was safe.

"And in the future, Abe, if you're ever tempted to do a little gambling, tell me about it beforehand. I can usually help a guy. If it doesn't crowd my interests, that is. You'd be amazed how little time passes, Abe, before I discover even your slightest indiscretion. Yours is not a particularly difficult scent to track."

"I suppose it isn't, Mr. Rothstein."

"No, Abe, it isn't. And that's dropped-death-on-toast in this racket. I wouldn't get in the ring with you, Abe."

"Yes, Mr. Rothstein. I understand."

And this time, as a matter of fact, he did.

"Good, Abe, good. How's the weather been out there? Nat Evans tells me it's turned a trifle windy."

You had to admire the Bankroll's brass, Abe admitted. He could inform you, without actually telling you, how the land lay.

"Yes, it's been breezy, but warm enough, and not a cloud bigger than a tablecloth for a week."

"Good, Abe, good, no clouds, glad to hear it. Well, I suppose you've got many matters to attend to now. I won't hold you up. I'll be expecting you in New York after the Series. You deserved a little vacation, Abe, but I've missed your graphic company quite a bit."

"Me too, Mr. Rothstein, missed your company that is. I'll be there. You can count on it."

"Good, Abe. And, say, Abe . . ."

"Yes, Mr. Rothstein?"

"Don't bet another dime on this Series. You'll lose more than everything if you do."

"Yes, Mr. Rothstein."

"Good night, Abe. Thanks for calling."

"Good night, Mr. Rothstein. Thanks for . . ."

But by then Rothstein really *had* hung up.

Attell sat on his bed, flexing the phone cord, letting relief ooze like dog's blood from his pores.

"Rothstein," Cohan liked to say, "can make an archduke

171

feel inadequate with a compliment. Nobody's better at sowing insecurity with reassurance."

Attell was glad he wasn't going to lose everything, though he resented Rothstein's presumptuous way of telling him. He was the former lightweight champion of the world, after all. People admired him who wouldn't puke on Rothstein's stairs.

Still he'd enjoyed hearing the Big Bankroll's voice again, and learning he hadn't queered their relationship permanently. And although Rothstein had warned him against betting any more on the Series, he'd said nothing about the bets that remained outstanding.

16

Game Five

Like the pivotal chapter of an overly florid romance, the fifth game evolved memorably, but mechanically.

For eight innings the White Sox performed flawlessly. In one inning they gave it all away.

Lefty Williams permitted four hits. Three came in the sixth, augmented by Jackson, Felsch, and Riisberg errors. The Reds got five more runs than they deserved, four more than they needed, and won 5–0.

A brief shower interrupted the third inning. Fans in my section sought cover beneath the pavilion. I remained seated, letting nature have its moment. A rainbow joined the skyline to the plains. Puddles formed in the lowlands of foul territory. For a moment I thought I saw a small fish leaping from one, but, obviously, I couldn't have.

Occasionally now, in those vaporous moments between waking and sleeping and waking again, a few memories of past pleasures slip my guard: of the joy I must once have felt before what I wanted to do became what I had to do.

That joy doesn't resemble what I now identify as happiness—a brief cessation of tension, a stunned compromise with reality. It's a much more sensual feeling, an almost physical sense that *nothing* is ever really lost for good.

One image jogs all such remembrances.

Joe Jackson's stance at the plate that final inning.

A stray gull floated in across the lake, making languid passes over the muddy infield. The crowd hushed. The sky brightened above the drifting clouds.

I don't know if my joy was as vibrant as my memory of it. I do know that I have spoken of it now as much as I care to.

In my mail slot, when I returned to the hotel, was a letter, the sole correspondence I would receive during the Series.

Dearest Sport,
    I do think of you always, and miss you more than love itself.
How does the southern coast of Mexico appeal, or Patagonia
even, wherever that may be?
                                                    Ever,
                                                    R.

That evening, as often occurs when I most desire solitude, it eluded me. I encountered an old Boston connection in the lobby. Past realities, and future possibilities, dictated a confab.

We were a third of the way through our cutlets, knee-deep in his increasingly pointed inquiries, when I bolted from the table as if slapped. I'm sure he suspected something gastric, but my distress was purely social.

173

I reached the street without retrieving my coat.

For the next two hours I roamed Chicago's back corridors, like an immigrant in the first flush of discovery. I'd earned the right to act arbitrarily, I felt. I hadn't fixed the Series just to swill guinea grub with bores.

I returned to my room at midnight, completely exhilarated. I'd outlasted the competition, both real and imaginary. I've often wondered how long it took my companion to realize I wouldn't be returning.

Until this very moment, perhaps?

17

A paternal twinge tugged me awake early the next morning. Even childless men experience them. My plot couldn't be expected to supervise itself.

The sun was inching up over the penthouses. Chambermaids were stirring resentfully in their ateliers. Both teams were approaching Indianapolis, having mounted their Pullmans as I'd abandoned my veal.

My decision not to accompany them was a conscious one. I wanted to avoid the welcoming mobs in Cincinnati, to enact the desertion I'd rehearsed so convincingly the night before.

On the train, Gandil and Riisberg rehashed their finances. Gandil's accounting had turned extemporaneously sidesaddle. He'd take the $10,000 he'd won yesterday, add the $10,000 I'd give him that evening, and shoot the moon on Cincinnati at even money. If he gave $10,000 to Riisberg, and $4,000 to the others, he'd clear twice what he'd make in any honest decade.

174

Only one detail threatened his arithmetic.

My absence.

I hadn't exactly promised I'd be on their train; I'd just said I'd be at the Sinton at five P.M. With the dough.

When I wasn't, Chick and Swede grew quietly edgy.

"It's ten past six, Chick. If he was coming, he'd be visible."

"Yeah, well . . ."

Riisberg waited patiently for the next line, before giving in and supplying it himself.

"Maybe he got here early and didn't wait."

"Or maybe . . ."

Again Gandil's prelude led nowhere, again Riisberg filled in the blank.

"The little bastard is pulling a Dutch switch."

"Well, I suppose . . ."

Gandil completed none of his sentences. Each trailed off like an Eddie Cicotte shine ball. Swede finished each for him, more eager for closure than significance.

It took twenty minutes for my absence to fix my fate. I'd be betrayed, as I'd hoped I would, given the same green lesson so recently dealt Attell.

Outside, the sun was slowly abandoning the pavement. The temperature had dropped an October ten degrees. Gandil and Riisberg floated affably toward the river, without meaning to, or meaning not to either.

"This feels . . ."

"Like something that's been happening too much lately. I know, Chick. I just had the same hot flash myself."

I could have made our appointment if I'd wanted to. But apparently I didn't want to. I ate a titanic breakfast, packed perfectly, amended my shoeshine. I'd have tubbed my un-

175

dies in my chamber pot if I'd had any castile soap. Despite my diddling, though, I still almost made the seven-fifteen. I reached the station just as it glided from the platform.

I bought a ticket for the ten-thirty and settled back to peruse the tabloids.

My procrastination didn't upset me. I often make decisions by gutting alternatives. I'd prefer to be more forthright, but can't seem to be.

As soon as I'd caught up on my crimes in print I phoned my actuaries, instructing them to let $60,000 ride on Chi tomorrow afternoon.

There were several reasons why upping my bet made no sense whatsoever. It rendered a straightforward wager ambiguous, risked losing much for the sake of winning more. Attell had washed out on a similar strategy. Not that I knew this, of course, or would have deferred to it if I had. I've always considered fate my sole precursor.

Still, something about this recklessness appealed to me. It felt both foreign and comfortingly familiar, as if I'd awakened in another man's bed, in his pajamas, yet felt more at home in his life than I ever had in mine.

Not until Chicago's foundries turned into Indiana's cornfields did my anxieties allay themselves. I turned my undivided attention to back issues of *Liberty Magazine.* Spotted cows grazed listlessly beside arid roadbeds. Narrow paths circled into leafy half-distances. My seatmate filled his handkerchief with bloody phlegm, while I concentrated on the implications of my daring.

I was going for broke, is what it amounted to. What is a gambler, after all, if not someone who gambles, one for whom loss is more than just another alternative to triumph?

176

18

Game Six

I drank a bit too much that evening. My next recollection is of the sixth game's first pitch. Twenty-four hours seem to have vanished from my résumé.

Two fantasies from that night *have* survived, though.

One is of Rose, slumbering serenely on her side, hip thrust forward, lips ajar, her breath as rhythmic as her heartbeat.

The other is of Rothstein, hovering in the shadows, gazing into the light, a silver curtain billowing past his ear.

Eventually these images always combine. I have no idea why.

For the first four innings Chicago played perfectly. Cincinnati played better. They were levitating with presumption, convinced they'd actually earned their previous victories. Every gambler dreads such self-delusion, the inferior opponent who's misplaced his limitations.

Dutch Reuther blanked Chicago. The Reds battered Dickie Kerr at will. They led 4–0 going into the fifth. I should have been worried, but wasn't.

In the fifth the White Sox scored a listless run. Riisberg walked, moved inconspicuously to third, scored moments later on an Eddie Collins fly. The stands grew hushed, as if by prearrangement.

In the sixth, Cincinnati's resolve crumbled. Weaver doubled. Jackson singled. Felsch doubled. All scored. The game was suddenly tied. The Reds never came close to untying it.

My eye caught a lovely one in front of me, sea-green, the tint of a sparrow's egg. Its owner was seated in the next row, five seats over, blotting her brow. When the score evened she turned to her companion, sensed my gaze, tilted her head to meet it, as women will to signal availability. Her shoulders were high, her neck slender, like a dancer's. Her companion was clearly a tradesman. I, on the other hand, was now precisely that audacious gambler I'd always imagined myself. I hoped my solitude added to my mystery.

It was a thrilling accent to the contest, her interest, her elegance. It made extending my gain an even more pressing imperative. My devotion to it reached quickly to my groin, though it was the most tenuous of half-flirtations imaginable.

Streams of late-afternoon sunlight pierced the clouds. Vendors' cries rose shrilly through the pall. Reds banners billowed down either line. It was now just a matter of waiting. The Reds could have ended it in the ninth, ended the Series, ended my dreams. How could I have been so sure they wouldn't?

In the tenth Weaver led off with a double. Gandil singled him home. The Reds went quickly in their half. And that was that. As dramatic as closing the screen door to the sun porch. The Series would continue. I'd won another $60,000.

I strained to see the green-eyed one in front of me. She was gone. It was only then that I realized she reminded me of someone, though try as I might I couldn't imagine who.

19

That evening I rang up Gandil at his flop. He answered promptly, with a truce-defying snarl.

"Congratulations, Chick. That's the suave batsmanship Comiskey and I expect of you."

"Up your brown, Sport. You'll be a man before your mother."

"Yes, well, it wouldn't surprise me in the least, Chick. Make a snazzy epitaph too, pithy, yet comprehensive. How do you think it would look carved on granite?"

"You sound awfully happy to me, Sport, for someone who's just lost more money than he's ever had."

"Just rollicking through the tears, Chick, though you needn't. I've got news here that will make me your favorite celebrity, unless you've got Mabel Normand there tooting on your root."

His silence said he didn't, but would like to.

"Chick? Chick? Are you still there, Chick? Aren't you going to ask me what happened to the money, Chick? That's always been my favorite part."

"I don't care about your fucking money, Sport. I'd just like to come up there and fry your fucking nuts off."

I'm easily charmed by the flamboyantly savage bulldoze. Chick's deserved full marks for specificity, conjuring up, as it did, crisp images of sheep shears and vegetable oil. Still, something about it sounded a trifle forced, as though he'd been reading it from the back of a rolled-oats box.

"I've got your money right here, Chick. That's what I'm trying to tell you. I missed my train last night. My cab broke down halfway to the station. I caught the Zephyr out this morning. It spent six hours on a siding at Terre Haute. That's French for 'hold your horses,' Chick. I had no way of reaching you. It was just bad luck. It cost me, too, Chick, plenty. I don't blame you for what happened today, Chick, for everything I lost. Imagine how anxious I am to win it back. That's why I'll give you all your money tonight, Chick. Plus a bonus. Meet me at the Garden of Palms at nine. I'm serious, Chick. This is more important to me than drawing my next ten breaths."

I was laying it on a trifle thick, I knew. But outlandishness now seemed my soundest strategy.

"I don't know, Sport. I'll think about it. I kind of doubt it, though. I believe you're just lying through your teeth again is what it is."

I swallowed hard, but held my tongue. He needed a little time to convince himself.

"If I do decide to come down there, though, and I'm not saying I will, but if I do, and you don't have the dough, all of it, for the whole Series, then imagine what will happen to your little scheme. No matter what you think, it will be even worse. We can beat these guys standing on our heads, Sport. Give that notion a quick spin through your wringer."

I knew he'd come then. His logic was proving no match for his longing.

"I have, Chick, very much so. That's why I want to meet with you tonight, to make up for any inconvenience I might have caused you."

"We'll see."

Then he hung up.

20

Game Seven

There are many things I don't know about that evening.
Only three have ever really mattered.

Were the other fixers there when I called?

Did they decide to win the seventh game right then?

Did Gandil go to the Garden of Palms to meet me?

Yes.

No.

Yes.

Those are my guesses. I have only intuition to base them
on. But that, and my preferences, seem enough.

Here are the two things I do know for sure about that
evening.

I didn't go to the Garden of Palms myself.

And I bet another $60,000 on the White Sox to win the
seventh game.

Which they did.

Eddie Cicotte pitched as he was able. The Reds played
like chumps. The final was 4–1. Chicago could have won by
any margin.

The Series stood 4–3. I was a quarter of a million, and
random change, ahead. Rothstein and I stood united by
prosperity, each, after his own particular fashion, unassaila-
ble. It was even better than all my dreams of it. The south
coast of Mexico drew closer by the moment.

21

There is an instant, in all equatorial climes, just before sunset, when the western sky lights up preternaturally. A protracted flash fills the air with greenish ether, signaling the beginning of yet another tropic night. In this way, in such realms, it is always brightest just before the dark.

A similar portent preceded that seventh game.

I'd won a fortune, won it heroically. The absence of other gamblers, the silence of the crowd, Gandil's belief that he was punishing me as he enriched me, all contributed to my escalating moxie.

Still I knew it wouldn't last, as travelers know lush sunsets aren't perpetual.

The second I sensed this, or a moment earlier, a familiar shadow passed across my lap. It neither moved, nor suggested it would again.

"Mr. Rothstein desires a confab with you, Sully. He'll ring you in your room right after dinner. If I were you I'd be squatting on the line."

He lingered another moment, but added nothing, before his shadow passed, returning my knees to sunlight.

"But you're not me, Nat," I yearned to scream at his receding backside. "And what's more, you never will be."

But by then I was quite alone in the park.

I returned placidly to my room at eight o'clock, there being no place else, apparently, that I wished to be. I hadn't hurried my dinner, though, as reluctant to toe Rothstein's line as to flout it. The phone wasn't ringing, didn't even look capable of ringing. Evans hadn't mentioned a specific time. "After dinner" covered an infinity in Rothstein's universe.

I ordered a glass of port and four macaroons, then snuggled up on the divan with the scandal sheets.

"Reds' Edge Narrows" was their collective theme.

Every few minutes I glanced up to see if the phone was still there. It always was.

Because I intended to take the red-eye back to Chicago, I set eleven as my curfew. At ten-fifty it became irrelevant. The shrillest ring imaginable bounced off every surface in the room.

"Hello."

"Hello, Sport, Arnold Rothstein here."

"How are you, Mr. Rothstein?"

"Fine, Sport, tip-top, couldn't be better. Don't suppose I have to ask you likewise? Details of your accomplishments reach us almost hourly."

I'd steeled myself against his breezy bluntness. Still it got through, making me feel the perpetrator of some hopelessly vulgar ruse, which I would now be required, but be completely unable, to defend.

"I can't say it's the way I would have handled it, Sport, one game at a time. Gamblers don't have to be bridge-jumpers, you know Sport. Nor is knifing Gandil the silk path to this prize."

He wasn't seeking enlightenment, or apology. He was flaunting his omniscience, making me squirm.

"I can explain everything, Mr. Rothstein. I—"

"No need, Sport. No use, either. Deeper thinkers have tested my resolve, playing both ends against my middle, as it were. I'm surprised you'd chance it, though. It doesn't seem your style."

Was this an insult, or faint praise? I didn't ask. It was his call, for his reasons.

"The time has come to put this gag to bed, Sport. I have a significant wish that Cincinnati take the Series. At four games to three this prospect looms equivocal. Clarify it. Give Gandil his money, every cent, tomorrow. You may want to stake everything on one game, but my father died fifteen years ago."

No blather softened his directive. He just said good night, then severed our connection.

I sat there, contemplating rejoinders, though I'd be unable to deliver any I might think of.

"Fuck you, kike," I finally whispered into the mouthpiece, then hung up and began stuffing my valise.

His call had lasted exactly three minutes. I had no trouble making my train, even less spotting Gandil in the smoker. He was sitting alone, staring out the window.

"Here it is, Chick, all of it, every penny."

I emptied my valise with a devil-may-care flourish.

"Not all, Sport, but enough, for now."

"Well, actually there is a bit more, Chick, if you stand by our agenda tomorrow."

He didn't answer, or do a count, but reached over and stuffed the bills into his pockets, then edged past me, up the aisle, toward the bar car.

When we reached Chicago I saw him standing beside Riisberg in the terminal. Both looked my way, neither acknowledged me.

An hour later I made my final bets of the Series.

Deference had overtaken my contacts. I'd hit them consecutively, with clashing strategies, and different teams. They, of course, didn't give a rat's ass who won. Bookies aren't gamblers, they're accountants with attitudes.

The odds had shifted radically overnight. The White Sox were now 8–5 for the eighth game.

There was a moment, as I recited my bets, when I was tempted to temper them, to hold a little back, just in case. I survived it, though, bet a full $100,000. I wanted to do something almost reckless just once in my life, to play that bottom card the rest of the world considers courage.

Rothstein had an arm in every town. Harry F. was his answer in Chicago.

Harry was a neat little shooter of the obsessive type most frequently encountered on psychiatric wards. He was eerily polite, unfailingly direct, with the dead eye of a cod in its third day on ice.

It was Harry's size that marked him truly murderous, though. He was five feet two, at best, his wrists as willowy around as umbrella handles. Yet Harry believed himself invincible, with a ferocity that soon convinced his victims he was.

"Could so tiny a figure brand himself homicidal," ran their reasoning, "unless history had already justified his claim?"

"Harry F. is so frightening," Rothstein often said, "because there's so little of him to be frightened by."

When Lefty Williams caught sight of Harry that bright October afternoon, his first impulse was to holler for the cops. Harry was squatting in the middle of Lefty's bed, eating chocolate cherries from a box as big as he was.

"Eeek!" squeaked the bimbo accompanying Lefty, a lobby lizard he'd recruited to suck him off.

"Can the cunt," said Harry F. tonelessly. "We got business."

185

"What the . . . what is . . . who are . . ."

"I said dump the quiff. You'll save yourself a fortune in dick salve."

The chippy was inclined to resist, until the dead spot in Harry's eye grew suddenly deader. The sound of her heels clattering down Lefty's stairs was the last either man ever heard of her.

This exit stripped one layer from Lefty's fear; he wouldn't be bashed before a woman. But it still left his major dread untended. Might he be about to be dismembered by a dwarf?

Harry F. had no such intention, of course. Instead he rose and smeared the remaining chocolates the length of Lefty's wall. A lesser mind might have added a little chuckle. But Harry F. believed in sticking to the basics.

He motioned Lefty to follow him to the kitchen.

"Give your oven a quick flick of the wrist, Williams. I got a layer cake in there could stand a little more warmth."

Any incongruity now seemed more than likely to Lefty. All he knew of ovens was how to turn one up. So he did.

Harry sat opposite him, tapping on the sideboard.

"Did Gandil give you any dough this morning, Lefty?"

"A thousand."

"Did he promise you any more if you lost today?"

"Fifteen hundred."

"Do you believe him?"

"Who knows."

"Bank on it, Lefty. It's going to happen. If you lose, you get it all. If you don't, you kiss forever."

Harry bounded out the door on this bullyrag, his tiny legs spinning helter-skelter. Lefty was left wondering if he'd actually been there. He knew *somebody* had been there, though. His nightmares had never been *that* explicit.

Lefty remained seated for several minutes, trying to put

his breathing back in gear. He'd forgotten about the oven almost entirely, until green smoke, and a vile odor, began oozing from it. The smell was unlike any he'd ever smelled before. Still, he identified it almost instantly. For the moment he realized that he smelled anything at all, he remembered he hadn't seen his cat since returning home.

22

Game Eight

Dark. Damp. Windy. The sky a drifting cushion of gray, more November than October, actually, the smell of newspapers burning in the stands, the prospect of brandy downed against a chill.

Bodies pressed involuntarily forward, for warmth, or baser comfort. Gulls blew in over second base. A day more ominous than anticipated. Yet I didn't resent its gloom. My mother died on a perfect spring morning.

It was surely the end of something, of Chicago's comeback, or Cincinnati's luck. One would end the Series, the other would sink my scam. Dreams that come true end as abruptly as those that perish.

On the field the fixers struck determined poses. Williams smirked as he unlimbered. If he feared for his life, he didn't show it.

Gleason paced the dugout. Comiskey sat stone still in his box. In the press room Ring Lardner revised his William Howard Taft imitation, a string of unrelated platitudes linked by blasts of gaseous jocularity. A little work on the lisp would make it inimitable.

187

"I feel like I've watched two Series already," he was telling Mathewson. "I'm curious to see if the third will be as beguiling."

The Chicago fans seemed convinced it would be. It was the Series' cheekiest crowd. You'd have thought the White Sox were about to clinch the argument, not one loss away from dog-daring oblivion.

I, meanwhile, knew exactly how the land lay. Or did I? I knew it was in the bag. I just didn't know if it would stay there. This put me as deep in the dark as the amateurs.

In New York, Rothstein whisked magnanimously through the Ansonia, angling for a seat beside the simulation board. He made no effort to conceal his presence this time, but ordered a corned beef sandwich, without crusts, and two bottles of Flexner's Dark. He was planning to stay until Williams tipped his hand.

Around the country, millions awaited the first pitch. The game, unfortunately, couldn't sustain their tension.

Lefty Williams threw fifteen pitches the first inning, each straighter than its predecessor, none with any discernible velocity. They split the plate's pale heart as though the Bankroll himself was flashing the signals.

Four of the first five Reds reached base, three scored. When Williams's fifteenth pitch proved his unseemliest, Kid Gleason shot from the dugout as if catapulted. A thin man with a suicide's neutral smile began whistling *Rigoletto* behind me.

Nothing could stop it. By the eighth the Reds led 10–1.

Attell left after the fourth, Evans an inning later. Comiskey stayed stuporously put. It was his stadium, and his team.

In the press box, Ring Lardner composed a burlesque headline:

CHICK & COMPANY: A PROFITABLE FULL-GAINER
HEADFIRST INTO THE SHITCAN

In the sixth he began typing his true copy.

REDS WORLD CHAMPS IN STARTLING UPSET

He filed his bogus story for future reference, though, to be conjured up if the facts came into fashion.

By the ninth the stands were filling up with ghosts. Bits of paper blew down the aisles, then up the empty runways. You could hear the players' voices against the wind. I believe I saw Eddie Cicotte light a cheroot in the bullpen.

I resented this all-too-abrupt return to normality, of course. Life wouldn't just go on, it already had.

And then suddenly, almost incongruously, it was over. Ray Schalk grounded to short. The umpires fled the field. The players followed. In twenty seconds the diamond was deserted. Just like that.

Ten days of intrigue; three months of planning; years beyond counting of passive musing in easeful solitude, until the dream of it had become more real than reality ever could be. Like anything else, and eventually everything else, it had ended.

I had won.

23

It took two minutes for the park to empty. Two attendants started tidying up my box, their conversation consisting of railings against the Wobblies. Tiny raindrops began decorating the seats.

I was tempted to linger in Comiskey's loge a few more minutes, to be the last to leave. But I didn't. I was ready to begin a life without symbolism. If I would cling to anything now, it wouldn't be to the past.

"You look like you just lost your wallet *and* your best friend," a fat usher informed me, steering me from his station.

I didn't answer. He wasn't serious, and I couldn't brag. Besides, I felt as if I probably had lost part of something.

Outside the streets were similarly deserted, no fans, no vendors, just ordinary life. I began walking deeper into the South Side, with no destination, just a yen. I wanted to be someplace, almost anyplace that the Series hadn't touched, someplace where the fact that it was over didn't matter.

When I reached a small park opposite a large church, I knew I'd found that place. I went into a tiny store and bought eight figs and a bottle of seltzer. Then I sat down in the park and tried to collect a few thoughts and banish some others.

The sky's gray deepened dramatically behind the trees. Calcified leaves dragged listlessly through clogged catch basins. A group of immigrant children eyed me suspiciously, sensing my displacement.

I felt detached from any reality I could identify, as I had on the day of my father's funeral. The rosary had been said, the mourners had left, the body lay decomposing beneath the ground. Everything had changed, yet nothing was really different. So where lay the point in moving on?

It was peaceful sitting in that little park, though, with the six-year-olds chanting their childish rounds, the shadows lengthening progressively over the churchyard. I sat there for a long time brooding on the timelessness of it all. It seemed like all I might ever need from life. It wasn't, of course. It was just all I ever wanted to need.

I didn't leave that park until half-past eight, when the cold and dark finally drove me from it. I've often wished I'd stayed on in that neighborhood, rented a small room above that little store, passed my remaining days watching those children playing Billy Buck and Cherries-in-the-Basket, monitoring their wistful weddings and vibrant funerals as they made their relentless way through that enormous church. I might have spared myself several decades of disillusion.

Of course, that's nonsense. Things are over no matter where they end. Over is over, life goes on, one must accompany it.

When I got back to the hotel it was as empty as the streets. All the gamblers had faded into history. Four messengers, clutching matching packages, stood impatiently outside my door.

For the next several hours I inventoried my take, counting it obsessively, as the city hit the sack outside my window. Each succeeding tally forced an even slower one, another methodical fingering of each sawbuck and C-note. I was falling, I'm afraid, half in love with the stuff. It seemed like something I might actually be able to count on.

Of course, I despised it too. It's every climber's sop.

When I finally got two totals to match (on the sixth try, just as the street sweeps began flooding Michigan Avenue), I stuffed it into my ancient buckskin kit and went to bed.

It was after midnight, so not totally pathetic. I thought briefly of calling Rose, but decided not to. Approval was no longer what I would seek.

191

I stripped to my skin and crawled beneath the sheets, pulling the quilt to within inches of my chin. The room was pure black, soundless, self-contained.

Just before I slept I removed the money from its pouch, spread it across the bed, adding another layer of insulation. Then I fell asleep and dreamed more dreams of Rothstein, in various settings, and shifting circumstances, each episode bleeding effortlessly into the next, exhilaratingly vivid, witheringly precise.

24

The next morning I awoke curiously unrefreshed. Mottled sunlight decorated my ceiling. Children's voices filled the streets far below. It was just another autumn weekday in Chicago. Except now I'd fixed the World Series, and made myself rich and formidable beyond imagining.

Before I could rationalize another hour in the rack, I threw off the covers, intending to rise. But I couldn't. Inertia had pinned me to my mattress. I didn't panic, though. I did what I always do when equivocation assails me—submitted to it, rationalizing a brief, and well-deserved, hiatus.

I lay there, blissfully inanimate, staring at the curtains. I didn't daydream, having run out of things to daydream about. I think I reflected principally on my socks.

It was forty-five minutes before I could finally rise, propelled by Gandil's imminent arrival. Where would I be, I've often asked my irresolute self, without the appointments I've made to force me through my schedule?

I will make an accounting now of the scam's financial outcome, of what I once considered the "crass" aspect of the Series.

The figures are approximate.

Rothstein made $1.2 million. Attell $320,000. Evans $40,000. Burns and Maharg nothing. Hal Chase probably snagged a few stray dollars. He usually did.

As for the players: Gandil made $35,000. Riisberg $15,000. Cicotte $10,000. Williams, Jackson, and Felsch $5,000 each. McMullin $2,500. Weaver nothing.

Each Red received a $4,881.55 winner's share, each White Sox got $3,254.37 for losing.

Comiskey cleared $185,433.47 in ticket receipts, and an untold sum from concessions.

I made $400,000, myself. Not as much as Rothstein, certainly, but much more than the others, and much much more, to be perfectly frank, than I'd have settled for.

I'd have liked my last meeting with Gandil to replicate the first one. I have a weakness for symmetry. It wasn't possible, though. We had the real money now, not just dreams of it.

"Well, Chick, did we, or didn't we?"

"I suppose we did, Sport."

The set of his jaw suggested getting down to business. I'd already separated his final cut. It wouldn't do to advertise mine.

I handed him the bills, wrapped in yesterday's sports pages. This wasn't irony, just carelessness. He began counting without a word.

"It's all there, Chick."

"I'm sure it is."

He went on, though. I walked to the window and looked

out at the street. The crowds below resembled those of previous mornings, all seemingly unaffected by my newly acquired wealth.

"What'll you do with it, Chick?"

"Spend it."

"On anything in particular?"

"Women, blue ruin, a new Buick."

"I see."

"What's that mean?"

"Just that, Chick. I understand."

"No you don't, Sport. You don't understand at all."

These were the last words that ever passed between us. I suspected they might be. Success never binds me to anyone like failure.

I should have checked deeper into his plans, I know. Concealing fruition is no easier than achieving it. And no tongue wags less discriminately than the new tycoon's. But I didn't. I intended to, even jotted it down on a little scrap of paper, which I promptly misplaced. I must have felt I'd grown immune to common cares.

I have no idea when our secret began unraveling. That moment seems as likely as any other.

As soon as Gandil left I felt ravenous. So I threw on my topcoat and went downstairs for a bite. I'd always imagined a celebrational feast in the Pump Room, or some equally swanky spot. But for some reason I didn't feel quite up to it that morning. So I pointed my toes toward the Strand Cafeteria instead.

The Strand was a joyless pork-and-beanery, its clientele consisting mainly of parole violators. Food there was a functional, not a stylistic, concern. It was precisely the atmosphere I'd gambled to escape. So there I trudged, since I no longer had to.

Rose once accused me of living in paradox. Living *for* paradox, I assured her, was closer to the point.

Still, I enjoyed my little fill-up in that dinky dive, among the steam tables and the unplaceable smells and the street monkeys. A stiff breeze rustled the oilcloth curtains. Temporarily penitent alcoholics dished up my belly cheer. The homey seediness made me feel almost elegant. If I'd contemplated this contradiction my life might have turned out differently. But I didn't. The overexamined life is no more livable than its opposite.

I walked slowly back to the hotel after lunch, wishing the day might somehow last forever. Or at least long enough to suggest my next move. Sparrows darted through leafless treetops. Young mothers pushed drooling children before them. Workmen worked, layabouts lay, taking the angled sun. The Series was growing more over by the minute. I decided to leave before it was *too* over.

I hailed a cab and headed straight to Union Station. I'd return to Saratoga, to Rose, to that reward. I've been back to Chicago only once since that afternoon. Perhaps I'll return again someday. Though with each passing year it seems less likely.

25

No bands had played me off from Saratoga; a matching indifference greeted my return. I wouldn't have had it otherwise. Fame was one luxury I still couldn't afford. Still, the *complete* lack of interest did annoy me. I felt I merited more.

As my train sped relentlessly east my misgivings multiplied proportionately. I'd wanted pluck and cunning to immortalize me, not greed and fear. But in the end it had all come down to the commonest denominators.

Perhaps my misgivings were sentimental. Rothstein wouldn't have had them. But then again, they didn't call him Sport.

I hadn't told Rose I was coming, wishing to savor my triumph before sharing it. I knew the risk in this, and accepted it.

My fellow passengers were the usual low-lid zekes: truss salesmen, novice pickpockets, pale teenage brides recently abandoned by pockmarked bosun's mates. None were types I'd ordinarily have sought out. Yet I found myself longing to confide in them, to tell them I'd done what I'd done. It was exhibitionism, pure and simple, and it terrified me. Not because I feared surrendering to it, but because I knew my accomplices would.

I arrived at dusk, sixteen days, almost to the hour, after leaving. It seemed decades. I called Rose from the station. She wasn't in.

I hadn't anticipated this possibility, but stayed calm. No

detail, apparently, was too minor to be counted on. She was probably out visiting friends, I told myself. She had no friends that I knew of, but sixteen days was plenty of time to make some.

I had a fleeting vision of her squirming between some dingo's thighs, her tongue crawling happily up his root. I banished this image, before it could work its will.

My driver asked if I'd just come from Chicago, wondered if I'd seen any of that "Series slosh."

"I don't think you missed much in the way of forthrightness, Sport. Everybody knows the Jews minced the onions."

My gullet snapped shut at his crack. He knew my name. He knew of the fix. He knew everything. Everybody knew everything. Warrants were even then being issued for my arrest. Descriptions of me were humming along the wires. Rose had fled, probably to Mexico. If I had any sense I'd follow her posthaste.

I didn't, of course, but simply settled a bit deeper into my seat, waiting for the hacker's remarks to explain themselves. Which they did, with unsettling speed.

Disappointed bettors always cry fix, and even more frequently blame their losses on "the Jews." And aren't such apes the likeliest of God's unfortunate to call every sap they inflict their theories on "Sport"?

Rose's absence was even more explainable. She'd moved, to roomier, much pricier digs, paying two months' rent on the prospect of an "inheritance." This cavalier action alarmed me. I hadn't gained my freedom for her benefit. But it also charmed me. I'd be needing somebody to make me spend my money. And it wasn't anything I hadn't known about her.

I found her bent over the table in our new kitchen, re-completing an ancient crossword she'd erased. She looked

197

even better than I remembered her, her cheekbones starkly chiseled and sweetly flushed, her eyes flashing with some emotion resembling expectancy. I spent three hours describing my exploits to her, making them seem even more triumphant than I now considered them. She clung to every phrase, laughed and shuddered in all the proper places. Only then did I realize her true worth. Every gambler needs a woman he can lie to.

We celebrated with a bottle of dago red, and a stroll beneath the stars without our slippers. Then we acted out my great fear from the taxi, with *my* privates replacing my ghostly rival's. I slipped into her as into another dream. She clung to me as if she, as least, believed in it.

November
1919

1

We didn't go to Mexico, of course. It was just one of those things you say you'll do, when you have to. Impossible tasks require tangible rewards. When I returned to Saratoga, though, I found I didn't want to retire, to rest on my laurels, any more than I wanted to buy baubles with my loot, the way Gandil would. I hadn't fixed the Series for common reasons after all, but to elevate myself. Now that I had, I found I wanted to rise even higher, to extend my gains, my momentum, my new life. Not knowing how, or even why, soon made me stuporous.

Rose didn't press me for an answer. I suppose she always knew.

The crossword I found her refinishing was one of hundreds she would solve that placid autumn, while I struggled with every success's ultimate question: Now what? Nothing had changed between us, except the tone, which is, of course, everything.

Our days passed in agreeably neutral diversions, so pleasantly that might have been the purpose. Rose made ambitious meals and pressed dead flowers between the pages of overdue library books. I slept until noon and ate heroic breakfasts and pedaled to the racetrack every afternoon to watch the sun set.

Each evening I recounted my money in sweet seclusion, in

the bedroom, latches locked, drapes drawn. Over cups of steaming English I stalked direction. No longer satisfied merely to resemble Rothstein, I now wanted to want exactly what Rothstein wanted. And what Rothstein always wanted was *more.*

I didn't scuttle the escape part of my dream entirely, however, just postponed it, placing it safely in my future—for later, when I really wanted to do it. I'd already forgotten the Series' shortcomings. Desire has no memory.

Despite my indecision I did manage a few simple tasks. I read eight papers daily, front to back, for baseball news. Every mention of the Series made me jump. Still, a day without any left me petulant.

When you're doing something big you don't think about afterward. Now I had to. Afterward was here.

Avoiding exposure wouldn't require secrecy I realized. Everybody already knew. It would require reticence. I assumed there would be some blather—in the papers, in the streets. I also assumed it would fade pretty quickly. I couldn't imagine anybody who *could* expose the fix who would want to. It was baseball.

Despite these assumptions, I grew increasingly apprehensive—about being discovered, about what to do next. Two unknowns in my life suddenly felt like two too many.

In the evenings Rose and I played hearts on the summer porch and made love in increasingly motivational positions. Gradually my desire for solitude reemerged. I've never really wanted to live alone, if the truth be known, but have always preferred living with a woman and ignoring her.

God knows how long we'd have perpetuated this charade (forever, if my first thirty-seven years are any indication) if a journalistic shock hadn't mercifully intervened, providing me with at least the illusion of direction. For one bright, weatherless morning, several weeks into our self-induced anaesthetization, the following story appeared in the *Herald Tribune:*

COMISKEY ANSWERS CRITICS

Buffeted by rumors of World Series irregularities, Chicago White Sox owner Charles Comiskey today issued the following statement:

"There is always a scandal of some kind following a big sporting event like the World Series. These yarns are manufactured out of whole cloth and grow out of bitterness to losing wagers. I believe my boys fought the battles of the recent Series on the level, as they always have. I would be the first to want evidence to the contrary, if there be any. I would give $20,000 for information to that effect."

It went on like that, but I couldn't. The term "Series irregularities" sounded like a death threat. The idea of a reward scared me spitless. Twenty grand can buy a universe of testimony, some of it even true.

I thumbed through it twice before sliding it Rose's way.

"Check this hen piss."

"I already have."

"You didn't say anything."

"And risk my reward?"

She stifled a grin to shield her little joke.

"Maybe we should head south," I suggested, yawning.

"Maybe we should," she answered, not asking where. Perhaps she hoped we'd mistake our way to Mexico.

Fleeing wasn't necessary, or even advisable. We weren't in any danger, couldn't have avoided it if we were. I just wanted to get away, to shake my bones. I hoped that just moving would provide me with some inspiration.

That night I skipped my count to fashion a strategy, worked three hours on it, without stopping. Here's what I came up with:

FORWARD

That's it. Details emerged, but none survived. Just after midnight I turned out the light, surrendering to the darkness, sat there listening to Rose's breathing, and my own.

Give it a year, I mused in summary. Aim high, take chances, make $400,000 into as much as it can be. You don't have to imitate Rothstein to surpass him. Try different things, until you find one. Become what you imagine yourself, or some equivalent.

The next morning, without looking back, or even wishing to, we boarded the Norfolk milk run to Miami.

We didn't stay on until Florida, however, but pulled up 60 percent short, in a Maryland shore town, Havre de Grace. They had a racetrack there, and a casino. I wanted to begin my new life in old circumstances. Rose's motive, if she had one, eluded me.

She expressed no disappointment along the way. When our weekend visit turned into a fortnight she took to knitting. I began to believe she actually wished me happiness, at no inconsiderable cost to her own. This was before I learned to distinguish acquiescence from approval, and to recognize the aliases female disgruntlement often travels under.

2

 "Sherbas looks the stayer in this one," said General Pershing, shaking a final drop from his foreskin.

"Maybe," I agreed sullenly, "though others have closed stronger at shorter distances."

We were standing shoulder to shoulder, Pershing and I, in the cool, lambent gloom of a Havre de Grace comfort station. Darky attendants rustled pointedly behind us. Captains of industry swept by, rearranging testicles.

Pershing had earned his unqualified opinion, I suppose, having picked three consecutive winners, at escalating odds. He needn't have trumpeted it quite so loudly, though. Even martinets should be modest about some things.

From the moment Red Casserly introduced us, on the meet's second day, I'd felt my prayers responded to. This could be the new scam I'd been hoping for. I'd return to the horses, and not have to risk my fortune betting them, either, but add to it by teaching hotshots how to. Pershing would be my prototype.

It was the perfect solution, my ticket to the top.

Nothing about it panned out, of course. All my handicapping theories quickly proved defective. I devised others, which flopped even faster. I'd apparently forgotten how perverse the track can be. Soon I was straining so hard to be my new self that I didn't feel like anybody.

Meanwhile, Pershing picked nothing but winners. They won for the wrong reasons of course, but they won. His assumption this was his due enraged me further. His ego

205

was sucking all the oxygen from my heart.

"Shall we rejoin the ladies?" he asked now, rezippering forcefully.

What choice do we have? I wondered, but bit my tongue. He was a man who liked suggesting the inevitable, making all his proposals sound like orders from the top.

"Where you studs been?" his "lady" asked us when we returned. "I and Rosie here have been pining for your attributes."

She was a pretty enough individual, for her purposes. Casserly had arranged her. Red clearly had plying in mind for the General. He wouldn't make a thin dime from me.

"Who do you fancy in *this* contest, my dear?" Pershing asked Rose now, coquettishly.

Rose smiled, but said nothing. Black Jack's novelty was wearing thin all around.

We were five days into the meeting, four days into my losing streak. If I'd wanted to impress Pershing with my handicapping, I surely had.

As my fiscal deficits deepened, my social defiance accelerated. I upped my bets instead of trimming them, a loser's trick. Pershing quickened his pace as well.

This particular day had been the cruelest so far. Three of my choices had trailed their fields. Pershing's companion had begun calling me Dragass Sullivan.

"Hey, Dragass, what's gonna run like it had three legs and orphan's cough this time?"

Detachment, of the commiserative sort, had settled over Rose. Our figuring for the seventh evolved in silence. Pershing stuck with Sherbas. I couldn't separate two overlays. So I bet both, hoping to double my chances. I doubled my losses instead.

Sherbas won by two open lengths, at 11–1. Casserly and

the tart gushed effusively. I couldn't even fake resignation. Pershing stared out at the track serenely, as if surveying the Argonne after a gas attack.

"By God and glory I truly like this sport. You feel solely responsible when you win, but free of all liability when you lose."

"Yes, General," I cooed benignly. "In that way it very much resembles war."

I bounced away on this barb, knowing it looked bitter, but feeling too bitter to care. I marched out back and claimed a bench reserved for solitaries. There I reviewed all my previous selections, quickly confirming what I'd been suspecting for days.

Pershing's winners had had the best form. Yet I'd dismissed them the instant he'd selected them. I'd wanted to *make* the truth, not bow to it. A familiar pang of self-recognition clamped my heart.

When I returned to the box, nobody acknowledged me. I didn't care. I was about to reclaim my territory, and my style.

"Excuse me if you would, ladies and gentlemen. I believe I've lost just about enough of everything for one meeting."

We shook hands all around, hoping to do it soon again. They seemed genuinely sad to surrender me, as I would have been to lose a similar mark.

As soon as Rose and I returned to our digs I called George M. Cohan in California, as I'd been imagining doing all week. I told him I'd like to come out and visit him. He said he couldn't think of anything he'd like better.

Rose and I packed in ten minutes. For the first time I noted the fierce impermanence of our surroundings, the wax-paper bureau linings, the two-spigot sinks. We ate a relaxed supper in the Captain's something-or-other, then stopped into Kresge's for some sunglasses. As we eased ourselves and our enthusiasms aboard our train, the late-November sun was just moments from its doom. We plied our qualms with palmy prospects at moving west. For Rose it meant beefy matinee idols and sugary beaches and a hard pitiless sun shining deep into long tropic evenings; it meant moving closer to Mexico. For me it meant moving so close to Mexico I might never have to move any closer.

But it also meant renovating my perspective. I'd never even considered California before. I'd been living the same life for so long it no longer felt like a choice I'd made, but like a decision made for me as I'd slithered from the womb. I'd need a complete change of scenery now, I realized, if I intended to move permanently up in class. In California things could be different. I could be my real self there, move spontaneously, freed by circumstance. I'd made my money, and my mark. I no longer needed to approach the world as its adversary.

They have palm trees in California. They make movies out there too.

3

While I'd cultivated slow horses and fast company in Havre de Grace, Comiskey had been busy freezing the fixers' checks. If the fix ever was brought to light, nobody could claim he hadn't tried to.

Rothstein heard of the reward while taking steam in a Lexington Avenue spritz stop. He wasn't worried. He'd padded his rear.

Attell found out from a cabana boy in Havana. He'd shifted his celebrations south to avoid the Bankroll's wrath. He wasn't worried, either. He was too drunk.

Bill Burns got the news in the Cathedral of Sighs. From where he sat, profitless, and aggrieved, in the ultimate pew, the notion of prattling for pay radiated potential.

Gandil learned from Riisberg. The day after the *Tribune* broke the story, Swede dialed Chick's number in a panic.

"What're we gonna do, Chick? The old man's after our asses."

"Nobody's going to talk, Swede. Nobody even knows about it."

"I do."

"They'd only be hurting themselves."

"Weaver wouldn't. He never got a cent."

"Who'd believe them?"

"A jury."

Riisberg had a worry for every calmative. Only his desire to be reassured finally permitted him to be.

Not until he hung up did Gandil allow himself his own reaction. He should have wrapped things up a little tighter, he now realized. Actually he should have wrapped them up period.

Eddie Cicotte read the story in his new outhouse. Each board in it had been paid for by the fix. When he reached the part about "evidence to the contrary," he ripped a page from the middle of his paper and put it to the best use he could think of.

Joe Jackson couldn't read. So he had his wife recite him the particulars. He was instantly intrigued, and thoroughly unfazed, and sat right down to dictate a rejoinder.

Dear Mr. Comiskey,

I have some interesting info for you on this World Series that you might like to get ahold of. That $20,000 you talked about could do the trick. But first off I want my Series share sent to me right off. It is rightfully mine as even you will admit to. Second of all I would request my salary be raised to $12,500 in 1920 on account of the terrific year I just had, what with .351 batting average, not to mention .375 during the Series, plus several good plays with the glove. The Series was fixed, like you said in the paper. If you want the straight dope on it write me quick.

Yours most sincerely,
J. Jackson

When Comiskey received this note he tossed it straight into his swill trap. He never even mentioned it to Austrian.

Rose and I remained oblivious to all these intrigues. The train speeding us west insulated us from common concerns. We slid past the continent's sad backyards, each mile a further lightening of our burdens. The air grew clearer as the Pacific became more possible. The sky reached closer to heaven every morning.

I'd be taking a stab at ordinary happiness out west, seeking contentment by not acting as if I needed it. California seemed the perfect spot for such ambitions. Gratification was said to be all but unavoidable there.

Rose and I made good use of our commute, playing Parcheesi, elaborating on our biographies. At every stop I jumped out for a local rag. None contained the news I both feared and would have killed for.

At night we ravished each other repeatedly in the sleeper, playing at the passion we both knew was sadly lacking. It sapped our energy, but didn't convince us. Rose's moaning brought occasional complaints from our neighbors. Their disapproval only served to spur us on.

I was trying hard to love her, to remember what I'd seen in her in Saratoga. But she didn't seem the same person she'd seemed in Saratoga. The only time I desired her now was when she wasn't there.

I'd promised myself I wouldn't recount the money on the train. The first day I didn't. The second night, around three, I gave in. After extricating myself from between Rose's inert hips, I excused myself on the pretext of dyspepsia, padding down to the smoker in my swagger-tail.

There I sat, alone, amid the ashtrays, reviewing my accounts with my back turned to propriety.

There was exactly $359,000 left, $41,000 less than I'd brought to Havre de Grace. What a relief! I'd pegged my losses at a cool fifty, minimum.

I retabulated the sums early the next night, then again the following morning, and later that afternoon. If our train had taken any longer to reach Los Angeles I'd have been ten-toeing it on the half hour by the weekend.

Only after we'd kissed off the Great Divide did a warning I'd received in Maryland register fully, like a wart suddenly revealing itself as tumor.

"Never desire what you can't have, Mr. Sullivan," Pershing had cautioned me as we'd parted, "lest your judgment become a captive to your longing."

4

Have I mentioned how I met the great George M.? Even if I have, it's a tale that bears repeating.

He used to favor the Back Bay with his gam operas. Jaunty Callahan introduced us at a run-through for *Broadway Jones*. That would make it 1908, or 1909. Cohan took to me instantly, as to some long-forgotten self.

"So refreshing to meet a bogtrotter with an adult name, Joe. Every mick I meet these days is called Socko, or Biffo, or Barfo, crack-handles best left to the shanty shams. Store up the dignity, Joe, and the chippiness. Soon you'll have enough of both to risk a middle initial of your own."

"Thanks, George," I shot back reflexively. "I'll do my best, and cite your influence. In the meantime, do us first-nighters a big favor, won't you? Can that caterwauling that opens the second act."

His grin said I'd struck the perfect tone. He was a hard-on who liked his ginger parried. We'd never be real friends; neither of us wanted that. He'd be my colorful contact in high places; I'd be his gentlemanly link to the streets. His seniority gave him the edge he always needed. It was a mateyness resembling Rothstein and Attell's.

When I first met him, I thought: Here you go, Sport. Soon you'll be ass-and-ankle with all the heavy timber.

It didn't work that way, of course. Progression was something I only *seemed* to want in those days.

Maybe it's not a story that bears *that* much repeating.

Cohan didn't meet our train in Los Angeles, as he'd promised to. I hadn't believed he would. It was just actor talk.

He sent Jesse Lasky's chauffeur instead. This was a typical Cohan ploy—standing us up, sending a surrogate, and borrowing that surrogate from a producer. It conveyed several unpleasant messages, all self-serving.

Lasky's chauffeur was graphically Mexican, and appropriately mute. He grabbed our bags without a word and bundled them through the terminal. I was too shocked to protest. Another journey had been sabotaged by arrival.

Out on the street the landscape was a different planet's entirely—shimmeringly, and unctuously, tropical. I suddenly didn't care where Cohan was, or where we were headed. I'd already achieved the lassitude I'd come west for. Rose peppered me with eager questions in the limousine. Meeting a movie star was her idea of living.

"Is your friend Mr. Cohan making a picture now, Sport?"

"I don't know."

"How many pictures has he made, all told?"

"I don't know."

"I wonder if he could get an amateur such as I a screen test?"

"A what?"

I'd been bragging about Cohan since Baltimore, to boost my flagging glamour in Rose's eyes. Apparently I'd done too good a job. Making your friends sound interesting can sometimes backfire with women.

"Hi-ho, you two, over here, over here!"

It was the great George M. himself, waving theatrically across the Mogambo's boundless dining room, snapping his fingers, beaming rhapsodically, a bravura performance. Two

213

parasitical types in double-breasted suits scrambled from his booth as we approached. One looked like an agent, the other didn't.

"Great to see you, Sport, been a million years, or six months at the very least."

"Yes it has, George. Just about."

"And this must be . . ."

"Rose."

"Of course. Rose. How delightful to finally meet you, Rose. I've heard so many wonderful things about you."

If Cohan had heard anything about Rose, wonderful or otherwise, it hadn't been from me. I hadn't mentioned her when I called him, just said I'd be bringing a woman along. Of course, in Cohan's eyes the mere fact that Rose was a woman was quite wonderful enough.

"Whatcha been up to, Sport?"

"Nothing much."

"Terrific. Wish I could say the same. Goldwyn's trying to squeeze three pictures out of me this year—two comedies and a melon-drama, as Sam likes to call them. We've already started one. I have a contract for a new revue back east. I'm in the middle of composing several tunes for that. Plus the Keiths have booked me into Indiana, or Missouri, or one of those places, an entire month's worth no less. And oh yes, I've agreed to write a series of articles for the Hearst rags. Didn't know the old hoofer was a litterateur, did you, Sport? Here's how that particular ruse came about. . . ."

He'd heard more than enough about me, apparently, in three syllables. Now he was free to do what he liked to do best—advertise himself. He spent the rest of the lunch doing so, interrupting only to flirt ritualistically with Rose.

I didn't mind. It was just Irishness. And it was Irishness I might actually be able to profit from. It could keep him from asking about the fix.

I knew he knew about it, would have to, if anybody did. He didn't mention it during the meal, though, shunned the entire subject studiously, with a pointedness that spoke volumes about his pique.

When the check came he grabbed it with hammy relish, then sent the waiter out to fetch our ride.

"Sorry I can't go back to Lasky's with you, Sport. I have a meeting at Paramount with Mayer. Actually, I'm not sure just how much time I'll be able to spare you this trip. Things are pretty hectic."

"That's okay, George, do what you can."

Consoling him wasn't necessary, of course. His regret wasn't genuine. He assumed picking up the check absolved him of any guilt.

"I'm so jealous, Sport. Of your leisure time, that is. Though I'm sure you've earned every second of it, from what I've heard. Remember, though, you and Rose are my guests out on this coast. I won't have you spending a single dime of that Series swag."

So there it was, disguised as generosity, his honeyed rebuke at having been excluded from the fix. I ignored it, as he expected me to. I knew he'd soon come looking for a payback. And that I'd give it to him. I was finally ready for us to be equals.

As Lasky's chauffeur led us resentfully from the restaurant, the two double-breasteds retook their places beside Cohan.

"Wasn't that Sport Sullivan?" I thought I heard one of them ask breathlessly. "The big-time gambler who's the brains behind Arnold Rothstein?"

215

5

We were guests at Lasky's residence, it turned out, a rococo villa halfway up the Hollywood Hills. Our suite was the size of Hartford; Cohan's was slightly larger. This was another standard Cohanism, showing his hospitality by divvying up another's.

Our first morning there proved typical of our stay. We were awakened at dawn by keening Mexican gardeners. They'd come to drain the moat. Swans stalked our veranda. Endless corridors opened onto vine-carpeted loggias. Bougainvillea. Mimosa. A privet hedge sculpted into a megaphone. Two trout pools!

After breakfast we went to Famous Players for a story conference. Cohan wanted us to see everything. Goldwyn was pressing him to adapt *Over There* to the screen. A doughboy returns to find his girl shtupping a shirker. Gradually (very gradually) she relents. With dancing. Goldwyn seemed to feel it was a common complaint. George M. balked at repeating himself. He wanted to make a picture where he got to ride a horse. There it sat, after two hours of vivid discourse (and cheese danish).

At noon Rose and I escaped to cover the lot. She thought she spotted Guy Newall and Ivy Duke practicing their smooching.

"I adored them in *The Garden of Resurrection*, Sport. They're married in real life, you know. I wonder who that is. Oh, this is fun."

I'd never seen her so animated. She was like a flapper who'd discovered a trapdoor to the universe.

216

I spied John Gilbert eating abalone in the canteen. I tried to sound excited about it, but it came out flat. I couldn't help wondering how he looked under all that lip foliage. Like the milkman's nephew, I'd lay odds.

That evening we went to a party at one of the Gishes' (I never did learn to tell them apart). Cohan loaned me tails. Rose rented a platinum lamé evening gown. We cadged Lasky's limo again, and his chauffeur. Can I remember every headliner who attended, or even seemed to?

Constance Talmadge (or was it Norma?), Richard Barthelmess (with his Guatemalan mistress), Nita Naldi, looking too intense to live, and a man named Walpole, rumored to be a viscount, but actually an ink-slinger, arriving cockeyed and addressing the assemblage plaintively.

"Where exactly does one go to peddle one's soul around here? Can any of you pretty people tell me? I've been all over town and haven't gotten a nibble. First chap puts five thousand dollars on the table gets the frigging thing, plus half my bummy and twenty pounds of whitefish."

Lon Chaney wandered by without his makeup, looking like a butcher who'd short-weight his own sister. Pearl White sat in a corner, wearing a camellia. Francis X. Bushman taught Rose to tango. I myself danced with a woman who claimed to be Gloria Swanson. I claimed to believe her.

Cohan spent an earnest hour quizzing William S. Hart on equestrianism. Just his eagerness made me saddle-sore. Around ten my old misgivings staged a comeback. Social evenings always raise my doubts. The commonest people seem threatening after sundown. And these weren't common people. Still, I'm sure the entire evening went just splendidly. Someday it may even feel that way.

I'd thought of launching my new life at that party, impressing the right people, or at least identifying them. But

217

the second I walked in I knew I wouldn't.

Dorothy Gish kissed me good night (or was it Lillian?), as did, I think, Ramon Novarro. Lasky's chauffeur turned up missing, so Cohan ferried us home. We made rude conjectures on the company the whole way back, inventing randy lyrics to obscure Christmas carols. The gatekeeper found the limousine the next morning, submerged in the moat. The chauffeur sent us a cryptic telegram from Guadalajara, claiming he'd been abducted by Zapatistas. I misplaced Cohan's collar studs, and was secretly glad.

The next day I awoke determined to begin doing business, whatever that business might be. I began by reading through all the Los Angeles papers, looking for Series news. Once again I couldn't find any.

At two we went to lunch at the Beverly Breezes, out back, beneath the midget palms. Each diner seemed unreasonably young, improbably successful, inordinately assured. All appeared to be speaking simultaneously.

"This," said Cohan, "is the native West Coast art—the soft sell."

After cigars we trekked out to Mack Sennett's new lot, a meadow just beyond Santa Anita. Two dozen cops chased three dozen pastry chefs. The significance eluded me. Sennett shot the same scene over and over, with no detectable variation.

On the sixth take a young man with a pie-shaped face pulled up a stool beside me. He said his name was Zeke Parcival and that he was an assistant director on Sennett's second unit. He said he'd heard I was the famous gambler Sport Solomon, who'd swept in all that velvet during the Series. I neither confirmed nor denied these suppositions.

Would I consider investing some of my winnings in a movie, an "ace pic" to be called *"Play Ball!"*? (He said it exactly like that—*"Play Ball,* exclamation point.") It was to be based on the life of Abner Doubleday. Selznick was wild about the concept. Griffith was interested in directing. There might even be a part in it for a *real* gambler.

I told him to call me the next day, though I already knew my answer. His lack of élan had hooked me. He couldn't possibly be that bumptious and lack sincerity. That was how I must have struck Rothstein.

I know I should have checked him out with Cohan. But I was in the mood for a heedless plunge. Hadn't I come out west to work on my spontaneity?

That night we attended a premier, a new Rod La Rocque romance. Klieg lights and autograph terriers, La Rocque supporting more makeup than Rose. Mae Murray swept in, bordered by two dwarfs. The King of Tonga followed her. Sixteen chorus girls spelled out "Hi, Your Highness!" with cue cards.

In the lobby Rose drank several green drinks, then several pink ones, then danced the two-step with a Bulgarian composer, whose name I forget, except that it rhymed with goulash. We finally met Lasky. He and Cohan conversed warily, like rival tailors plotting each other's bankruptcy.

Rose and I drove to the beach at midnight and frolicked self-consciously in the breakers. Then we made tentative love in the tall grass above the tree line. A very romantic concept, but, like so many such, better contemplated than attempted, what with the goose flesh and the cockleburrs and so on. I couldn't give it my full attention, anyway. I was too busy thinking of my potential deal with Parcival.

We drove back at two, getting lost among the canyons. We

219

didn't arrive until four. The first hint of dawn was tinting the horizon. Cohan's lamp pierced his drapes, flooding the garden.

The next day I gave Zeke Parcival $10,000 in $100 bills. He'd peddled up from Westwood on his Schwinn. We sat on the marble terrace overlooking the trout ponds. The sound of goldfish surfacing punctuated our chat.

He wanted to outline the scenario for me. I demurred. I hate descriptions of movies, even those I'm financing. I told him I was indifferent to the details, that I was betting on him, that's what made me a gambler. He didn't argue, seemingly anxious for any deal. He said he'd begin shooting in Stockton in February. I said, "Give me a call, I'll drop by." I tried to sound casual about it. He didn't mention the gambler's role again.

The longer we talked, the more excited I became. He remained scrupulously aloof, put the money in a battered hardtack tin, securing it to his pants leg with leather thongs. This struck me as eccentric, even for Hollywood.

He peddled down the endless driveway to the road. I sat on the porch, alone, watching the sun set over the city. Rose joined me. We whiled away the hour before dinner playing dominoes. For a few moments she seemed like the girl I'd once believed her to be. Then it was time to go.

The next day we were invited, Cohan, Lasky, Rose, and myself, to Douglas Fairbanks's for late brunch and tennis. I almost believed I belonged in such places by then, might even have tried to strike up another movie deal.

We arrived at noon. Spirited doubles were just beginning. Mary Pickford and Bill Tilden versus Fairbanks and Charles Chaplin, the farceur. Fairbanks was deeply tanned, as aggressively vital as his legend. Chaplin was small, earnest, with a stubborn swatch of unruly ginger hair. He played with graceful, surprisingly uncomic attentiveness. Tilden remained stylishly remote, only his strokes belying his reticence. Pickford was tiny, chatty, ebullient, clearly anxious to escape the solemn contest. She collared Rose as soon as we arrived and headed out on a lengthy tour of the grounds.

Cohan replaced her on the court. A new set began. We would rotate like this, one set each. Lasky and I settled into lawn chairs and were served piña coladas by a tiny, dainty Negro, whose features looked hand-tooled from onyx.

"Five thousand says the lens louses take it," Lasky said, so casually I thought I might have misheard him. But no, he was proposing such a wager. Was this another aspect of his garish hospitality, or just his odd way of dismissing any sum under five figures?

"Make it ten thousand and you're on," I said combatively. If I was to be patronized, it wouldn't be on the cheap.

Tilden was the world's premier player, Cohan one of Manhattan's deftest amateurs. Even if Fairbanks was twice Cohan's match (which he wasn't), Chaplin would have to be one-quarter Tilden's (which he couldn't be) to hang me out. It was a lock.

Cohan served first, running through his paces at love. My blood pumped in rhythm to his strokes. This was how I'd imagined it out here, lazing in the sun, soaking up the elegance, cashing spontaneous bets with men of exotic significance.

"I noticed Zeke Parcival poking around the grounds the other day," Lasky said.

Was it his tone, or Parcival's name, that stiffened my neck? I felt as if a strange tongue had just been rammed into my ear.

"Yes, we met on Sennett's lot a few days ago," I said hopefully.

Out on the court the teams were changing ends.

"Queer bird, Zeke. Used to do a little yardwork for me, nice touch with the peat moss. Bit of a charlatan, though, I'm afraid. Likes to let on he's a producer. Doesn't know a pentagraph from his bunghole, of course, but he can locate any exit with found money. Not that anybody's ever been dumb enough to give him any. Hope he wasn't pestering you."

"Not at all," I answered flatly, struggling to swallow. "Actually, peat moss was the very soul of our discourse."

Lasky rambled on for several more minutes, dissecting Parcival's character. I heard little of it. My brain had simply seized. By the time it thawed, Tilden and Cohan were three games down. They lost 6–4. I just sat there, incredulous, yet unsurprised. It seemed the logical extension of all the cruel facts I'd been hearing.

"I'll take your marker," Lasky said, reaching for his racket.

Cohan slumped down next to me, barely perspiring.

"You might be the only schmuck in California," I told him icily, "who could lose at doubles with Tilden as your partner."

I hoped my rebuke sounded more lighthearted than it was.

"Are you kidding?" Cohan asked, reaching for a Bushmills. "Tilden tanked it. He never beats a pretty boy socially. He's got the hots for Fairbanks, for lemons' sake. Everybody in this hemisphere knows that."

Some vague sense of Lasky's clip must have dawned on him then, for he leaned forward and gazed straight into my eyes. He didn't ask me to acknowledge it, though, sparing me at least that level of embarrassment.

I eventually got my chance on the court, as soon as I trusted myself to stand. Cohan and I got meat-axed. Apparently Big Bill wasn't that taken with my charms.

By then, of course, the whole exercise seemed academic. Lasky gave me no chance to get even. I never requested one. He was the sort who only bets with local knowledge.

I was surprised by how well I still covered the court, and by the extent to which this vestige consoled me. I only wished Rose was there to witness it.

Long before she returned I'd discounted this latest setback, two setbacks actually, ten grand to Parcival, a matching sum to Lasky. I wrote both off as preliminary expenses. I might have asked how much more seed money I'd be requiring, but apparently I was having too much fun to care.

The next day Lasky spoke to me for the final time.

I was counting big bills into his palm in his conservatory. Japanese beetles hovered over every frond. Nasturtium funnels swayed gently in the breeze. There was a clear sense of some season in the California air, though it was difficult to tell exactly which.

"Parcival's a fagella also," Lasky informed me, apropos of nothing. "Look at the fancy handle he gives himself, and how neat he keeps that silly little mustache."

He paused, not for a response, but to allow a fresh thought to fall into place.

"I hope you're enjoying your visit to my estate, Mr. Sullivan, and that you'll feel free to stay on as long as conceivable."

I assured him that I was, and that I would. But in truth the setting had lost much of its appeal for me. I'd thought I'd enjoy not hearing about the Series, then the first eel who mentioned it had had me on toast.

That night I began studying an enormous atlas in Lasky's library. It suddenly struck me how many places I'd never visited.

6

If I'm unaware something is happening, I tend to believe it isn't. Yet offstage intrigue was all the rage that autumn.

In Boston, Bill Burns was nursing second thoughts, not about canarying, but about how to do it anonymously.

In Georgia, Joe Jackson was awaiting Comiskey's call. Joe wasn't having second thoughts, though. He was still busy sorting out his first.

In Key West, Comiskey and Austrian were trawling for tarpon. They'd done all they could.

And in New York, Rothstein was buying up apartment buildings. He, too, was treating the Series as a turning point.

Chicago's sportswriters knew they couldn't expose the fix. It wouldn't be good for business. They assumed the fixers would take care of it for them.

"It's as inevitable as a punch-up at a dago wedding," Lardner believed. "Braggers will brag, gripers will gripe, soon stoolies will be taking numbers to spill their guts."

Only Hugh Fullerton yearned to put a flame to the fuse. This was Pulitzer material.

Fullerton was a cheerful night-court type with a purposefully disheveled exterior. He knew where all the bodies were buried though, and that his bosses preferred any order to chaos.

"I only *write* for the dreary things," he told inquisitors. "I rarely read them. They sell soap. You wrap fish in them. Beyond that, I don't take them all that seriously."

Hugh took baseball very seriously, though. He'd been covering it in Chicago for years, in the pages of the *Herald and Examiner*. To him it represented everything America was supposed to be, but wasn't. He resented the way it had begun to be manipulated. The Series had been the last straw. What bothered him most was the blatancy of it all, the assumption that moneyed interests could conspire to keep it quiet.

He knew they could, of course. Unless he did something to stop them.

So two days after Comiskey's bluff appeared in the *Tribune*, Hugh locked himself in a *Herald and Examiner* storage closet to bat out a twelve-take indictment, naming names, speculating on motives. When he finished he skipped downstairs to the city room and dropped it on the sports editor's desk. Then he went home and took a long soak in sulphanaphthol.

Three days later, the sports editor, a deracinated Yankee who incorrectly believed himself executive material, summoned Fullerton to his carrel. Hugh's onionskins sat on his desk, unedited. Without looking up, the editor motioned him to remove them.

"We can't use this" was all he ever said.

Fullerton retrieved them, then headed back upstairs, free now to do what he'd intended to do all along.

I had no idea this exposé had been muffled. (It was months before I even learned one existed.) If I had it wouldn't have comforted me anyway. It had been written. Bad news always works its way forward. Publication is just the lettering on the tombstone.

The day after I squared Lasky's bet, I drove up the coast to check on Gandil. I wasn't looking forward to seeing Chick again. He'd always made me jittery. Just thinking about him now makes my palms sweat.

The sun pointed me north to Calistoga, the ocean a constant presence to my left. Undulant fields ran to implausibly sudden cliffs, surrendering to rolling whitecaps at every chance. I encountered few cars, and no pedestrians. In California people are either rehearsing or at the beach by mid-morning.

Calistoga was the precise jerkwater I'd imagined it, all wooden shacks and tar-papered abjectness. It looked like six blocks of Indianapolis dropped in the middle of Valhalla.

At Spud's Sunoco I received grudging directions to Chick's. His fame apparently cut several ways even here.

The house itself was a social climber's fantasy, a rabbit warren being refurbished to house a Hapsburg. Workmen scurried along its mansards, turning asphalt into slate. Wrought-iron accents rose at every cornice. Two excavations dominated the front yard. Twin swimming pools perhaps? Or matching mausoleums?

I squatted in my benzene buggy, sweating, agog. Gandil himself wasn't present. Only the new Buick in his driveway confirmed his tenancy. "Chick G." was stenciled phosphorescently to its grillework.

I'd seen more than enough in five seconds. I spun right around and sped back to Los Angeles, reaching its outskirts just as the sun kissed the ocean. I knew it would take forever to forget what I'd seen that day, the menacing evidence of Chick's indiscretion. I also knew I'd *better* forget it. My only alternative was to do something about it. And I couldn't.

7

Cohan never told me why he introduced me to Warren Harding. I suspect it was to make up for introducing me to Jesse Lasky.

Our California sojourn was clearly winding down. Like a fading passion, it was persisting solely on inertia. It lacked only the final straw.

To speed things along I raised Harding's name one morning. The *Times* had said he'd be gracing town that weekend. Cohan's response materialized forty-eight hours later.

"Skip down to Gutfarb's with me for a pig's whistle, Sport. I'd like to introduce you to your country's next potentate."

It was a listless Sunday, edging up on noon. Rose and I had sought refuge in the refectory, fleeing the constant California sun, and that moribund feeling vacation weekends can inspire. Cohan had burst in on us unannounced, freshly scrubbed, oppressively cheerful, the ingenue who'll catch diphtheria between the acts.

"You mean Keaton, George? Or that hoof-and-mouther Jolson? Or has Metro arranged for Zukor's nephew to take the palm?"

He smiled reflexively, without conviction. Only he was allowed to make real jokes in his presence. He seemed wistful about something, though, having surely sensed my disillusion with the area, and calculated it against his remaining chances to show off.

"I mean Harding, Sport. The money boys have lured him out to Malibu. We'd better get there before they've divvied up the corpse."

On the drive out, Cohan was his full unbridled self, turning the air blue with upbeat speculation. He had enough enthusiasm for both of us, which was lucky. Rose stayed home. She said Republicans bound her bowels tighter than Gruyère.

Gutfarb's house was a model of overstatement, not in bad taste precisely, just in that oppressive good taste a touch of bad taste might have mitigated. Gutfarb was a mysterious figure around Hollywood, a squat, dour Litvak with an engagingly skewered toupee. He held no title that anyone was aware of; he was just important.

"Out here," Cohan informed me as we fled the city, "a producer is anyone with a phone and a bottle of celery tonic."

Manny knew people, is what it amounted to. So it was thought advisable to know Manny.

The bash was in full swing when we arrived. Half-breed maids circulated "medallions" of something modish. Unemployed actors dispensed seltzer and emoted. We made our sly way down the clay path to the pool.

Many faces looked familiar, others seemed like they should have. All exuded money, but just shopping, not looking to be bought.

The object of their acquisitiveness stood meekly by the diving board, *at* the party, not *in* it. He was a midwesterner, a bureaucrat, a Gentile. These were coast-dwellers, movie people, Jews.

"He looks like a cossack," I heard one tiny mogul mutter.

"Not a cossack, Lou," his companion shot back instantly, "the guy who *sends* the cossacks."

Whatever their differences, Harding and his suitors shared two attributes. Both had undue influence, and wanted more.

Gutfarb propelled us urgently toward the great man, who was standing beside his campaign manager, Harry Daugherty. Daugherty was believed to be the brains behind Harding, or such brains as there were. Later he would have himself appointed Attorney General.

Harding seemed relieved to see us. Most of the high rollers had glommed his hand, flashed him a smile, then left him hanging. They'd fulfilled their minimum ambition, pressed the flesh of a potential head of state. Cohan emulated them now, convinced he could lunch out at Lindy's on it for weeks. I longed to do likewise, but didn't. A morbid fascination with Harding's banality held me fast.

"That boy Cohen is one fine entertainer, yessiree," he bellowed at me now, seemingly eager to talk to anyone.

"It's Cohan, I believe, Senator, two syllables, long a."

I rarely correct mispronunciations, and never pedantically. But Harding's tone made me eager to deflate him.

"Co-han then," he drawled, taking my barb constructively. "I never miss a single one of his serials, do I, Harry? He can quick-draw with the best of them. This is a treat for a country boy like me, meeting all you movie people. Except I haven't met as many actors as I'd expected, or actresses, either, getting straighter to my point. I was hoping to meet that Po-lo Negri woman in my wanderings, though I expect her Eye-tye boyfriends keep her busy."

I turned my eye from the wink that surely followed.

"Are you an actor, Mr. . . . ?"

"No, actually, I'm not, Senator Harding, I'm in finance."

"Are you now? And what did you say your name was again?"

"Sullivan. Joseph Sullivan."

"Well, thank God, Sullivan, I thought I'd see bees pee out here before I met another non-Israelite."

"Cohan isn't Jewish, Senator."

"He isn't?"

"No, he's Irish."

"Oh."

"Irish Catholic."

He stopped talking then, and also breathing, struggling to fix us Romans in his hierarchy. After a few moments he turned back to Daugherty, as if satisfied.

"You know, Sullivan," Daugherty broke in suddenly, sounding anxious to put all this small talk to bed, "this professor in the White House at present is trying to feed our country to the foreigners. As a finance man I'm sure you've caught that wind. The Senator would like to put a stop to him. I'm sure you would too. The Senator has met many fine people at this gathering who feel likewise. Many have made generous contributions to his campaign. The smallest we've received so far has been two thousand dollars."

I've met a fair number of pigeon-pluckers in my travels. So I'm used to feeling strange fingers on my wallet. They'd generally sought much humbler sums, though, and always with more roundabout cons. This Daugherty character was a revelation. Beneath his jaunty Presbyterian heartiness lurked a Hell's Gate bait-and-switch man.

"One thing's for sure, though, Mr. Sullivan, when the Senator does take his place on Pennsylvania Avenue there'll be no more talk of legislating sports wagering. Or of investigating unproven fix allegations, either."

Did a smile jog his jaw at this hint, or was he just having

trouble digesting his blintz? The idea that he might actually have a sense of humor hadn't occurred to me.

"The Senator's been thinking of forming a wagering commission too, Mr. Sullivan. Might that be something you'd be interested in serving on?"

Coercion supposedly rarefies at higher levels. You couldn't tell by me. Daugherty could have stripped the corpse while comforting the widow. He was the cudgel incarnate.

My first instinct was to laugh right in his face. Instead I found myself reaching for my checkbook. Hadn't the other big cheeses anted up? Didn't substantial influence carry a substantial price tag?

"Will three thousand be enough, Mr. . . . ?"

"Daugherty."

"Mr. Daugherty?"

"It's a start, and a winsome one at that. Make it out to Warren Gamaliel Harding. The Senator will endorse it over to his campaign committee later."

Before I could recap my pen a teeny specter stole up beside me. He might easily have been lurking beneath a chafing dish. He whisked the check from my fingers and fled the scene.

"Thank you, Randolph," Daugherty barked at his compact memory. "And make a note that Mr. Sullivan is interested in the wagering post."

Harding just stood there throughout this exchange, beaming into the middle distance. Now he and Daugherty began moving back toward the house. Two fresh limousines were churning up the driveway. I didn't take their abrupt exit personally, of course, having already factored in the attention span of statesmen.

"Orange juice and soda, my dear," I instructed a ravish-

ing waiter, who was holding his head in perpetual left profile. "And don't spare the citrus, or the sincerity. It's for the
Republic."

Then I picked up some goobers and a radish curl and
ambled poolward to keep my fellow king-makers company.

That night I dreamed Harding appointed me Secretary of
Agriculture. I can't imagine a more repulsive job in real life,
yet I seemed to enjoy it while asleep. Everybody had to do
exactly as I told him, and I had my own masseuse.

I never heard from either Harding or Daugherty again, of
course, or from any of their henchmen. Not that it mattered.
By the time they were in any position to make good on their
offer, I was in no position to do anything about it myself.

I awoke the next morning craving solitude. Social occasions always deplete me. Nothing I say at them sounds like
anything I want to say.

Rose's leg lay flat against my thigh, its warmth relieving
my distress, at least in part.

I slipped quietly from the bed to avoid waking her,
dressed quickly, tiptoed down the marble staircase. The
house was still, cool, strangely unresonant. I walked straight
through the front door, down the driveway to the road.

It was just past dawn, a time I usually avoid on principal.
But today its starkness steadied my nerves. I walked a great
distance, haphazardly, in a new direction, embankment dew
curling the cuffs of my corduroys. It felt enlivening to be
alone, like the old times, before the fix.

I walked without pausing until I reached a tree-lined hill.
A small group of boys was playing ball there, in December,
at dawn. There was nobody else around, no buildings, no
cars, just several boys hitting a ball and catching it.

I watched them for twenty minutes, sitting beneath an aspen, pulling cornsilk through my teeth. It aroused too many emotions in me to separate: love of the game's simplicity, grief that such directness was now lost to me, and, of course, intransigence. I knew I'd gone too far to retreat a single inch.

I turned to touch my money, to recount it, but I couldn't. It wasn't there.

After a while I got up and walked back to the house. It wasn't as late as I'd imagined. Everybody was still asleep. I made a pot of mocha and sat out on the portico, drinking cup after cup, wishing somebody, almost anybody, would wake up.

That afternoon Rose proposed her own political excursion, to Santa Monica, to hear John Reed flog the lefties. She was trying to make some sort of league with me I knew, and at the same time tweak my nose. Reed was a Harding for swashbucklers.

I gave in easily, always anxious for the cheap compromise. Besides, I owed her one. You have to let them decide something every once in a while.

On our drive down we talked around the usual issues.

"Cohan's never been married, has he, Sport?"

"I wonder."

"I can see why you're so friendly."

"Can you?"

"You're so alike in so many ways."

"Are we?"

"Mexico's his most ideal spot, he told me."

"Is it?"

"Do you think you're richer than him?"

"I wonder."

The Bolshies had appropriated a bandbox for their rave-up. We arrived just as Reed took the stage. The setting sun cast an appropriate glow behind him.

His message neatly paralleled Harding's. Stripped of its bushwah, it promised revenge, followed by power. His partisans weren't the downtrodden I'd expected though, but younger versions of Harding's plush contributors. They could easily have been their children.

Only a few memories survive the evening's rhetoric: a tramp band butchering various international anthems; tense bodies swaying raggedly to the strains; glazed eyes gleaming longingly from every corner; a new moon rising slowly beyond the banyans.

Their dogma clearly had the power to change everything, I could see. Though I doubted they'd have the patience to implement it. Even I was moved. I, who never make common cause with any faith. I was caught up in the improbability of it all, the weepy notion of casting off our shackles, even those of us with no shackles to cast off.

I dropped ten dollars into Reed's soiled panama.

"Bless you, comrade," he mumbled, gazing into my pupils. "You'll be remembered when we put the fence-sitters to the wall."

I doubted it, but appreciated the sentiment.

Rose wanted to join the torchlight parade beachward. But I'd had enough bogus brotherhood for one evening. So I broke from the crowd and headed back to the car, like a delinquent fleeing a distant relative's wedding.

Rose insisted on taking the wheel on the way back, driving at great speed, poking her head out the window periodically, for the rush of it. If we'd had a convertible she'd have been standing on the throttle. Later, in bed, she mounted me with equal fervor. I was abashed, but did my best. I didn't

234

dream of Reed, leaving that to her. I don't believe I dreamed of anything actually. Ten bucks doesn't buy that many reveries.

I bolted straight awake at 3:00 A.M. Rose wasn't beside me. The light was on again in Cohan's room. I thought I saw shadows flashing past it, but that was probably just the dream I didn't have.

The next morning I lay alone in the gloom, trying to figure out what had gone wrong in California.

I began, as usual, with a cash-up.

I'd dropped thirty grand in just over a month, having relaxed too much to make up for never relaxing. I'd probably overadapted to the climate as well, forcing my wishes on too hospitable an environment.

When I sauntered into the refectory at ten-thirty it was to pronounce our West Coast sojourn officially finished. Neither Cohan nor Lasky seemed surprised. Rose betrayed no emotion whatsoever. I seemed to be the only one who really cared. Still, it was time. The flawless weather had begun to disorient me. Cozy visions of Manhattan Christmases beckoned me east. I could *seek* warmth there, not be hounded relentlessly by it.

Nobody asked me where I intended to go. I told them anyway.

"I'm heading back east," I announced in singsong, "to old New York, to do all those things I should have done ages ago."

I hoped my bluntness masked my disappointment, or at least suggested that I had some idea what any of those things might be.

235

8

IS BASEBALL BEING RUN FOR GAMBLERS?
by Hugh Fullerton

> Professional baseball has reached a crisis. Charges that ball-
> players are bribed and games sold out are made without
> refutation. The recent World Series was fraught with such
> rumors. Yet the men who run baseball do nothing about it.
> They keep silent, hoping it will all blow over. The time has
> come for open talk. . . .

We were four days back in Manhattan, Rose and I, when a
muted version of Fullerton's charges ran in the *New York
World.* He'd had to come east himself to get anything into
print. We'd ensconced ourselves in a suite at the Ansonia,
the hotel where Rothstein had watched the Series. I passed
my afternoons porthole-browsing on Fifth Avenue, or playing Mah-jongg and cribbage by the fire. It was my idea of
consummate contentment, contemplating change without actually having to make it.

Fullerton's story refocused my attention. It wasn't much.
But it meant the possibility of exposure still existed.

The morning it ran I experienced its first effect. I saw
Abe Attell walk into the foyer of Burlingame's. It couldn't
have been anyone but Abe. Few men that short were that
modish.

I trailed him through Handkerchiefs into Hosiery, then
across that minefield of intimacy known as Foundations. I
finally lost him in Cosmetics, among the mirrors. Only then
did I realize it couldn't have been Abe. Abe had hair.

236

The next day I put my vacillation in cold storage, committing myself to at least the idea of containment. I hired a detective.

I've always been a bit on the furtive side, a listener at transoms, a steamer of mail. Secrets empower me—having mine, discovering others'. Still, I'd never required soft-shoe help before, had no idea how to acquire it. In the spirit of fresh beginnings, I dialed uptown.

"Excelsior Detective."

"I want to hire . . ."

"Come on over."

"When?"

"Now."

"Who . . . ?"

"Dwayne."

Dwayne?

Could his curtness be construed as efficiency? Or his monicker as a tongue-in-cheek alias? When I reached 1703 Broadway I decided that they couldn't. Nor could Dwayne's obesity be translated as worldliness, or his cheap suit as the mark of a focused mind. All Dwayne's shortcomings were just shortcomings. Plus he babbled.

"How may we be of service to you, Mr. Sullivan?"

"I'm interested in having a particular individual followed, a number of individuals, actually."

"Fine, very fine indeed. You came to absolutely the correct place then, Mr. Sullivan. Surveillance is our primary specialty here at Excelsior, tailing, observation, playing the shadow without a source. We utilize the very shrewdest modern techniques at it too, employ the latest doodads to sniff out the mischief. I wouldn't have it any other way. Ask anybody in the field, anybody that knows his apples, that is. They'll put our name right at the top. Why, I remember one time in 1914, or was it '15? Let me think, '14. No '15. No '14. It was just after I passed that kidney stone, I remember that much. So '15 then, the early part, February, or was it March? Well anyway, we got a midnight call from a society stiff on Riverside, wanted us to gumfoot a burrhead been planting his sister. Imagine if you will . . ."

I was mesmerized by his monologue. Might he eventually recount every experience he'd ever had? To avoid finding out, I asked for his credentials, which he couched in two interminable anecdotes, pointless, except as blatant self-promotion. He was sliding smoothly into a third when I jerked him back my way.

"The men I want followed are baseball players, Dwayne, and individuals of that stripe."

"Baseball, isn't that just something. A grand game. And talk about coincidences. My brother Leo was a crackerjack horsehider at Fairleigh Dickinson. Rarely misses a Giants game, Leo. Of course, he's on the road a good bit in this racket. Our agency thinks nothing of . . ."

And there was Dwayne's method in its essence: plucking extraneous threads from my instruction, then weaving equally irrelevant monologues from them. He seemed to need to extemporize to keep breathing. It promised to be a very long morning indeed, unless I got my talent for brusqueness back in gear.

"The first person I'd like you to tail is Charles Comiskey."

"Comiskey, the noted sausage magnate. The meat business is another of our specialties, Mr. Sullivan. One time the renowned Lithuanian belly broker—"

"Not sausages, Dwayne, baseball. The White Sox, from Chicago. Comiskey owns them."

"Of course he does, why certainly, fine and dandy, the

White Sox, the owner. Going straight to the top is always the best strategy, Mr. Sullivan. A treasured client of ours, the proprietor of a garter facility in Sheepshead Bay . . ."

He was incorrigible. My interruptions grew increasingly more brutal, though nothing I said seemed to affect his feelings particularly. He apparently didn't have any.

"There are nine guys I'd like to have tailed."

"No problem, we—"

"Six ballplayers, two gamblers, plus Comiskey."

"Ah yes, gamblers. I once—"

"One week apiece. Learn everything they do, where they go, who they see, no matter what."

"Thoroughness, an Excelsior hallmark, clients often find . . ."

To caulk his tongue I read him my preferred list: each fixer (except Gandil), Attell, Burns, and Comiskey. I'd decided to keep Rothstein to myself.

We agreed on his fee, almost as an afterthought. Then he showed me to the door, his closing line as characteristic as his opening.

"You'll never regret choosing Excelsior, Mr. Sullivan. It's an old Latin word, the root of which . . ."

Why, you ask, did I make this monkey my Pinkerton?

Because I needed to know, but was afraid to.

I spent the rest of the afternoon locked in my bathroom, revising my hairstyle, making cosmetic changes in lieu of real changes. The result was a quasi boy's school bob with Marie Dresslerish overtones.

Rose didn't notice, at least not out loud. She'd recently begun emulating my enigmaticism. I didn't bite. I knew too much about silence to be fooled.

During the night I slept the wrong way on my head, re-

239

verting my locks to their usual lank insouciance. I left them that way.

The real reason I hadn't seen Attell was that Abe was still busy hot-timing it in Havana.

He'd been intending to leave for weeks, theoretically. But there always seemed to be new sambas to be sambaed, fresh doxies to be shagged, lush dreams of extended glory to be slumbered through. The soft climate cradled Abe's inertia in its palm.

It also primed his ego. Attell was still a hero in the tropics, where the concept "former" champion went unrecognized. Days passed so languidly there, in fact, that no one ever seemed a "former" anything.

"They won't be calling me the Bankroll's Mascot on Broadway anymore," Abe reasoned tersely. "I wish I was there to pass the boys some crow."

The New York papers took a week to reach Havana in those days. It wasn't until December 19 that Fullerton's charges caught up with the Little Champ. So formidable was his hangover that morning, however, that he could barely tell the comics from the obituaries. He couldn't even place the snoring señorita beside him. Yet Fullerton's innuendos quickly pierced his bottle-ache. He'd have to head right home, if he could only find his pants.

At eight that evening he wrangled the last cabin on the S.S. *Mariposa.* Five days later it slid silently through the Narrows, depositing the Little Hebrew on 57th Street. It was Christmas Eve.

Abe didn't wait for his luggage, but flagged a cab to Rothstein's penthouse. He'd spent the entire passage rehearsing his alibi, convincing himself the Bankroll would buy it. Why, then, were his hands quivering so violently?

For his part, Rothstein *was* willing to forgive. It was the forgetting part he wasn't so crazy for. He'd always liked Abe, liked him still; and various uses for the Little Champ still existed. Rothstein had kept close tabs on Abe in Havana. The cab driver who plucked him from the dock was a trusted employee.

Rothstein had passed the afternoon huddling with the new police commissioner. At five he'd instructed his chef to begin filleting the shad. He hadn't settled on a tone to take with Attell. He needed to crank Abe, not to crack him. Shortly after six the ideal approach occurred to him. When Abe walked sheepishly through the vestibule, leaking slush from his silly planter's hat, Rothstein extended both arms in rhetorical welcome.

"Abe, Abe, my old friend, it's so good to see you again. Where have you been keeping yourself, you and that lovely tan of yours?"

"I just got back from Havana, Arnold. I—"

"Havana! One of my top favorite capitals. The green surf beating urgently against the Presidio, the nights full of swaying palms and tropical impulse. I don't get down there nearly as often as I'd like anymore, Abe. Jesus, I envy your mobility. Did you have any luck at the dice cribs?"

"I didn't do that much gambling, Arnold, I—"

"Smart boy, reluctant to plow your winnings back to the house. I don't blame you, you sly momzer, you. I heard how well you did with the Series. What a master stroke. I couldn't have organized it any better myself."

"Arnold, I—"

"Of course, I cashed in a bit on the event myself. I have you to thank for that. You orchestrated everything so beautifully. I was able to benefit from your foresight long-distance. What's your pleasure, Abe?"

"Scotch and water, Arnold, please."

"Of course, has it ever been anything but? And what do you hear from Carl Zork and the Levi brothers in the meantime?"

"To be truthful, Arnold, I haven't seen them since October. I—"

"Shrewd, Abe, shrewd. Those Izzies were never in your bracket. Cigar? These beauties were ten more years in Havana than even you, Abe. Tell me, what are your plans now that you're back in the States?"

"Well, Arnold. I had sort of hoped that you and I—"

"You bet, you and I, I and you, we two. Wherever your wandering heart may lead you, Abe, I only hope I'll be included on the agenda. I can't tell you how much I've missed you, Abe. There aren't many around like you. Never have been, never will be again, either."

"Arnold, I—"

"In fact I've got a new project of my own in the works, Abe. Something I began diddling around with just before you left. I'd like to tell you about it over dinner if I could. Is shad still a favorite? I know how you always doted on André's interpretation, the flesh augmented by fledgling asparagus tips, baked murphies peeking out from their little jackets. . . ."

And so it went, Rothstein easing Attell's anxiety, making his excuses for him, labeling his betrayal diligence. By the time they'd negotiated the gazpacho Attell was convinced Rothstein's admiration was genuine. He'd even begun resenting its limitations.

Throughout dinner the lathering continued, Rothstein outlining his plans for a new speakeasy, soliciting Attell's advice. Attell was febrilely enthusiastic, and quick to suggest impractical embellishments. Rothstein listened atten-

242

tively, interrupting only for the occasional reinforcement.

"Marvelous, Abe. Christ, why didn't I think of that? Singing croupiers! I'll get the boys on it right away."

Attell couldn't get enough of it. Rothstein could almost smell his perfervidity rising. The courses multiplied, the plans expanded. Before the baked Alaska arrived Attell had forgotten he could die.

As they retired to the library, Rothstein excused himself to urinate. Attell stood warming himself by the fire, surveying the spotlit portraits of Rothstein's ancestors (dour Latvians brashly depicted as Puritan totems). The wide window on the far wall framed the black, roiling Hudson far below. Attell thought he saw the *Mariposa* swaying at its mooring. It seemed two lifetimes since he'd walked its pitted decks. The snow swirled in riotous circles through the fog banks.

"All this could be yours," he told himself, staring out at the city.

Was that Rothstein he felt creeping up behind him?

"All that could be yours, Abe," Rothstein whispered in his ear.

Was he echoing Attell's thought, or just anticipating it?

Too late, Attell realized they weren't alone, felt himself gripped, calf and wrist, as if by God. The window burst open, cold air rushed in like oblivion. In one motion Attell was propelled out into the night, and soundlessly gave himself over to it. The dark streets rushed up at him, then stopped. His neck snapped. His lips brushed the building's concrete crust. He was being suspended by his ankles, wrong side up, two hundred feet from the end of the world. Snowflakes invaded his nostrils, mixing with drippings from his recently discharged bowels. He thought he heard carolers harmonizing below, their trilling punctuated by Rothstein's droning monologue.

"Was the shad up to your expectations, Abe? I hope so. André takes such pride in it. And I in André. Here's a little anecdote for you, Abe, something for your files. A certain Jewboy used to caddy for the shkotzim, up in Bronxville. They treated him like shit, as you can imagine. 'Hey, Ikey, clean my mashie; hey, heebie, draw me a phosphate.' He took it, of course, for the tips. Like the moyl, eh, Abe?

"Anyway, this particular yiddle promised himself that when he grew up he'd never treat his caddy like that. Which he didn't. In fact, the first time he ever played golf, which was at Pompano Link and Racquet, incidentally, he treated the kid hauling his bag almost princely, like another human being. By the eighth hole the pissant thought he owned him. He was tossing clubs, razzing his swing, cutting farts. The poor bastard had to chase him off with a niblick."

Rothstein paused here, whether for effect or nostalgically, who could tell?

"I carried my own fucking bags the last ten holes, Abe."

One of Attell's handlers gasped at this, his grip on Abe's ankles weakening noticeably.

"All that could be yours, Abe, what you were looking at before, or this, what you're looking at now. It's up to you. I like you, Abe. We've had some good times. Everything I told you tonight is true. I'm going to do all those things, and then some. You can come along, Abe, but only for the ride. It's very warm in here, the chairs are soft, the fire high. I think it's quite cold out there, Abe. Am I wrong? Very windy, wet, quite unpleasant. You can't hurt me, Abe. If we were boxing you could. But we're not boxing. I can hurt you a couple of thousand ways, though. And I will. The next time you fuck with me, you little pork punisher, I'll put a bullet in your brain so fast you'll think you came that way. But what am I saying, Abe? Next time? First time. There was no other

244

time. Past is past. The future is ours. Am I right, Abe? Or am I right?"

Rothstein paused again, to emphasize his point. His thugs lowered Attell another notch. He tried to scream, but nothing came. A church bell tolled twelve times across 64th Street. It had become Christmas.

"Save yourself, Abe."

To which notion Attell assented enthusiastically, shaking his head hard enough to risk salvation. Only by the taste of his own tears did he realize he'd begun weeping. Then, just as abruptly as he'd exited it, he regained the room, in one intestine-wrenching yank. How firm the floor now felt beneath him, how wonderfully and permanently actual. He lay across it, heaving, drenched, as Rothstein's henchmen vanished into the walls. Rothstein himself stood by the fire, nursing a smile. After a moment he moved back toward Attell, arms outstretched, parodying concern.

"Abe old friend, outside? On such a night? You could catch your death from cold. Here, accept a hot towel, and some jodhpurs. The tailoring may not exactly thrill you, but you'll appreciate the dryness. Here's some cognac, too, for solace. When you're ready, let's resume our conversation."

Which they did, in newly intimate tones. Rothstein was again conciliation's soul. It was as if the intervening episode had never taken place. Attell didn't speak, though he was occasionally able to nod. He'd gotten the message. Being outside was one thing, being inside something else. The longer he was inside, the less being outside seemed advisable.

Just before he nodded off, seated upright before the pointed orange flames, he had a violent intuition that he'd been had. Rothstein couldn't have dropped him, gory and indelible, to the pavement. Rothstein rarely left traces, and never in his own territory.

By then, however, no discrepancy seemed that relevant. For with all his remaining strength, Attell had reembraced subservience. To be Rothstein's second now seemed more than sufficient to him. It seemed preferable.

The last sound Abe heard before he drifted off to sleep was the soothing voice of Rothstein's public self.

"Happy Chanukah, my dear Little Champ," it said paternally. "May all your dreams be either auspicious or abbreviated."

Then all was silence.

9

The holidays passed pleasantly. I had no family. Rose detested hers. We were grateful for each other's company, and formalized this gratitude with lots of presents.

I received two racing books, a ruffled dickey, and a florid painting of an improbable equatorial sunset. I already owned the books, the dickey itched, and the painting was hideous. These inadequacies didn't anger me, though; they embarrassed me, a shame Rose wisely chose to read as gratitude.

I gave her several diamond settings, a chinchilla wrapper, and a first edition of Keats. This last was more for the woman I wished her to be than for the woman she actually was. She took my yearning as flattery.

As she leafed unconvincingly through the book a $2,000 check fluttered poetically to her lap. I thought she'd vacate her skin acknowledging its appropriateness. Women like Rose feign indifference to money, but it's all they really care about.

246

We took Christmas dinner in the hotel dining room. Only two other tables were occupied. Midway through our goose, two brittle octogenarians shuffled tentatively through the holly arch, looking as frail as last year's wrapping paper. Only the warm sentiments of the season seemed to be keeping them alive. Naturally they sat down next to us. Our waiter circled the large room impatiently, as the nativity ice sculpture melted slowly into its basin.

Rose spent the next week returning her presents. I kept mine. Even bad love is love. When I asked her how she'd spent her two grand, she said she hadn't.

"I'm looking for something appropriately deluxe, Sport, something memorable."

Three days later, during one of my periodic frisks of her handbag, I learned she'd found it. It was a bank account, dated December 26, with an opening balance of $3,100. She'd raised the extra $1,100, I assumed, by hocking my presents. I'd paid $1,200 for the lot.

No further mention of the Series marred our holidays. More than usual, this calm unnerved me. Only the promise of a new decade offset the tension. I've always been a sucker for clean slates.

"You've got a Monday-morning mentality," Rose once informed me. She was right. I treasure symmetry, and while any shock seems to derail my resolve, that resolve seems endlessly renewable.

This particular New Year exuded promise. I'd been drifting since the Series I knew, trying on my new life for size. My next fresh start might just be my last.

I consumed far too much Dom Pérignon on New Year's Eve, though, rendering the decade's first twenty-four hours unusable. I wouldn't stoop to date my fresh start from the second, either. And besides, it wasn't a Monday.

On January 3 the new decade kicked off in earnest. Babe Ruth was sold by the Red Sox to the Yankees.

Two implications attended this transaction. It meant another Bostonian would be moving his campaign south, and that Harry Frazee was even broker than I'd imagined.

Frazee was the diminutive owner of the Red Sox, a backer of Broadway flops, a poacher of chorus girls. To fund his various diversions he often sold promising players to Colonel Rupert.

I'd met Harry several times over the years, and been progressively less impressed. He not only was, but actually seemed, like someone who *sold* things. His peddling of Ruth smacked of terminal self-cannibalization. Could there be something in this for me?

I called Harry at the Lambs Club the next morning for an appointment.

"Sure thing, Sport. I'm tossing a little soirée tonight in fact. You'll be the only other Beantowner in attendance. We'll show these Babylonian wide-mouths a cultivated thing or three."

He was aware, clearly, of my part in the Series. It seemed to elevate me in his judgment. I was no longer the punk mick he'd half-tolerated in Boston, but a fellow New Englander, a confrere.

Could there be something in me for him?

Two dozen finaglers filled Frazee's duplex that evening, polluting the air with Manhattan-style rapacity. I hardly got to talk to Harry, never mind grift him. I'm not sure who did.

The evening wasn't a total loss, however. I met a man who

248

raised marmosets for carnivals, and another who turned coffee grounds into lanolin. I also met T. Fortune Ryan, the noted stock diddler.

Ryan was a classic fox-and-hounds Hibernian, brisk and wry, a regular dazzler. While the other thieves pitched Frazee for loose change, Ryan and I huddled in a corner, swapping hyperboles. He seemed as fascinated by my trade as I was by Wall Street. Soon we only had ears for each other. He was convinced the stock market was about to redouble itself.

"Millions," he argued persuasively, "didn't perish in Europe for nothing."

This was exactly the inside noise I'd come to hear. The new year was already paying plush dividends. Ryan was Rothstein with a foreskin.

We made a dinner date for the following Monday. He suggested Saturday. I wouldn't hear of it.

> The charge that these fix rumors are from disgruntled gamblers isn't true. I heard them before a single game was played.
>
> —Hugh Fullerton, *New York World*
> January 7, 1920

Fullerton had waited three weeks to write a follow-up, marshaling his facts, checking the legalities. He closed with a chilling prescription:

> An independent investigator should be appointed.

I didn't see this black dispatch, thank the Lord. I was too busy researching Ryan. It's curious how many such flashes I missed that winter, considering how obsessed I'd grown with their appearance. Two days later, I missed still another.

Ray Schalk was interviewed by the *Cicero Daily Sentinel*

and bled vague hints of the fix to its reporter. The next morning this individual got a call.

"Owen Drib?"

"Speaking."

"Ray Schalk's got something he wants to tell you, Drib."

Schalk took the phone. He didn't hesitate, but sprang compliantly to his task.

"I played to the best of my ability during the Series. I feel every man on our club did likewise. There wasn't a single moment in all the games when we did not try. How anyone can say differently, if he saw the Series, is a mystery to me."

Proprietarily, the first voice retook the line.

"Got that, Owen?"

"But . . ."

"Put it in your next column, Drib, under 'Retractions,' or you'll be fox-trotting with our shysters straight through Judgment Day."

"But . . ."

There weren't going to be any buts about it, though, for Owen Drib was now talking to thin air.

10

Of all my huddles with the mighty that fatal winter, my confab with T. Fortune Ryan proved the drollest.

Ryan owned a limestone townhouse on East 87th Street, a potent metaphor for the remoteness of his thought. At eight sharp his butler led us into its drawing room, for Ryan had insisted I bundle Rose along.

"Women round off the race's rougher edges, I believe, Sullivan. I need to expose my own consort to wider society."

Even in the context of his aloofness this was a chilling remark. Who calls any woman "my consort," or demeans her as requiring renovation? And what "wider society" did Ryan think Rose represented, anyway? Rock-bottom society?

He let us stew among his etchings before joining us, then acted as if it had been *we* who'd kept *him* waiting. He wore a Savile Row three-piecer and calfskin brogues, his flesh and hair glowing in cheeky unison. He looked like God's half brother.

His "consort" was already pacing the dining room, brusquely ordering the placement of the trivets. She was a pale, thin individual with dramatically accented cheekbones, her plaited locks supporting a turquoise mantilla.

Today I'd consider such touches sadly studied, but that evening they seemed the soul of *dernier cri.* I remember thinking she was much younger than Ryan, though not as young as she'd have liked to be. Major components of her face seemed poised for a fall.

Ryan appeared in most particulars as remembered, gracious, witty, expansive. Still, his sums didn't quite equal their previous parts. He seemed more restrained, less eager to swap impertinences, as if he'd had second thoughts about sharing himself with me.

"Have you ever visited Brazil, Mr. Sullivan?" Dolly asked me (for Dolly, indeed, was our hostess's name).

"No, actually, I haven't."

"Dolly," Ryan cut in, "I don't think Mr. Sullivan cares to discuss South America."

The rich tend to grow reticent in their living rooms, I've noticed. Familiar surroundings seem to put them on their guard. This proved particularly true of Ryan that evening. Within minutes Dolly was calling all our tunes.

"I have. Visited Brazil, that is. Countless times. It's one of my absolute favorite lands. My last journey there was absolutely heavenly. Carnival in Rio was especially dithering. They kill pigs and hoist their noggins up on pikes. Such fêtes! But the last two weeks were rather a botheration. A rich landowner's son fell hopelessly in love with me and made my existence a cornucopia of inconvenience."

She didn't look Ryan's way as she spoke, rarely acknowledged him in any way, in fact, except by omission. Whenever he chided her, as he often did, she rambled on as if he wasn't even there. It was a practiced gesture. Soon she had all of us aping it, addressing each other as if no other soul were present.

"How much money do you think Fortune has, Mr. Sullivan? And isn't that an ideal name for Fortune, incidentally? Fortune? It can mean almost anything you want it to, can't it?"

By now I'd become the sole focus of her jabbering, though hardly a willing one. I assumed it had something to do with the seating.

"Dolly, please, I'm sure Mr. Sullivan doesn't . . ."

Ordinarily I resent domestic sparring. But Ryan's intervention held the promise of some relief. Dolly buzzed right through it, though, without a pause.

"Lots, plenty, a multitude. Enough to fill up this depressing tomb with currency. But he's not the only one with abundant resources around here, no indeed. My father has extensive holdings in the Transvaal, which he's been signing over to me in droves lately, ever since his heart last attacked him. He's nearing eighty, Daddy is. And I'm his only child."

"Is that so?"

"Yes, Mr. Sullivan, it is. And my mother has one of the less encouraging cancers."

252

I hardly knew how to greet this lurid news. All Dolly's conversation seemed impervious to response. I retreated to an interrogation of her meal ticket.

"Are there any particular stocks you're enthusiastic about now, Mr. Ryan, from an appreciation standpoint, that is?"

Ryan smiled, without answering, as if I'd just complimented him on the fragrance of his hair pomade.

"That's a lovely brooch you're wearing, my dear," he informed Rose. "It prompts memories of a piece my late mother treasured, a virgin tourmaline wreathed by dainty flecks of garnet."

Rose looked befuddled, but stayed calm, eager to prove she could deflect deflections with the best of them.

"I understand the new Ziegfeld show's enthralling," she finally gushed. "I met him in California, a short customer, but oh what etiquette!"

Our four-handed dialogue proceeded like this, no component intersecting, or achieving any point. It was only as we were leaving, in fact, that anything even remotely direct got said.

Ryan had hustled us to the cloakroom like a bouncer. He pressed a wrinkled card to my palm as Rose buttoned her raglan.

"A list of issues which will reward you as you deserve, Mr. Sullivan."

I felt my flesh flush expectantly at this gift. The long evening of evasive chatter had borne fruit.

"I'll call you when the baseball season opens, Mr. Ryan," I replied. "You can count on me for some dope of equal value."

Dolly interrupted to say goodbye. We didn't kiss, though her fingers lingered pointedly on my wrist. As my hand reached uncertainly for the door she risked a gesture that sent the blood straight to my privates. With premeditated nonchalance she reached up to her mantilla and loosened it, sending her hair cascading luxuriantly to the floor. A thrilling toss of her head arranged each strand. I longed to salute this most female of gestures by burying my face completely in its results.

"I've been thinking of having my tresses trimmed radically, Mr. Sullivan, in the current gypsy mode. Do you believe I should surrender to this impulse?"

"Oh no," I protested theatrically, as though she'd just suggested self-immolation. "Leave it precisely as it is," and here I paused coquettishly, "forever."

I was about to elaborate on this torrid advice when a familiar tug at my elbow cut me short. Moments later I found myself out on the sidewalk, drawing on my gloves, tightening my muffler. I wasn't aware of having moved either foot.

During the next week I took significant positions in all of Ryan's stocks, feeling audacious, yet oddly provident. I was applying proven strategies to fresh possibilities, launching my new life.

Only two of the twenty ever traded higher, and those not for long. I created my own small depression within the great paper prosperity swirling about me. Only when I read in the *Times* that Ryan had bad-mouthed Federal Can did a hint of what he'd done to me bubble forth.

Though I'd had a previous clue.

One dreary evening, late in January, as I sat studying the mounting evidence of my impoverishment, Rose asked me if I'd been "attracted to that Dolly person."

She'd never asked me about her before, or about any woman, actually. But even I know how low the fires of female jealousy can be banked. I translated "attracted to" to mean "contacted."

"Of course not, she's not my type. What makes you ask?"

"Something about her presentation, I suppose, her cinched waist, her gaudy hardware, or just the tough sell she was giving you on her resources."

"She was?"

"She was. Must you be oblivious to only the most obvious signals, Sport?"

"You don't have to worry—I'm not going anywhere."

"I'm not worried. I'm sure she foists herself on every stiff dick she meets. I bet Ryan's got some dandy ways of dealing with it."

She paused, as if savoring the possibilities, though in retrospect her silence seemed aimed directly at me.

"I was just wondering," she said.

Two weeks later I sold every stock Ryan had stuck me with, keeping only the Federal Can. When I finally sold that, deep into the next autumn, it brought exactly one shiny dime on my dollar.

11

One good thing about stock walloping, it leaves you precious little time for anything else. How many fix stories did I miss during my flutter?

The day it ended, Dwayne's first report hit my mailbox, sans stamps. Here are its findings, in their entirety:

Subject: C. Comiskey
Profession: Owner, Chicago White Sox

Age: 60

Background: Subject has spent entire life in baseball, signed
    by Dubuque at 19, player/manager St. Louis at 24, top
    salary, $8,000. Jumped National League to Players Asso-
    ciation 1880 (a player-run scheme). League folded 1881.
    Returned to St. Louis, helped form American League,
    with White Stockings as charter member.

Surveillance: At home all of January. One visitor, Alfred
    Austrian, January 11, 13, 14, 17, 21, 22, 25.

Summary: No interests except baseball; wealthy, reclusive,
    more eager to rise above associates than with them.

It wasn't much for my $600, though the precision of
Dwayne's prose did impress me, particularly the Players
Association part. It helped explain the depth of Comiskey's
contempt for his underlings.

I called Dwayne for further details.

"Excelsior Detective."

"Dwayne?"

"Speaking."

"Sport Sullivan here. I just got your report on Comiskey.
It's quite precise, and . . . intriguing. But it does seem a bit
short on the activities side."

"So's he."

"Yes, well, I can see that, but how about his office, what
happens there?"

"You didn't ask."

"I know, perhaps I should have. How about phone calls?
Did he get any phone calls?"

"You didn't request a tap."

"But this report doesn't tell me what he did."

"He didn't do anything."

He had me there. I knew what I needed to know. I needed

to know about the fix, who was talking, or intended to. But I couldn't tell Dwayne that. I couldn't tell anyone.

"Mr. Sullivan?"

"Yes."

"Did you see that story in yesterday's *Tribune?*"

"What story?"

"This story:

" 'Charles Riisberg, Chicago White Sox shortstop, announced today in San Francisco that he was retiring from baseball to open a restaurant. Riisberg expressed dissatisfaction with his major league salary. Chicago outfielder Joe Jackson earlier announced he had returned his contract unsigned, and would quit baseball unless his salary demands were met.' "

"Is that all?"

"That's it."

"Hmmm."

"Should I gumshoe these guys, Mr. Sullivan?"

"Yes, Dwayne, that's probably advisable."

"Both of them?"

"No, just Riisberg, just a week's worth."

"Okay, Mr. Sullivan."

"And Dwayne."

"Yes, Mr. Sullivan."

"Forget the biographical details from now on. For my purposes all these guys were born yesterday."

"Okay, Mr. Sullivan."

"And Dwayne."

"Yes, Mr. Sullivan."

"Stop calling me Mr. Sullivan, will you please? I keep thinking my father's listening in on the line."

"Sure, Sport."

"Thanks, Dwayne."

I perused the papers thoroughly the next week. One by one the other fixers returned their contracts. I had no idea what this meant, but it didn't seem promising. I hoped Dwayne's report on Riisberg would enlighten me.

Thus did another January spin seamlessly into another February. One-twelfth of the new year had already evaporated. Shin-deep slush clogged Manhattan's pitiless byways. Soft coughing echoed along our carpetless corridors. The sky became a solid sheet of gray until sunset, only darkness relieving the tenacity of the gloom.

I found I missed playing the stock market, despite my reverses. I missed its expansiveness, its grown-up feeling. Still, it wasn't the upgrade I'd been looking for. It was just paper passion, not street stuff.

The approaching baseball season had always brightened my past Februarys. But I couldn't imagine it brightening this one. I couldn't even imagine there being another season now, last year's having obliviated all successors. I was wrong about that, too. They were going to have another season, with or without me. The world took no more heed of my feelings now than it ever had.

On Valentine's Day, Babe Ruth's mitts dominated the tabloids, sweeping snow from home plate at Yankee Stadium. It was another sign that the return of spring was imminent.

I gave Rose a box of nougats to mark the holiday. She gave me nothing, claiming she'd let the day's significance slip her gaze. I claimed I almost had.

I withheld my second gift then, a gold locket pressed from the remains of previous sentiments. Ryan's tourmaline reference had inspired it. I'd paid $2,600 for this bauble, overspending in precise proportion to my ambivalence. I was hoping to buy an option on Rose's affection. I can't say her forgetfulness disappointed me, though. I hadn't bothered to have the gaudy thing inscribed.

12

If I was surprised at baseball's persistence, I was shocked at my bum luck's. It had leaped both coasts and decades, providing little for my dwindling bankroll but more shrinkage.

And how did I propose to buck this trend? By accentuating it, need you ask?

I began the evening of Valentine's Day, after a suspicion I'd muffled for months snuck under my guard.

"This is the good life you've always aspired to, Sport. This is all of it."

My entire life didn't flash before me then, just enough of it to prove I'd been flirting with exoticism, living by chance. If I intended to rise above my chronic station, I now knew, plotting would have to play some part in my plans.

It was on this insight that I anchored my miscalculation.

A casino.

In retrospect it seems the dizziest notion conceivable. But at that point it seemed God's absolute ideal. It involved gambling, after all, and subterfuge, seemed a chance to boost my nonexistent extroversion, while rousing and taming a city full of hardheads. After hours of poking it from every angle I detected no flaw. Rose, when consulted, pronounced it "ludicrous"—another plus.

The following morning the prospect still intoxicated me. So I called Salvatore Luciana to float it.

And that was my *real* mistake.

Luciana would soon become Luciano, Salvatore was even then proving himself "Lucky." He survived so many hits he seemed perpetually a beginner. But he was in full bloom even then. Rothstein already had him on the short list.

They shared several characteristics, those natty felons—silken willfullness, placid savagery, the assumption that every advantage would eventually turn their way. But their presentations were stark opposites. Where Rothstein behaved compensatorily, for example, Luciana was unaware compensation was necessary.

We met.

Among the more mixed blessings of that period was that every hood seemed suddenly to know me. Luciana said he'd be "honored" to buy me lunch. I suggested splitting it.

We met at Diamond's, on West 58th Street. He sat alone, at a rear table, eyeing the door, his black hair matted to his thought box, every feature looking recently stripped and buffed. Nothing about him encouraged small talk. I kept it short.

"It'll be a top-flight joint, Mr. Luciana, a regular throb palace. I'll super the gambling, you'll keep the peace. We'll split expenses. How's that sound?"

He was alleged to be something of a gambler himself, although I couldn't see it. All that scar tissue argued otherwise. No gambler courts violence that impertinently. Perhaps he was just Lucky to be alive.

"We might be interested. We'll have to think about it. Give us a week."

One Camel followed another, each clutched, like life itself, between his teeth. All his gestures were similarly flamboyant, the feisty touches of the novice punk ascendant. By then I was sure I'd made a mistake, was willing to eat my necktie to get out of it.

"We'll need a little jingle up front, though, to calm some consciences."

"How much?"

"Twenty thousand, for licenses, and goodwill. I'll put up half."

Whether it was fear, or to impress him, or simply because I had it, I pulled ten grand from my hip pocket, tossing it, and my casino hopes, his way.

"That's all I can manage just now, Mr. Luciana. I have other expenses."

He scooped it, as an adder might a field mouse, making an instant bulge of it in his silk suit's inside drawer.

"We'll get to work on it right away. We'll call you tomorrow."

He'd made the door, and turned the corner, before I could answer, his little legs churning, the rest of his body following, as though he had no bones.

I didn't expect to see my ten grand again, and in this, at least, I wouldn't be disappointed. Two apes at adjoining tables trailed him out. His *we,* I assumed.

All the next week I rationalized this fleecing as an investment, and as an investment in my serenity it proved invaluable. It helped me forget Fullerton's stories, for one thing, and the green lesson Ryan had so recently given me. At $10,000 I figured I'd gotten off pretty light. He could have asked for much more. I could have been carrying it.

I scouted casino locations all the rest of the week, priced furniture, passed a giddy evening designing period costumes for the doormen (Beefeater getups with little muskrat hats). But mostly I dreamed about the money I'd make, even

261

though I still had no idea how to spend the money I had.

Luciana didn't call the next morning, of course, or the next, or forever. I feigned indifference. What was his type to my type, after all?

It was three weeks before I admitted our meeting's consequences, another before I owned up to its lesson. Betting on sports was what I did best. Anything else seemed to squeeze the boodle from my bones.

I had one further misgiving, I'll admit. I felt Luciana disdained me.

When I finally did encounter him again, weeks later, on Amsterdam Avenue, he neither altered his path nor softened his expression. His blank stare neatly summarized his opinion of me; my evasion of it admitted that he was right.

13

Subject: Charles Riisberg.
Day One: Up, 7:47; breakfast, papers. To Gondolph's Butchers, 9:52; eye roast, bratwurst. To post office, 10:39; 2-cent stamps. To Wells Fargo Bank, 10:58; 45 minutes with L. Keck, Credit Expediter. To Continental Restaurant Supply, 11:47 . . .

There were seven entire days of this. How did Dwayne stand it? Riisberg was opening a hash house is what it amounted to, making the dreary preparations such dreary dreams are heir to.

I called Dwayne immediately to express my satisfaction, and to tell him to begin bloodhounding Cicotte.

The holdouts didn't faze Comiskey. He figured intimidation would quickly wilt their will. When he was ready to launch some he called Kid Gleason.

"Get Jackson," the Kid advised him without hesitating. "He's the dumbest, but the ablest. Nail him and the others' glands will follow."

The Kid didn't particularly like skunking on his boys, but was too proud of his insight not to share it.

Comiskey trusted Gleason's hunch implicitly. If anyone knew weakness, it was the Kid. And besides, his assessment was too harsh not to be accurate.

The next day Comiskey sent his wiliest negotiator, and his opaquest contract, to Savannah. Fillius was the negotiator's name; the contract was known as "the nut-crusher."

Fillius was a tall, skeletally thin southerner who rarely spoke, except to haggle, and seldom socialized, except to booze. He was an undertaker's son who'd drunk himself out of law school.

"He has the mortician's watery eye," Comiskey noted on first meeting him, "and the advocate's itchy palm. I have need of such a type. They're free of conscience."

Fillius arrived in Savannah on February 21, at 11:00 A.M., having begun sucking up the nose paint just before daybreak. All-day drinking no longer fazed him particularly, though, veteran funnel-mouth that he was. He was clear-eyed, level-headed, relatively hygienic. One comb and two garlic cloves would render him socially acceptable.

He flagged a taxi to Jackson's bungalow on McKee Street. Joe's wife was at the chiropodist, indulging her bunions. The big man himself was sitting beside the coal crib, whittling. Fillius skipped up the stairs and launched right into his spiel.

"Show him you like him," Gleason had advised. "Affec-

263

tion disarms Joe. Like myself, he is an orphan."

"Hiya, Joe. Junior Fillius here, from out Vidalia way, a lawyer by trade, a big fan of yours by inclination. I've done a lot of work for different ballplayers around these parts. So when I heard about your problems with the White Sox, I said to myself, 'Junior,' I said, 'here's your chance to give the great Joe Jackson a little stand-behind. You may never get another in this lifetime.' Pardon my presumptuousness, Joe, but that's a heck of a deal of woodwork you've got going. A beaver, ain't it?"

Jackson looked momentarily befuddled. Each of Fillius's claims had left him another response behind, with no notion of which to address first.

"It's a pheasant," he said finally, almost defensively, holding it at arm's length to the light. "At least I think it is."

"And a fine example of its type too, Joe. Fill me in on the White Sox now, won't you? I think I can help you along those lines. What seems to be the major bone of contention?"

"The what?"

"What's the beef, Joe?"

"The dough, the cheap bastards, that's the major bone with me."

"I'm hardly surprised."

"Any other club would love to have me, and pay me what I'm worth, the cheap bastards."

Jackson seemed shocked at his own dander. He hadn't griped openly before, simply rejected his contract, referring the one reporter who'd called to Mrs. Jackson.

Fillius wasn't surprised though. Celebrity whining was bleached bones to him.

"Absolutely, Joe, couldn't agree with you more. But are you going to sit out the whole season now, or what? How will

264

you make a living, Joe? Excuse me for prying. I only ask in the interest of your interests."

He was probing the soft tissue of Jackson's resentment here, courting his indignation.

"I've got a few bucks saved. The wife and I could open up a dry-cleaning joint."

Joe's eyes rolled involuntarily at this prospect. Was that his future self he saw squatting over by the icehouse door, oxidizing shit stains from the deputy mayor's tuxedo pants?

"I won't sign for what Comiskey's offering, though, that's for sure. It aint' right. Any other team would love to have me, and pay me double."

"What if you hurt yourself, Joe, burnt your thumbs off with cleaning fluid or something like that? You might never play again."

"Fellow can hurt himself sitting in bed nowadays, bub. Comiskey could solve that on a hand gallop. Just trade me. Any other team would love to have me."

And there it was, Fillius thought smugly, the superfluous point made three sentences running. His liver shrank a crucial half centimeter.

"That's just it, Joe. Comiskey can't trade you. He tried. I thought you knew that. There's lots of evil talk around about the Series, Joe. None of it true, naturally. Still, there you are. The other teams don't want you, Joe. I already checked."

Fillius knew he was taking a big chance here. But the terror in Jackson's pupils bulked his courage.

"I don't know what you're talking about, mister. Nobody told me any shit like that."

"I'm sure they didn't, Joe. They try to keep all the heavy rag from the athletes. That's what attorneys are for. Luckily, before I came down here this morning I drew up a fiduciary covenant, *in media res,* with corollary ancillaries and prenatal overtones. It guarantees you can be traded to any team you want, Joe. After you've put in another year with Comiskey, that is. It's a sweet deal, Joe, even has *droit du seigneur* stipulations, like the compacts I devised in the Rabbit Maranville matter."

Fillius was laying it on a bit thick here, he knew. He wasn't even sure who Rabbit Maranville was.

"How much do I get?"

"Well, for the coming year, Joe, just the stipulated amount, but that's merely *a priori.* And it's a nifty investment in your future, collaterally speaking. After all, you can't play baseball if no team will have you. That's a simple matter of tort. And this document here guarantees every team in baseball *has* to want you, Joe, no matter what kind of foul rumors they've been hearing."

Fillius could feel himself getting carried away now, victim again of his chronic compulsion to amuse himself.

"But what about that letter I sent Comiskey? How come he never even answered it?"

Isn't it astounding, Fillius thought, reaching for his fountain pen. Everybody has doubts. This man's anxieties are as pathetic as my own, and he a genius, in his own deficient realm.

"Don't worry about that, Joe. I'll grease those skids when I get back to Vidalia."

It progressed naturally from there, almost like something Jackson had been hoping for. There was a little more fencing on the money, and some carping about Comiskey's character, but by the time Mrs. Jackson had returned from her toe overhaul, Joe's signature had fixed their futures through the '20s.

Fillius was long gone and lonesome by then, of course,

bent on an early rendezvous with Blottoville. He'd call it dinner for two and bill Comiskey accordingly.

The next day, Jackson's signing became public. Within a week the other fixers followed. Riisberg was the last. The idea of opening a restaurant still appealed to him; the prospect of operating one had begun to feel like purgatory. He couldn't imagine tolerating that many strangers nightly.

"I could make more money tilting games anyway," he told his wife, "especially with Gandil hanging up the ax."

For Chick, indeed, was quitting baseball. By mid-March that much was obvious. He'd made his pile, settled his scores, grown eager to cede the low road to those who belonged there.

The day after Riisberg signed, Comiskey drove out to his ballpark. He hadn't seen it since the last game of the Series.

It was a dark, chilly Monday on the forward edge of March. The park sat immobilized by winter, paint peeling from its seats, mysterious drips echoing along its runways.

Comiskey went up and sat behind the first base dugout. Some springtime sun and a coat of paint would put this all straight, he thought, though nothing could make it what it had been. Absolutely nothing.

He'd enjoyed playing with the fixers' spirits, he had to admit. But he no longer wanted to employ them.

Maybe he should just can them all and be done with it, he thought, start over again, like after the Players Association. He'd gotten this far without catering to vermin. What was the point in being on top if those under you got to call the tune?

But it was too late for such gestures, he knew, had been too late for quite some time now. He was as trapped by

267

circumstance as the rest of them. He forced himself to remain seated for several minutes, basking in the melancholy he'd come to shake. Then he stood and walked slowly back down the aisle. He wouldn't return until April at the very earliest, or until some thaw had made at least the illusion of renewal supportable.

14

March isn't really a month, is it? It's more an interlude between seasons, lacking definition, and thus purpose, its days defying recollection.

That March was particularly elusive. I seemed to be sitting around perpetually in my woollies, waiting for something, almost anything, to happen. But what? I'd already gotten everything I wanted. I wasn't like those sad souls I saw haunting the bus kiosks, so divorced from the reality of their dreams that they no longer even knew what to hope for.

On March 3, Cohan called, fresh from Hollywood, armed with enough scandal for ten whisper sheets.

"Chaplin's caught cupid's itch from Marion Davies, Lasky's got an Apache dancer baby-bound, and De Mille's made Izzy Mayer the ghoul pool of the century: a hundred thousand on whose mother kisses the clouds first."

He paused pregnantly, anticipating my skepticism.

"I have personal knowledge of all these tidings, too, Sport. They're not just bitchy rumors concocted by minty underlings."

Something in his tone suggested yearning, for New York, for fresh action. "I'm back on the right coast," it seemed to say, "ready to draw on all the accounts I've paid into."

I had no news for him, at least none I wished to share. He didn't mind, always eager to fill in any gap.

"My hondling with Goldwyn has hit an impasse, too, Sport. He'd rather steal two bucks than make ten million. That's okay, though. Now I can loaf across the spring with you. We'll take in a few doubleheaders, you and I."

The phrase "take in" had a decided spin to it, whose gist required no etymologist to decipher.

"Also my price now escalates a droll twenty-five percent. Overcharging makes the nickel-nursers drool for you."

We agreed on lunch the following day.

The next morning, ten on the dot, he called, as antici-pated, to cancel.

"I have a couple of bankrollers here to velvet, Sport. I'm thinking of sending *Only a Mother* off to yokeldom."

Even in slack times Cohan kept several pots roiling. Fuss-ing was *his* antidote to futility.

"Let's meet tomorrow at the bicycle races, Sport. We'll get in some plunging practice then."

"Sure, George, tomorrow, at noon."

Female giggling undercut his fib, a sound he should have, and could have, kept from me. I wasn't angered, just hurt. He was the closest thing I had to a friend.

The morning papers were full of baseball news. None concerned the fix, even subliminally. Spring training had broken out among the mangroves. To commemorate it the *Times* ran a picture of the White Sox in Waco.

I ordered room-service hash and spent the rest of the day dipping into Macaulay. Rose was out pricing motor cars. She wanted to hit Carolina for the azalea season, whatever that was.

Six-day bicycle racing seems glamorous in retrospect. It wasn't. It was just folk dancing with pedals. The action continued unabated around the clock. No matter what time you got there, it was the middle.

Cohan ignored its drawbacks. Misgivings stood little chance with him. He created small islands of contentment within every disappointment he encountered.

We started betting immediately, with no clue.

I'd lost $500 before my bum had warmed my bench. Sweating figures in colorful costumes circled the track, to what purpose even they seemed uncertain. Anxious coaches hectored them in tongues. Some sort of teamwork seemed involved.

We stayed four hours. I slipped into it, as I will. The general idea was disconcertingly familiar.

Cohan, pronouncing himself "enchanted," suggested returning within the week, "for some serious flutter."

"I'll call a friend in Nice, Sport. He'll put me wise to the nuances."

I was willing. This could be exactly the new scam I'd been hoping for. It was a game, after all, and an uncommon one. I'd already determined it could be beaten. I assume anything I'm not familiar with can be beaten.

I spent the next week researching it in depth, what depth there was. Mostly it seemed to involve genetics and vendettas. A Castilian bellhop filled me in between split shifts.

"Don't bribe the French, even if they'll talk to you. They'll take your money and buy hats with it. The same with the Italians. They'd like to cheat, but get distracted. Don't

270

even talk to the Germans. You know what they are. Stick to the Spanish—we honor our word."

I took his council for what it was and stood him a scotch.

I didn't notice much else that week. Spring training had commandeered the sports pages, rendering my previous felony old news. I consoled myself by buying a new leather ledger, and by calling Cohan to postpone our date.

The next day I started attending the bicycle races alone. At first the results seemed dishearteningly arbitrary. Only gradually did unexpected patterns begin to emerge.

I ran into Luciana the very first evening, or rather spied him in time to avoid running into him. He was lolling around the mezzanine with his accomplices, as if awaiting the official sign at Jamaica.

I don't think he noticed me; I'm sure his drillers didn't. There were four of them—Augie Orgen (the shooter), Eddie Diamond (Legs' brother), Kid Dropper (the shylock), and Vannie Higgins (Big Bill Dwyer's arm). Their demeanors, which were jocularly murderous, sent me bouncing like sixty toward the john. I rarely think of myself as rabbit-hearted, but their predatoriness put the fear of God straight in me. I spent the rest of the evening rationalizing their presence, and rereading the first two pages of my cycling notes.

Comiskey didn't go to spring training that year. For the first time in forty years he didn't go south at all. He spent the rest of March plotting repairs to his stadium. Occasionally he'd glance at a scouting report. Any mention of a fixer sapped his interest.

Most nights he stayed peacefully at home, listening to his Caruso records, retiring early. He was working hard to keep his rage in check. The Austrians sometimes came over for

271

dinner, which was invariably Salisbury steak. Mrs. Austrian would try gallantly to buck the conversation, though it always worked its way back to the Series.

At nine, Comiskey would pronounce himself exhausted, presenting the Austrians with their hard-earned clue to scram. They always took it, no questions asked.

On St. Patrick's Day it reached sixty degrees in the city. Rose and I watched the parade from the Tiffany Building. Discordant bugle corps slogged through ankle-deep slush. Tipsy spectators aped my race's crudest defects.

"I've never particularly enjoyed being Irish," I told Rose, "though I wouldn't want to be anything else."

"You're thrilled to your eyeteeth to be Irish," she shot back. "It's those other spuds you wish had different genes."

That evening I visited Rothstein's new casino, on the corner of Madison and 90th. He'd done it exactly as I would have. The public rooms were insolently elegant, damask drapes balanced by smoked Florentine mirrors. The color strategy alternated charcoal with chocolate. Mexican tiles made each hopper a fiesta.

The hootch flowed freely, the dice racks hummed, the clientele resembled a pushier version of the Brook's—Trollope characters with hyperactive thyroids.

I'd been there barely twenty minutes when Attell strolled in. I nearly fainted.

I'd presumed Abe was still fleeing Rothstein's wrath, or else defunct from it. Yet there he stood, banty as Barnum, prowling the Bankroll's new pen like he owned it.

I couldn't bear to face this irony sober. So I scrammed.

When I got home I gave Rose an efficient hosing, our first such encounter in weeks. She seemed to enjoy it.

272

The next several days I spent ignoring my cycling statistics, briefly exchanging one obsession for another, lugging street maps and measuring tapes all across the East Side. I wasn't renewing my search for a casino location, just checking to see if Rothstein's could be improved on.

It could not.

15

March 26, 1920
Waco, Texas
9:17 p.m.

Dear Mr. Sullivan,

I been camped out on this boob Cicotte's porch two weeks now. He ain't done nothing your average corpse couldn't manage. The man is tedious. In Michigan he shoveled horse biscuits sixteen hours daily, down here he does likewise, but with baseballs. I'm not sending you a report because there's nothing to report on. This guy could hypnotize concrete. Do you have something particular you want me to look for? If not, I suggest pulling me off. We're proud of our patience at Excelsior, but this is bughouse.

Yours most sincerely,
Dwayne (the detective)

It wasn't exactly what I'd been paying for; it was better. It meant Cicotte was no immediate threat to me. I sat right down and wrote Dwayne a bread-and-butter.

Dear Dwayne,

Thanks loads for your very helpful letter. You did the right thing. I'm glad I decided to hire you. Please start hawkshawing

Lefty Williams as of this date. I suspect he'll make your eve-
nings a little livelier.

> *Best personal regards,*
> *Sport (the gambler)*

It took me a week to figure out bicycle racing. When I did I called Cohan to inform him. He answered as if he'd been sitting on the phone.

"Great news, Sport. A little curtain-raiser for our baseball exploits, *n'est-ce pas?*"

"Well . . ."

"No false modesty now, kiddo. We'll debut your philosophy Thursday at the Wintergarden."

Once, too many years ago, I made a lengthy study of parimutuel favoritism. My figures covered five thousand races. Favorites never lost eight straight. A fortune could be made betting progressions, or so I thought.

My records were accurate; only their scope lacked rigor. Open progressions are a pit, one exception obliterating a million rules. I was just nineteen, a greenhorn at my trade. My bosses hadn't impressed me. They disdained detail as much as my father revered it.

A week after I completed my research, seven straight favorites lost at Narragansett. The next day I committed a year's savings to science.

I bet $100 on the first favorite, which ran seventh. I moistened my lips and doubled my action. Fourth. I doubled again. This favorite, my last, placed, closing fast, nosed at the wire. Ten straight choices had lost. I'd tapped out.

It no longer surprises me when the worst thing that can happen does. What does still surprise me, as it surprised me that sunny afternoon at Narragansett, is how a disaster's inevitability only provokes me to defy it.

I knew I'd lose the moment I entered the track. I didn't know how, only what. I could smell it in the air, as a parent senses menace for a child. Yet I persisted. I had to see it through.

A similar fatalism pervaded my bicycle endeavor. I'd marshaled my statistics, classified them, analyzed them. Yet somehow I felt as doomed as doomed could be.

From the start I lost instinctively, unremittingly, by tiny margins, by ludicrous margins, on fouls, through accidents, in every manner possible, and a few even fate might call contrived. Reversals of logic grew dizzyingly dramatic. I'd tapped a vein of incorrigible arbitrariness, which I stubbornly refused to step aside for. If anything, I picked up the pace.

At first Cohan mimicked me, betraying the layman's blind reverence for expertise. But gradually his allegiances drifted; he began taking his own chances. He didn't finish the day ahead; my humiliation wouldn't be *that* complete. But he did make the odd successful stab, all the while keeping up a stream of annoying banter. He couldn't permit himself a bad time.

I wish I could recall the evening's details. They were probably quite picturesque. I do remember one Andalusian cyclist breaking his femur, and several harpies going for each other's eyeballs in the loge.

I lost $35,000 in just seven hours, my bluntest reversal yet. It was the pasting's character which really panicked me, though. I'd absorbed it betting on something I knew little, and cared nothing, about.

I stayed in bed for three days after that, convinced I'd contracted something aptly lethal. I longed to put a match to my statistics, but couldn't bear to. They represented too much work to junk. I stuck them instead into my filing cabinet, thus obliterating them as effectively as by combustion.

Cohan called constantly during this period. I told Rose to say I was out. I could have borne his scorn, but not his solace, and even less his pointed avoidance of the entire abject episode.

Rose, in her Roseish way, managed to distract me. The afternoon after I took to bed she embarked on a lavish pillage of Fifth Avenue. Each evening she spread her take across my lap, admiration for her taste being part of my tariff.

"Look, Sport, a precious little smock from Beauregarde's. Everybody on the Continent is wearing them."

"Very nice."

"And don't you just love this darling cloche from Lily of Lille? She's the Queen of England's personal chapeaurier, you know."

"Very nice."

No one could have drawn solace from my compliments. I doubt she even heard them.

I wasn't spending any money on myself, of course, being far too busy losing it. I'd never been particularly interested in *things* anyway. They require dusting, and repair. I've always preferred looking at possessions to possessing them.

"You're a queer bird," Cohan once informed me, back in the Boston days.

"How so, George?" I asked, not that I needed to.

"You seem to want just enough to keep from wanting more."

Rose was more conventional in her desires. She wanted the *stuff.* Where was the simple girl I'd wooed in Saratoga, I

276

kept asking myself, knowing full well that girl had never existed.

Rose's purchases ceased the day I emerged from bed. She'd blown over $3,000 in just five days of rag-trawling. But at least she had her geegaws to amuse herself with, and the satisfaction of not taking her pleasure from denying it.

That evening a figure from my past reentered my life briefly. My brother Eugene appeared in our lobby, asking to see me. When he called on the house phone Rose hung up on him. She thought it was a joke. She didn't even know I had a brother.

That's how I knew it *was* Eugene. Few people realized he existed. None who did would stoop to imitate him. I struggled to sweep his features from my psychology, as I'd done so successfully for so many years. I told myself he'd only come for a handout. Whatever he sought, he must have found it elsewhere. He didn't return, at least not in person.

Thus did March slip imperceptibly into April, as so many anonymous Marches had before it; so unobtrusively, in fact, that we'd hit the cusp of Easter before I even realized Lent had run its course. The harbor breezes softened, as in tradition. Banal street clatter began sifting through our walls. Suddenly we were only eight days from the baseball season. Another event I'd long expected had snuck up on me.

Where had my Manhattan idyll gotten itself off to? I wondered. I'd been back east exactly three months, and had exactly nothing to show for it. Meanwhile my stake had shrunk another 20 percent. The whole world seemed to be moving on without me, even though I was the one who was supposed to be making the progress.

The day after the bike bust I thought of abandoning gambling entirely. I'd start a real business, something with inventory, and hours. I could have a real office then, and, by extension, a real home. That's what I could raise myself up to, normality.

The whole idea was ridiculous, of course. I'd be like *them* then.

I was simply drifting, I had to admit, as I'd drifted for so many years before the fix. My only hope was that returning to baseball might anchor me, without turning all my cravings back to stone. The new season was here, after all. Something, or its equivalent, would have to be done about it.

16

On April 7, the White Sox opened the decade in Philadelphia, beating the A's 6–2. Cicotte allowed four hits. Jackson hit two homers. Riisberg made several unlikely fielding plays. They seemed eager for vindication, or at least higher odds.

No paper had mentioned the Series in weeks. I'd begun to believe the exposure threat had passed.

The approach of spring *was* reviving my ambitions. I could feel it now. The days grew longer, the air softer, blue light stretched from sky, to ground, then back again. Even my enthusiasm for baseball seemed to be rekindling itself— for its consistencies, and my command of them.

In every family there is one who answers the phone. In ours it was Rose. But this particular call, for whatever reason, fell to me. It came during the season's second week.

"Sport?"

"Speaking."

"Sullivan?"

"The same."

It wasn't an accent, or a style, I was familiar with. This ignorance froze my tongue behind my teeth.

"Dempsey could go south against Miske, you know, skeezix. Doc Kearns wants to gas with you on that."

Our conversation didn't survive this cryptic tease. Before he could elaborate, I slammed the receiver down.

The very idea was ant paste incarnate, of course. Dempsey was just approaching his prime, Miske wouldn't have one. No book would make a price on such a bout. Nor would Kearns, Dempsey's manager, permit a fix. He knew the straight path was the plushest one with this boy.

Despite my doubts, though, the notion held some appeal for me. The heavyweight championship was even less fixable than the Series.

Dempsey's mitts dominated Costello's Gym the next morning, pummeling the heavy bag with cauliflower logic. No human, I figured, could absorb such punishment and live. Jack's glowing torso was the focus of every envy. Heavyweight champions are what God must have intended.

I asked a second where Doc Kearns was hiding.

"Downstairs with a ten-percenter, Mac. They're lining up vaudeville dates for the Mauler. You could join them in fifteen minutes or so. First rat hole on your right."

Something in his manner alarmed me. His helpfulness seemed just a hair excessive. And his eyes had found mine, though mine had searched the crowd.

I loitered upstairs another half an hour, reacquainting myself with the conviviality of such dumps. Camaraderie infests the surliest fight venues, an agreeableness physical mayhem only accentuates.

Dempsey left at noon. Showered, powdered, dapper, beaming, he plowed through the back-patters and the lobby gows, out into the feathery Manhattan sunlight. I doubted Miske would survive to retire.

As he swept past me I stifled an urge to address him.

"Hiya, champ," I'd blurt out companionably, sharing in his eminence by acknowledging it.

"Hiya, pal," he'd growl back instinctively, marking me forever as his intimate.

I held my tongue, though, and this time appropriately. To claim equality with him risked branding myself his inferior.

All the glamour fled the building with him. It suddenly felt like a place that used to be thrilling. I'd lingered too long in such joints to cling to this one. So I descended to Kearns's crib on the trot.

I knocked once, firmly, to assert myself. Doc opened the door, looking remarkably like himself, a tense little terrier I'd encountered often in previous lives. He didn't seem surprised to see me. It was as if he'd been waiting.

"Don't hang around my boy like the butter-and-egg man, Sport. There's no percentage in it. I ain't quite the lollipop Comiskey is."

It was the set speech of a road-company tommy-buster, a small man used to standing behind big men. The obligatory door slamming followed. Standing an inch closer would have cost me my schnozz.

Just before the room disappeared forever, the helpful second glanced up from his knuckle-wrapping. His smirk made every kind of sense.

Isn't it inspiring, I thought, lurching back to street level, how many nobodies you can offend without remembering them, and how long they'll lurk in the shadows to get even?

I should have suspected his servility, I suppose. Seconds

280

are rarely that cooperative. They're too close to the power not to have any.

When I got home I poured myself three scotches, lining them up like sentries on my portmanteau. Luckily, Rose was fast asleep. Her inquiries would only have salted the sting. I sat down and smoked a couple of slow cheroots, turning my latest humiliation, and its perpetrator, over in my memory.

What a sad fucking sack he was in retrospect, how unworthy of both my worry and my rancor, and how easy to quash when my sweet time came to do so.

I convinced myself to forget about boxing too. It was a scabby-eyed life full of gonifs and rattle-caps, its vivid characters better recollected than encountered.

After an hour of musing, my hootch had evaporated, along with the memory of the takedown that obliged it. I immersed myself in the past week's baseball stories, which I'd had the good sense to clip and save.

17

I was hardly alone, that April, in my bamboozlement. Riisberg had waited a week to begin finagling, then gone at it like a double-chin after pogie bait. By May he was fixing promiscuously. Swede wasn't a delicate character to begin with. His success put him high on his horse. The threat of discovery never even occurred to him.

Every gambler fears this level of presumptuousness. It's one thing to try to fix something, quite another to try to fix everything. Riisberg was tilting the equilibrium. He needed comeuppance.

The man with the ginger hair was waiting for Happy Felsch outside McGaffigan's. The setting sun shone in every window on Michigan Avenue.

"Felsch."

Happy spun a neat ninety degrees, hand outstretched, in nonspecific welcome.

"We're watching you, Hap. We can get you with a whistle."

Felsch's lips straightened, though his arm remained extended. His antagonist swaggered off toward the lake.

It took three rounds of boilermakers to blunt Happy's terror.

"You know, Violet," he told his wife that evening over her pimiento mystery loaf, "it tickles me the way some fans like to fun with us. Why this one fellow I met outside McGaff's this afternoon . . ."

Two days later Cicotte found a note pinned to his pillow.

E.C.:
   You shouldn't go south quite so often, liver lips. You might consider stopping. You could live longer.

It wasn't signed. Cicotte recognized Lefty Williams's brand of teasing, though. He curled the note into a thin, rigid cone and used it to sweep a June bug from his windowsill.

Two days later, Lefty himself got the message.

He awoke in his cubbyhole in Detroit. A manila envelope was slithering beneath his door, like a live thing. It was the sort of folder druggists store lapsed prescriptions in.

Lefty opened it with sleep-tinged curiosity.

Inside were two photographs, one of the stove in his

282

kitchen, the other of a corpse without its skin. The torso had been neatly drawn and quartered, a baseball cap stenciled to its skull.

Williams's stomach got the point before his brain did. Two hours later every fixer shared the gist. Menace had found its medium. Williams had added two and two and gotten infinity.

I never learned who made these vivid threats. By then it seemed irrelevant. Individual fears had begun to feel communal.

Had I seen the White Sox play that spring I'd have understood. Their brazenness contradicted decency. They were throwing everything. But I hadn't seen them play. I'd been too busy.

I'd gone several times to Rothstein's, losing heavily. I'd traipsed with Rose through both the Bronx Zoo and Central Park. We'd spent one dreary afternoon in the endless Metropolitan, and an even drearier one navigating the Hudson on a paddle-wheeler.

"We're going to get out and enjoy life," Rose had threatened me. "We're going to do things, not just plan them."

I'd also opened several small bank accounts, each forcing me to recalculate my worth (260 Gs and fading like my confidence). I reorganized my address book. I placed daily calls to Dwayne. I was just waiting, waiting for that second shoe to drop.

When I awoke the shining morning of April 30, though, I knew nothing could keep me from the ballpark. And nothing did.

The White Sox were visiting Yankee Stadium.

Could I believe what I saw?

Yes.

No.

Williams didn't survive the second. Riisberg booted everything. Felsch looked wobble-jawed just butt-ending the bench. They lost 10–1. By the third inning the crowd was knitting nooses. Every third crack referred knowingly to the Series.

When I'd seen enough, and heard too much, I rose to leave, like a concert-goer ditching the Scarlatti. I was two steps from salvation when my name rang through the park.

"Sport! Sport Sullivan!"

The words pierced my heart, then my memory.

"Hold up a minute, Sport. I just want to ask you one simple question."

I recognized him instantly, as one would a former self. He dated from my novice days in Boston, though I couldn't recall his name, or his pretext.

"Are you scramming because they're dumping like amateurs, Sport, or are you steamed because you and Baruch don't have a piece?"

"That's two questions, you puss-brained shanty mick," I longed to remind him, though for the sake of my remaining dignity, I didn't.

What had brought on this heavy wave of razzing? I couldn't help wondering. Had my Series scam emptied that many pockets?

I had to smile.

Baruch?

I went straight from the park to the 42nd Street library, eager to regain my composure in a cool and soothing place. I also wanted to check the Chicago papers, for Series buzz. Seeing the White Sox again hadn't cost me any more money, just some additional peace of mind. I'd rather pay in cash.

Before sitting down with the *Tribune* though, I stopped in at "City Directories," humoring an urge to see Rose's name in print. I hoped the world's corroboration might make her seem more real to me.

She wasn't listed in Saratoga, or in Albany either. I began tearing through every book in the room, as though I needed to. But she wasn't anywhere.

I tried to calm myself, to focus on specifics. But there were too many specifics to choose from. There was my shrinking bankroll, and Fullerton's stories, and Comiskey's reward. There was Gandil's house, and Riisberg's gall, and Rothstein's casino. And of course there was my own perfectly agreeable life with Rose, which promised to keep right on getting more agreeable until it strangled me.

A bindle stiff held the squeaking seat beside me, wearing the *Louisville Courier* on his knees. I bent my neck to evade his aroma. As I did my eyes caught the headline they were meant to:

DERBY FIELD EXPANDS TO ELEVEN

So this was what my life had evolved to then—taking career cues from the lap camouflage of rumdums.

When I opened the next directory, Rose's name leaped from it. Utica. She'd never mentioned *that* burg before, though a hint of an *a* clung to many of her *o*'s.

I sat staring at her initials on the page. "R.A." How official they looked, how murderously impersonal, how suggestive of any person she might be.

I knew then that fixing the Derby was unavoidable. For that reason it seemed destined to succeed. I'd *have* to return to baseball if it didn't. I was fast running out of sure things to fail at.

18

I'd wanted to see the Derby all my life. I'd only been
waiting until I deserved to.

The trip proved unworthy of the wait. It was like the last
months of my marriage, ritual deprived of motive—numbing, inevitable, remorseless.

Only four scattered images remain with me.

Someone, probably me, arguing shrilly with a bellhop, a
birthmark snaking vindictively along his cheek, enraging
me further by moving me. He sorted mail throughout, denying me his attention. The source of my anger? An ice bucket
undelivered to my room.

The sharp scent of a fat girl in a Posey Street chinky eats,
her perspiration undiluted by Kresge sachet. Did I lie with
this lump, or merely fear I might?

The crowd roaring the Derby field home, a ritualistic
clamor, more reflex than emotion. I didn't actually *see* the
race. My view was blocked.

A hot tropical wind filling the dark southern streets. Another summer edging up the delta.

That's it.

Not much to wait all those years for, I'll admit.

The morning before the race itself I went to the receiving
barn. It was a clear, brisk sunup with a hint of fall about it. I
carried a list of the Derby starters, clipped by candlelight
from Stingo's Famous Green Card. Twenty thousand in hundreds lined my skivvies. Did I intend to tempt a jockey with
this wad, or grease a trainer? I seem to recall some notion of

drugging the favorite. But who, exactly, would the favorite have been? And where were my mojo and hypodermic?

I stood fifty feet from the Calumet barn, in the shade of an ancient copper beech. Hot-walkers shuffled in narrow, easy loops, puffs of steam curling from their fretting charges. Hooves struck stone. Shanks slapped bits. I knew suddenly that I couldn't fix this race. It was the most sporting of events, after all. I'd have to bet it.

The evening before the race I attended the Festive Derby Gala, which was as "festive" as advertised, though by invitation only. My cutaway got me suavely past the Pinkertons. I probably could have snuck in anywhere that year, though as a metaphor for my life it cut too deep.

All the swells had gotten it up for this affair—old money and new, horsey types, nightlifers. There were even a few second-string sovereigns milling about. I wandered casually among them, sipping soda water, resenting my boredom. When a sallow-eyed Brahmin mistook me for a Widener I suddenly got the joke. My new status placed such fêtes beyond my longings.

"I didn't go to Harvard, you bloodless faggot," I advised him. "I went two years to Our Lady of Perpetual Regret High School before I quit to run mattress-backs on the street. I believe that's where I met your mother."

I whirled and strode dramatically from the ballroom, trailing skeins of tousled dignity in my wake. The blue blood's stammer atrophied into speechlessness. You could have hung a brakeman's lantern from his pout. I didn't look back, though. It did little for Lot's wife.

The moment my heels hit the macadam I felt emancipated. I'd taken two lessons in one day on how out of my element I'd gotten myself. I'd tried something new; it hadn't

287

worked. Now I was free to go back to all the old things that didn't work either.

I needed no pillow powder to reach slumberland that evening. The coming day couldn't possibly be my enemy. Imagine my shock when it proved to be just that.

I lost every race on the Derby card; didn't even come close. The main event took my twenty grand and sneered at it. I was sure I'd win. It meant too much to me not to.

Nor were my indignities restricted to the betting windows. A society stiff sloshed mint julep over my saddle shoes. I couldn't conjure a cab to my train, had to lug my bags fifteen blocks to the station. The train itself was two hours late. When it arrived the seats were ass-jammed with ordinaries. I went straight to the smoker and took a long drag from my flask. We'd barely cleared the platform before I craved another. I can only guess at how many followed.

Just before I took the liquid count, two soothing revelations swam up to comfort me.

I'd definitely be returning to baseball. And I wouldn't have to fail at anything else to permit me to.

"Your Series sweep gets cleaner on every telling," Rose once chided me.

"What on earth are you talking about, my little cinnamon bun?"

"Have you forgotten all the ways it went cockeyed, Sport? Or do you just leave them out to annoy me?"

She wasn't picking a fight, just venting a little rancor, as lovers smelling the final curtain will.

"You're not half as romantic as you imagine yourself, Sport," she informed me. "In fact, it's only in your head that you have any real heart at all."

19

The day after I returned from Kentucky, this headline appeared in the *Times:*

DETECTIVES TO POLICE GAMBLING DENS AT MAJOR LEAGUE PARKS

The story added few details; none impressed me. It didn't seem to be connected to the Series. And I was too busy plotting my return to those same parks.

Two days later the inevitable sequel appeared:

FORTY-SIX GAMBLERS ARRESTED AT COMISKEY PARK

None of these "gamblers' " names sounded familiar to me; they didn't sound like they'd be familiar to anyone. But their pinch got the message across neatly.

Three days later a third bulletin confirmed it. The following letter appeared on the editorial page of the *Chicago Tribune,* bordered in black, like a prominent advertiser's obituary.

Dear Sir,
    Baseball must be cleaned up at once.
    It makes no difference who is hit in the investigation, from the president of either league down to the clubhouse batboy. The game must be protected.
    There is a perfectly good grand jury in this county. Those who possess evidence of gambling in last fall's Series must come forward. Justice must be done.

Yours sincerely,
Fred M. Loomis

Loomis was a prominent Chicago old boy; his opinions were never entirely his own. The cannons were being rolled out to the high ground.

I spent the rest of May plotting my return to baseball. I wanted it to be serpentine, inviolable, unprecedented. It would have to prove that I'd backtracked voluntarily.

Oh Jesus.

I rented a small room at the back of the Ansonia, spent several hours there every morning, plotting, drinking lime juice, practicing my signature, trying to fall back in love with Rose in my head. Nothing worked. The trees were shedding their buds along 74th Street. Staring at them gave me comfort, but few ideas.

It was a small room, with little furniture, and less light. It cost $8 monthly, in advance.

I'd been going there almost a week when Dwayne's report on Williams hit my mail slot. It consisted of a lengthy list of Lefty's assignations, his life apparently having no other side.

I sent Dwayne a wire commending him on his diligence, and dismissing him. The fixers' indiscretions no longer threatened me. I'd soon be back monitoring them in person.

During this period I read no papers at all. One in particular I didn't read was the *Herald and Examiner.* It was in that rag, the day after Dwayne's dismissal, that this story ran under Hugh Fullerton's byline:

> Big gamblers are still operating in the boxes behind the players' bench. . . .

But here I find I cannot continue. Do I need to? Those few

290

words made the next thousand superfluous. Only two sentences really mattered anyway:

> The young stars have so far proven immune. But how long before youngsters like Babe Ruth are infected. . . .

20

Historians dwell on his hat size. But it was the Babe's bum which really took the cake. Viewed in profile, undraped, its gelatinous bulk accentuated by locomotion, Ruth's keister assumed its own imperial logic. It looked imposing enough to lead the league in several departments.

I stood in the clubhouse doorway the next morning, gauging its volume. The Babe had just emerged from the shower; his street weeds lay in folds at his feet. He was facing his locker, excavating a nostril, his legs thinner than an ingenue's, his torso as hairless as a herring's.

I'd slammed three doors to signal my arrival, cleared my throat, jangled my key ring. He remained resolutely oblivious. Addressing him didn't seem possible, remaining silent risked being judged a voyeur.

The clubhouse clock finally rescued me. Ruth wheeled to read it. Our eyes met. My glance dropped involuntarily to his crotch. Here was size that rendered his rump's inconsequential. I suddenly appreciated the full irony of his nickname.

"Hiya, bub."

"Hello, Mr. Ruth."

I rarely enter clubhouses. My devious line precludes it. Ballplayers will bend over for almost any price, but few will take the freight right where they live. Ruth seemed the exception. He appeared no more at home in his element than I did.

"Mr. Ruth, I wonder if I might have just a moment?"

"Sure, bub, sure. My fans can always bump an autograph off the Babe."

"Well, thank you, Mr. Ruth, but—"

"Babe."

He was mistaking my distance for deference. To call him Babe risked having him call me Sport.

"Babe, thank you, but that's not actually what I had in mind here. I'm not really a fan, you see. That is, I am a fan, of course, of yours, of the Yankees, that goes without saying, but I'm not *just* a fan, if you get my meaning. Actually I'm here today in a business sort of capacity. Not *real* business exactly, but . . ."

"Sure, bub, sure. I get your twist. Listen, calm down, will you? You're putting my steam glands in a lather. Why don't you just sit down there and tell the Babe all about it. I'll get dressed while we talk. I got a cooz outside could make John R. Corpse cream his intimates."

He was right. I *was* pressing my throttle, babbling on with neither design nor discrimination. Naked men always unnerve me, appearing too familiar, yet not quite familiar enough.

"No, of course not, Mr. Ruth. Babe, that is. I understand completely. I know how much effort it takes to do anything as well as you play baseball. I'm that way myself, very much so in fact. Your teammates will tell you that, if you ask them. About me, that is. I've had dealings with quite a number over the years. On this club, and others, mostly great stars like yourself, who put so much into the game, but don't get back nearly what they've invested. Now you take—"

"Ain't that the hard cheese and then some, bub? The Babe don't get ten cents on *his* dollar."

"Exactly, Babe. Exactly my point. And I'd like to see something done about that, right now, as soon as possible. Now you just imagine . . ."

Was I pitching him too fast here, pushing too hard? I didn't want to sound like I was desperate, like I *needed* it.

"Do my pits smell at all suspicious from where you're sitting, bub? Do you catch anything too offensive over there?"

"No, Babe, I can't say that I do. But, as I was saying, suppose you had a bad game occasionally, a bad game for you, that is—no hits, a couple of errors, a throw to the wrong base. Nobody could hold it against you, could they? After all . . ."

"They better not."

"After all, you've put the Yanks in the driver's seat all by yourself."

"Haven't I? And aren't I entitled to an occasional gray day once in a while? These other guys have two or three a week."

"Precisely, Babe. Exactly my point. Now Babe, do you know who you're playing Wednesday afternoon?"

He put his pinky to his chin then, as though I'd just asked him to recite the first book of the *Iliad*.

"St. Louis?"

"Well, no, not exactly. I believe you play St. Louis *next* week, Babe. Actually it's Detroit, the Tigers. Let me check my schedule here. Yes, Detroit. And who knows? That game could be the very off day we've been speaking of."

"Sure, who knows? It could happen anytime, to anyone."

"Right. And just to make sure we understand each other

completely, Babe, here's a small token of my esteem and anticipation."

I took $2,000 in hundreds from my pocket then, hoping my speed compensated for my crassness. He didn't seem to notice.

"Gee, thanks, bub. That's awfully white of you. Could I fix you up with a couple of on-the-cuffs for Wednesday? Or maybe this broad outside's got a sister you can plug."

"Thanks no, Babe. I prefer to make my own way through this universe. You'll learn that about me soon enough. We'll probably be seeing a lot of each other from now on."

"I hope so, pal. You seem like a regular type of guy. And if you ever *do* need any house seats . . ."

"I'll be sure to let you know, Babe. Now, I really must be running along. I'm having a snort with Justice Brandeis at the Biltmore."

Nothing seems too easy when you're doing it. Still, I sensed this particular sale was made too quickly. He'd been too friendly, too amenable, too willing to treat my odd proposal as commonplace.

Yet I needed to be encouraged, so I was. I left the stadium feeling weightless and authoritative. Ruth was the whole team. I could manipulate it through him, then move on to other stars, other teams, other areas. I'd use my new mastery of baseball to distance myself permanently from it.

The five-day wait for Ruth's slump passed blithely. I made my bets, planned successors, awoke early, spent long days in delectable solitude. I even enjoyed my nights on the town with Rose. This is the best sort of waiting, I've always felt, waiting for the sure thing. I could have stood a solid year of it. Its flawlessness almost atoned for all that followed.

The Yankees won 13–2. Ruth hit two home runs, reached base three other times, played impeccably in the field. He may have had better games in his career, but not in my presence.

I lost $18,000 to the odds commissioners, plus most of my renewed enthusiasm to reality. I'd bet intelligently. The Tigers were a fair team with good pitching, the Yankees a mediocre crew with one star. My reasoning had been perfect, just incorrect.

Some men consider themselves inviolable from the get-go, only to discover their fallibility along the way. I never thought I'd require such reappraisal, until that moment.

Was I the meticulous enigma who'd fixed last October's Series? Or the pathetic shlub who'd botched every shake-down since?

I sat in the stands, after the final out, wondering. All I could think of was how I must have struck the Babe—like a seedy putz desperately pushing his dumb luck. I was embarrassed for this man, and he was me. I stared at my hands. They seemed older, wrinkled, devoid of muscle. My cuffs were frayed, my shoes scuffed. I waived further examination, fearing the results.

I spent the rest of the week picking on Rose. I also went a couple of times to Rothstein's where I pilfered some silverware. I read my file of fix stories every night (alternately mourning their brevity, then their existence). Mostly I fantasized vengeance on the Babe. Perhaps I could lace his hot dogs with strychnine, I thought, or write letters to the editors accusing him of dishonesty.

Years later I had his betrayal explained in detail. A guy who used to hang with Slaveship Hoolihan at the Polo Grounds put me straight on the particulars. He'd looked me up in a bar in my new neighborhood, anxious to chew over

295

the "good old days in the grifter trade." I figured I owed my history a few moments, and he was paying.

He had the forced heartiness of all marginal old acquaintances. His shrunken face made me feel even older. Right off he started in on "the Ruth razzle."

Did I ever get to the Bambino, or even try to? It seemed important to him.

I told him what had happened, understating my losses, jollying the consequences. He seemed relieved, having clearly come to talk more than to listen. I was still curious enough to give him his head.

"He pulled the same clip on me, Sport, in '26 or '27. He went south on every gink who ever greased him."

"How'd he stay alive?"

"Who'd bother? He didn't mean anything by it. He never bragged. He even gave one guy his money back."

"He *what?*"

"He just didn't get it, Sport. He thought we just liked him. He didn't know he was supposed to *do* anything for it."

It made a certain kind of sense. No matter how little you take for granted, it's too much.

I had a sudden urge to track Ruth down then, like a bounty hunter, to shame my money, and a belated apology, from him. But his bones had long since been gnawed through by the bad disease, rogue corpuscles accomplishing what no strong-arm would have dared to.

I could imagine taking weeks to recover from this latest loss. But I couldn't afford to. Letting the stain set would have cost me too much time. So after a single evening of sulky rationalization I got right back on it, transferring my comeback hopes to an even less appropriate vehicle.

"Mr. Cobb?"

"What's your problem?"

The visitors' clubhouse was much smaller than the Yankees'. Cobb was much meaner than Ruth. Other than that, everything matched.

"I'm a great admirer of yours. . . ."

"Everybody seems to be these days."

"I'm sure they do. It's just that I thought maybe you and I—"

"—could scratch each other's back until the fun starts. What's your angle, Jim?"

"Well, I couldn't help noticing that you haven't struck out since—"

"—three weeks ago tomorrow, in Philadelphia."

"And most years you only strike out—"

"—fifteen or twenty times, at most."

"So I'd imagine the odds would be pretty stiff against your striking out twice tomorrow afternoon." (They were 30–1; I'd gotten three separate estimates.)

"I'd imagine they would be."

I'd intended to approach him more forcefully, but his own force precluded this. All the bluster I'd been rehearsing emerged now as apology.

"And since Thormahlen is pitching tomorrow, and since he never fans anyone, I figured . . ."

"Put a thousand dollars in hundred-dollar bills in a six-by-nine envelope. Slip it under my door at two-fifteen. I sleep in private."

He'd left little room for embellishment, or doubts. I nodded gravely, extending my hand.

"What's your name, Jim?"

"Sullivan."

"*Sport* Sullivan?"

"That's correct."

297

"What took you so long, Sullivan? I've been expecting you since Gandil took the gas."

It was more of a taunt than a question. Before I could bandy it he'd faded out the door.

I had nothing on for the next couple of hours, so I trailed him to an Eighth Avenue gag-and-run. He ate alone, head down, like a post-holer. He apparently did everything alone. I could see why. He'd only glanced at me once during our run-in, and then just to make sure I wasn't carrying.

When he fled the joint I entered and took his booth. I had the fish cakes, which were tolerable, then hot-footed it back to the hotel for the dough.

It was a promising scam. I probably could have squeezed 40–1 from it. (I was a popular item with the wise guys in those days. They'd have made me a nice price on the Lions against the Christians.) But trailing Cobb was as far as I ever went with it. I didn't put the $1,000 in the six-by-nine envelope, didn't slip anything under Ty's hotel door that evening.

I couldn't afford another betrayal is what it amounted to. And this dodge already smelled like last month's socks.

Still, my real reason for passing on Cobb was a personal one. I couldn't stand the guy. And where's the point in talking your way into heaven if your guardian angel turns out to be a putz?

So back I went to the slide rule and the eyeshades. Only Tris Speaker, among the game's untouchables, remained. Beyond him lay only the sad second tier. I was determined, for obvious reasons, not to slip there.

Tris and his Indians wouldn't be visiting New York until mid-July, however. Which gave me three whole weeks to devise a new strategy. While I worked at it I kept religiously to my digs, pacing the floorboards, staring like a moon cow through the bars across the air shaft. I wanted to concoct a scam no setback could monkey with, an undeniable thing. It might be very much like my Series scam, actually. Yes, very much like my Series scam indeed.

I'm not sure how Rose passed these hidden weeks. I saw her every day, though just in passing. She was edging farther into the margins of my life.

Occasionally I considered starting up fresh with her, taking her to Roseland for an hour or two of fox-trotting, then to Rumpelmayer's for a round of frozen novelties. We'd have a nice talk, and some handholding, and a tonsil swab. Soon everything between us would be as it had been in the old days. Then I remembered we hadn't had any old days. And the next day Rothstein cut Abe Attell off at the knees.

21

Mock impulsiveness defined the Bankroll's élan. He made unexpected events seem inevitable, unavoidable occurrences appear arbitrary. One felt pedestrian trying to anticipate him, or deciding not to.

He summoned Attell to his office on June 26, the hottest evening, by ten degrees, of the season. It was six months since they'd opened shop. Attell knew how well they'd been doing; he kept both sets of books. He assumed Rothstein wanted to cut him in on the velvet. In a sense he was right.

"Abe, I'm letting you go," Rothstein announced, without preliminary. Attell's haunches had hardly settled on the davenport.

"You'll be paid through the end of the month. After that I'll have no further need of your services."

Rothstein's tone was eerily neutral, betraying no emotion Attell was familiar with. He seemed to have invented one just for the occasion.

"It's been pleasant working with you. Keep in touch."

Attell lacked the words to respond. Those that emerged seemed drawn from earlier embarrassments.

"I thought you liked me, Arnold."

"Liking has nothing to do with it, Abe. You know that. It's just business."

"But Arnold, you and me, we . . ."

"I'm sure you'll do quite nicely on your own, Abe, no matter what brand of chintzing you turn your talents to. You're an able enough chap. I wish you every success. Now, if you'll excuse me."

Rothstein rose and swept imperiously from the room, certain Attell wouldn't linger long over his emotions. Abe loathed solitude, especially when enforced.

Rothstein could have explained his reasons for axing Abe, but felt abstraction was the harsher punishment in this case. He'd done what the street expected of him, disciplined a muzzler, after draining all his worth. He'd also distanced himself from the fix, discrediting Attell's testimony before Abe could even give it.

Within hours, he knew, the Little Champ would be out regaling the shine boys. Now all who heard him would have good reason to mistrust him, to call his bleat "the errand boy's revenge."

The most startling aspect of Attell's dismissal, from my viewpoint at least, was not how it happened, but how I learned of it. Rose told me.

"Your little pal Abie is painting your name all over

300

Broadway, Sport. You'd better clot him before he puts it up in lights."

She'd cadged $500 from me that morning for a bunting bender. I'd succumbed easily, hoping to buy a day alone with my dreams. But she was back before the maid had flipped the coverlets. I hadn't seen her so animated since we'd last discussed Mexico.

"What are you talking about, my precious one? Nobody on Broadway even knows my name."

This was no longer true, of course. But I'd always prided myself on my anonymity, no matter how involuntary.

I certainly wasn't going to have to pry any details from her. She'd run into a "friend" on 57th Street. They'd chewed the rag over finger food at Schrafft's. Her "friend" had filled her in on Attell's squawk.

I wasn't surprised, just shocked. I'd been expecting something like this, just not *exactly* this.

I listened attentively, even nodded once or twice. It meant I'd have to postpone the Speaker fix, I knew, augmenting my fabled reputation for deferral.

Still, I could continue *planning* the Speaker fix. I'd have the best of both worlds then. Feverish preparation for an indeterminate event. I launched it now by asking Rose to scram.

"Excuse me, dear," I said, ushering her over the threshold. "I have a month's worth of unpaid milliner's bills to catch up on."

I worked late into the soft part of the evening, feeling dangerously, yet propitiously, revived. I revamped the figures for the Speaker fix, the dates, the tone. I was making much of nothing, the way I like to. I intended to quit at eight, but two phone calls kept me pumping well past midnight.

301

"Sport?"

"Speaking."

"That little kike is peaching on you, Mickey. They'll come looking for your ass before his tongue dries."

"Who is this? What are you talking about?"

"He's in McEvoy's most afternoons with an *a* in them. Give his lip a little ear when you've got time. You're not doing much else with that sad vaudeville you call a life."

I didn't recognize his accent, which seemed feigned. It could have been Evans, or perhaps Burns, or even Gandil. It might even have been my brother, Eugene. Actually by that point it could have been almost anyone. I couldn't imagine there were still those who didn't know.

No sooner had he hung up than the damn phone rang again.

"Sullivan?"

"Right."

"Abe Attell here. We met last summer, in Saratoga."

I was too stunned to answer. I guessed I wouldn't have to. He sounded like he was revving up for a tongue run. When none materialized, I prodded him ever so daintily.

"Yes, I remember."

"Good."

Another pause.

"Did you call for anything in particular, Mr. Attell?"

"Yeah."

"What was it you wanted to talk about?"

More silence.

"Mr. Attell?"

No response.

"Abe?"

Nothing.

I severed the connection.

Was he drunk, or shot on hop, or just a victim of the vagaries of technology? Maybe it wasn't even him. I thought of calling him back, but couldn't. I didn't have his number. I decided not to look for it either. My best chance, I guessed, lay in pretending it hadn't even happened.

22

The next morning dawned demonically bright. I awoke at six and scuttled from my roost. I only rise before noon when I'm excited. Or frightened. This morning I was both. I'd been dreaming the fix was unraveling.

I sat beside the window watching the sun flood lower Broadway. Rose stirred occasionally, moaning in her sleep. Her presence still had the power to surprise me.

She looked more beautiful asleep than awake, her body angled intriguingly beneath the counterpane, her lips framing thin membranes of saliva. In repose she seemed the least treacherous being imaginable, incapable of even contemplating betrayal.

By then, of course, her beauty had become purely theoretical, having lost all its power to beguile me. I could imagine having wanted her, I just couldn't imagine ever having loved her.

I knew then that it was time to leave New York. In seven months there I'd done nothing with my roll but lighten it. I didn't want to squat in this steamy room all summer, letting fears of disclosure eat cankers in my heart.

I woke Rose at eight to tell her we were going. At first she seemed agreeable, even pleased. Only as she dressed did her misgivings stage a comeback. She voiced a few, which I ignored.

We packed quickly. Leaving fast is often the only way I *can* leave.

I had no idea where we were headed, though some notion of the mountains seemed appropriate. Someplace farther than Chicago, but short of California, someplace with canyons, but no newspapers, where I could perfect the details of the Speaker scam at my leisure, dangle my toes in trout streams, pick berries, douse campfires.

We didn't discuss our destination in the cab, an evasion that hung menacingly in the air. I think Rose hoped we'd end up in Mexico, but feared suggesting it, lest I agree to go without meaning it.

I bought two one-way tickets to Chicago, intending to decide our final destination there. We played pinochle most of the way, inventing improbable biographies for our traveling companions. One effeminate youth became an exiled Romanov count, heading west to lease his borscht recipe to the Wrigleys.

We reached Chicago shortly after midnight. The streets were sublimely quiet, devoid of traffic. I felt a sudden urge to show Rose the sights, to don a broad-brimmed tour director's cap and steer her breathlessly through the town. I might even run her cheekily past the stadium.

We checked into the Warner, the Ansonia of the Loop. She retired immediately, while I ordered a ham-and-onion sandwich, eating it slowly, watching the dark clouds roll in over the lake. My New York behavior had instantly become my Chicago behavior. I'd traveled a thousand miles to sit beside another window, and look out at another street.

Occasionally small figures materialized far below, their muffled voices rising slowly to my ears. Once a bottle smashed against the pavement. The breezes blew the curtains across the room. Rose's scent wafted appealingly through the dark, not as appealingly as on previous occasions, of course, but appealingly enough. Her back was turned to me. I couldn't see her features, had to imagine them.

She wasn't there the next morning when I awoke. A note was pinned to her pillow.

"Gone shopping, opening account at Field's, suspect stay indefinite."

This was the first I'd heard of it, but she was right. I'd done nothing to extend our journey west, and seemed unlikely to.

Rose had a gift for the laconic minor insight, for cutting straight to the bone of my discursiveness. I'd asked her often to be less telegraphic. She'd always refused.

"You don't need to save on stationery," I'd tell her. "I like a little detail mixed in with my pith."

"But I do need to hoard my remaining time," she'd say to me. "And my brand of detail seems to slide right past your ears."

What response could I have made to such an analysis, that wouldn't have held our decline up to the light?

I mooned away most of that first day designing a Chicago schedule. As long as Rose was predicting a lengthy stay, we might as well have one.

I could perfect the Speaker scam here as well as anywhere. I didn't need bighorn sheep and acres of loco weed to inspire me. I could also keep an ear out for talk of last year's Series. I hurried to finish unpacking before the stores closed. I needn't have. Rose didn't return until well after midnight.

The White Sox spent most of July in Chicago. I saw all their games. It's what I'd really returned for, I now knew. Another shot at them. Alone. They were percolating more judiciously, winning often, losing with greater tact. I could easily imagine starting in with them again.

I waited a discreet week before surrendering to this temptation. Then on Monday, July 10, I trailed Eddie Cicotte from the park to his rooming house. Not the seamy scratch-castle Gandil had invaded, but a tonier dump, with venetian blinds.

"He ain't in," Eddie's landlady informed me graciously. I knew better, and pitched my camp on his stoop to make my point. Ten minutes later Cicotte came floating through the vestibule, like Vernon Castle. He took one step down, I one step forward. Without a word he wheeled and disappeared back inside. I knew he wouldn't reappear until I'd scrammed. His expression said he couldn't really help me, that he had little enough help left for himself.

I waited three days before pitching my second choice.

Joe Jackson's wife couldn't swim. Happy Felsch wouldn't. So when an urge to dunk stole inexplicably over Joe, he was forced to satisfy it solo. On his next trip to the lake I fell in step beside him.

"Hello, Joe. Don't suppose you remember me by any chance?"

"Sure I do, pal. You're the joker who promised us all that necessary during the Series."

"Yes, well . . . apropos of moolah, Joe, I'm sure I can get you more than the Swede been delivering lately."

"Whatever happened to all that Series bacon anyway, pal? Me and Hap only got five thousand apiece."

His tone wasn't petulant, just curious, like a four-year-old examining a corpse.

"I thought you got it, Joe. I gave it to Gandil."

"I don't believe so, pal. I'm pretty dumb, but I retain things."

He stopped talking then, and also walking, as if his doubts had suddenly spread into his feet.

"Are you sure it didn't wind up in your pocket, pal?"

And just about then, at 10:15 A.M., July 13, 1920, I'd had more than enough of Joe Jackson's leeriness, of everyone's leeriness, in fact. He was treating me like a salesman, like a commission man. And I no longer cared if he bought.

"It's been nice seeing you," I told him, implying otherwise. "Give me a holler if you're ever interested in improving yourself."

Then I sauntered off in the general direction of the Loop.

Happy Felsch wasn't my last chance, I just wished he was. That evening, in Naylor's Speakeasy, I ran my basic spiel past his silly grin.

"How's it going, Hap? Haven't seen you since Hoover was in nappies."

"You betcha, how's yourself, been quite a while, yessiree."

He clearly had no idea who I was. I pressed my luck by getting brutally to the point.

"I'm the guy who bankrolled the Series, Hap. I know you've been bagging again lately. Whoever's running it is getting you on the cheap."

Was there any way I could have said this without alarming him? His lips straightened, as if injected with formaldehyde.

"I don't know what you're talking about, mister. You've

probably got the wrong guy entirely. You better scram now while you still can."

He pronounced each syllable of this threat separately. This tickled me. To make Felsch even momentarily unhappy was a coup.

I was quickly depleting my short list of fallbacks. None of those remaining inspired much confidence.

Who'd want to proposition McMullin? He was too sad. I'd never trusted Williams. Weaver seemed irrelevant. Which left Riisberg. I could call him, or forget it. I called.

"Of course I'll see you, Sullivan. I owe you that much."

We met at a Hungarian restaurant on the South Side— strolling fiddlers, sneering captains, the whole roll. It was such a fussy little dump it made me ashamed of being hungry.

Riisberg had come a long way in nine months, ordering Veal Marengo and a Salade Livonière. I had chopped beef and a beer. The evening doesn't rate remembering; I certainly shouldn't have to recount it.

He wanted to rub my nose in it, so he did.

"Where's that little mince Evans you used to cotton with, Sport? I thought you two were a sister act." And "I'm not sure I need a shagger just now, Sport. I'm copping more cash than you promised us in October."

That sort of thing.

I took it, two hours' worth, plus a cigar. Swede had always been a great hater; now he was a disciplined one. When we parted I felt like my shoes were filled with blood.

The rest of the month passed uneventfully. My latest failure was too complete to take seriously, like a bad joke told in code.

308

I took up my plans for the Speaker fix again. I found I liked Chicago, especially since I no longer *had* to be there. It was no place to dodge either killing heat or rumors. Yet somehow I managed to avoid both.

I began reading *all* the papers again, expecting the worst. I thought it would emerge gradually, in print, from the east. Instead it evolved swiftly, through channels, from across town.

23

Eddie Collins seemed the least likely of snitches. Unless you knew him. Then he seemed the most likely. Eddie was cool, rational, gifted, a Columbia man. He had options. When Riisberg dropped three straight to St. Louis in early July, he decided to exercise them. He'd finally had enough. He marched into Comiskey's office to take his stand.

Comiskey's receptionist, a goiterous churl with menopausal resentments, was appalled at Collins's presence. Players *never* visited Mr. Comiskey. He *couldn't* be there.

Collins persisted, with cloying courtesy. Eddie was never rude. That was his whole point.

The snake finally put him through to the boss.

Comiskey was even more annoyed. *Players Never Came to His Office.* He hadn't toiled thirty years in obscurity to blur distinctions. Perhaps he could deny he was in. He knew he shouldn't, though. Collins was his team's lone remaining asset.

"Wonderful to see you, Eddie. Great of you to drop by. What a fine surprise, pleased as punch, tickled to death. I imagine you know how thrilled we are at the year you're having for us. Yes we are. Couldn't be happier."

"Six of your boys are white-eyeing on you, Mr. Comiskey. There were seven. One retired. They queered the Series last October, too."

Collins curled his thumbs through his belt loops, daring rebuttal.

There was none. Comiskey's neutral expression never wavered. Except for the slow, measured heaving of his chest he could have been dead. Collins didn't know what to do. He'd anticipated several responses, none of them blankness.

"Mr. Comiskey, did you hear me?"

Comiskey fingered his temple, sighed, turned to the window. He was wondering if he could change the subject somehow, as if nothing had been said.

"Yes, Eddie, I heard you. This is terrible news, just terrible. You haven't told anybody else about it, have you?"

"No, Mr. Comiskey, I haven't."

"Good. I mean, that's just as well. I hope you won't for the time being. Until I've had some time to investigate the matter thoroughly. Yes, this is most distressing news, most distressing. I'm shocked. I don't know what else to say."

He rose and walked slowly around his desk. Eddie took a tentative half-step backward, narrowly avoiding a collision with an umbrella stand. He'd had a sudden vision of Comiskey prostrate before him, burying uncontrollable sobs in the creases of his knickerbockers.

Comiskey had no such intention, of course; he just wanted to ease Collins out the door.

"Thanks for coming by, Eddie. I appreciate it, I really do. You'll be hearing from me about this matter presently."

The heavy brass lock clicked funereally behind Collins. He

310

hadn't precisely been pushed out into the hall, or had he?

The receptionist stared disdainfully into her filing cabinet, refusing to gloat.

Eddie had no idea what to do now. Comiskey had known everything, that much was obvious. Maybe everybody knew. Maybe everybody had always known. Maybe that was the way the world worked after all. Maybe everyone had always known this except him.

Comiskey knew what he had to do now. He just didn't want to do it. His hand paused briefly over his phone, as if he still had options.

"What's Alfred's number over at the Regency Club, Nadine?"

He'd been relying a bit too heavily on Austrian lately, he knew. But what the hell. Did it matter that some now called him the Mouthpiece's Lapdog? As he dialed the first reassuring digit he decided that it didn't.

Moments later Kid Gleason walked into Commissioner John Heydler's office. He too had had enough. His whole team was disintegrating around him. He wanted to get on the record before it all came out. A faint aura of decay had begun trailing the Kid lately. Old men were now crossing the street to avoid him.

He wouldn't mention Comiskey unless they made him. The flunky who took his statement expressed no shock. He simply promised the appropriate steps would be taken. Gleason didn't ask what these steps were. He was too anxious to make the entire incident a memory.

Within seconds, Heydler was on the horn to Austrian. But Austrian's line was busy. Heydler dialed Comis-

key reflexively, before remembering that Comiskey
no longer mattered. He hung right up and tried Austrian
again.

Austrian fielded Comiskey's call on his rubdown table.
A sullen muscleboy was kneading his hairy back with
peppermint oil. Austrian dismissed him with a greasy finger
wag.

Comiskey blurted out his bad news in monotone. Austrian
had grown immune to Comiskey's panics by now. But this
one put him Johnny-at-the-rat-hole.

"Collins won't do anything, Charles. He's just buying
himself some heinie insurance. I'll read him a few chapters
from the catechism."

"He might talk to the papers, Alfred, to Fullerton, to
Lardner even. Christ on a cruller."

"It's not his style, Charles. Everybody has a style. This
isn't Eddie's."

Austrian had begun calling Comiskey "Charles" recently.
Comiskey pretended not to notice.

"I hope you're right, Alfred, for both our sakes."

Austrian couldn't miss this collusive inference. Comiskey
was even more frightened than he seemed.

"There's only two months left in the season, Charles.
Attendance is up. We could win the thing. It's working out
just lovely. In December we'll peddle their butts to the rag-
men, for top dollar too. Don't get distracted by the minor
points."

He knew Comiskey longed for such reassurance, though
he probably shouldn't have said "we" so many times. He
didn't mention his doubts. Comiskey didn't pay him to have
doubts.

Austrian intended to have his true reaction later, after he

312

hung up. But he didn't have time. Heydler's call followed Comiskey's by four seconds.

"Alfred?"

"John?"

"Kid Gleason was just in here tossing up his lunch."

"Jesus Mary and be seated."

Black language wasn't Austrian's idiom. He could feel the situation slipping beyond his call.

"Attell's been talking too. He's varnishing the landscape with overtone."

Suddenly all the figures added up. Austrian spit out the totals.

"Forget Gleason. He's nothing. Attell too. Rothstein's behind this. He thinks he knows something we don't. He's wrong. Sit tight. I'm going to teach that Broadway boy a lesson."

He hung up then, as if he, not Heydler, had placed the call.

He settled back on his massage table, chin on elbow, feeling pleased with himself. His tone had been reassuring, his message precise. He'd sounded as certain as all lawyers are supposed to sound. In fact, he had no idea what Rothstein was up to. Except that it was something that could cut his annual income in half.

The next day I put my pastoral dreams to the acid test, packed two bratwurst sandwiches and a copy of *Roughing It,* and bought a day ticket to the wilds of Batavia.

When I arrived I hiked up a large hill and sat in the deep grass, like in the linocuts. I gave it a full shot too—picked some flowers, stared at the clouds, kicked at an anthill. It was all as idyllic as I'd always heard it was, and in half an hour I was ready to scream bloody murder.

313

So much for the consolations of the bucolic life, I admitted to myself, settling back on my drop cloth for an eyeshut.

When I awoke I knew exactly what I had to do. I'd been dreaming I'd fixed the *upcoming* World Series.

The Indians were about to win the pennant. Speaker would be my contact. I could control it by controlling him. I had half my score left. I'd start from there.

We'd go straight to Saratoga, Rose and I, spend the month, take the waters, get the feel. This time I'd do it right, without accomplices.

It was a thrilling conceit, and a feasible one. I fairly floated back to my train on its prospects. Returning to Saratoga was the jakest part. All the high rollers were sure to be there. If I still intended to number myself among them, I should be there too.

24

I*f I still intended to number myself among them.* It sounds so pathetic now, so irrelevant to almost any dream.

Saratoga looked as poised as always when we returned, though something important was clearly missing. The reason, perhaps.

The first night I stepped out for a racing form. I knew all the stores were closed, but went anyway. In my mind I saw myself entering a deserted shop, its lights dim, yet bright against the twilight. Canned goods lined the shelves, dope sheets covered the counters. My hand reached for one, but fell short.

The streets were quiet, unseasonably cool. I circled the block, peering in back-lit windows. No figures were visible. I needed to be alone, to reorient myself. I stood looking up at our room. Rose's shadow slid slowly past the shade. I could almost imagine being with her.

Steel-blue flags flapping over the infield lake, trailing jockeys whistling encouragement to their mounts, gamblers in bowlers, gamblers with cigars, rust-brown cognac on the Gideon Putnam porch, the Brook aglow against the purple evening sky, the rain, the past.

One scene paints the month in miniature.

Thomas Edison stands in the winner's circle, in the rain, sheets of water cutting the gray air between us. He is alone, flanking the winner, uncertain in his purpose, yet buoyed by its novelty. The race has been named for him.

"The Thomas Alva Edison Purse, Three-Year-Olds and Up, Non-Winners of Two Races, Ever."

Steam shoots from the winner's nostrils, a mediocre animal, indifferent to its triumph. The jockey, winded, seems anxious to be off. The crowd looks a thousand miles away. I alone defy the downpour to hug the rail.

Edison grabs the reins. Fear tints his excitement. His grin is an attack. A bulb flashes. The photographer sprints for cover. The jockey leaps off. The horse is led back to its barn. Edison is left standing with no hand to shake, mud oozing over his puttees.

"I'll be playing that beast's number the next five nights," he shouts. "At what's-his-name's casino, on the north side, you know, that Jew who fixed the World Series last October."

The lake, calm, and red, at dawn. Hands skimming hips in unlit auction barns, deep in the night, far from the gavel. Money brushing palms in dim casinos, Mendelssohn trios, the pale orange sun, a quick breeze knifing the morning air, the scent of love hanging in the balance, the pines, the dark.

25

We stayed the entire month. I lost steadily. It didn't matter. I was about to fix another World Series.

I'd forgotten how I dread the gut of summer. It's alleged to keep the spring's recurring promise, but spring would last all year if left to me. I've always preferred that one promise follow another anyway.

The heat hung over the town like a punishment. Within its torpor we struggled to create our new life. I longed for Saratoga to revive me, to show Rose I could be passionate about something. I'd apparently forgotten we'd met there.

We went to the track every afternoon. At dusk we swam in obscure corners of the lake. The world seemed to have receded from our caring. Occasionally we visited a casino, though never the Brook.

I worked every evening on my Series plan, under a blue lamp, overlooking the street. Its outline never exceeded two pages. I made few changes. It was mostly heavy thinking disguised as industry.

I was trying to reduce my duplicity to its essentials, to make it immune to failure. It was like pressing my wishes repeatedly through cheesecloth.

Gradually I lengthened my nights into daybreak, as I always do when I'm reverting to solitude. It was peaceful. I could concentrate. Across the room Rose kept her own particular counsel, whistling like a newborn through pursed lips.

During the second week I stopped reading the papers again, determined to stop worrying about the immutables.

Here's some of what I missed:

August 8, *New York World:*

COMMISSIONER HINTS CLEANUP WARRANTED

August 13, *Chicago Tribune:*

AUSTRIAN ADMITS CHICAGO PERFORMANCE PUZZLING

August 16, *New York Times:*

COLLINS BLASTS TEAMMATES' INDIFFERENCE

I'm often asked how it all came out in the end. Was it "a bolt from the blue," or "in one fell swoop," or some similar bromide? It wasn't. It was just the inevitable becoming actual, like Gandil's greed, or Rose and me, like water seeping through mortar, the press of time.

One day, toward the end, I chanced upon Rothstein in his element. His limousine breezed past me outside the track. He was perched on the back seat, looking imperiously blasé. He didn't see me, or at least acknowledge me.

I hadn't encountered him in a year, though his image had been a constant and disquieting presence. He looked grander, more elegant, more detached, in most particulars more imposing than memories of him.

I came close to pointing him out to Rose. Luckily I didn't. She'd have known everything then.

That night I couldn't work on my plan, couldn't even think of it. I took a long walk down by the society stables, listened to the stallions calling wistfully to the trees,

317

watched the August clouds racing past the moon.

The next morning I bought my first paper in weeks, thumbed purposefully toward its middle. There, on the sports pages, was what I was after.

CHICAGO D.A. SUMMONS GRAND JURY ON SPORTS GAMBLING

It mentioned no names, though its fevered prose fairly pulsed with insinuation. I could read between the lines as though I'd written them.

It didn't scare me as much as I'd thought it would, though. I'd run as far as I intended to for now, having grown tired of edging out the back door and calling it ambition.

I turned down George Street to the Paddock Café, a small one-armer I'd always intended to sample. I wanted to breakfast alone there with my misgivings. I couldn't have resisted any confidant, and the slightest condolence would have made me feel I'd earned it.

I downed a boiled egg and half a cup of mocha, then skimmed through the rest of the morning's news. The Indians had moved four up on the White Sox. They'd be visiting Boston the first week of September.

Contradictory news had broken, as usual, in tandem. The last act's scenery had just grown visible through the scrim.

26

Of course, I returned to Boston. I always knew I would. The city seemed a village after my travels, a smug backwater stunted by familial antagonisms, a gray town to hide gray dreams in, my home.

We left Saratoga the morning of getaway day. I had even less desire to see the track shuttered than usual, having dropped more money on the horses than any distraction warranted. My roll had shrunk to a flat two hundred grand.

Our train retraced the previous August's route. I spent the entire trip in the parlor car, polishing my series plan. As we edged through Boston's seedier precincts, Rose and I conducted this symptomatic exchange.

"Where shall we stay, Rosie love?"

"How long?"

"A few days, a week perhaps."

"I've heard the Barclay's nice."

"It is, though somewhat noisy."

It wasn't, but Rose detested clatter.

"A friend once stayed at the Essex. He dubbed it deluxe."

Her "he" was to punish my imperiousness. The "deluxe" was pure ostentation.

"That's odd. Most women I know find it tacky."

I'd only asked her preference to appease her, and on the off chance that it might actually match my own. She was too stiff-necked, though, to fade without a fight.

"How about the Buckminster?"

And there it was, forever memorialized, at least in *her* mind, as her choice.

"A nice suggestion—all the top people stay there. It's pricey, but absolutely worth it."

In fact it was doss-house cheap, with its foolscap window shades and forty-watt bulbs. Rose didn't itemize its defects, though. Perhaps she'd already begun numbering the days.

I spent our first night showing her the sights, which saddened me, as only old enthusiasms can. I begged off early and returned to the hotel, encouraging Rose to continue, which she did.

I passed the rest of the week in rhapsodic seclusion, reading Montaigne, sipping Darjeeling. It was a useful hiatus for my prefelonious purposes, evoking the great calm looming chaos often brings.

On September 3, the Indians arrived in Boston.

Many of that year's setbacks seem the cruelest. My confrontation with Tris Speaker probably was. I'm not sure I've gotten over it yet.

I called him at the Kenmore to set a time. He suggested toting some deadeye to his room, and was abrasively specific about the brand.

In appearance he eclipsed all possible preconception, embodying some grand matinée idol rendition of athleticism, all sinewy limbs and quick, reflexive movement. I extended my hand for a quick fin flip, just as his paw reached for the comfort of the booze. Without thanks, or even acknowledgment, he poured a rouser.

"Well, Tris," I began sheepishly, cracking my knuckles, "I'm sure you must have heard through the stovepipe . . ."

But what's the point in recreating this last embarrassment? It was just my old shoes with a new set of laces. I larded it with the usual seductive selling points—its ease, its rewards, its discretion. Speaker remained appropriately unimpressed. I thought for a silly second I might have hypnotized him.

Then he began to laugh.

It started softly, in the marrow of his chest, like the rolling sound that precedes the summer thunder. Then it erupted in a stream of brutal spasms, his neck reddening, his body rocking. I had no reaction. He couldn't help himself, I refused to. If I'd allowed myself any response it would have been murder.

As I turned to leave he regained momentary control of

himself, just enough to permit a gratuitous explanation.

"That New York kahoona already beat you to it, Moiphy. Except it's the Brooklyn boys who'll be going in the tank."

We ditched the Buckminster early the next morning, moving clear across town, into my father's house. I'm tempted to say "moving *back* into my father's house," except Rose had never been there, and I'd never really left.

The building had brought no offers in my absence. I'd been too distracted to shave the price. It appeared as left— dowdy, dark, forbidding, no furniture rearranged, no mementos disposed of. The food I'd left had calcified on the countertops. Each nook reeked of a cheap and inviolable permanence.

I assumed our stay would be brief, unable to imagine otherwise. We stayed through September, our days passing as if no implication attended them. I puttered, Rose sunned herself, achieving some tantalizingly unlikely angles in her dogged pursuit of the glare.

In the evenings she went to the library, or so she said. As soon as she left I'd take a long walk in the opposite direction. Often, when I returned, I'd dance alone to my Argentine tango records. Then I'd count my money. Rose had begun lifting occasional bills from my wallet. I'd have given them to her if she'd asked. Though I understood very well why she didn't.

One evening, toward the end, we went to see Rachmaninoff at the Athenaeum. Three Chopin ballades opened the program, followed by a Brahms sonata, then some miniatures by Satie. The Chopin was magisterial, the sonata emotive, but it was the French pieces that truly seized my heart. Their exotic simplicity revived my flagging enthusiasm, transporting me to some tree-lined avenue in Vienna, or

321

Lisbon, or Mexico City even. I could live there as I'd always imagined living, alone, daring intrigues not yet dreamed of. Rose was staring pensively at the stage. For an instant I could see why I'd once wanted her. It's always in the eyes.

When we returned home I gave it one more try, just to be sure.

My former wife once accused me of cultivating misgivings, of keeping ledgers with all her defects blissfully annotated. To avoid this charge I couched Rose's final test as an anecdote, of the sort one longs to tell the woman one never meets.

"Once, when I was twelve," I began casually, as if lapsing into a favorite bedtime story, "I was awakened by music of an unearthly sort, very close, yet far away, very clear, yet quite distorted. I'd never heard anything even remotely like it before. It disoriented me in an exhilarating sort of way. I lay completely still, in the absolute darkness, imagining I didn't know where I was, imagining I was no longer even me, imagining my real life was just about to begin. Eventually, after ten minutes, or several hours, I fell back to sleep."

I paused, to check her reaction, to see if she was listening, or even pretending to. She was filling in another crossword, smiling, nodding.

"The next afternoon I was playing alone in the yard. I heard the same music. It was coming from a neighbor's Victrola. It was just a popular song of the moment, an ordinary tune, one I'd heard countless times before without noting it."

I glanced over at her again, without expectation. She kept scribbling away, as if I'd been reciting the alphabet.

"That's quite an interesting story, Sport. I once had a similar experience. During a piano lesson with a crone my mother set on me . . ."

I couldn't listen. I hadn't bared my heart for the sake of matching anecdotes, but in the unlikely hope of actually being heard. When she finished I launched into yet another allegory, of a purely punitive sort.

"Another time I saw an impossibly beautiful girl on the street, the most beautiful girl I've ever seen. For three days I could think of nothing but her. Through discreet inquiries I learned she peddled geegaws at Kazenmeier's. I hurried there to buy a packet of peacock feathers. In the neutral light of forced reacquaintance, she was more than disappointing—she was brassy, chatted incessantly, with bilious banality. The elegant ambiguity of her laughter was really the edgy cackle of chronic apprehension. She was the sort of woman who'd never really hear anything I said. She was, in a word, common."

Rose didn't look up from her puzzle. In fact, she bent further to her task. Only a twitch in her jaw suggested she'd even heard me. It was enough. I straightened my legs and took the stairway express to quiltville.

The next morning, violent regressiveness took hold of me. I'd begun imagining I could resume my career in Boston. Not as before, of course, but on a grander, bolder scale— leasing confederates, expanding into commerce, finance, even politics. I was just reshaping my stunted ambitions, of course, revising improbabilities. But in the arid serenity of my father's house my timidity felt positively audacious.

It is to weep.

I spent the next four days plotting my reimprisonment, simultaneously scanning the newspapers for escape routes. I might actually have activated this plan (or what's worse, stayed on indefinitely dreaming of it) had the fatal news not hit the streets and saved me.

I remember that day as if I'd invented it.

September 21, 1920, a cool morning with a high, lucid sky, the season with several days to run, Cleveland to meet Brooklyn in the Series. Someone may fix it; it won't be me.

I've descended to breakfast in a sedentary mood, my father's robe brushing my calves reassuringly, the papers piled neatly inside the doorway. I bend to lift one. Blood rushes to my brain. I have a brief premonition of what I'm about to learn. I often experience such portents; my entire life sometimes seems to have been one.

I open the *Transcript* to the sports page. A crow screeches from the bushes. A stray branch scrapes the kitchen window. It was there, in its place.

> CHICAGO GRAND JURY SUBPOENAS PLAYERS
> ON SERIES FIX

I didn't read on, didn't have to. I'd been waiting a full year, after all.

It was over.

27

But of course nothing is ever really over. Nothing, that is, that cannot leave a clue. One aspect was fading, another emerging. In the interim, several morbid symptoms flourished.

It rained all day. I took several naps. That night we had the first frost of the season.

I had no direct reaction to the headline, unless vacancy

can be considered a response. For the next few days I led a genuinely carefree life, took long walks, did chores, read, listened with both ears to the gramophone. It was an ideal existence, for a certain kind of person. Only its ordinariness testified to my panic.

I might have embraced it forever if Rothstein hadn't come to see me.

He simply showed up one starless night, knocked once, almost tentatively. I assumed it was Rose. Yet when I opened the door, there he stood, grinning sheepishly, smaller than life.

If I'd expected him I'd have spent the whole day fretting. But I hadn't. His appearance was too unlikely to unnerve me.

We chatted softly, on neutral topics—meteorology, home ownership, the Balkan Wars. We were like strangers visiting a mutual acquaintance's grave. One of us would have to get to the point, we both knew. Neither of us expected it to be me.

"What will you do with yourself now, Sport, now that your put-up is losing all its stuffing?"

"I thought I'd start up here again in Boston, Mr. Rothstein. I've truly missed it."

"Really, Sport? Do you think that's wise? Have you slipped one noose just to neck up to another?"

"I suppose not."

"No, Sport. I don't believe you have. I truly don't."

"I suppose not."

I was repeating myself, out of panic.

"How about Mexico, Sport? Mexico's a swell place, particularly in the morbid months. I understand you and Rose have been discussing it for ages."

The true genius of men like Rothstein, I've often thought,

325

lies in their ability to make the arbitrary sound mandatory. How could he have known Rose even existed, never mind the subject of our most intimate divergence?

"Yes, we've discussed it, on and off."

"I could help you down there, Sport, make some arrangements, talk to some people. A year in the tropics might make you a world of difference. That's my reading. Everything here could clarify itself by then. Of course, I know I can trust your discretion on this, Sport, a man like you, I'm very sure of that."

"Of course, Mr. Rothstein. I know the score."

My agreeableness was sliding quickly toward subservience. I started to dig in my heels, to save myself, but my defiance emerged with characteristic diffidence.

"What happened, Mr. Rothstein?"

I couldn't imagine asking anyone such a question. Yet there it was. I was at the edge.

His answer sounded solidly premeditated, as if he recognized his fate in my predicament, had spent long nights burrowing sleeplessly into damp bedclothes, imagining what it might feel like to be me.

"You need somebody to know, Sport. And nobody does."

"*You* know, Mr. Rothstein. I know you do."

He smiled then, as if I'd just made his point.

"You can live like a prince on a dollar a day in Mexico, Sport. That's one hundred thousand days, with matching nights thrown in gratis. Plus it's warm."

He took a deep breath then, as if struggling for control.

"Do you think I enjoy living like this, Sport, just because you think you might? Plotting every fucking minute, wearing these monkey rigs, piling up dough so fast I can't even breathe from it?"

I was stunned at his vehemence. It sounded genuine.

"Guys like you are a dollar a carload, Sport. You feel one way, want to feel another. I don't want to feel any way. So I don't."

I felt a metaphor coming on, and I was right.

"I see all the noses pressed to my window, Sport, wondering what it's like to be inside. I myself wonder what it's like to be outside, to just imagine things."

I didn't want to hear any of this, but seemed fated to.

"It was impossible from the start, Sport."

"No it wasn't, Mr. Rothstein. I made it work. I fixed the Series."

"You didn't fix anything, Sport. I was one step in your size nines all the way. I did it. That's why it worked. You never could have done it. Not alone. I kept you in it to smooth the edges. You were useful. I liked you. It was amusing. But you botched it. Now it's unraveling. Still, it was different. I made some money. And it won't hurt me. I've made very sure of that."

If he derived any pleasure from disillusioning me he didn't show it. He seemed, in fact, to be more disenchanted than I was.

"Look what you did with the money, Sport. You gave it back. In six months you'd be touching asshole bottom. And who's to say you're not right? At least now you get to go to Mexico with your plans, while I have to stay on here impersonating myself."

I didn't answer. I couldn't. I could barely breathe. I felt as if my stomach had vacated the room. I wanted him to vanish then, from my home, from the world. I wanted to run upstairs and fall into a dreamless sleep, regain my balance by embracing pure unconsciousness.

327

He must have sensed my change of mood, for he began easing himself from the room, much as he'd entered it, on a cheeky wave of self-obfuscating banter.

"There are far worse places than Mexico, Sport. Boston, for instance. It's not as if there are that many choices. The trick is to pick one and stick with it. Actuality isn't all it's cracked up to be, Sport."

I'd be given several useful contacts in Mexico. He'd made train reservations. They were paid for. He didn't promise me a job on my return, though implicit in his offer was this likelihood. Only after he left did I realize how much this pleased me, how close it felt to what I'd wanted all along.

He shook my hand, keeping one eye on the clock, then stepped through the door, and down the gravel path. Beneath the gas lamp stood the cab he'd kept waiting. Even as his figure diminished in the dusk the reality of him faded from my memory. I simply couldn't retain it.

On our first meeting, fourteen months before, I'd been struck by the remoteness of his manner. On our second encounter, over the phone, it was the adamancy of his will that most impressed me. That evening, in my parlor, during our third, and final, conversation, it was his ordinariness that sounded the major chord.

It wasn't common ordinariness, of course. Still, it was ordinariness. I wanted to remember this, to think of it every time I thought of him. I knew I wouldn't, though. And even if I did I'd call it a distortion, a banality he only achieved in my presence.

In the years since, I've settled on two ways of thinking of him: as he was—a man of undisputed powers with unexpected limitations, a heightened version of myself, perhaps; and as I would have him—a man who keeps to himself, a man who makes things work, a man who knows.

I went to bed as soon as he left, surrendering completely to my dreams. They weren't the sort of dreams I was used to having, but more like blurred visions of my past and present mingling. They kept changing shape and texture, like stick figures drawn in smoke.

In the morning I awoke to the bright sun and quiet. It took only moments to shake the night from my mind. I felt great sadness, but also great relief. A new life seemed both possible and necessary. What it would be I didn't know, didn't want to know. Perhaps it would be no particular life at all, just a series of random episodes unencumbered by relevance, a life like most men seem to lead.

Rose wasn't beside me. At first I thought she'd left during the night. Then I realized I hadn't seen her since dinner. Some of her clothes were missing, and all her luggage. But these weren't my main concerns. I ran immediately to the drawer where I kept my stash. One hundred thousand dollars was gone, exactly half.

She'd left no note, not even a venomously restrained kiss-off. She was leaving all the filling in to me. We wouldn't be going to Mexico together, it seemed, at least not that year. What wasn't clear was whether I would ever see her again.

In fact I did not.

28

It took me ten minutes to pack, a world's record. I've always preferred traveling light, though naturally I'd rather do the lightening myself.

I didn't leave right away though. I wanted to spend one

more night in my father's house, alone, for the symmetry of it.

I awoke the next morning before dawn. It was only the *eve* of the first Series game, so my departure wouldn't be *that* ironic.

In the first sad blue light of October I removed my father's atlas from its shelf, sat in his favorite chair with it propped against the windowpane. His frayed curtains blew freely across the room, as he'd never allowed them to. Damp smells of unattended age filled every corner.

I pointed at random to a remote spot on the map, La Pesca, a tiny town with no roads leading to it, one hundred miles north of Tampico. The name suggested a vaguely undefined ardor, balmy days and crisp nights, endless possibilities if one cared to indulge in them. I'd never been to Mexico, knew nothing of it.

I could imagine La Pesca clearly, though—Indian sharecroppers leading small burros to the surf, the town square sprinkled hourly against the sun, myself seated in a second-story louver, gazing steadily out across the blue boundless sea. I resisted these images, then surrendered to them. Rothstein was right about that. Anticipation might be all I'd ever have.

I ate breakfast, read the papers, walked in the garden, wrote the agent a note suggesting any price be taken. Then I went upstairs for my luggage—a Gladstone for my clothes, a grab-all for my papers.

I missed Rose, but not terribly. I knew I'd soon get used to it. Her absence might limit my happiness, but no more than her presence ever had.

When I stepped outside I got a sharp surprise. A package

was sitting on the threshold, a flat, square bundle wrapped in greengrocer's paper, a note stuck like a summons to its side.

Some reading material to lighten your journey south.
—A.R.

I was tempted to open it, but didn't. I knew that's what he would have wanted.

I took the same route to the station as always, encountered no dogs, no pigeons, nothing living, actually. A few houses had disappeared in my absence, some stores had changed hands, the pavement weeds had grown several inches higher.

The station was alive with travelers, pilgrims to the Series. For a moment I was tempted to join them, but refrained. It no longer seemed to have anything to do with me.

I gathered my bags and plunged heedlessly against the tide. My train lay waiting patiently beyond it. As I drew closer a familiar figure swept past me, a form too compactly dapper to be anybody but Attell. He was switching trains, to Montreal, to the chilly exile Rothstein had prescribed for *him*.

It would have been just like Rothstein to arrange our passing, I thought. But even more like me to credit him with it.

My train was almost empty. We'd pick up passengers along the way, unlikely traveling companions for an improbable journey: laconic ranch hands in gator-skin boots, blowsy teenage whores fresh off the Mississippi riverboats. I found myself pining for their company, as long as they kept their distance, and their tongues.

Series fans swirled hysterically past my window. Rose

wasn't among them. I took the last $100,000 from my valise and began counting it, reaching $20,000 before I forced myself to stop.

Then I picked up Rothstein's package and opened it. It contained a typed report from Dwayne, the detective.

Subject: Joseph Sullivan
Profession: Numbers runner
Date: January 11, 1920–September 26, 1920
Subject born in Boston, 1882, claims to have been married, but never was. One brother, Eugene, 36. No other living relatives. Subject left school at 14 to run numbers for Jocko Kielty. Worked for Kielty 22 years, without advancement. Resigned July 1919. Moving across the country since—New York, Los Angeles, Chicago—to no apparent purpose, accompanied by Rose ———, a prostitute from Utica, N.Y.

There was more of this, all untrue. Rothstein had written his own note at the bottom.

Nothing is the way it seems, is it, Sport? Most things are the opposite. That's how you know. We're too smart to be gamblers, Sport. But we're too cheeky to be anything else. Just don't imagine it could have been different, or that you owe your history more unhappiness. Stuff your dreams back inside your head now, enjoy Mexico, and keep your mouth shut.

I closed the cover, tore it up, opened the window, scattered the pieces to the wind.

Attell's train pulled out just before mine did. I gave it a wave, then closed my eyes and imagined again the dark heart of Mexico, cool evenings in lush mountain towns, flat beaches stretching languorously to the sea.

For a moment an unlikely image mingled with these, of myself walking tentatively toward Gandil, in the Buckmin-

332

ster lobby, just fifteen months earlier. I smiled at the improbability of what had happened since, that his cockeyed smile could have led me to this window, to this hour, this fate. Who would have guessed it? For that was one thing Rothstein was dead wrong about.

I *had* fixed the Series.

And I'd done it on my own.

The train gave an almost imperceptible lurch then, like brain and heart skipping simultaneous beats. It was only the wheels disengaging themselves, though, beginning their slow roll toward the redolent glades of La Pesca. For a moment I felt we might be moving backward, toward Boston, or Saratoga, or even Chicago. But Boston was already disappearing, and Saratoga's season had ended long ago, and Chicago was just the scene of last year's Series. No, we were clearly moving forward, moving south, to Mexico, to the reward my dreams had dealt me.

December
1920

Some will know the end of this story, others will guess it. Cicotte confessed; Jackson, Felsch, and Williams followed quickly.

On October 22, 1920, thirteen indictments were handed down: the eight players, Abe Attell, Bill Burns, Nat Evans, Hal Chase. And me.

The trial began on June 27, 1921, and lasted five weeks. Attell and I were tried *in absentia.* The jury deliberated two hours, finding each defendant innocent on every count. Attell and I could return if we wanted to. I didn't want to. I'd worried little about the outcome, assuming Rothstein would take care of it.

One week later, all the players were banned from baseball for life. None ever played another game. That's the one thing I hadn't known, what nobody could have known. The last fix had been put in by professionals.

After the first death there are sometimes others, it turns out.

Chick Gandil became a plumber in Calistoga, Eddie Cicotte a game warden in Michigan. Joe Jackson opened a package store in Greenville, Lefty Williams a pool hall in Chicago. Swede Riisberg and Happy Felsch fronted bars, in San Francisco and Milwaukee, respectively. Fred McMullin

337

moved to Los Angeles, and disappeared.

Comiskey never finished in the first division again. Gleason managed three more years, then retired. Bill Burns moved to west Texas, for the climate. Abe Attell stayed on Broadway, for the company. All are gone now. Only one preceded them.

On November 4, 1928, Arnold Rothstein was shot between the left cheek and earlobe during a poker game in the Park Central Hotel on West 56th Street.

As for me, I stayed in Mexico.

It was the most foreign place I'd ever visited. I immediately felt at home there. The years slipped by almost imperceptibly. Whole decades have left no visible trace.

My life's second half has often seemed an appendix to the first. That's as it should be, I suppose. Perhaps it's what I was seeking all along, a great distance from which all events appear hypothetical.

Mexico wasn't as I'd envisioned it, of course, though its reality was often as vivid as my imaginings. My houses were more wood than adobe, the heat more oppressive than comforting, the endless intrigues so thick with repercussion that no real gambler would have had any complaint.

In any event I've long since forgotten my dreams of it. I've long since forgotten most of my dreams, actually, except the one dream the rest were meant to induce, the dream of my perfect scam.

It is the only dream no disappointment can ever tamper with. It has changed somewhat, but only as my life has changed, and then mainly in its nuances.

It no longer steals on me in the moments preceding sleep, but greets me now as I flee the night's entanglements, in those increasingly lengthy intervals before I summon the will to rise.

In the pure tropic silence I can almost swim in it, as the black turns deeper blue against the dawn.

I am alone. I am calm. I have prepared well. My path of flight awaits me. I have approached Gandil. I haven't allowed him to speak. I haven't contacted Burns. I go to Saratoga to await the Series. I meet a beautiful woman, leave her, win the necessary capital at the races. I go to Chicago. I am even more alone. I bet, collect, flee—to the mountains perhaps, somewhere vast, foreign, someplace not unlike where I am today.

I do not go to Rothstein. I never even see Rothstein. And that is the real difference.

Perhaps it wouldn't have made any actual difference, but it might have, and that's all that matters now.

The end of the dream remains as it has always been, except for one significant detail.

I do none of these things, but only imagine them, keeping it all a dream.

Instead I take long walks, sketch, read voraciously, sitting in my lush, untended garden, staring up through the swaying jacarandas, picturing again all the loveliest scenes as they could have been, and as, no doubt, they someday will be, in some country, in some year, in this brief life whose realest parts are what we dream of it, in this best of dreams, which is, at last, my own.